and his worldwide bestselling Discworld® series

"Think J.R.R. Tolkien with
a sharper, more satiric edge."
Houston Chronicle

"Pratchett is always clever, always funny,
and always surprisingly timely. His obvious delight in
the silliness of human nature makes his stories witty,
and his emphasis on fun overall helps to sweeten the
bite of his deadly sharp social commentary. . . .
His world is more than just an alternate universe—
it's a delirious roller-coaster ride that never allows
the reader to even consider getting off."
Philadelphia Inquirer

"Pratchett's wry wit is as good as gold. . . .
His novels are clever, wry, and insightful,
and his fictional Discworld easily mirrors the
real world on many levels. . . . Hilarious."
Boston Globe

"Good news for lovers of wit, originality, and a
crackling good story. . . . Pratchett [is] one of the
smartest and funniest comic writers working today . . .
Funny and thought-provoking and entirely enjoyable."
Minneapolis Star Tribune

"A master of laugh-out-loud fiction . . . Pratchett has
created an alternate universe full of trolls, dwarfs,
wizards, and other fantasy elements, and he uses
that universe to reflect on our own culture with
entertaining and gloriously funny results. It's an
accomplishment nothing short of magical."
Chicago Tribune

"Mad magic, wild adventures, hilarious characters
and situations, and enchanting prose.
Most writers would have been reduced to
repeating themselves by now; Pratchett finds a
mother lode of ore every time he returns to the vein."
San Francisco Chronicle

Terry Pratchett

Thud!

A Novel of Discworld®

HARPER

An Imprint of HarperCollinsPublishers

This is a work of fiction. Names, characters, places, and incidents are products of the author's imagination or are used fictitiously and are not to be construed as real. Any resemblance to actual events, locales, organizations, or persons, living or dead, is entirely coincidental.

HARPER

An Imprint of HarperCollins*Publishers*
195 Broadway
New York, New York 10007

Copyright © 2005 by Terry and Lyn Pratchett
Terry Pratchett® and Discworld® are registered trademarks.
ISBN 978-0-06-233498-5

First Harper premium printing: November 2014
First HarperTorch mass market printing: September 2006
First HarperCollins hardcover printing: October 2005

Visit Harper paperbacks on the World Wide Web at
www.harpercollins.com

10 9 8 7 6 5 4 3 2 1

The first thing Tak did, he wrote himself.
The second thing Tak did, he wrote the Laws.
The third thing Tak did, he wrote the World.
The fourth thing Tak did, he wrote a cave.
The fifth thing Tak did, he wrote a geode, an egg of stone.

And in the twilight of the mouth of the cave, the geode hatched, and the Brothers were born.

The first Brother walked toward the light, and stood under the open sky. Thus he became too tall. He was the first Man. He found no Laws, and he was enlightened.

The second Brother walked toward the darkness, and stood under a roof of stone. Thus he achieved the correct height. He was the first Dwarf. He found the Laws Tak had written, and he was endarkened.

But some of the living spirit of Tak was trapped in the broken stone egg, and it became the first troll, wandering the world unbidden and unwanted, without soul or purpose, learning or understanding. Fearful of light and darkness it shambles forever in twilight, knowing nothing, learning nothing, creating nothing, being nothing . . .

—From 'Gd Tak 'Gar' (The Things Tak Wrote), *trans. Prof. W. W. W. Wildblood. Ankh-Morpork: Unseen University Press. AM$8. In the original, the last paragraph of the quoted text appears to have been added by a much later hand.*

Him who mountain crush him no
Him who sun him stop him no
Him who hammer him break him no
Him who fire him fear him no
Him who raise him head above him heart
Him diamond

—Translation of troll pictograms found carved on a basalt slab in the deepest level of the Ankh-Morpork treacle mines, in pig-treacle measures estimated at 500,000 years old.

***T**hud* . . .

. . . that was the sound the heavy club made as it connected with the head. The body jerked, and slumped back.

And it was done, unheard, unseen: the perfect end, a perfect solution, a perfect story.

But, as the dwarfs say, where there is trouble you will always find a troll.

The troll saw.

It started out as a perfect day. It would soon enough be an imperfect one, he knew, but just for these few minutes, it was possible to pretend that it wouldn't.

Sam Vimes shaved himself. It was his daily act of defiance, a confirmation that he was . . . well, plain Sam Vimes.

Admittedly, he shaved himself in a mansion, and while he did so his butler read out bits from the *Times*, but they were just . . . circumstances. It was still Sam Vimes looking back at him from the mirror. The day he saw the Duke of Ankh-Morpork

1

in there would be a bad day. "Duke" was just a job description, that's all.

"Most of the news is about the current . . . dwarfish situation, sir," said Willikins, as Vimes negotiated the tricky area under the nose. He still used his granddad's cutthroat razor. It was another anchor to reality. Besides, the steel was a lot better than the steel you got today. Sybil, who had a strange enthusiasm for modern gadgetry, kept on suggesting he get one of those new shavers, with a little magic imp inside that had its own scissors and did all the cutting very quickly, but Vimes had held out. If anyone was going to be using a blade near his face, it was going to be *him*.

"Koom Valley, Koom Valley," he muttered to his reflection. "Anything *new*?"

"Not as such, sir," said Willikins, turning back to the front page. "There is a report of that speech by Grag Hamcrusher. There was a disturbance afterwards, it says. Several dwarfs and trolls were wounded. Community leaders have appealed for calm."

Vimes shook some lather off the blade. "Hah! I bet they have. Tell me, Willikins, did you fight much when you were a kid? Were you in a gang or anything?"

"I was privileged to belong to the Shamlegger Street Rude Boys, sir," said the butler primly.

"Really?" said Vimes, genuinely impressed. "They were pretty tough nuts, as I recall."

"Thank you, sir," said Willikins smoothly. "I pride myself I used to give somewhat more than I got if we needed to discuss the vexed area of turf issues with the young men from Rope Street. Stevedore's hooks were their weapon of choice, as I recall."

"And yours . . . ?" said Vimes, agog.

"A cap-brim sewn with sharpened pennies, sir. An ever-present help in times of trouble."

"Ye gods, man! You could put someone's eye out with something like that."

"With care, sir, yes."

And here you stand now, in your pinstripe trousers and butlering coat, shiny as schmaltz and fat as butter, Vimes thought, while he tidied up under the ears. And I'm a duke. How the world turns.

"And have you *ever* heard someone say 'let's have a disturbance'?" he said.

"Never, sir," said Willikins, picking up the paper again.

"Me neither. It only happens in newspapers." Vimes glanced at the bandage on his arm. It had been quite disturbing, even so.

"Did it mention I took personal charge?" he said.

"No, sir. But it does say here that rival factions in the street outside were kept apart by the valiant efforts of the Watch, sir."

"They actually used the word 'valiant'?" said Vimes.

"Indeed they did, sir."

"Well, good," Vimes conceded grumpily. "Do they record that two officers had to be taken to the Free Hospital, one of them quite badly hurt?"

"Unaccountably, not, sir," said the butler.

"Huh. Typical. Oh, well . . . carry on."

Willikins coughed a butlery cough. "You might wish to lower the razor for the next one, sir. I got into trouble with her ladyship about last week's little nick."

Vimes watched his image sigh, and lowered the razor. "All right, Willikins. Tell me the worst."

Behind him, the paper was professionally rustled. "The headline on page three is: 'Vampire Officer For The Watch?,' sir," said the butler and took a careful step backwards.

"Damn! Who told them?"

"I really couldn't say, sir. It says you are not in favor of vampires in the Watch, but will be interviewing a recruit today. It says there is a lively controversy over the issue."

"Turn to page eight, will you?" said Vimes grimly. Behind him, the paper rustled again.

"Well?" he said. "That's where they usually put their silly political cartoon, isn't it?"

"You *did* put the razor down, did you, sir?" said Willikins.

"Yes!"

"Perhaps it would also be just as well if you stepped away from the washbasin, too, sir."

"There's one of me, isn't there . . ." said Vimes grimly.

"Indeed there is, sir. It portrays a small, nervous vampire and, if I may say so, a rather larger-than-life drawing of yourself leaning over your desk, holding a wooden stake in your right hand. The caption is 'Any good on a stakeout, eh?,' sir, this being a humorous wordplay referring, on the one hand, to the standard police procedure—"

"Yes, I think I can just about spot it," said Vimes wearily. "Any chance you could nip down and buy the original before Sybil does? Every time they run a cartoon of me, she gets hold of it and hangs it up in the library!"

"Mr., er, Fizz does capture a very good likeness, sir," the butler conceded. "And I regret to say that her ladyship has already instructed me to go down to the *Times* office on *her* behalf."

Vimes groaned.

"Moreover, sir," Willikins went on, "her ladyship desired me to remind you that she and Young Sam will meet you at the studio of Sir Joshua at eleven sharp, sir. The painting is at an important stage, I gather."

"But I—"

"She was very specific, sir. She said if a commander of police cannot take time off, who can?"

On this day in 1802, the painter Methodia Rascal woke up in the night because the sounds of warfare were coming from a drawer in his bedside table. Again.

One little light illuminated the cellar, which was to say that it lent different textures to the darkness and divided shadow from darker shadow.

The figures barely showed up at all. It was quite impossible, with normal eyes, to tell who was talking.

"This is not to be talked about, do you understand?"

"Not talked about? He's *dead*!"

"This is dwarf business! It's not to come to the ears of the City Watch! They have no place here! Do any of us want *them* down here?"

"They do have dwarf officers—"

"Hah. *D'rkza*. Too much time in the sun. They're just short humans now. Do they *think* dwarf? And Vimes will dig and dig and wave the silly rags and tatters they call laws. Why should we allow such a violation? Besides, this is hardly a mystery. Only a troll could have done it, agreed? I said, are we agreed?"

"That is what happened," said a figure; the voice was thin and old and, in truth, uncertain.

"Indeed, it was a troll," said another voice, almost the twin of that one, but with a little more assurance.

The subsequent pause was underlined by the ever-present sound of the pumps.

"It could only have been a troll," said the first voice. "And is it not said that behind every crime you will find the troll?"

There was a small crowd outside the Watch House in Pseudopolis Yard when Commander Sam Vimes arrived at work. It had been a fine sunny morning up until then. Now it was still sunny, but nothing like as fine.

The crowd had placards. BLOODSUCKERS OUT!!,

Vimes read, and NO FANGS! Faces turned toward him with a sullen, half-frightened defiance.

He uttered a bad word under his breath, but only just.

Otto Chriek, the *Times* iconographer, was standing nearby, holding a sunshade and looking dejected. He caught Vimes's eye and trudged over.

"What's in this for you, Otto?" said Vimes. "Come to get a picture of a jolly good riot, have you?"

"It's news, Commander," said Otto, looking down at his very shiny shoes.

"Who tipped you off?"

"I just do zer pictures, Commander," said Otto, looking up with a hurt expression. "Anyvay, I couldn't tell you even if I knew, because of zer Freedom of the Press."

"Freedom to pour oil on a flame, d'you mean?" Vimes demanded.

"Zat's freedom for you," said Otto. "No-vun said it vas *nice*."

"But . . . well, you're a vampire, too!" said Vimes, waving a hand toward the protesters. "Do *you* like what's been stirred up?"

"It's still news, Commander," said Otto meekly.

Vimes glared at the crowd again. It was mostly human. There *was* one troll, although, admittedly, the troll had probably joined in on general principle, simply because something was happening. A vampire would need a masonry drill and a lot of patience before it could put a troll to any trouble. Still, there was one good thing, if you could call it that—this little sideshow took people's minds off Koom Valley.

"It's strange that they don't seem to mind *you*, Otto," he said, calming down a little.

"Vell, I'm not official," said Otto. "I do not haf zer sword und zer badge. I do not threaten. I am just a vorking stiff. And I make zem laff."

Vimes stared at the man. He'd never thought about that before. But yes . . . Little fussy Otto, in his red-lined black opera cloak with pockets for all his gear, his shiny black shoes, his carefully cut widow's peak and, not least, his ridiculous accent that grew thicker or thinner depending on whom he was talking to, did not look like a threat. He looked funny, a joke, a music-hall vampire. It had never previously occurred to Vimes that, just possibly, the joke was on other people. Make them laugh, and they're not afraid.

He nodded to Otto and went inside, where Sergeant Cheery Littlebottom was standing—on a box—at the too-high duty officer's desk, her chevrons all shiny and new on her sleeve. Vimes made a mental note to do something about the box. Some of the dwarf officers were getting sensitive about having to use it.

"I think we could do with a couple of lads standing outside, Cheery," he said. "Nothing provocative, just a little reminder to people that *we* keep the peace."

"I don't think we'll need that, Mister Vimes," said the dwarf.

"I'm not interested in seeing a picture in the *Times* showing the Watch's first vampire recruit being mobbed by protesters, Corp—Sergeant," said Vimes severely.

"I thought you wouldn't be, sir," said Cheery. "So

I asked Sergeant Angua to fetch her. They came in the back way half an hour ago. She's showing her the building. I think they're down in the locker room."

"You asked *Angua* to do it?" said Vimes, his heart sinking.

"Yessir?" said Cheery, suddenly looking worried. "Er . . . is there a problem?"

Vimes stared at her. She's a good, orderly officer, he thought, I wish I had two more like her. And she deserved the promotion, heavens knew, *but*, he reminded himself, she's from Uberwald, isn't she? She should have remembered about the . . . thing between them and werewolves. Maybe it's my fault. I tell 'em that all coppers are just coppers.

"What? Oh, no," he said. "Probably not."

A vampire and a werewolf in one room, he thought, as he headed on up the stairs to his office. Well, they'll just have to deal with it. And that'll be just the *first* of our problems.

"And I took Mr. Pessimal up to the interview room," Cheery called after him.

Vimes stopped in mid-stair.

"Pessimal?" he said.

"The government inspector, sir?" said Cheery. "The one you told me about?"

Oh yes, thought Vimes. The *second* of our problems.

It was politics. Vimes could never get a handle on politics, which was full of traps for honest men. This one had been

sprung last week, in Lord Vetinari's office, at the normal daily briefing . . .

"Ah, Vimes," said his lordship, as Vimes entered. "So kind of you to come. Isn't it a beautiful day?"

Up until now, Vimes thought when he spotted the two other people in the room.

"You wanted me, sir?" he said, turning to Vetinari again. "There's a Silicon Anti-Defamation League march in Water Street, and I've got traffic backed up all the way to Least Gate—"

"I'm sure it can wait, Commander."

"Yes, sir. That's the trouble, sir. That's what it's doing."

Vetinari waved a languid hand. "Full carts congesting the street, Vimes, is a sign of progress," he declared.

"Only in the figurative sense, sir," said Vimes.

"Well, at any rate I'm sure your men can deal with it," said Vetinari, nodding to an empty chair. "You have so many of them now. Such an expense. Do sit down, Commander. Do you know Mr. John Smith?"

The other man at the table took the pipe out of his mouth and gave Vimes a smile of manic friendliness.

"I don't believe wwwe have had the pleasure," he said, extending a hand. It should not be possible to roll your double-yous, but John Smith managed it.

Shake hands with a vampire? Not bloody likely, Vimes thought, not even one wearing a badly hand-knitted pullover. He saluted instead.

"Pleased to meet you, sir," he said crisply, standing to attention. It really was an *awful* garment, that pullover. It had a queasy zigzag pattern, in many strange, unhappy colors. It looked like something knitted as a present by a colorblind aunt, the sort of thing you wouldn't dare throw away in case the garbage collectors laughed at you and kicked your trash cans over.

"Vimes, Mr. Smith is—" Vetinari began.

"President of the Ankh-Morpork Mission of the Uberwald League of Temperance," said Vimes. "And I believe the lady next to him to be Mrs. Doreen Winkings, treasurer of same. This is about having a vampire in the Watch, isn't it, sir? Again."

"Yes, Vimes, it is," said Vetinari. "And, yes, it is *again*. Shall we all be seated? Vimes?"

There was no escape, Vimes knew, as he sagged resentfully into a chair. And this time he was going to lose. Vetinari had cornered him.

Vimes knew all the arguments for having different species in the Watch. They were good arguments. Some of the arguments against them were bad arguments. There were trolls in the Watch, *plenty* of dwarfs, one werewolf, three golems, an Igor, and, not least, Corporal Nobbs,* so why not a vampire? And the League of Temperance was a fact. Vampires wearing the League's Black Ribbon ("Not One Drop!") were a fact, too. Admittedly, vampires who had sworn off blood could be a bit weird, but they were intelligent and clever and, as such, a potential asset to society. And the Watch was the most visible arm of government in the city. Why not set an example?

---

*This was a bit of a slur on Nobby, Vimes had to admit. Like many other officers, Nobby was human. It was just that he was the only one who had to carry a certificate to prove it.

Because, said Vimes's battered but still functional soul, you hate bloody vampires. No messing about, no dissembling, no weasel words about "the public won't stand for it" or "it's not the right time." *You* hate bloody vampires, and it's *your* bloody Watch.

The other three were staring at him.

"Mr. Vimes," said Mrs. Winkings. "Ve cannot help but notice that you still haf not employed any of our members in the Vatch . . ."

Say "Watch," why don't you? Vimes thought. I know you can. Let the twenty-third letter of the alphabet enter your life. Ask Mr. Smith for some, he's got more than enough. Anyway, I have a new argument. It's copper-bottomed.

"Mrs. Winkings," he said aloud, "no vampire has *applied* to join the Watch. They're just not mentally suited to a copper's way of life. And it's Commander Vimes, thank you."

Mrs. Winkings's little eyes gleamed with righteous malice.

"Oh, are you sayink vampires are . . . stupid?" she said.

"No, Mrs. Winkings, I'm saying they're intelligent. And there's your problem, right there. Why would a clever person want to risk getting their nadg—their head kicked in on a daily basis for thirty-eight dollars a month plus allowances? Vampires have got class, education, a von in front of their name. There's a hundred better things for them to be doing than walking the streets as a cop. What do you want me to do, *force* them to join the force?"

"Wwwouldn't they be offered officer rank?" said

John Smith. There was sweat on his face, and his permanent smile was manic; rumor had it he was finding the pledge very hard going.

"No. Everyone starts on the street," said Vimes. That wasn't entirely true, but the question had offended him. "And on the Night Watch, too. Good training. The best there is. A week of rainy nights with the mists coming up and the water trickling down your neck and odd noises in the shadows . . . well, that's when we find out if we've got a real copper—"

He knew it as soon as he said it. He'd walked right into it. They must have found a candidate!

"Vell, zat is good news!" said Mrs. Winkings, leaning back.

Vimes wanted to shake her and shout: You're not a vampire, Doreen! You're *married* to one, yes, but he didn't become one until a time when it is beyond human imagining that he could possibly have wanted to bite you! All the *real* Black Ribboners try to act normal and unobtrusive! No flowing cloaks, no sucking, and definitely no ripping the underwired nightdresses off young ladies! Everyone knows John Not-A-Vampire-At-All Smith used to be Count Vargo St. Gruet von Vilinus! But now he smokes a pipe and wears those horrible woolen sweaters, and he collects bananas and makes models of human organs out of matchsticks, because he thinks hobbies make you more human! But you, Doreen? You were born in Cockbill Street! Your mum was a washerwoman! No one would ever rip your nightdress off, not without a crane! But you're so . . . *into* this, right? It's a *damn* hobby. You try to look more like vampires than vampires do! Incidentally, those fake pointy teeth rattle when you talk!

"Vimes?"

"Hmm?" Vimes became aware that people had been speaking.

"Mr. Smith has some good news," said Vetinari.

"Indeed, yes," said John Smith, beaming manically. "Wwwe have a recruit for you, Commander. A vampire wwho *wwants* to be in the Wwwatch!"

"Ant, of course, zer night vill *not* prezent a problem," said Doreen triumphantly. "Ve *are* zer night!"

"Are you trying to tell me that I *must*—" Vimes began. Vetinari cut in quickly.

"Oh, no, Commander. We all fully respect your autonomy as head of the Watch. Clearly, you must hire whomsoever you think fit. All I ask is that the candidate is interviewed, in a spirit of fairness."

Yeah, right, thought Vimes. And politics with Uberwald will become just that bit easier, won't it, if you can say you even have a Black Ribboner in the Watch. And if I turn this man down, I'll have to explain why. And "I just don't like vampires, okay?" probably won't do.

"Of course," he said. "Send him along."

"He is, in fact, she," said Lord Vetinari. He glanced down at his paperwork. "Salacia Deloresista Amanita Trigestatra Zeldana Malifee . . ." He paused, turned over several pages, and said, "I think we can skip some of these, but they end 'von Humpeding.' She is fifty-one, *but*," he added quickly, before Vimes could seize on this revelation, "that is no age at all for a vampire. Oh, and she'd prefer to be known simply as Sally."

The locker room wasn't big enough. Nothing like big enough. Sergeant Angua tried not to inhale.

A large hall, that was fine. The open air, even better. What she needed was room to breathe. More specifically, she needed room not to breathe vampire.

Damn Cheery! But she couldn't have refused, that would have looked bad. All she could do was grin and bear it and fight down a pressing desire to rip out the girl's throat with her teeth.

She must know she's doing it, she thought. They must *know* that they exude this air of effortless ease, confident in any company, at home everywhere, making everyone else feel second-class and awkward. Oh, my. Call me Sally, indeed!

"Sorry about this," she said aloud, trying to force the hairs on the back of her neck not to rise. "It's a bit close in here." She coughed. "Anyway, this is it. Don't worry, it always smells like this in here. And don't bother to lock your locker, all the keys are the same and anyway most of the doors spring open if you hit the frame in the right way. Don't keep valuables in it, this place is too full of coppers. And don't get too upset when someone puts holy water or a wooden stake in there."

"Is that likely to happen?" said Sally.

"Not likely," said Angua. "*Certain.* F'rinstance, I used to find dog collars and bone-shaped biscuits in mine."

"Didn't you complain?"

"What? No! You *don't* complain!" snapped Angua, wishing she could stop inhaling right now. Already she was sure her hair was a mess.

"But I thought the Watch was—"

"Look, it's nothing to do with what you . . . what *we* are, okay?" said Angua. "If you were a dwarf, it'd be a pair of platform soles or a stepladder or something, although that doesn't happen so much these days. Mostly they try it on *everyone*. It's a copper thing. And then they'll watch what you do, you see? No one cares if you're a troll or a gnome or a zombie or a vampire," *much*, she added to herself, "but don't let them believe you're a whiner or a snitch. And actually the biscuits were pretty good, to tell you the truth—ah, have you met Igor yet?"

"Many times," said Sally. Angua forced a smile. In Uberwald, you met Igors all the time. Especially if you were a vampire.

"The one here, though?" she said.

"I don't think so."

Ah. That was a relief. Angua normally avoided Igor's laboratory, because the smells that emanated therefrom were either painfully chemical or horribly, suggestively organic, but now she'd snuff them up with relief. She headed for the door with slightly more speed than politeness required, and knocked.

It creaked open. Any door opened by an Igor would creak. It was a knack.

"Hi, Igor," said Sally cheerfully. "Gimme six!"

Angua left them chatting. Igors were naturally servile, vampires were naturally not. It was an ideal match. At least she could go and get some air now.

The door opened.

"Mr. Pessimal, sir," said Cheery, ushering in a man not much taller than she was into Vimes's office. "And here's the office copy of the *Times* . . ."

Mr. Pessimal was neat. In fact, he went beyond neat. He was a folding kind of person. His suit was cheap but very clean, his little boots sparkled. His hair gleamed, too, even more than the boots. It had a center parting and had been plastered down so severely that it looked as though it had been painted on his head.

All the city's departments got inspected from time to time, Vetinari had said. There was no reason why the Watch should be passed over, was there? It was, after all, a major drain on the city coffers.

Vimes had pointed out that a drain was where things went to *waste*.

Nevertheless, Vetinari had said. *Just* "nevertheless." You couldn't argue with "nevertheless."

And the outcome was Mr. Pessimal, walking toward Vimes.

He *twinkled* as he walked. Vimes couldn't think of another way to describe it. Every move was . . . well, neat.

Shovel purse and spectacles on a ribbon, I'll bet, he thought.

Mr. Pessimal folded himself onto the chair in front of Vimes's desk and opened the clasps of his briefcase with two little snaps of doom. With some ceremony, he donned a pair of spectacles. They were on a black ribbon.

"My letter of accreditation from Lord Vetinari, Your Grace," he said, handing over a sheet of paper.

"Thank you, Mr. . . . A. E. Pessimal," said Vimes, glancing at it and putting it on one side. "And how can we help you? It's Commander Vimes when I'm at work, by the way."

"I will need an office, Your Grace. And an oversight of all your paperwork. As you know, I am tasked to give his lordship a complete overview and cost/benefit analysis of the Watch, with any suggestions for improvement in every aspect of its activities. Your cooperation is appreciated but not essential."

"Suggestions for improvement, eh?" said Vimes cheerfully, while behind A. E. Pessimal's chair Sergeant Littlebottom shut her eyes in dread. "Jolly good. I've always been known for my cooperative attitude. I did mention about the duke thing, did I?"

"Yes, Your Grace," said A. E. Pessimal primly. "Nevertheless, you are the Duke of Ankh-Morpork and it would be inappropriate to address you in any other way. I would feel disrespectful."

"I see. And how should I address *you*, Mr. Pessimal?" said Vimes. Out of the corner of his eye he saw a floorboard on the other side of the room lift almost imperceptibly.

"A. E. Pessimal will be quite acceptable, Your Grace," said the inspector.

"The *A* standing for—?" Vimes said, taking his eyes off the board for a moment.

"Just *A*, Your Grace," said A. E. Pessimal patiently. "A. E. Pessimal."

"You mean you weren't named, you were *initialed*?"

"Just so, Your Grace," said the little man calmly.

"What do your friends call you?"

A. E. Pessimal looked as though there was one major assumption in that sentence that he did not understand, so Vimes took a small amount of pity on him.

"Well, Sergeant Littlebottom here will look after you," he said with fake joviality.

"Find Mr. A. E. Pessimal an office somewhere, Sergeant, and let him see any paperwork he requires." As much as possible, Vimes thought. Bury him in the stuff, if it keeps him away from me.

"Thank you, Your Grace," said A. E. Pessimal. "I shall need to interview some officers, too."

"Why?" said Vimes.

"To ensure that my report is comprehensive, Your Grace," said Mr. A. E. Pessimal calmly.

"I can tell you anything you need to know," said Vimes.

"Yes, Your Grace, but that is not how an inquiry works. I must act completely independently. *Quis custodiet ipsos custodes?* Your Grace."

"I know that one," said Vimes. "Who watches the watchmen? Me, Mr. Pessimal."

"Ah, but who watches you, Your Grace?" said the inspector with a brief little smile.

"I do that, too. All the time," said Vimes. "Believe me."

"Quite so, Your Grace. Nevertheless, I must represent the public interest here. I shall try not to be obtrusive."

"Very good of you, Mr. Pessimal," said Vimes,

giving up. He hadn't realized he'd been upsetting Vetinari so much lately. This felt like one of his games. "All right. Enjoy your hopefully brief stay with us. Do excuse me, this is a busy morning, what with the damn Koom Valley thing and everything. Come in, Fred!"

That was a trick he'd learned from Vetinari. It was hard for a visitor to hang on when their replacement was in the room. Besides, Fred sweated a lot in this hot weather; he was a champion sweater. And in all these years he'd never worked out that when you stood outside the office door, the long floorboard seesawed slightly on the joist and rose just where Vimes could notice it.

The piece of floorboard settled again, and the door opened.

"Don't know how you do it, Mr. Vimes!" said Sergeant Colon cheerfully. "I was just about to knock!"

After you'd had a decent earful, thought Vimes. He was pleased to see A. E. Pessimal's nose wrinkle, though.

"What's up, Fred?" he said. "Oh, don't worry, Mr. Pessimal was just leaving. Carry on, Sergeant Littlebottom. Good morning, Mr. Pessimal."

Fred Colon removed his helmet as soon as the inspector had been ushered away by Cheery, and wiped his forehead.

"It's heating up out there again," he said. "We're in for thunderstorms, I reckon."

"Yes, Fred. And you wanted what, exactly?" said Vimes, contriving to indicate that while Fred was always welcome, just now was not the best of times.

"Er . . . something big's going down on the street,

sir," said Fred earnestly, in the manner of one who had memorized the phrase.

Vimes sighed. "Fred, do you mean something's happening?"

"Yes, sir. It's the dwarfs, sir. I mean the lads here. It's got worse. They keep going into huddles. Everywhere you look, sir, there's huddlin' goin' on. Only they stops as soon as anyone else comes close. Even the sergeants. They stops and gives you a *look*, sir. And that's makin' the trolls edgy, as you might expect."

"We're not going to have Koom Valley replayed in this nick, Fred," said Vimes. "I know the city's full of it right now, what with the anniversary coming up, but I'll drop like a ton of rectangular building things on any copper who tries a bit of historical recreation in the locker room. He'll be out on his arse before he knows it. Make sure everyone understands that."

"Yessir. But I ain't talking about all that stuff, sir. We all *know* about that," said Fred Colon. "This is something different, fresh today. It feels bad, sir, makes my neck tingle. The dwarfs know something. Something they ain't sayin'."

Vimes hesitated. Fred Colon was not the greatest gift to policing. He was slow, stolid, and not very imaginative. But he'd plodded his way around the streets for so long that he'd left a groove, and somewhere inside that stupid, fat head was something very smart that sniffed the wind and heard the buzz and read the writing on the wall, admittedly doing the last bit with its lips moving.

"Probably it's just that damn Hamcrusher who has got them stirred up again, Fred," he said.

"I hear them mentioning his name in their lingo, yes, sir, but there's more to it, I'll swear. I mean, they looked really uneasy, sir. It's something important, sir, I can feel it in my water."

Vimes considered the admissibility of Fred Colon's water as Exhibit A. It wasn't something you'd want to wave around in a court of law, but the gut feeling of an ancient street monster like Fred counted for a lot, one copper to another.

He said, "Where's Carrot?"

"Off, sir. He pulled the swing shift *and* the morning shift down at Treacle Mine Road. Everyone's doin' double shifts, sir," Fred Colon added reproachfully.

"Sorry, Fred, you know how it is. Look, I'll get him on it when he comes in. He's a dwarf, he'll hear the buzz."

"I think he might be just a wee bit too tall to hear this buzz, sir," said Colon, in an odd voice.

Vimes put his head on one side.

"What makes you say that, Fred?"

Fred Colon shook his head. "Just a feeling, sir," he said. He added, in a voice tinged with reminiscence and despair, "It was better when there was just you and me and Nobby and the lad Carrot, eh? We all knew who was who in the old days. We knew what one another was thinking . . ."

"Yes, we were thinking, 'I wish the odds were on our side, just for once,' Fred," said Vimes. "Look, I know this is getting us all down, right? But I need you senior officers to tough it out, okay? How do you like your new office?"

Colon brightened up.

"Very nice, sir. Shame about the door, 'course."

Finding a niche for Fred Colon had been a problem. To look at him, you'd see a man who might well, if he fell over a cliff, have to stop and ask directions on the way down. You had to *know* Fred Colon. The newer coppers didn't. They just saw a cowardly, stupid, fat man, which, to tell the truth, was pretty much what was there. But it wasn't *all* that was there.

Fred had looked retirement in the face, and didn't want any. Vimes had got around the problem by giving him the post of custody officer, to the amusement of all,* and an office in the Watch Training School across the alley, which was much better known as, and probably would forever be known as, the Old Lemonade Factory. He'd thrown in the job of Watch liaison officer, because it sounded good and no one knew what it meant. Vimes had also given him Corporal Nobbs, who was another awkward dinosaur in today's Watch.

It was working, too. Nobby and Colon had a street-level knowledge of the city that rivaled Vimes's own. They ambled about, apparently aimlessly and completely unthreatening, and they watched and they listened to the urban equivalent of the jungle drums. And sometimes the drums came to them. Once, Fred's sweaty little office had been the place where bare-armed ladies had mixed up great batches of Sarsaparilla and Raspberry Lava and Ginger Pop. Now the kettle was always on and it was open house for all his old mates, ex-watchmen and old cons—sometimes the same individual—and Vimes happily

---

* As in "Ol' Fred thought he said *custard* officer and volunteered!" Since this is an example of office humor, it doesn't actually have to be funny.

signed the bill for the doughnuts consumed when they dropped by to get out from under their wives' feet. It was worth it. Old coppers kept their eyes open, and gossiped like washerwomen.

In theory, the only problem in Fred's life now was his door.

"The Historians' Guild say we've got to preserve as much of the old fabric as possible, Fred," said Vimes.

"I know that, sir, but . . . well, 'The Twaddle Room,' sir? I mean, really?"

"Nice brass plate, though, Fred," said Vimes. "It's what they called the basic soft drink syrup, I'm told. Important historical fact. You could stick a piece of paper over the top of it."

"We do that, sir, but the lads pull it off and snigger."

Vimes sighed. "Sort it out, Fred. If an old sergeant can't sort out that sort of thing, the world has become a very strange place. Is that all?"

"Well, yes, sir, really. But—"

"C'mon, Fred, it's going to be a busy day."

"Have you heard of Mr. Shine, sir?"

"Do you clean stubborn surfaces with it?" said Vimes.

"Er . . . what, sir?" said Fred. No one did perplexed better than Fred Colon. Vimes felt ashamed of himself.

"Sorry, Fred. No, I *haven't* heard of Mr. Shine. Why?"

"Oh . . . nothing, really. 'Mr. Shine, him Dia-

mond!' Seen it on walls a few times lately. Troll graffiti; you know, carved in deep. Seems to be causing a
buzz among the trolls. Important, maybe?"

Vimes nodded. You ignored the writing on the
walls at your peril. Sometimes it was the city's way
of telling you if not what was on its bubbling mind
then at least what was in its creaking heart.

"Well, keep listening, Fred. I'm relying on you
not to let a buzz become a sting," said Vimes with
extra cheerfulness to keep the man's spirits up. "And
now I've got to see our vampire."

"Best of luck, Sam. I think it's going to be a
long day."

Sam, thought Vimes, as the old sergeant went out.
Gods know he's earned it, but he only calls me Sam
when he's really worried. Well, we all are.

We're waiting for the *first* shoe to drop.

Vimes unfolded the copy of the *Times* that Cheery
had left on his desk. He always read it at work, to
catch up on the news that Willikins had thought
unsafe to hear whilst shaving.

Koom Valley, Koom Valley. Vimes shook out the
paper and saw Koom Valley everywhere. Bloody,
bloody Koom Valley. Gods damn the wretched
place, although obviously they had already done
so—damned it and then forsaken it. Up close it was
just another rocky wasteland in the mountains. In
theory, it was a long way away, but it seemed to be
getting a lot closer lately. Koom Valley wasn't really
a place now, not anymore. It was a state of mind.

If you wanted the bare facts, it was where the
dwarfs had ambushed the trolls and/or the trolls
had ambushed the dwarfs, one ill-famed day under

unkind stars. Oh, they'd fought one another since Creation, as far as Vimes understood it, but at the Battle of Koom Valley that mutual hatred became, as it were, Official, and, as such, had developed a kind of mobile geography. Where any dwarf fought any troll, there was Koom Valley. Even if it was a punch-up in a pub, it was Koom Valley. It was part of the mythology of both races, a rallying cry, the ancestral reason why you couldn't trust those short, bearded/big, rocky bastards.

There had been plenty of such Koom Valleys since that first one. The war between the dwarfs and the trolls was a battle of natural forces, like the war between the wind and the waves. It had a momentum of its own.

Saturday was Koom Valley Day, and Ankh-Morpork was full of trolls and dwarfs and you know what? The further trolls and dwarfs got from the mountains, the more that bloody, bloody Koom Valley mattered. The parades were okay; the Watch had gotten good at keeping them apart, and anyway they were in the morning, when everyone was still mostly sober. But when the dwarf bars and the troll bars emptied out in the evening, hell went for a stroll with its sleeves rolled up.

In the bad old days, the Watch would find business elsewhere, and only turned up when stewed tempers had run their course. Then they'd bring out the hurry-up wagon and arrest every troll and dwarf too drunk, dazed, or dead to move. It was simple.

That was then. Now there were too many dwarfs and trolls—no, mental correction—the city had been *enriched* by vibrant, growing communities of dwarfs and trolls . . . and there was more . . . yes, call it venom in the air. Too much ancient politics, too many chips handed down from shoulder to shoulder. Too much boozing, too.

And then, just when you thought it was as bad as it could be, up popped Grag Hamcrusher and his chums. Deep-downers, they were called, dwarfs as fundamental as the bedrock. They'd turned up a month ago, occupied some old house in Treacle Street, and had hired a bunch of local lads to open up the basements. They were "grags." Vimes knew just enough dwarfish to know that "grag" meant "renowned master of dwarfish lore," but Hamcrusher had mastered it in his own special way. He preached the superiority of dwarf over troll, and that the duty of every dwarf was to follow in the footsteps of their forefathers and remove trollkind from the face of the world. It was written in some holy book, apparently, so that made it okay, and probably compulsory.

Young dwarfs listened to him, because he talked about history and destiny and all the other words that always got trotted out to put a gloss on slaughter. It was heady stuff, except that brains weren't involved. Malign idiots like him were the reason you saw dwarfs walking around now not just with the "cultural" battle-axes but heavy mail, chains, morningstars, broadswords . . . all the dumb, in-your-face swaggering that was known as "clang."

Trolls listened, too. You saw more lichen, more clan graffiti, more body carving, and much, much bigger clubs being dragged around.

It hadn't always been like this. Things had loosened up a lot in the last ten years or so. Dwarfs and trolls as races would never be chums, but the city stirred them together, and it had seemed to Vimes that they had managed to get along with no more than surface abrasions.

Now the melting pot was full of lumps again.

Gods damn Hamcrusher. Vimes itched to arrest him. Technically, he was doing nothing wrong, but that was no barrier to a copper who knew his business. He could certainly get him under "Behavior Likely To Cause A Breach Of The Peace." Vetinari had been against it, though. He'd said it'd only inflame the situation, but how much worse could it get?

Vimes closed his eyes and recalled that little figure, dressed in heavy black-leather robes and hooded so that he would not commit the crime of seeing daylight. A little figure, but with big words. He remembered: "Beware of the troll. Trust him not. Turn him from your door. He is nothing, a mere accident of forces, unwritten, unclean, the mineral world's pale, jealous echo of living, thinking creatures. In his head, a rock; in his heart, a stone. He does not build, he does not delve, he neither plants nor harvests. His nascence was a deed of theft and everywhere he drags his club he steals. When not thieving, he plans theft. The only purpose in his miserable life is its ending, relieving from the wretched rock his all-too-heavy burden of thought. I say this in sadness. To kill the troll is no murder. At its very worst, it is an act of charity."

It was about that time that the mob had broken into the hall.

That was how much worse it could be. Vimes blinked at the newspaper again, this time seeking anything that dared suggest that people in Ankh-Morpork still lived in the real world—

"Oh, damn!" He got up and hurried down the stairs, where Cheery practically cowered at his thundering approach.

"Did we know about this?" he demanded, thumping the paper down on the Occurrences Ledger.

"Know about what, sir?" said Cheery nervously.

Vimes prodded a short, illustrated article on page four, his finger stabbing at the page.

"See that?" he growled. "That pea-brained idiot at the Post Office has only gone and issued a Koom Valley stamp!"

The dwarf looked nervously at the article. "Er . . . *two* stamps, sir," she said.

Vimes looked closer. He hadn't taken in much of the detail before the red mist descended. Oh yes, two stamps. They were very nearly identical. They both showed Koom Valley, a rocky area ringed by mountains. They both showed the battle. But in one, little figures of trolls were pursuing dwarfs from right to left, and in the other, dwarfs were chasing trolls from left to right. Koom Valley, where the trolls ambushed the dwarfs and the dwarfs ambushed the trolls. Vimes groaned. Pick your own stupid history, a snip at ten pence, highly collectible.

"'The Koom Valley Memorial Issue,'" he read. "But we don't *want* them to remember it! We want them to forget it!"

"It's only stamps, sir," said Cheery. "I mean, there's no law against stamps . . ."

"There ought to be one against being a bloody fool!"

"If there was, sir, we'd be on overtime every day!" said Cheery, grinning.

Vimes relaxed a little. "Yep, and no one could build cells fast enough. Remember the cabbage-scented stamp last month? 'Send your expatriate sons and daughters the familiar odor of home'? They actually caught fire if you put too many of them together!"

"I still can't get the smell out of my clothes, sir."

"There are people living a hundred miles away who can't, I reckon. What did we do with the bloody things in the end?"

"I put them in No. 4 evidence locker and left the key in the lock," said Cheery.

"But Nobby Nobbs always steals anything that—" Vimes began.

"That's right, sir!" said Cheery happily. "I haven't seen them for weeks."

There was a crash from the direction of the canteen, followed by shouting. Something in Vimes, perhaps the very part of him that had been waiting for the first shoe, propelled him across the office, down the passage, and to the canteen's doorway at a speed that left dust spiraling on the floor.

What met his eyes was a tableau in various shades of guilt. One of the trestle tables had been knocked over. Food and cheap tinware were strewn across the floor. On one side of the mess was troll Constable Mica, currently being held between troll Constables Bluejohn and Schist; on the other was dwarf Constable Brakenshield, currently being lifted off the ground by probably human Corporal Nobbs and definitely human Constable Haddock.

There were watchmen at the other tables, too, all

caught in the act of rising. And, in the silence, audible only to the fine-tuned ears of a man searching for it, was the sound of hands pausing an inch away from the weapon of choice and very slowly being lowered.

"All right," said Vimes in the ringing vacuum. "Who's going to be the first to tell me a huge whopper? Corporal Nobbs?"

"Well, Mr. Vimes," said Nobby Nobbs, dropping the mute Brakenshield to the floor, ". . . er . . . Brakenshield here . . . picked up Mica's . . . yes, picked up Mica's *mug* by mistake, as it were . . . and . . . we all spotted that and jumped up, yes . . ." Nobby speeded up now, the really steep fibs now successfully negotiated, ". . . and that's how the table got knocked over . . . 'cos," and here Nobby's face assumed an expression of virtuous imbecility that was really quite frightening to see, "he'd have really hurt himself if he'd taken a swig of troll coffee, sir."

Inside, Vimes sighed. As stupid, lame excuses went, it wasn't actually a *bad* one. For one thing, it had the virtue of being completely unbelievable. No dwarf would come close to picking up a mug of troll espresso, which was a molten chemical stew with rust sprinkled on the top. Everyone knew this, just as everyone knew that Vimes could see that Brakenshield was holding an axe over his head and Constable Bluejohn was still frozen in the act of wrenching a club off Mica. And everyone knew, too, that Vimes was in the mood to sack the first bloody idiot to make a wrong move, and probably anyone standing near him.

"That's what it was, was it?" said Vimes. "So it

wasn't, as it might be, someone making a nasty remark about a fellow officer and others of his race, perhaps? Some little bit of stupidity to add to the mess of it that's floating around the streets right now?"

"Oh, nothing like that, sir," said Nobby. "Just one of them . . . things."

"Nearly a nasty accident, was it?" said Vimes.

"Yessir!"

"Well, we don't want any nasty accidents, do we, Nobby . . ."

"Nosir!"

"*None* of us want nasty accidents, I expect," said Vimes, looking around the room. Some of the constables, he was grimly glad to see, were sweating with the effort of not moving. "And it's so easy to have 'em, when your mind isn't firmly on the job. Understood?"

There was a general muttering.

"I can't hear you!"

This time there were audible riffs on the theme of "Yessir!"

"Right," snapped Vimes. "Now get out there and keep the peace, because as sure as hell you won't do it in here!" He directed a special glare at Constables Brakenshield and Mica, and strode back to the main office, where he almost bumped into Sergeant Angua.

"Sorry, sir, I was just fetching—" she began.

"I sorted it out, don't worry," said Vimes. "But it was *that* close."

"Some of the dwarfs are really on edge, sir. I can smell it," said Angua.

"You and Fred Colon," said Vimes.

"I don't think it's just the Hamcrusher thing, sir. It's something . . . dwarfish."

"Well, I can't beat it out of them. And just when the day couldn't get any worse, I've got to interview a damned vampire."

Too late Vimes saw the urgent look in Angua's eyes.

"Ah . . . I think that would be me," said a small voice behind him.

Fred Colon and Nobby Nobbs, having been rousted from their lengthy coffee break, proceeded gently up Broad Way, giving the ol' uniform an airing. What with one thing or another, it was probably a good idea not to be back at the Yard for a while.

They walked like men who had all day. They did have all day. They had chosen this particular street because it was busy and wide and you didn't get too many trolls and dwarfs in this part of town. The reasoning was faultless. In lots of areas, right now, dwarfs or trolls were wandering around in groups or, alternatively, staying still in groups in case any of those wandering bastards tried any trouble in *this* neighborhood. There had been little flare-ups for weeks. In these areas, Nobby and Fred considered, there wasn't much peace, so it was a waste of effort to keep what little was left of it, right? You wouldn't try keeping sheep in places where all the sheep got eaten by wolves, right? It stood to reason. It would look silly. Whereas in big streets like Broad Way there was lots of peace, which, obviously, needed keeping. Common sense told them this was true. It was as plain as the nose on your face, and especially the one on Nobby's face.

"Bad business," said Colon, as they strolled. "I've never seen the dwarfs like this."

"It always gets tricky, Sarge, just before Koom Valley Day," Nobby observed.

"Yeah, but Hamcrusher's really got them on the boil and no mistake." Colon removed his helmet and wiped his brow. "I told Sam about my water, and he was impressed."

"Well, he would be," Nobby agreed. "It would impress anyone."

Colon tapped his nose. "There's a storm coming, Nobby."

"Not a cloud in the sky, Sarge," Nobby observed.

"Figure of speech, Nobby, figure of speech." Colon sighed and glanced sideways at his friend. When he continued, it was in the hesitant tones of a man with something on his mind. "As a matter of fact, Nobby, there was another matter about which, per say, I wanted to speak to you about, man to—" there was only the tiniest hesitation, "—man."

"Yes, Sarge?"

"Now you know, Nobby, that I've always taken a pers'nal interest in your moral well-being, what with you havin' no dad to put your feet on the proper path . . ."

"That's right, Sarge. I would have strayed no end if you hadn't," said Nobby virtuously.

"Well, you know you was telling me about that girl you're goin' out with, what was her name, now . . ."

"Tawneee, Sarge?"

"That's the . . . bunny. The one you said worked in a club, right?"

"That's right. Is there a problem, Sarge?" said Nobby anxiously.

"Not as such. But when you was on your day off last week, me an' Constable Jolson got called into the Pink PussyCat Club, Nobby. You know? There's pole-dancing and table dancing and stuff of that nature? And you know ol' Mrs. Spudding what lives in New Cobblers?"

"Ol' Mrs. Spudding with the wooden teeth, Sarge?"

"The very same, Nobby," said Colon magisterially. "She does the cleaning in there. And it appears that when she come in at eight o'clock in the morning ae-em, with no one else about, Nobby, well, I hardly like to say this, but it appears she took it into her head to have a twirl on the pole."

They shared a moment of silence as Nobby ran this image in the cinema of his imagination and hastily consigned much of it to the cutting-room floor.

"But she must be seventy-five, Sarge!" he said, staring at nothing in fascinated horror.

"A girl can dream, Nobby, a girl can dream. O'course, she forgot she wasn't as limber as she used to be, plus she got her foot caught in her long drawers and panicked when her dress fell over her head. She was in a bad way when the manager came in, having been upside down for three hours, with her false teeth fallen out on the floor. Wouldn't let go of the pole, too. Not a pretty sight, I trust I do not have to draw you a picture. Come the finish, Precious Jolson had to rip the pole out top and bottom and we slid her off. That girl's got the muscles of a troll, Nobby, I'll swear it. And then, Nobby, when we was bringing her 'round behind the scenes, this young lady wearing two sequins and a bootlace comes up and says she's a friend of yours! I did not know where to put my face!"

"You're not supposed to put it anywhere, Sarge. They throw you out for that sort of thing," observed Nobby.

"You never told me she was a pole dancer, Nobby!" Fred wailed.

"Don't say it like that, Sarge." Nobby sounded a little hurt. "This is modern times. And she's got class, Tawneee has. She even brings her own pole. No hanky-panky."

"But, I mean . . . showin' her body off in lewd ways, Nobby! Dancing around without her vest and practic'ly no drawers on. Is that any way to behave?"

Nobby considered this deep metaphysical question from various angles.

"Er . . . yes?" he ventured.

"Anyway, I thought you were still walking out with Verity Pushpram? That's a handy little seafood stall she runs," Colon said, sounding as though he was pleading a case.

"Oh, Hammerhead's a nice girl if you catch her on a good day, Sarge," Nobby conceded.

"You mean those days when she doesn't tell you to bugger off and chases you down the street throwing crabs at you?"

"Exactly those days, Sarge. But good or bad, you can never get rid of the smell of fish. And her eyes are too far apart. I mean, it's hard to get a relationship goin' with a girl who can't see you if you stand right in front of her."

"I shouldn't think Tawneee can see you if you're up close, either!" Colon burst out. "She's nearly six feet tall and she's got a bosom like . . . well, she's a big girl, Nobby." Fred Colon was at a loss. Nobby Nobbs and a dancer with big hair, a big smile, and . . . general bigitigy? Look upon this picture, and on this! It did your head in, it really did.

He struggled on. "She told me, Nobby, that she'd been Miss May on the centerfold of *Girls, Giggles and Garters*! Well, I mean . . . !"

"*What* do you mean, Sarge? Anyway, she wasn't just Miss May, she was the first week in June as well," Nobby pointed out. "It was the only way they had room."

"Err . . . well, I ask you," Fred floundered, "is a girl who displays her body for money the kind of wife for a copper? Ask yourself that!"

For the second time in five minutes, what passed for Nobby's face wrinkled up in deep thought.

"Is this a trick question, Sarge?" he said at last. "'Cos I know for a fact that Haddock has got that picture pinned up in his locker and every time he opens it he goes, 'Pwaor, will you look at th—'"

"How did you meet her, anyway?" said Colon quickly.

"What? Oh, our eyes met when I shoved an IOU in her garter, Sarge," said Nobby happily.

"And . . . she hadn't just been hit on the head, or something?"

"I don't think so, Sarge."

"She's not . . . ill, is she?" said Fred Colon, exploring every likelihood.

"No, Sarge!"

"Are you *sure*?"

"She says perhaps we're two halves of the same soul, Sarge," said Nobby dreamily.

Colon stopped with one foot raised above the pavement. He stared at nothing, his lips moving.

"Sarge?" said Nobby, puzzled by this.

"Yeah . . . yeah," said Colon, more or less to himself. "Yeah. I can see that. Not the same stuff in each half, obviously. Sort of . . . sieved . . ."

The foot landed.

"I say!"

It was more of a bleat than a cry, and it came from the door of the Royal Art Museum. A tall, thin figure was beckoning to the watchmen, who strolled over.

"Yessir?" said Colon, touching his helmet.

"We've had a burglareah, officer!"

"Burglar rear?" said Nobby.

"Oh dear, sir," said Colon, putting a warning hand on the corporal's shoulders. "Anything taken?"

"Years. I rather think that's hwhy it was a burglareah, you see?" said the man. He had the attitude of a preoccupied chicken, but Fred Colon was impressed. You could barely understand the man, he was that posh. It was not so much speech as modulated yawning. "I'm Sir Reynold Stitched, the curator of Fine Art, and I was hwalking through the Long Gallereah and . . . oh, dear, they took the Rascal!"

The man looked at two blank faces.

"Methodia Rascal?" he tried. "*The Battle of Koom Valley*? It is a priceless work of art!"

Colon hitched up his stomach. "Ah," he said, "that's serious. We'd better take a look at it. Er . . . I mean, the locale where it was situated in."

"Years, years, of course," said Sir Reynold. "Do come this hway. I am given to understand that the modern hWatch can learn a lot just by looking at the place where a thing was, is that not so?"

"Like, that it's gone?" said Nobby. "Oh, *years*. We're *good* at that."

"Er . . . Quite so," said Sir Reynold. "Do come this way."

The watchmen followed. They had been inside the museum before, of course. Most citizens had, on days when no better entertainment presented itself. Under the governance of Lord Vetinari it hosted fewer modern exhibitions these days, since his lordship held Views, but a gentle stroll among the ancient tapestries and rather brown and dusty paintings was a pleasant way of spending an afternoon. Plus, it was always nice to look at the pictures of big pink women with no clothes on.

Nobby was having a problem. "Here, Sarge, what's he going on about?" he whispered. "It sounds like he's yawning all the time. What a galler rear?"

"A gallery, Nobby. That's very high-class talkin,' that is."

"I can hardly understand him!"

"Shows it's high class, Nobby. It wouldn't be much good if people like *you* could understand, right?"

"Good point, Sarge," Nobby conceded. "I hadn't thought of that."

"You found it missing this morning, sir?" said Colon, as they trailed after the curator into a gallery still littered with ladders and dust sheets.

"Years indeed!"

"So it was stolen last night, then?"

Sir Reynold hesitated.

"Er . . . not necessarileah, I'm afraid. We have been refurbishing the Long Gallereah. The picture was too big to move, of course, so hwe had it covered in heavy dust sheets for the past month. But when we took them down this morning, there hwas only the frame! Observe!"

The Rascal occupied—or rather, *had* occupied—an actual frame some ten feet high and fifty feet long, which, as such, was pretty close to being a work of art in its own right. It was still there, framing nothing but uneven, dusty plaster.

"I suppose some rich private collector has it now," Sir Reynold moaned. "But how could he keep it a secret? The mural is one of the most recognizable paintings in the hworld! Every civilized person hwould spot it in an instant!"

"What did it look like?" said Fred Colon.

Sir Reynold performed that downshift of assumptions that was the normal response to any conversation with Ankh-Morpork's Finest.

"I can probableah find you a copy," he said weakly. "But the original is fifty feet long! Have you *never* seen it?"

"Well, I remember being brought to see it when I was a kiddie, but it's a bit long, really. You can't really *see* it, anyway. I mean, by the time you get to the other end you've forgotten what was happening back up the line, as it were."

"Alas, that is regrettableah true, Sergeant," said Sir Reynold. "And hwhat is so vexing is that the hwhole *point* of this refurbishment hwas to build a special circular room to hold the Rascal. His ideah, you know, hwas that the viewer should be *hwholly* encircled by the mural and feel right in the *thick* of the action, as it hwere. You hwould be there in Koom Valleah! He called it panoscopic art. Say hwhat you like about the current interest, but the extra visitors hwould have made it possible to display the picture as hwe believe he intended it to be displayed. And now this!"

"If you were going to move it, why didn't you just take it down and put it away nice and safe, sir?"

"You mean *roll it up*?" said Sir Reynold, horrified. "That could cause *such* a lot of damage. Oh, the horror! No, hwe had a very careful exercise planned for next hweek, to be done with the utmost diligence." He shuddered. "hWhen I think of someone just *hacking* it out of the frame I feel quite faint—"

"Hey, this must be a clue, Sarge!" said Nobby, who had returned to his default activity of mooching about and poking at things to see if they were valuable. "Look, someone dumped a load of stinking ol' rubbish here!"

He'd wandered across to a plinth, which did, indeed, appear to be piled high with rags.

"Don't touch that, please!" said Sir Reynold, rushing over. "That's *Don't Talk to Me About Mondays!* It's Daniellarina Pouter's most controversial hwork!

You didn't move anything, did you?" he added nervously. "It's literalleah priceless, and she's got a sharp tongue on her!"

"It's only a lot of old rubbish," Nobby protested, backing away.

"Art is greater than the sum of its mere mechanical components, Corporal," said the curator. "Surely you hwould not say that Caravati's *Three Large Pink Women and One Piece of Gauze* is just, ahem, 'a lot of old pigment'?"

"What about this one, then?" said Nobby, pointing to the adjacent plinth. "It's just a big stake with a nail in it! Is this art, too?"

"*Freedom*? If it hwas ever on the market, it hwould probableah fetch thirty thousand dollars," said Sir Reynold.

"For a bit of wood with a nail in it?" said Fred Colon. "Who did it?"

"After he viewed *Don't Talk to Me About Mondays!*, Lord Vetinari graciousleah had Ms. Pouter nailed to the stake by her ear," said Stitched. "However, she did manage to pull free during the afternoon."

"I bet she was mad!" said Nobby.

"Not after she hwon several awards for it. I believe she's planning to nail herself to several other things. It could be a very exciting exhibition."

"Tell you what, then, sir," said Nobby cheerfully. "Why don't you leave the ol' big frame where it is and give it a new name, like *Art Theft*?"

"No," said Sir Reynold coldly. "That would be foolish."

Shaking his head at the way of the world, Fred Colon walked right up to the wall so cruelly—or cruelleah—denuded of its covering. The painting had been crudely cut from its frame. Sergeant Colon was not a high-speed thinker, but that point struck him as odd. If you've got a month to pinch a painting, why botch the job? Fred had a copper's view of humanity that differed in some respects from that of the curator. Never say that people wouldn't do something, no matter how strange it was. Probably there were some mad rich people out there who *would* buy the painting, even if it meant only ever viewing it in the privacy of their own mansion. People could be like that. In fact, knowing that this was their big secret probably gave them a lovely, tight little shiver inside.

But the thieves had slashed the painting out as if they didn't care about making a sale. There were several ragged inches all along the— just a moment . . .

Fred stood back. A Clue. There it was, right there. He got a lovely, tight little shiver inside.

"This painting," he declared, "this painting . . . this painting which isn't here, I mean, obviously, was stolen by a . . . *troll*."

"My goodness, how can you tell?" said Sir Reynold.

"I'm very glad you asked me that question, sir," said Fred Colon, who was. "I have detected, you see, that the *top* of the circular muriel was cut really close to the frame." He pointed. "Now, your troll would easily be able to reach up with his knife, right, and cut along the edge of the frame at the top and down a bit on each side, see? But your average troll don't bend that well, so when it come to cutting along the bottom, right, he made a bit of a mess of the job and left it all jagged. Plus, only a troll could carry it away.

A stair carpet's bad enough, and a rolled-up muriel would be a lot heavier than that!"

He beamed.

"Well done, Sergeant!" said the curator.

"Good thinking, Fred," said Nobby.

"Thank you, Corporal," said Fred Colon generously.

"Or it could have been a couple of dwarfs with a stepladder," Nobby went on cheerfully. "The decorators have left a few behind. They're all over the place."

Fred Colon sighed.

"Y'see, Nobby," he said, "it's comments like that, made in front of a member of the public, that are the reason why I'm a sergeant and you ain't. If it was dwarfs, *it would be neat all 'round*, obviously. Is this place locked up at night, Mr. Sir Reynold?"

"Of course! Not just locked, but barred! Old John is meticulous about it. And he lives in the attics, so he can make this place like a *fortress*."

"This'd be the caretaker?" said Fred. "We'll need to talk to him."

"Certainly you may," said Sir Reynold nervously. "Now, I think hwe may have some details about the painting in our storeroom. I'll, er, just go and, er, find them . . ."

He hurried off toward a small doorway.

"I wonder how they got it out?" said Nobby, when they were alone.

"Who says they did?" said Fred Colon. "Big place like this, full of attics and cellars and odd corners, well, why not stash it away and wait awhile? You get in as a customer one day, see, hide under a sheet, take out the muriel in the night, hide it somewhere, then go out with the customers next day. Simple, eh?" He beamed at Nobby. "You've got to outsmart the criminal mind, see?"

"Or they could've just smashed down a door and pushed off with the muriel in the middle of the night," said Nobby. "Why mess about with a cunning plan when a simple one will do?"

Fred sighed. "I can see this is going to be a complicated case, Nobby."

"You should ask Vimesy if we can have it, then," said Nobby. "I mean, we already know the facts, right?"

Hovering in the air, unsaid, was: *Where would you like to be in the next few days? Out there, where the axes and clubs are likely to be flying, or in here, searching all the attics and cellars very, very carefully? Think about it. And it wouldn't be cowardice, right? 'Cos a famous muriel like this is bound to be part of our national heritage, right? Even if it is just a painting of a load of dwarfs and trolls having a scrap.*

"I think I *will* do a proper report and suggest to Mr. Vimes that maybe we should handle this one," said Fred Colon slowly. "It needs the attention of mature officers. D'you know much about art, Nobby?"

"If necessary, Sarge."

"Oh, come on, Nobby!"

"What? Tawneee says what she does is Art, Sarge. And she wears more clothes than a lot of the women on the walls around here, so why be sniffy about it?"

"Yeah, but . . ." Fred Colon hesitated here. He knew in his heart that spinning upside down around a pole wearing a costume you could floss with definitely was not Art, and being painted lying on a bed wearing nothing but a smile and a small bunch of grapes was good solid Art, but putting your finger on why this was the case was a bit tricky.

"No urns," he said at last.

"What urns?" said Nobby.

"Nude women are only Art if there's an urn in it," said Fred Colon. This sounded a bit weak even to him, so he added: "Or a plinth. Both is best, o'course. It's a secret sign, see, that they put in to say that it's Art and okay to look at."

"What about a potted plant?"

"That's okay if it's in an urn."

"What about if it's not got an urn *or* a plinth *or* a potted plant?" said Nobby.

"Have you one in mind, Nobby?" said Colon suspiciously.

"Yes, *The Goddess Anoia* Arising from the Cutlery*," said Nobby. "They've got it here. It was painted by a bloke with three *i*'s in his name, which sounds pretty artistic to me."

"The number of *i*'s is important, Nobby," said Sergeant Colon gravely, "but in these situations you have to ask yourself: 'Where's the cherub?' If there's a little fat pink kid holding a mirror or a fan or similar, then it's still okay. Even if he's grinning. Obviously you can't get urns *everywhere*."

"All right, but supposing—" Nobby began

The distant door opened, and Sir Reynold came hurrying across the marble floor with a book under his arm.

---

*Anoia is the Ankh-Morpork Goddess of Things That Get Stuck in Drawers.

"Ah, I'm afraid there is no copy of the painting," he said. "Clearly, a copy that did it justice hwould be quite hard to make. But, er, this rather *sensationalist* treatise has many detailed sketches, at least. These days every visitor seems to have a copy, of course. Did you know that more than two thousand four hundred and ninety individual dwarfs and trolls can be identified by armor or body markings in the original picture? It drove Rascal quite mad, poor fellow. It took him sixteen years to complete!"

"That's nothing," said Nobby cheerfully. "Fred here hasn't finished painting his kitchen yet, and he started twenty years ago!"

"Thank you for that, Nobby," said Colon coldly. He took the book from the curator. The title was *The Koom Valley Codex*. "Mad how?" he said.

"hWell, he neglected his other hwork, you see. He hwas constantly moving his lodgings, because he couldn't pay the rent and he had to drag that huge canvas with him. Imagine! He had to beg for paints in the street, hwhich took up a lot of his time, since not many people have a tube of burnt umber on them. He said it talked to him, too. You'll find it all in there. Rather dramatized, I fear."

"The painting *talked* to him?"

Sir Reynold made a face. "hWe believe that's hwhat he meant. hWe don't really know. He did not have any friends. He hwas convinced that if he hwent to sleep at night he hwould turn into a chicken. He'd leave little notes for himself saying 'You are not a chicken,' although sometimes he thought he hwas lying. The general belief is that he concentrated so much on the painting that it gave him some kind of brain fever. Toward the end he hwas sure he hwas losing his mind. He said he could hearh the battle."

"How do you know that, sir?" said Fred Colon. "You said he didn't have any friends."

"Ah, the incisive intellect of the policeman!" said Sir Reynold, smiling. "He left notes to himself, Sergeant. All the time. hWhen his last landlady entered his room, she found many hundreds of them, stuffed in old chicken-feed sacks. Fortunately, she couldn't read, and since she'd fixed in her mind the idea that the lodger hwas some sort of genius and therefore might have something she could sell, she called in a neighbor, a Miss Adelina Happily, hwho painted hwatercolors, and Miss Happily called in a friend hwho framed pictures, hwho hurriedly summoned Ephraim Dowster, the noted landscape artist. Scholars have puzzled over the notes ever since, seeking some insight into the poor man's tortured mind. They are not in order, you see. Some are very . . . odd."

"Odder than 'You are not a chicken'?" said Fred.

"Yes," said Sir Reynold. "Oh, there is stuff about voices, omens, ghosts . . . he also hwrote his journal on random pieces of paper, you know, and never gave any indication as to the date or hwhere he hwas staying, in case the Chicken found him. And he used very guarded language, because he didn't hwant the Chicken to find out."

"Sorry, I thought you said he thought *he* was the chic—" Colon began.

"hWho can fathom the thought processes of the sadleah disturbed, Sergeant," said Sir Reynold wearily.

"Er . . . and *does* the painting talk?" said Nobby Nobbs. "Stranger things have happened, right?"

"Ahah, no," said Sir Reynold. "At least, not in my time. Ever since that book hwas reprinted, there's been a guard in here during visiting hours, and he says it has never uttered a hword. Certainlyeah it has always fascinated people and there have always been stories about hidden treasure there. That is hwhy the book has been republished. People love a mystereah, don't they?"

"Not us," said Fred Colon.

"I don't even know what a Mister Rear is," said Nobby, leafing through the *Codex*. "Here, I heard about this book. My friend Dave who runs the stamp shop says there's this story about a dwarf, right, who turned up in this town near Koom Valley more'n two weeks after the battle, an' he was all injured 'cos he'd been ambushed by trolls, an' starvin,' right, an' no one knew much dwarfish, but it was like he wanted them to follow him, and he kept sayin' this word over and over again, which turned out, right, to be dwarfish for 'treasure,' right, only when they followed him back to the valley, right, he died on the way, an' they never found nothin,' an' then this artist bloke found some . . . thing in Koom Valley and hid the place where he'd found it in this painting, but it drove him bananas. Like it was haunted, Dave said. He said the government hushed it up."

"Yeah, but your mate Dave says the government always hushes things up, Nobby," said Fred.

"Well, they do."

"Except he always gets to hear about 'em, and *he* never gets hushed up," said Fred.

"I know you like to point the finger of scoff, Sarge, but there's a lot goes on that we don't know about."

"Like what, exactly?" Colon retorted. "Name me one thing that's going on that you don't know about. There— you can't, can you?"

Sir Reynold cleared his throat. "That is certainly one of the theories," he said, speaking carefully, as people tended to after hearing the Colon-Nobbs Brains Trust crossing purposes. "Regrettably, Methodia Rascal's notes support just about any theory one may prefer. The current populariteah of the painting is, I suspect, because the book does indeed revisit the old story that there's some huge secret hidden in the painting."

"Oh?" said Fred Colon, perking up. "What kind of secret?"

"I have no idea. The landscape hwas painted in great detail. A pointer to a secret cave, perhaps? Something about the positioning of some of the combatants? There are all kinds of theories. Rather strange people come along with tape measures and rather hworryingly *intent* expressions, but I don't think they ever find anything."

"Perhaps one of them pinched it?" Nobby suggested.

"I doubt it. They tend to be rather furtive individuals who bring sandwiches and a flask and stay here all day. The sort of people who love anagrams and secret signs and have little theories and pimples. Probably quite harmless except to one another. Besides, hwhy steal it? We *like* people to take an interest in it. I don't think that kind of person hwould hwant to take it home, because it hwould be too large to fit under the bed. Did you know that Rascal hwrote that sometimes in the night he heard screams? The noise of battle, one is forced to assume. So sad."

"Not something you'd want over the fireplace, then," said Fred Colon.

"Precisely, Sergeant. Even if it hwere possible to have a fireplace fifty feet long."

"Thank you, sir. One other thing, though. How many doors are there in this place?"

"Three," said Sir Reynold promptly. "But two are always locked."

"But if the troll—"

"—or the dwarfs," said Nobby.

"Or, as my junior colleague points out, the dwarfs tried to get it out—"

"Gargoyles," said Sir Reynold proudly. "Two hwatch the main door constantleah from the building opposite, and there's one each on the other doors. And there are staff on during the day, of course."

"This may sound a silly question, sir, but have you looked everywhere?"

"I've had the staff searching all morning, Sergeant. It hwould be a very big and very heavy roll. This place is full of odd corners, but it hwould be very obvious."

Colon saluted. "Thank you, sir. We'll just have a look around, if you don't mind."

"Yes, for urns," said Nobby Nobbs.

Vimes eased himself into his chair and looked at the damned vampire. She could have passed for sixteen; it was certainly hard to believe that she was not a lot younger than Vimes. She had short hair, which Vimes had never seen on a vampire before, and looked, if not like a boy, then like a girl who wouldn't mind passing for one.

"Sorry about the . . . remark down there," he said. "It's not been a good week and it's getting worse by the hour."

"You don't have to be frightened," said Sally. "If it's any help, I don't like this any more than you do."

"I am *not* frightened," said Vimes sharply.

"Sorry, Mr. Vimes. You smell frightened. Not *badly*," Sally added. "But just a bit. And your heart is beating faster. I am sorry if I have offended you. I was just trying to put you at your ease."

Vimes leaned back. "Don't try to put me at my ease, Miss von Humpeding," he said. "It makes me nervous when people do that. It's not as though I have any ease to be put at. And do not comment on my smell, either, thank you. Oh, and it's Commander Vimes, or 'sir,' understand? Not 'Mister Vimes.'"

"And I would prefer to be called Sally," said the vampire.

They looked at each other, both aware that this was not going well, both uncertain that they could make it go any better.

"So . . . 'Sally' . . . you want to be a copper?" said Vimes.

"A policeman? Yes."

"Any history of policing in your family?" said Vimes. It was a standard opening question. It always helped if they'd inherited some idea about coppering.

"No, just the throat biting," said Sally.

There was another pause.

Vimes sighed.

"Look, I just want to know one thing," he said. "Did John Not-A-Vampire-At-All Smith and Doreen Winkings put you up to this?"

"No!" said Sally. "I approached them. And if it's any help to you, I didn't think there'd be all this fuss, either."

Vimes looked surprised.

"But you *applied* to join," he said.

"Yes, but I don't see why there has to be all this . . . interest!"

"Don't blame me. That was your League of Temperance."

"Really? *Your* Lord Vetinari was quoted in the newspaper," said Sally. "All that stuff about the lack of species discrimination being in the finest traditions of the Watch."

"Hah!" said Vimes. "Well, it's true that a copper's a copper, as far as I'm concerned, but the fine traditions of the Watch, Miss von Humpeding, largely consist of finding somewhere out of the rain, mumping for free beer 'round the backs of pubs, and always keeping two notebooks!"

"You don't want me, then?" said Sally. "I thought you needed all the recruits you could get. Look, I'm probably stronger than anyone on your payroll who isn't a troll, I'm quite clever, I don't mind hard work, and I've got *excellent* night vision. I can be useful. I *want* to be useful."

"Can you turn into a bat?"

She looked shocked. "What? What kind of question is *that* to ask me?"

"Probably among the less tricky ones," said Vimes. "Besides, it might *be* useful. Can you?"

"No."

"Oh, well, never mind—"

"I can turn into a *lot* of bats," said Sally. "One bat is hard to do, because you have to deal with changes in body mass, and you can't do that if you've been Reformed for a while. Anyway, it gives me a headache."

"What was your last job?"

"Didn't have one. I was a musician."

Vimes brightened up.

"Really? Some of the lads have been talking about setting up a Watch band."

"Could they use a cello?"

"Probably not."

Vimes drummed his fingers on his desk. Well, she hadn't gone for his throat yet, had she? That was the problem, of course. Vampires were fine right up until the point where, suddenly, they weren't. But, in truth, right now, he had to admit it: he needed anyone who could stand upright and finish a sentence. This damn business was taking its toll. He needed men out there all the time, just to keep the lid on things. Oh, right now it was just scuffles and stone throwing and breaking windows and running away, but all that stuff added up, like snowflakes on an avalanche slope. People needed to see coppers at a time like this. They gave the illusion that the whole world hadn't gone insane.

And the Temperance League was pretty good and very supportive of its members. It was in the interests of all members that no one found themselves standing in a strange bedroom with an embarrassingly full feeling. They'd be watching her . . .

"We've got no room for passengers in the Watch," he said. "We're too pressed right now to give you any more than what is laughingly known as on-the-job training, but you'll be on the streets from day one . . . er, how *are* you with the daylight thing?"

"I'm fine with long sleeves and a wide brim. I carry the kit, anyway."

Vimes nodded. A small dustpan and brush, a vial of animal blood, and a small card saying:

Help, I have crumbled and I can't get up. Please sweep me into a heap and crush vial. I am a Black Ribboner and will not harm you. Thanking you in advance.

His fingers rattled on the desktop again. She returned his stare.

"All right, you're in," Vimes said at last. "On probation, to start with. Everyone starts that way. Sort out the paperwork with Sergeant Littlebottom downstairs, report to Sergeant Detritus for your gear and orientation lecture, and try not to laugh. And now you've got what you want, and we're not being official . . . tell me why."

"Pardon?" said Sally.

"A vampire wanting to be a copper?" said Vimes, leaning back in his chair. "I can't quite make that fit, 'Sally.'"

"I thought it would be an interesting job in the fresh air, which would offer opportunities to help people, Commander Vimes."

"Hmm," said Vimes. "If you can say that without smiling, you might make a copper after all. Welcome to the job, lance constable. I hope you have—"

The door slammed. Captain Carrot took two steps into the room, saw Sally, and hesitated.

"Lance Constable von Humpeding has just joined us, Captain," said Vimes.

"Er . . . fine . . . hello, miss," said Carrot quickly, and turned to Vimes. "Sir, someone's killed Hamcrusher!"

Ankh-Morpork's Finest strolled back down toward the Yard.

"What *I'd* do," said Nobby, "is cut the painting up into little bits, like, oh, a few inches across?"

"That's diamonds, Nobby. It's how you get rid of stolen diamonds."

"All right, then, how about this one? You cut the muriel up into bits the size of ordinary paintings, okay? Then you paint a painting on the other side of each one, an' put 'em in frames, an' leave 'em around the place. No one will notice extra paintings, right? An' then you can go an' pinch 'em when the fuss has died down."

"And how do you get *them* out, Nobby?"

"Well, first you get some glue, and a really long stick, and—"

Fred Colon shook his head. "Can't see it happening, Nobby."

"All right, then, you get some paint that's the same color as the walls, and you glue the painting to the wall somewhere it'll fit, and you paint over it with your wall paint so it looks just like the wall."

"Got a convenient bit of wall in mind, then?"

"How about inside the frame that's there already, Sarge?"

"Bloody hell, Nobby, that's clever," said Fred, stopping dead.

"Thank you, Sarge. That means a lot, coming from you."

"But you've still got to get it out, Nobby."

"Remember all those dust sheets, Sarge? I bet in a few weeks' time a couple of blokes in overalls will be able to walk out of the place with a big white roll under their arms and no one'd think twice about it, 'cos they'd, like, be thinkin' the muriel had been pinched weeks before."

There were a few moments of silence before Sergeant Colon said, in a hushed voice: "That's a very dangerous mind you got there, Nobby. Very dangerous indeed. How'd you get the new paint off, though?"

"Oh, that's easy," said Nobby. "And I know where to get some painters' aprons, too."

"Nobby!" said Fred, shocked.

"All right, Sarge. You can't blame a man for dreaming, though."

"This could be a feather in our caps, Nobby. And we could do with one now."

"Your water playing up again, Sarge?"

"You may laugh, Nobby, but you've only got to look around," said Fred gloomily. "It's just gang fights now, but it's going to get worse, you mark my words. All this scrapping over something that happened thousands of years ago! I don't know why they don't get back to where they came from if they want to do that!"

"Most of 'em come from here now," observed Nobby.

Fred grunted his disdain for a mere fact of geography.

"War, Nobby. Huh! What is it good for?" he said.

"Dunno, Sarge. Freeing slaves, maybe?"

"Absol—well, okay."

"Defending yourself against a totalitarian aggressor?"

"All right, I'll grant you that, but—"

"Saving civilization from a horde of—"

"It doesn't do any good in the long run is what I'm saying, Nobby, if you'd listen for five seconds together," said Fred Colon sharply.

"Yeah, but in the long run, what does, Sarge?"

"Say that again, paying attention to every word, will you?" said Vimes.

"He's dead, sir. Hamcrusher is dead. The dwarfs are sure of it."

Vimes stared at his captain. Then he glanced at Sally and said: "I gave you an order, Lance Constable von Humpeding. Go and get joined up!"

When the girl had hurried out, he said: "I hope you're sure about it as well, Captain . . ."

"It's spreading through the dwarfs like, like—" Carrot began.

"Alcohol?" Vimes suggested.

"Very fast, anyway," Carrot conceded. "Last night, they say. A troll got into his place in Treacle Street and beat him to death. I heard some of the lads talking about it."

"Carrot, wouldn't we *know* if something like that had happened?" said Vimes, but in the theater of his mind, Angua and Fred Colon uttered their cassandraic warnings again. *The dwarfs knew something. The dwarfs were worried.*

"Don't we, sir?" said Carrot. "I mean, I've just told you."

"Why aren't his people shouting it in the streets? Political assassination and all that sort of thing? Shouldn't they be screaming bloody murder? Who told you this?"

"Constable Ironbender and Corporal Ringfounder, sir. They're steady lads. Ringfounder's up for sergeant soon. Er . . . there was something else, sir. I did ask them why we hadn't heard officially, and Ironbender said . . . you won't like this, sir . . . he said the Watch wasn't to be told." Carrot watched Vimes carefully. It was hard to see the change of expression on the commander's face, but certain small muscles set firmly.

"On whose orders?" said Vimes.

"Someone called Ardent, apparently. He's Hamcrusher's . . . interpreter, I suppose you could say. He says it's dwarf business."

"But this is Ankh-Morpork, Captain. And murder is Murder."

"Yes, sir."

"And we are the City Watch," Vimes went on. "It says so on the door."

"Actually, it mostly says COPERS ARE BARSTUDS on the door at the moment, but I've got someone scrubbing it off," said Carrot. "And I—"

"That means if anyone gets murdered, we're responsible," said Vimes.

"I know what you mean, sir," said Carrot carefully.

"Does Vetinari know?"

"I can't imagine that he doesn't."

"Me neither." Vimes thought for a moment. "What about the *Times*? There's plenty of dwarfs working there."

"I'd be surprised if they passed it on to humans, sir. I only got to hear about it because I'm a dwarf, and Ironbender really wants to make sergeant, and, frankly, I overheard them, but I doubt if the printing dwarfs would mention it to the editor."

"Are you telling me, Captain, that dwarfs in the Watch would keep a murder *secret*?"

Carrot looked shocked. "Oh no, sir!"

"Good!"

"They'd just keep it secret from humans. Sorry, sir."

The important thing is not to shout at this point, Vimes told himself. Do not . . . what do they call it . . . go postal? Treat this as a learning exercise. Find out why the world is not as you thought it was. Assemble the facts, digest the information, consider the implications. *Then* go postal. But with precision.

"Dwarfs have always been law-abiding citizens,

Captain," he said. "They even pay their taxes. Suddenly they think it's okay not to report a possible murder?"

Carrot could see the steely glint in Vimes's eyes.

"Well, the fact is—" he began.

"Yes?"

"You see, Hamcrusher was a deep-down dwarf, sir. I mean *really* deep-down. Hated coming to the surface. They say he lived at sub-sub-basement level . . ."

"I know all that. So?"

"So how far down does our jurisdiction go, sir?" said Carrot.

"What? As far down as we like!"

"Er . . . Does it say that anywhere, sir? Most of the dwarfs here are from Copperhead and Llamedos and Uberwald," said Carrot. "Those places have surface laws and underground laws. I know it's not the same here but . . . well, it's how they see the world. And, of course, Hamcrusher's dwarfs are *all* deep-downers, and you know how ordinary dwarfs think about them."

They come bloody close to worshiping them, Vimes thought, pinching the bridge of his nose and shutting his eyes. It just gets worse and worse.

"All right," he said. "But this is Ankh-Morpork, and we have our own laws. There can be no harm in us just checking up on the health of Brother Hamcrusher, can there? We can knock on the door, can't we? Say we've got good reason to ask? I know it's only a rumor, but if enough people believe a rumor like that, we will *not* be able to keep a lid on it."

"Good idea, sir."

"Go and tell Angua I want her along. And . . . oh, Haddock. And Ringfounder, maybe. You come, too, of course."

"Er . . . not a good idea, sir. I happen to know most deep-downers are nervous about me. They believe I'm too human to be a dwarf."

"Really?"

Six feet three inches in his stockinged feet, thought Vimes. Adopted and raised by dwarfs in a little dwarf mine in the mountains. His dwarfish name is Kzad-bhat, which means Head Banger. He coughed. "Why on earth should they think that, I wonder?" he said.

"All right, I know I'm . . . *technically* human, sir, but size has traditionally never been a *dwarfish* definition of a dwarf. Hamcrusher's group aren't happy about me, though."

"Sorry to hear it. I'll take Cheery, then."

"Are you mad, sir? You know what they think about female dwarfs who actually *admit* it!"

"All right, then, I'll take Sergeant Detritus. They'll believe in *him* all right, won't they?"

"*Could* be said to be a bit provocative, sir—" Carrot began doubtfully.

"Detritus is an Ankh-Morpork copper, Captain, just like you and me," said Vimes. "I suppose *I'm* acceptable, am I?"

"Yes, sir, of course. I think you worry them, though."

"I do? Oh." Vimes hesitated. "Well, that's good. And Detritus is an officer of the law. We've still got some law here. And as far as I'm concerned, it goes deep. All the way down."

Bloody stupid thing to say, Vimes thought five minutes later, as he walked through the streets at the head of the little squad. He cursed himself for saying it.

Coppers stayed alive by trickery. That's how it *worked*. You had your Watch Houses with the big blue lights outside, and you made certain there were always burly watchmen visible in the big public places, and you swanked around like you owned the place. But you didn't own it. It was all smoke and mirrors. You magicked a little policeman into everyone's head. You relied on people giving in, knowing the rules. But in truth, a hundred well-armed people could wipe out the Watch, if they knew what they were doing. Once some madman finds out that a copper taken unawares dies just like anyone else, the spell is broken.

Hamcrusher's dwarfs don't believe in the City Watch? That could turn out to be a problem. Maybe bringing a troll along *was* provocative, but Detritus was a citizen, gods damn it, just like everyone else. If you—

"Duddle-dum-duddle-dum-duddle-dum!"

Ah, yes. No matter how bad things were, there was always room for them to get just that little bit worse . . .

Vimes pulled the smart brown box out of his pocket and flipped it open. The pointy-eared face of a small green imp stared up at him with that wistful, hopeless smile, which, in its various incarnations, he'd come to know and dread.

"Good morning, Insert Name Here! I am the Dis-Organizer Mark Five, the Gooseberry™. How may I—" it began, speaking fast in order to get as much said as possible before the inevitable interruption.

"I swear I switched you off," said Vimes.

"You threatened me with a hammer," said the imp accusingly, and rattled the tiny bars. "He threatens state-of-the-Craft technomancy with a hammer, everybody!" it shouted. "He doesn't even fill in the registration card! That's why I have to call him Insert Nam—"

"I thought you'd got rid of that thing, sir," said Angua, as Vimes snapped the lid shut. "I thought it had had an . . . accident."

"Hah!" said a muffled voice from the box.

"Sybil always gets me a new one," said Vimes, making a face. "A *better* one. But I *know* this one was turned off."

The box's lid thrust upwards.

"I wake up for alarms!" the imp shrieked. "*Ten colon forty-five colon Sit for Damn Portrait!*"

Vimes groaned. The portrait with Sir Joshua. He'd get into trouble for this. He'd already missed two sittings. But this dwarf thing was . . . important.

"I won't be able to make it," he mumbled.

"Then would you like to engage the handy-to-use Bluenose™ Integrated Messenger Service?"

"What does that do?" said Vimes, with deep suspicion. The succession of Dis-Organizers he had owned had proved quite successful at very nearly sorting out all the problems that stemmed from owning them in the first place.

"Er . . . basically, it means me running with a message to the nearest clacks tower *really fast*," said the imp hopefully.

"And do you come back?" said Vimes, hope also rising.

"Absolutely!"

"Thank you, no," said Vimes.

"How about a game of Splong!™, specially devised for the Mark Five?" pleaded the imp. "I have the bats right here. No? Perhaps you would prefer the ever-popular 'Guess My Weight in Pigs'? Or I could whistle one of your favorite tunes? My iHUM™ function enables me to remember up to one thousand five hundred of your all-time—"

"You could try learning to use it, sir," said Angua, as Vimes once again shut the lid on the protesting voice.

"Did use one," said Vimes.

"Yup. As a doorstop," rumbled Detritus, behind him.

"I'm just not at home with technomancy, all right?" said Vimes. "End of discussion. Haddock, nip along to Moon Pond Lane, will you. Present my apologies to Lady Sybil, who will be at Sir Joshua's studio there. Tell her I'm very sorry, but this has come up and it needs careful handling."

Well, it does, he thought, as they headed onwards. It probably needs more careful handling than I'm going to give it. Well, to hell with that. It comes to something if you have to tread carefully even to find out if there's *been* a murder.

Treacle Street was just the kind of area the dwarfs colonized—on the *edge* of the less pleasant parts of town, but not all the way there. You tended to notice the dwarf outposts. A patchwork of windows testified to a two-story house having been turned into a three-story house while remaining exactly the same height; there was an excess of small ponies pulling small carts; and, of course, all the really short people wearing beards and helmets was a definite clue.

Dwarfs dug down, too. It was a dwarf thing. Up here, far from the river, they could probably get to sub-basement level without being up to their necks in water.

There were a lot of them out and about this morning. They weren't particularly angry, insofar as Vimes could tell when the available area of expression between eyebrows and mustache was a few square inches, but it wasn't usual to see dwarfs just standing around. They tended to be somewhere, working hard, usually for one another. No, they weren't angry, but they *were* worried. You didn't need to see faces to sense that. Dwarfs as a whole weren't happy about newspapers, regarding such news as a lover of fine grapes would regard raisins. They got their news from other dwarfs, to ensure that it was new and fresh and full of personality, and no doubt it grew all kinds of extras in the telling. This crowd was waiting uncertainly for news that it was going to become a riot.

For now, it parted to let them through. The presence of Detritus caused a wake of muttering, which the troll cleverly decided not to hear.

"Feel that?" said Angua, as they walked up the street. "Through your feet?"

"I don't have your senses, Sergeant," said Vimes.

"It's a constant thud, thud, underground," said Angua. "I can feel the street shaking. I think it's a pump."

"Pumping out more cellars, maybe?" said Vimes. Sounded like a big undertaking. How far down could they go? he wondered. Ankh-Morpork is mostly built on Ankh-Morpork, after all. There's been a city here since *forever*.

It wasn't just a random crowd, when you looked closely. It was also a queue, along one side of the street, moving very slowly toward a side door. They were waiting to see the grags. *Please come and say the death words over my father . . . please advise me on the sale of my shop . . . please guide me in my business . . . I am a long way from the bones of my grandfathers, please help me stay a dwarf . . .*

This was not the time to be *D'rkza*. Strictly speaking, most Ankh-Morpork dwarfs were *D'rkza*; it meant something like "not really a dwarf." They didn't live deep underground and only come out at night, they didn't mine metal, they let their daughters show at least a *few* indications of femininity, they tended to be a little slipshod when it came to some of the ceremonies. But the whiff of Koom Valley was in the air, and this was no time to be *mostly* a dwarf. So you paid attention to the grags. They kept you on the straight seam.

And, until now, that had been fine by Vimes. Up until now, though, the grags in the city had stopped short of advocating murder.

He *liked* dwarfs. They made reliable officers, and dwarfs tended to be naturally law-abiding, at least in the absence of alcohol. But they were all watching him. He could feel the pressure of their gaze.

Standing around watching people was, of course, Ankh-Morpork's leading industry. The place was a net exporter of penetrating stares. But these were the wrong kind. The street felt not exactly hostile but alien. And yet it was an Ankh-Morpork street. How could he be a stranger here?

Maybe I shouldn't have brought a troll, he thought. But where does that lead? Pick your own copper from a chart?

Two dwarfs were on guard outside Hamcrusher's house; they were more heavily armed than the average dwarf, insofar as that was possible, but it was probably the black-leather sashes they wore that were doing the trick of keeping the mood subdued. These declared to all who recognized them that they were working for deep-down dwarfs and, as such, partook a little of the magic, mana, awe, or fear that they engendered in the average, backsliding dwarf.

They started to give Vimes the look of all guards everywhere, which, in summary, is this: The default position is that you're dead; only my patience stands in the way. But Vimes was ready for it. Any five hells you cared to name knew that he'd used it himself often enough. He countered with the aloof expression of someone who didn't notice guards.

"Commander Vimes, City Watch," he said, holding up his badge. "I need to see Grag Hamcrusher immediately."

"He's not seeing anyone," said one of the guards.

"Oh. So he *is* dead, then?" said Vimes.

He *felt* the answer. He didn't even have to see Angua's little nod; the dwarfs had been dreading the question, and were sweating.

To their shock and horror, and also somewhat to his own surprise, he sat down on the steps between them and pulled a packet of cheap cigars out of his pocket.

"I won't offer one to you lads, because I know that you aren't allowed to smoke on duty," he said convivially. "I don't allow my boys to do it. The only reason I can get away with it is that there's no one to tell me off, haha." He blew a stream of blue smoke. "Now, I am, as you know, head of the City Watch. Yes?"

The two dwarfs, staring straight ahead, nodded imperceptibly.

"Good," said Vimes. "And that means you, that's *both* of you, are impeding me in the execution of my duty. That gives me, oooh, a whole *range* of options. The one I'm thinking of right now is summoning Constable Dorfl. He's a golem. Nothing impedes *him* in the execution of his duty, believe me. You'll be picking bits of that door off the floor for *weeks*. And I wouldn't stand in his way, if I was you. Oh, and it'd be lawful, which means that if anyone puts up a fight it gets really interesting. Look, I'm only telling you this because I've done my share of guarding over the years, and there are times when looking tough works and there are times—and this, I suggest, is one of them—when going and asking the people *inside* what you should do next is a very good career move."

"Can't leave our post," said one of the dwarfs.

"Don't worry about that," said Vimes, standing. "I'll stand guard for you."

"You can't do that!"

Vimes bent down to the dwarf's ear.

"*I* am Commander of the Watch," he hissed, no longer Mr. Friendly. He pointed at the cobblestones. "*This* is my street. I can stand where I like. *You* are standing on *my* street. It's the public highway. That means that there are about a dozen things I could arrest you for, right now. That would cause trouble, right enough, but you would be bang in the middle of it. My advice to you, one guard to another, is to hop off smartly and speak to someone highe—further up the ladder, okay?"

He saw worried eyes peering out from between the rampant eyebrows and the luxuriant mustache, spotted the tiny little tells he'd come to recognize, and added: "Off you go, ma'am."

The dwarf hammered on the door. The hatch slid back. Whispering transpired. The door opened. The dwarf hurried in. The door closed. Vimes turned, took up station beside it, and stood to attention slightly more theatrically than necessary.

There were one or two outbreaks of laughter. Dwarfs they may be, but in Ankh-Morpork people always wanted to see what would happen next.

The remaining guard hissed: "We're not allowed to smoke on duty!"

"Oops, sorry," said Vimes, and removed the cigar, tucking it behind his ear for later. This got a few more chuckles. Let 'em laugh, said Vimes to himself. At least they're not throwing things.

The sun shone down. The crowd stood still. Sergeant Angua stared at the sky, her face carefully blank. Detritus had settled into the absolute, rock-like stillness of a troll with nothing to do right now. Only Ringfounder looked uneasy. This probably was not a good time and place to be a dwarf with a badge, Vimes thought. But why? All we've been doing in the last couple of weeks is trying to stop two bunches of idiots from killing one another.

And now this. This morning was going to cost him an earful, he thought, although Sybil never shouted when she told him off. She just spoke sadly, which was a lot worse.

The bloody family portrait, that was the trouble. It seemed to involve an awful lot of sittings, but it was a tradition in Sybil's family, and that was that. It was more or less the same portrait, every generation: the happy family group against a panorama of their rolling acres. Vimes had no rolling acres, only aching feet, but as the inheritor of the Ramkin wealth, he was, he'd learned, also the owner of Crundells, a huge stately home out in the country. He'd never even seen it yet. Vimes didn't mind the countryside if it stayed put and didn't attack, but he liked pavement under his feet and didn't much care for being pictured as some kind of squire. So far, his excuses for avoiding the interminable sittings had been reasonable, but it was a close-run thing . . .

More time passed. Some of the dwarfs in the crowd wandered off. Vimes didn't move, not even when he heard the hatch in the door open for a moment and then slide back. They were trying to wait him out.

"Tcha-tcha-rumptiddle-tiddle-tiddle-tiddle-tchum-chum!"

Without looking down, maintaining the stolid

thousand-mile stare of a guard, Vimes pulled the Dis-Organizer out of his pocket and raised it to his lips.

"I *know* you were turned off," he grunted.

"Pop up for alarms, remember?" said the imp.

"How do I stop you doing that?"

"The correct form of words is in the manual, Insert Name Here," said the imp primly.

"Where is the manual?"

"You threw it away," said the imp, full of reproach. "You always do. That's why you never use the right commands, and that is why I did not 'go away and stick my head up a duck's bottom' yesterday. You have an appointment to see Lord Vetinari in half an hour."

"I will be busy," muttered Vimes.

"Would you like me to remind you again in ten minutes?"

"Tell me, what part of 'stick your head up a duck's bottom' didn't you understand?" Vimes replied, and plunged the thing back into his pocket.

So . . . it had been half an hour. Half an hour was enough. This was going to be drastic, but he'd seen the looks the dwarfs were giving Detritus. Rumor was an evil poison.

As he stepped forward, ready to go and summon Dorfl and all the problems that invading this place would entail, the door opened behind him.

"Commander Vimes? You may come in."

There was a dwarf in the doorway. Vimes could just make out his shape in the gloom. And for the first time he noticed the symbol chalked on the wall over the door: a circle with a horizontal line through it.

"Sergeant Angua will accompany me," he said. The sign struck Vimes as vaguely unsettling; it seemed to be a stamp of ownership that was rather more emphatic than, for example, a little plaque saying MON REPOS.

"The troll will stay outside," said the figure flatly.

"Sergeant Detritus will stand guard, along with Corporal Ringfounder," said Vimes.

This restatement of fact seemed to pass muster, suggesting that the dwarf probably knew a lot about iron but nothing about irony. The door opened further, and Vimes stepped inside.

The hall was bare, except for a few stacked boxes, and the air smelled of— what? Stale food. Old, empty houses. Sealed-up rooms. Attics.

The whole house is an attic, Vimes thought. The thud, thud from below was really noticeable here. It was like a heartbeat.

"This way, if you please," said the dwarf, and ushered Vimes and Angua into a side room. Again, the only furnishings were more wooden boxes and, here and there, some well-worn shovels.

"We do not often entertain. Please be patient," said the dwarf, and backed out. The key clicked on the lock.

Vimes sat down on a box.

"Polite," said Angua. Vimes put one hand to his ear and jerked a thumb toward the damp, stained plaster. She nodded, but mouthed the word "corpse" and pointed downwards.

"Sure?" said Vimes.

Angua tapped her nose. You couldn't argue with a werewolf's nose.

Vimes leaned back against a bigger box. It was comfort itself to a man who'd learned to sleep leaning against any available wall.

The plaster on the opposite wall was crumbling, green with damp and hung with dusty old spiderwebs. Someone, though, had scratched a symbol in it so deeply that bits of the plaster had fallen out. It was another circle, this time with two diagonal lines slashed through it. Some passion there; not what you'd expect around dwarfs.

"You are taking this very well, sir," said Angua. "You must know this is deliberate discourtesy."

"Being rude isn't against the law, Sergeant." Vimes pulled his helmet over his eyes and settled down.

The little devils! Play silly buggers with me, will they? Try to wind me up, will they? Don't tell the Watch, eh? There are no no-go areas in this city. I'll see to it they find that out. Oh yes.

There were more and more deep-downers in the city these days, although you very seldom saw them outside the dwarf areas. Even there, you didn't see deep-downers themselves, you just saw their dusty black sedan chairs being muscled through the crowds by four other dwarfs. There were no windows; there was nothing outside that a deep-downer could possibly want to see.

The city dwarfs regarded them with awe, respect, and, it had to be said, a certain amount of embarrassment, like some honored but slightly loopy relative. Because somewhere in the head of every city dwarf there was a little voice that said, *You should live in a mine, you should be in the mountains, you shouldn't walk under open skies, you should be a* real *dwarf.* In other words, you shouldn't really be working in your uncle's pigment-and-dye factory in Dolly Sisters. However, since you *were*, you could at least try to *think* like a proper dwarf. And part of that meant being guided by the deep-downers, the dwarfs' dwarfs, who lived in caves miles below the surface and never saw the sun. Somewhere down there in the dark was true dwarfishness. They had the knowing of it, and they could guide you . . .

Vimes had no problem with that at all. It made as much sense as what most humans believed, and most dwarfs were model citizens, even at two-thirds scale.

But deciding that murder could be kept in the family? thought Vimes. Not on my Watch!

After ten minutes, the door was unlocked and another dwarf stepped inside. He was dressed as what Vimes thought of as "standard city dwarf," which meant basic helmet, leather, chain mail, and battle-axe/mining pick, but hold the spiky club. He also had a black sash. He looked flustered.

"Commander Vimes! What can I say? I do apologize for the way you have been treated!"

I bet you do. Aloud, Vimes said: "And who are you?"

"Apologies again! I am Helmclever, and I am the . . . the nearest word is, perhaps, 'daylight face'? I do those things that have to be done aboveground. Do come into my office, please!" He trotted off, leaving them to follow him.

The office was downstairs, in the stone-walled basement. It looked quite cozy. Crates and sacks were piled up against one wall. There wasn't much food in deep caves, after all; the simple life for dwarfs down below happened because of quite complex lives for a lot of dwarfs above. Helmclever looked like little more than a servant, making sure that his masters got fed, although he might have thought the job was rather grander than that. A curtain in the corner probably concealed a bed; dwarfs did not go in for dainty living.

A desk was covered in paperwork. Beside it, on a small table, was an octagonal board covered in little playing pieces. Vimes sighed. He hated games. They made the world look too simple.

"Oh, do you play at all, Commander?" said Helmclever with the hungry look of a true enthusiast. Vimes knew the type, too. Show polite interest, and you'll be there all night.

"Lord Vetinari does. It's never interested me," said Vimes.* "Helmclever's not a common dwarf name. You're not related to the Helmclevers in Tallow Lane, are you?"

He'd meant it as no more than a bit of noncontroversial icebreaking, but he might as well have cursed. Helmclever looked down and mumbled: "Er, yes . . . but to a . . . grag, even a novice, all of dwarfdom is his . . . family. It would not be . . . really not be . . ." He faltered into silence, and then some other part of his brain took over. He looked up, brightly. "Some coffee, perhaps? I shall fetch some."

Vimes opened his mouth to say no, but didn't. Dwarfs made good coffee, and there was a smell of

---

*Vimes had never got on with any game much more complex than darts. Chess in particular had always annoyed him. It was the dumb way the pawns went off and slaughtered their fellow pawns while the kings lounged about doing nothing that always got to him; if only the pawns united, maybe talked the rooks around, the whole board could've been a republic in a dozen moves.

it wafting from the next room. Besides, the nervousness radiating off Helmclever suggested he'd been drinking a lot of it today. No harm in encouraging him to have more. It was something he told his officers: people got worried around coppers if the officer knew his stuff, and jittery people gave too much away.

While the dwarf was gone, he took in more of the room, and his eye spotted the words *The Koom Valley Codex* on the spine of a book half-concealed in the paperwork.

That bloody valley again, with added weirdness this time. Actually, Sybil had bought a copy, along with most of the reading population of the city, and had dragged him along to look at that poor man's wretched picture in the Royal Art Museum. A painting with secrets? Oh yes? And how come some mad young human artist a hundred years ago knew the secret of a battle fought thousands of years before? Sybil said that the book claimed he'd found something on the battlefield, but it was haunted, and voices drove him to believe he was a chicken. Or something.

When the mugs were brought in, with just a little spilled on Helmclever's desk because his hand was shaking, Vimes said: "I must see Grag Hamcrusher, sir."

"I'm sorry, that is not possible."

The answer came out flat and level, as if the dwarf had been practicing. But there was a flicker in his eyes, and Vimes glanced up at a very large grille in the wall.

At this point, Angua gave a little cough. Okay, thought Vimes, someone's listening.

"Mr. Helm . . . clever," he said, "I have reason to suppose that a serious crime has been committed on Ankh-Morpork soil." He added: "That is to say, under it. But Ankh-Morpork's, anyway."

Once again, Helmclever's strange calm gave him away. There was a hunted look in his eyes.

"I am sorry to hear it. How may I assist you to solve it?"

Oh well, thought Vimes, I did say I don't play games.

"By showing me the dead body you have downstairs," he said.

He was obscenely pleased at the way Helmclever deflated. Time to press home . . .

He took out his badge.

"My authority, Mr. Helmclever. I *will* search this place. I would prefer to do so with your permission."

The dwarf was trembling, with fear or anxiety or probably both.

"You will *invade* our premises? You cannot! Dwarf law—"

"This is Ankh-Morpork," said Vimes. "All the way to the top, all the way to the bottom. Invasion is not the issue. Are you really telling me I cannot search a basement? Now take me to Grag Hamcrusher or whoever is in charge! Now!"

"I— I refuse your request!"

"It wasn't a request!"

And now we reach our own little Koom Valley, Vimes thought, as he stared into Helmclever's eyes. No backing down. We both think we're right. But *he's* wrong!

A movement made him glance down. Helmclever's trembling finger had teased out the spilled coffee into a circle. As Vimes stared, the dwarf's fingers drew two lines across the circle. He looked back up, his eyes bulging with anger, fear . . . and just a hint of something else . . .

"Ah. Commander Vimes, is it?" said a figure in the doorway.

It might have been Lord Vetinari speaking. It was that same level tone indicating that he had noticed you and you were, in some small way, a necessary chore. But it was coming from another dwarf, presumably, although he wore a rigid, pointed black hood, which brought him up to the height of the average human.

Elsewhere he was completely shrouded—and that was a well-chosen word—in overlapping black-leather scales, with just a narrow slit for the eyes. Were it not for the quiet authority of the voice, the figure in front of Vimes could be mistaken for a very somber Hogswatch decoration.

"And you are—?" said Vimes.

"My name is Ardent, Commander. Helmclever, go about your chores!"

As the "daylight face" scuttled off at speed, Vimes turned in his seat and allowed his hand to brush across the sticky symbol, wiping it out. "And do *you* want to be helpful, too?" he said.

"If I can be," said the dwarf. "Please follow me. It would be preferable if the sergeant did not accompany you."

"Why?"

"The obvious reason," said Ardent. "She is openly female."

"What? So? Sergeant Angua is very definitely not a dwarf," said Vimes. "You can't expect everyone to conform to *your* rules!"

"Why not?" said the dwarf. "You do. But could we just, together, for a moment, proceed to my office and discuss matters?"

"I'll be fine, sir," said Angua. "It's probably the best way."

Vimes tried to relax. He knew he was letting himself get steamed up. Those silent watchers in the street had got through to him, and the look he'd gotten from Helmclever needed some thinking about. But—

"No," he said.

"You will not make that small concession?" said Ardent.

"I am already making several big ones, believe me," said Vimes.

The hidden eyes under the pointy cowl stared at him for a few seconds.

"Very well," said Ardent. "Please follow me."

The dwarf turned and opened a door behind him, stepping into a small, square room. He beckoned them to follow and, when they were inside, pulled a lever.

The room shook gently, and the walls began to rise.

"This is—" Ardent began.

"—an elevator," said Vimes. "Yes, I know. I saw them when I met the Low King in Uberwald."

The dropping of the name did not work.

"The Low King is not . . . respected here," said Ardent.

"I thought he was the ruler of all dwarfs?" said Vimes.

"A common misconception. Ah, we have arrived."

The elevator stopped with barely a jerk.

Vimes stared.

Ankh-Morpork was built on Ankh-Morpork. Everyone knew that. They had been building with stone here ten thousand years ago. As the annual flooding of the Ankh brought more silt, so the city had risen on its wall until attics had become cellars. Even at basement level today, it was always said, a man with a pickaxe and a good sense of direction could cross the city by knocking his way through underground walls, provided he could also breathe mud.

What had this place been? A palace? The temple of a god who'd subsequently slipped everyone's memory? It was a big space, dark as soot, but there was a glow that managed to show beautiful vaulting in the roof above. A strange glow.

"Vurms," said Ardent. "From the deep caves in the mountains around Llamedos. We brought them with us, and they breed very fast here. They find your silt quite nourishing. I'm sure they shine more, too."

The glow moved. It did not illuminate much, but it showed the shape of things, and it was heading toward the elevator, flowing over the wonderful ceiling.

"They head for heat and movement, even now," said the hooded dwarf.

"Er . . . why?"

Ardent gave a little laugh.

"In case you die, Commander. They think you are some rat or small deer that has tumbled into their cave. Nourishment is rare in the Deeps. Every breath you exhale is food. And when eventually you expire, they will . . . descend. They are very patient. They will leave nothing but bones."

"I was not *intending* to expire here," said Vimes.

"Of course not. Follow me, please," said Ardent, leading them past a big, round door. There were more doors on the other side of the room, and several gaping tunnel mouths.

"How far down are we?"

"Not far. About forty feet. We are good at digging."

"In this city?" said Vimes. "Why aren't we trying to breathe underwater? And calling it water is giving it the best of it."

"We are very good at keeping water out, too. Alas, it appears we are less good at keeping out Samuel Vimes." The dwarf stepped into a smaller room, its ceiling thick with brilliant vurms, and motioned to a couple of dwarf-sized chairs. "Do sit down. Can I offer you refreshment?"

"No, thank you," said Vimes. He sat down gingerly on a chair that brought his knees up almost to his chin. Ardent sat down behind a small desk made of stone slabs and, to Vimes's amazement, took off his headgear. He looked quite young, with a beard that was actually trimmed. Angua watched him, breathing slowly.

"How far do all these tunnels run?" Vimes said.

"I don't propose to tell you," said Ardent levelly.

"So you're undermining my city?"

"Oh, Commander! You've been to the caves in Uberwald. You've seen how dwarfs can build? We are craftsmen. Do not think that your house is about to collapse."

"But you're not just building basements! You're mining!" said Vimes.

"In a sense. We would say we are mining for holes. Space, Commander, that is what we are digging for. Yes, we are mining for holes. Although our bores have found deep treacle, you will be interested to hear—"

"You can't do this!"

"Can we not? But we are doing it nevertheless," said Ardent calmly.

"You are burrowing under other people's property?"

"Rabbits burrow, Commander. *We* dig. And, yes, we are. How far down does ownership go, after all? And how far up?"

Vimes looked at the dwarf. Calm down, he thought. You can't deal with this. This is too big. It's something for Vetinari to decide. Stick to what you know. Stick to what you *can* deal with.

"I'm investigating reports of a death," he said.

"Yes. Grag Hamcrusher. A terrible misfortune," said Ardent, with a calmness that was enraging.

"I've heard it was a vicious murder."

"That would be a fair description."

"You admit it?" said Vimes.

"I'll choose to assume that by that you mean 'do I admit there has been a murder,' Commander. Yes. There has. And we are dealing with it."

"How?"

"We are discussing the appointment of a *zad-*

krdga," said Ardent, folding his hands. "That is 'one who smelts.' One who finds the pure ore of truth in the dross of confusion."

"*Discussing?* Have you sealed off the scene of the crime yet?"

"The smelter may order that, Commander, but we already know that the crime was committed by a troll."

Ardent's face now bore an expression of amused contempt that Vimes longed to remove.

He said: "How do you know this? Was it witnessed?"

"Not as such. But a troll's club was found beside the body," said the dwarf.

"And that's all you have to go on?" Vimes stood up. "I've had enough of this. Sergeant Angua!"

"Sir?" said Angua, beside him.

"Let's go. We're going to find the murder scene while there's still any clues left to find!"

"You have no business in the lower areas!" snapped Ardent, standing up.

"How are you going to stop me?"

"How are you going to get past locked doors?"

"How are *you* going to find out who murdered Hamcrusher?"

"I told you, a troll's club was found!"

"And that's *it*? 'We found a club, so a troll did it?' Is anyone going to believe that? You're prepared to start a war in my city with a piece of flimflam like that? Because, believe me, that's what's going to happen when this gets out. Try it and I'll arrest you!"

"And start a war in your city?" said Ardent.

Dwarf and man glared at each other while they

caught their breath. On the ceiling above them, vurms congregated, feasting on spittle and rage.

"Why would anyone but a troll strike down the grag?" said Ardent.

"Good! You're asking questions!" Vimes leaned across the desk. "If you really want answers, unlock those doors!"

"No! You cannot go down there, Blackboard Monitor Vimes!"

The dwarf could not have put more venom in the words "child murderer."

Vimes stared.

Blackboard monitor. Well, he had been, in that little street school, more than forty-five years ago. Mum had insisted. Gods knew where she'd sprung the penny a day it cost, although most of the time Dame Slightly had been happy to accept payment in old clothes and firewood, or, preferably, gin. Numbers, Letters, Weights, Measures; it was not what you'd call a rich curriculum. Vimes had attended for nine months or so, until the streets demanded he learn much harder and sharper lessons. But, for a while, he'd been trusted to hand out the slates and clean the blackboard. Oh, the heady, strutting power of it, when you're six years old!

"Do you deny it?" said Ardent. "You destroy written words? You admitted as much to the Low King in Uberwald."

"It was a joke!" said Vimes.

"Oh? Then you *do* deny it?"

"What? No! He was impressed by my titles, and I just threw that one in for . . . fun."

"Then you deny the crime?" Ardent persisted.

"Crime? I cleaned the blackboard so that new things could be written on it! How is that a crime?"

"You did not care where those words went?" said Ardent.

"Care? They were just chalk dust!"

Ardent sighed and rubbed his eyes.

"Busy night?" said Vimes.

"Commander, I understand that you were young and may not have realized what you were doing, but *you* must understand that to us you appear to be proud of being complicit in the most heinous of crimes: the destruction of words."

"Sorry? Rubbing out 'A is for Apple' is a capital crime?"

"One that would be unthinkable for a true dwarf," said Ardent.

"Really? But I have the trust of the Low King himself," said Vimes.

"So I understand. There are six venerable grags below us, Commander, and in their eyes, the Low King and his kind have strayed from the true seam. He is," Ardent rattled off a sentence in staccato dwarfish, too fast for Vimes to catch it, and then translated: "Wishy-washy. Dangerously liberal. Shallow. He has seen the light."

Ardent was watching him carefully. Think hard. From what Vimes could remember, the Low King and his circle had been pretty crusty types. But *these* people think they're soppy liberals.

"Wishy-washy?" he said.

"Indeed. I invite you, therefore, to derive from that statement something of the nature of those I serve below."

Ah, thought Vimes. There's something there. Just a hint. Friend Ardent is a thinker.

"When you say 'he has seen the light' you *sound* as if you mean 'corrupted,'" he said.

"Something like that, yes. Different worlds, Commander. Down here, it would be unwise to trust your metaphors. To see the light is to be blinded. Do you not know that in the darkness, the eyes open wider?"

"Take me to see these people down below," said Vimes.

"They will not listen to you. They will not even look at you. They have nothing to do with the World Above. They believe it is a kind of bad dream. I have not *dared* tell them about your 'newspapers,' printed every day and discarded like rubbish. The shock would kill them."

But dwarfs invented the printing engine, Vimes thought. Obviously, they were the wrong kind of dwarf. I've seen Cheery throw stuff in the wastepaper basket, too. It seems like nearly all dwarfs are the wrong sort, eh?

"What exactly is your job, Mr. Ardent?" said Vimes.

"I am their chief liaison with the World Above. The steward, you could say."

"I thought that was Helmclever's job?"

"Helmclever? He orders the groceries, relays my orders, pays the miners, and so on. The chores, in fact," said Ardent disdainfully. "He is a novice, and his job is to do what I tell him. It is *I* who speaks to the grags."

"You talk to bad dreams on their behalf?"

"You could put it that way, I suppose. They would

not let a proud word-killer become a smelter. The idea would be abominable."

They glared at each other.

Once again, we end up in Koom Valley, Vimes told himself. They won't—

"Permission to make a suggestion?" said Angua quietly.

Two heads turned. Two mouths said: "Well?"

"The . . . smelter. The seeker of the truth. Must they be a dwarf?"

"Of course!" said Ardent.

"Then what about Captain Carrot? He's a dwarf."

"We know of him. He is an . . . anomaly," said Ardent. "His claim to dwarfishness is debatable."

"But most dwarfs in the city accept that he's a dwarf," said Angua. "And he's a copper, too."

Ardent flopped back into his seat. "To your dwarfs here, yes, he is a dwarf. He would be unacceptable to the grags."

"There's no dwarf law that says a dwarf can't be more than six feet tall, sir."

"The grags *are* the law, woman," Ardent snapped. "They interpret laws that go back for tens of thousands of years."

"Well, ours don't," said Vimes. "But murder is murder anywhere. The news has got out. You've already got the dwarfs and the trolls simmering nicely, and this will bring it all right to the boil. Do you *want* a war?"

"With the trolls? That is—"

"No, with the city. A place inside the walls where the law doesn't run? His lordship won't accept that one."

"You would not dare!" said the dwarf.

"Look into my eyes," said Vimes.

"There are far more dwarfs than there are watchmen," said Ardent, but the amused expression had fled.

"So what you are telling me is that law is just a matter of numbers?" said Vimes, standing up. "I thought you dwarfs practically *worshiped* the idea of law. Is numbers all it is? I'll swear in more men, then. Trolls, too. They're citizens, just like me. Are you sure every dwarf is on your side? I'll raise the regiments. I'll have to. I know how things are run in Llamedos and Uberwald, but they are not run like that here. One law, Mr. Ardent. That's what we've got. If I let people slam their front door on it, I might as well shut down the Watch."

Vimes walked to the doorway. "That's my offer. Now I'm going back to the Yard—"

"Wait!"

Ardent sat staring at the desktop, drumming his fingers on it.

"I do not have . . . seniority here," he said.

"Let me talk to your grags. I promise to rub out no words."

"No. They will not talk to you. They do not talk to humans. They are waiting below. They had word of your arrival. They are frightened. They do not trust humans."

"Why?"

"Because you are not dwarfs," said Ardent. "Because you are . . . a sort of bad dream."

Vimes put his hand on the dwarf's shoulder.

"Then let's go downstairs, where you can talk to

them about nightmares," he said, "and you can point out which one is me."

There was a long silence until Ardent said: "Very well. This is under protest, you understand."

"I'll be happy to make a note of that," said Vimes. "Thank you for your cooperative attitude," he added.

Ardent stood up and produced a ring of complex keys from his robes.

Vimes tried to keep track of the journey, but it was hard. There were twists and turns, in dim tunnels that seemed all alike. There was not a trace of water anywhere. How far did the tunnels go? How far down? How far out? Dwarfs mined through granite. They could probably *stroll* through river mud.

In fact, in most places, the dwarfs hadn't so much mined as cleaned house, taking away the silt, tunneling from one ancient, dripping room to another. And, somehow, the water went away.

There were things, glittering, possibly magical, half-seen in dark archways as they passed. And odd chanting. He knew dwarfish, in a the-axe-of-my-aunt-is-in-your-head kind of way, and it didn't sound like that at all. It sounded like short words rattled out at very high speed.

And with every turn he felt the anger coming back. They were being led in circles, weren't they? For no reason other than pique. Ardent forged ahead, leaving Vimes to blunder along behind and occasionally bump his head.

His temper was bubbling. This was nothing more than a bloody runaround! The dwarf didn't care about the law, about him, about the world above. They undermine our city and they don't obey our laws! There had been a damn murder. He admits it! Why am I putting up with this . . . this stupid play-acting!

He was passing yet another tunnel mouth, but this one had a piece of board nailed across it. He pulled out his sword, yelled, "I wonder what's down here?," smashed the board, and set off down the tunnel with Angua following.

"Is this wise, sir?" she whispered, as they plunged along.

"No. But I've had it up to here with Mr. Ardent," Vimes growled. "I tell you, another twisty tunnel and I'll be back here with the heavy mob, politics or not."

"Calm down, sir!"

"Well, everything he says and does is an insult! It makes my blood boil!" said Vimes, striding onwards and ignoring the shouts of Ardent behind him.

"There's a door ahead, sir!"

"All right, I'm not blind! Just half-blind!" Vimes snapped.

He reached out. The big, round door had a wheel in its center, and dwarf runes chalked all over it.

"Can you read them, Sergeant?"

"Er . . . 'Mortal Danger! Flooding! No Entry!'" said Angua. "More or less, sir. They're pressure doors. I've seen these used before, in other mines."

"Chained shut, too," said Vimes, reaching out. "Looks like solid iron—ow!"

"Sir?"

"Gashed my hand on a nail!" Vimes rammed his hand into a pocket, where, without fail, Sybil saw to it that a clean handkerchief was lodged on a daily basis.

"A nail in an iron door, sir?" said Angua, looking closely.

"A rivet, then. Can't see a thing in this gloom. Why they—"

"You *must* follow me. This is a mine! There are dangers!" said Ardent, catching up with them.

"You still get flooding?" said Vimes.

"It is to be expected! We know how to cope! Now, stay close to me!"

"I'll be more inclined to do that, *sir*, if I thought we were taking a direct route!" said Vimes. "Otherwise I might look for shortcuts!"

"We are nearly there, Commander," said Ardent, walking away. "Nearly there!"

Aimless and hopeless, the troll wandered . . .

His name was Brick, although currently he couldn't remember this. His head ached. It really *ached*. It was der Scrape that did it. What did dey always say? When you sinkin' to where you was cookin' up Scrape, you was so low even der cockroaches had to bend down to spit on you?

Last night . . . what had happenin'? What bits did he see, what bits did he do, what bits in der thumpin,' scaldin' cauldron of his brain were real? The bit with der giant wooly elephants, *dey* prob'ly weren't real. He was pretty sure there weren't any giant wooly elephants in dis city, 'cos if der were, he would've seen 'em before, and dere'd be big steamin' turds in der streets an' similar, you wouldn't miss 'em . . .

He was called Brick because he had been born in the city, and trolls, being made of metamorphorical rock, often take on the nature of the local rocks. His hide was a dirty orange, with a network of horizontal and vertical lines; if Brick stood up close to a wall, he was quite hard to see. But most people didn't see Brick anyway. He was the kind of person whose mere existence is an insult to all decent folk, in their opinion.

Dat mine wi' dem dwarfs, was *dat* real? You go an' find a place to lie down and watch der pretty pichturs, suddenly you're in dis dwarf hole? That couldna bin real! Only . . . word on der street was dat some troll had got into a dwarf hole, yeah, and *everyone* was lookin' for dat troll an' not to shake him by der han' . . . Der word said der Breccia wanted to find out *real* hard, and by der sound of it dey were not happy. Not happy that some dwarf who'd been puttin' der bad word on the clans was *off'ed* by a troll? Were dey mad? Actually, it didn't matter if dey was mad or not, 'cos dey had ways of asking questions dat didn't heal for months, so he better be keepin' out dere way.

On der oder hand . . . a dwarf wouldn't know one troll from anoder, right? And no one else had seen him. So act normal, right? He'd be fine. He'd be fine. Anyway, it couldna bin him . . .

It occurred to Brick—yeah, dat's my name, knew it all der time—that he still had a bit of the white powder at the bottom of the bag. All he needed to do now was find a startled pigeon and some alcohol, any alcohol at all, and he be fine. Yeah. Fine. Nothin' to worry about at all . . .

Yeah.

When Vimes stepped out into the brilliant daylight, the first thing he did was draw a deep breath. The second thing he did was draw his sword, wincing as his sore hand protested.

Fresh air, that was the stuff. He'd felt quite dizzy down there, and the tiny cut on his hand itched like mad. He'd better get Igor to take a look at it. You could probably catch *anything* in the muck down there.

Ah, that was better. He could feel himself cooling down. The air down there had made him feel really strange.

The crowd was a lot more like a mob now, but he saw at the second glance that it was what he thought of as a plum-cake mob. It doesn't take many people to turn a worried, anxious crowd into a mob. A shout here, a shove there, something thrown *here* . . . and with care, every hesitant, nervous individual is being drawn into a majority that does not, in fact, exist.

Detritus was still standing like a statue, apparently oblivious to the growing din. But Ringfounder . . . damn. He was arguing hotly with people at the front of the crowd. You *never* argued! You never got drawn in!

"Corporal Ringfounder!" he bellowed. "To me!"

The dwarf turned as a halfbrick sailed over the heads of the mob and clanged off his helmet. He went over like a tree.

Detritus moved so fast that he was halfway through the crowd before the dwarf hit the cobbles.

His arm dipped into the press of bodies and hauled up a struggling figure. He spun around, thudded back through the gap that hadn't had time to close yet, and was beside Vimes before Ringfounder's helmet had stopped rolling.

"Well done, Sergeant," said Vimes out of the corner of his mouth. "Did you have a plan for the next bit?"

"I'm more der tactical kind, sir," said Detritus.

Oh, well. At times like this you didn't argue, and you didn't step back. Vimes pulled out his badge and held it up.

"This dwarf is under arrest for assaulting a Watch officer!" he shouted. "Let us through, in the name of the law!"

And, to his amazement, the crowd went quiet, like a lot of children when they sense that *this* time the teacher is really, really angry. Perhaps it was the words on the badge, he thought. You couldn't rub *them* out.

In the silence, another halfbrick dropped out of the free hand of the dwarf in Detritus's very solid custody. Years later, Vimes would shut his eyes and still be able to recall the crunch it made when it hit the ground.

Angua stood up, with the unconscious Ringfounder in her arms.

"He's concussed," she said. "And I suggest, sir, that you turn around, just for a moment?"

Vimes risked a glance. Ardent—or, at least, a leather-shrouded dwarf that could have been him—was standing in the shadows of the doorway. He had the attention of the crowd.

"We're being *allowed* to go?" he said to Angua, nodding to the figure.

"I think the going is the thing, sir, don't you?"

"You've got that right, Sergeant. Detritus, keep a grip on that little bugger. Back to the nick, all of us."

The crowd parted to let them through, with barely a murmur. The silence followed them all the way back to the Watch house . . .

. . . where Otto Chriek of the *Times* was waiting in the street, iconograph at the ready.

"Oh no, you don't, Otto," said Vimes, as his squad approached.

"I'm standing on the public highway, Mr. Vimes," said Otto meekly. "Smile, please—"

And he took a picture of a troll officer holding a dwarf up in the air.

Oh well, said Vimes to himself, that's page one sorted out. And probably the bloody cartoon, too.

One dwarf in the cells, one in the tender, loving care of Igor, Vimes thought, as he trudged up the stairs to his office. And it's only going to get worse. Those dwarfs were *obeying* Ardent, weren't they? What would they have done if the dwarf had shaken his head?

He landed in his chair so hard that it rolled back a foot.

He'd met deep-down dwarfs before. They'd been weird, but he'd been able to deal with them. The Low King was a deep-downer, and Vimes had got on with him well enough, once you accepted that the fairy-tale dwarf in the Hogfather beard was an astute politician. He was a dwarf with a vision. He dealt with the world. Ha, "he'd seen the light." But those in the new mine . . .

He hadn't seen them, even though they were sitting in a room made brilliant with the light of hundreds of candles. That seemed odd, since the grags themselves were completely shrouded in their pointy black leather. But maybe it was some mystic ceremony, and who'd look for sense there? Maybe you got a more holy dark in the midst of light? The brighter the light the blacker the shadow?

Ardent had spoken in a language that *sounded* like dwarfish, and out of the dark hoods had come answers and questions, all barked out in the same harsh, brief syllables.

At one point, Vimes was asked to repeat the meat of his statement made up above, which had seemed too far away now. He'd done so, and there'd been a long-drawn-out discussion in what he'd come to think of as Deep Dwarf. And all the time he felt that eyes he could not see were watching him very hard indeed. It didn't help that his head had been aching like mad and there were shooting pains going up and down his arm.

And that was it. Had they understood him? He didn't know. Ardent had said that they agreed with considerable reluctance. Had they? He hadn't a clue, not a clue, to what had really been said. Would Carrot be given access to a crime scene that had not been interfered with in any way? Vimes grunted. Huh. What do *you* think, boys and girls?

He pinched the bridge of his nose, and then stared

at his right hand. Igor had gone on at length about "tiny invithible biting creatureth" and used some vicious ointment that probably killed anything of any size or visibility. It had stung like seven hells for five minutes, but the sting had gone and seemed to have taken the pain with it. Anyway . . . what mattered was that the Watch was officially on this case.

His eye was caught by the top sheet of paperwork in his in-tray.* He groaned as he picked it up.

To: His Grace Sir Samuel Vimes, Commander of the Watch
From: Mr. A. E. Pessimal, Inspector of the Watch

Your Grace:

I hope you will not mind giving me as soon as possible the answers to the following questions:

1) *What is Corporal "Nobby" Nobbs for? Why do you employ a known petty thief?*
2) *I timed two officers in Broad Way earlier, and in the space of one hour they made no arrests. Why was this an economic use of their time?*
3) *The level of violence used by troll officers against troll prisoners appears excessive. Could you please comment upon this?*

. . . and so on. Vimes read on with his mouth open. All right, the man wasn't a copper—definitely

---

*Vimes maintained three trays: In, Out, and Shake It All About; the last one was where he put everything he was too busy, angry, tired, or bewildered to do anything about.

not—but surely he had a fully functional brain? Oh, good grief, he'd even spotted the monthly discrepancy in the petty-cash box! Would A. E. Pessimal understand if Vimes explained that Nobby's services over the years more than made up for the casual petty theft, which you accepted as a kind of mild nuisance?

Would *that* be an economic use of *my* time? I think not.

As he put the paper back in the tray, he spotted a sheet underneath, in Cheery's handwriting. He picked it up and read it.

Two dwarfs and one troll had handed in their badges this morning, citing "family reasons." Damn. That was seven officers lost this week. Bloody Koom Valley, it got everywhere. Oh, it couldn't be fun, heavens knew, being a troll holding the line against a bunch of your fellow trolls and *defending* a dwarf like the late Hamcrusher. It probably wasn't any funner being a dwarf hearing that some troll street gang beat up your brother because of what that idiot had said. Some people would be asking: Whose side are you on? If you're not with us, you're against us. Huh. If you not an apple, you're a banana . . .

Carrot came in quietly and placed a plate on the desk.

"Angua told me all about it," he said. "Well done, sir."

"What do you mean, well done?" said Vimes, looking at his healthy sandwich lunch. "I nearly started a war!"

"Ah, but they didn't know you were bluffing."

"I probably wasn't." Vimes carefully lifted the

top of the bacon, lettuce, and tomato sandwich, and smiled inwardly. Good old Cheery. She knew what a Vimes BLT was all about. It was about having to lift up quite a lot of crispy bacon before you found the miserable skulking vegetables. You might never notice them at all.

"I want you to take Angua down there with you again," he said. "And . . . yes, Lance Constable von Humpeding. Our little Sally. Just the job for a vampire who fortuitously has arrived in the nick of time, eh? Let's see how good she is."

"Just those two, sir?"

"Er, yes. They both have very good night vision, yes?" Vimes looked down at his sandwich, and mumbled: "We can't take any artificial light down there."

"A murder investigation in the *dark*, sir?"

"I had no choice!" said Vimes hotly. "I know a sticking point when I see one, Captain. No artificial light. Well, if they want to play silly buggers, I'm their boy. You know about mines, and both the ladies have got night vision built in. Well, the vampire has, and Angua can practically see with her nose. So that's it. Do the best you can. The place is full of those damn glow beetles. They should help."

"They've got vurms?" said Carrot. "Oh. Well, I know some tricks there, sir."

"Good. They say a big troll did it and ran away. Make of that what you will."

"There might be some protests about Sally, sir," said Carrot.

"Why? Will they spot she's a vampire?"

"No, sir, I don't think they—"

"Then don't tell 'em," said Vimes. "You're the . . .

smelter, it's up to you what, er, tools you use. Seen this?"

He waved the report about the three officers he was trying not to think of as deserters.

"Yes, sir. I was meaning to talk to you about that. It might help if we changed the patrols a bit," said Carrot.

"How do you mean?"

"Er . . . it would be quite easy to arrange the patrol schedules so that trolls and dwarfs don't have to go on the beat together, sir. Um . . . some of the lads say they'd be a bit happier if we could . . ."

Carrot let the sentence die away in the stony glare.

"We've never paid any attention to an officer's species when we do the roster, Captain," said Vimes coldly. "Except for the gnomes, of course."

"There's your precedent, then—" Carrot began.

"Don't be daft. A typical gnome room is about twice the size of a shoebox, Captain! Look, you can see this idea is nuts. Dangerous nuts, too. We'd have to patrol troll with troll, dwarf with dwarf, and human with human—"

"Not necessarily, sir. Humans could patrol with either of the others."

Vimes rocked his chair forward. "No, they couldn't! This is not about common sense, this is about fear! If a troll sees a dwarf and a human patrolling together, he'll think: 'There's the enemy, two against one.' Can't you see where this is going? When a copper's in a tight corner and blows his whistle for backup, I don't want him demanding that when it arrives it's the right damn shape!" He calmed down a little, opened his notebook, and tossed it on the desk. "And talking of shapes, do you know what this means? I spotted it in the mine, and a dwarf called Helmclever scrawled it with some spilt coffee, and you know what? I think he was only half-aware that he'd done it."

Carrot picked up the notebook and regarded the sketch solemnly for a moment.

"Mine sign, sir," he said. "It means 'The Following Dark.'"

"And what does *that* mean?"

"Er . . . that things are pretty bad down there, sir," said Carrot earnestly. "Oh dear." He put the notebook down slowly, as if half-afraid that it might explode.

"Well, there has been a murder, Captain," Vimes pointed out.

"Yes, sir. But this might mean something worse, sir. Mine sign is a very strange phenomenon."

"There was a sign like it over the door, only there was just one line and it was horizontal," Vimes added.

"Oh, that'd be the Long Dark rune, sir," said Carrot dismissively. "It's just the symbol for a mine. Nothing to worry about."

"But this other one is? Is it anything to do with grags sitting in a room surrounded by lighted candles?"

It was always nice to surprise Carrot, and this time he looked amazed. "How did you work that out, sir?"

"It's only words, Captain," said Vimes, waving a hand. "'The Following Dark' doesn't sound good. Time to stay brightly lit, maybe? When I met them, they were surrounded by candles. I thought maybe it was some kind of ceremony."

"Could be," Carrot agreed, carefully. "Thank you for this, sir. I'll go prepared."

As Carrot reached the door, Vimes added, "One thing, Captain?"

"Yes, sir?"

Vimes didn't look up from the sandwich, from which he was daintily separating fragments of the L and the T from the crispy B.

"Just remember you're a copper, will you?" he said.

Sally knew something was up as soon as she got back into the locker room, in her shiny new breastplate and soup-bowl helmet. Coppers of various species were standing around trying to look nonchalant. Coppers are never any good at this at all.

They watched as she approached her locker. She opened the door, therefore, with due care. The shelf was full of garlic.

Ah. It starts, and so soon, too. Just as well she'd been prepared . . .

Here and there, behind her, she heard the faint coughs and throat clearings of people trying not to laugh. And there was smirking going on; a smirk makes a subtle noise if you're listening for it.

She reached into the locker with both hands and pulled out two big fat bulbs. All eyes were on her, all coppers were motionless as she walked slowly around the room.

The reek of garlic was strong on one young constable, whose big grin was suddenly caked with nervousness at the corners. He had the look about him of the kind of fool who'd do anything for a giggle.

"Excuse me, Constable, but what is your name?" she said meekly.

"Er . . . Fittly, miss . . ."

"Are these from you?" Sally demanded. She let her canines extend just enough to notice.

". . . er, only a joke, miss . . ."

"Nothing funny about it," said Sally sweetly. "I like garlic. I *love* garlic. Don't you?"

"Er . . . yeah . . ." said the unhappy Fittly.

"Good," said Sally.

With a speed that made him flinch, she rammed a bulb into her mouth and bit down heavily.

The crunching was the only sound in the locker room.

And then she swallowed.

"Oh dear, where *are* my manners, Constable?" she said, holding out the other bulb. "This one's yours . . ."

Laughter broke out around the room. Coppers are like any other mob. The table's been turned, and this way around it's funnier. It's a bit of a laugh, a bit of fun. No harm done, eh?

"Come on, Fittly," said someone. "It's only fair. She ate hers!" And someone else, as someone always does, began to clap and urge "Eat! Eat!" Others took it up, encouraged by the fact that Fittly had gone bright red.

"Eat! eat! eat! eat! eat! eat! eat! eat! eat!eat!eat!—"

A man without an option, Fittly grabbed the bulb, forced it into his mouth, and bit it hard, to the accompaniment of cheers. A moment later, Sally saw his eyes widen.

"Lance Constable von Humpeding?"

She turned. A young man of godlike proportions* was standing in the doorway. Unlike the armor of the other officers, his breastplate shone and the chain mail was quite devoid of rust.

"Everything all right?" The officer glanced at Fittly, who'd dropped to his knees and was coughing garlic across the room, but somehow quite failed to see him.

"Er, fine, sir," said Sally, puzzled, as Fittly began to throw up.

"We've met already. Everyone calls me Captain Carrot. Come with me, please."

Out in the main office, Carrot stopped and turned. "All right, Lance Constable . . . you had a bulb already prepared, right? Don't look like that, there's a vegetable barrow out in the square today. It's not hard to work out."

"Er . . . Sergeant Angua did warn me . . ."

"So . . . ?"

"So I carved a garlic out of a turnip, sir."

"And the one you gave Fittly?"

"Oh, that was a carved turnip, too. I try not to touch garlic, sir," said Sally. Oh gods, this one really was attractive . . .

"Really? Turnip? He seemed to take it badly," said Carrot.

"I put a few fresh chili seeds in it," Sally added. "About thirty, I think."

---

*The better class of gods, anyway. Not the ones with the tentacles, obviously.

"Oh? Why did you do that?"

"Oh, you know, sir," said Sally, radiating innocence. "A bit of a laugh, a bit of fun. No harm done, eh?"

The captain appeared to consider this.

"We'll leave it at that, then," he said. "Now, Lance Constable, have you ever seen a dead body?"

Sally waited to see if he was serious. Apparently, he was.

"Strictly speaking, no, sir," she said.

Vimes fretted through the afternoon. There was, of course, the paperwork. There was always the paperwork. The trays were only the start. Heaps of it were ranged accusingly along one wall, and gently merging.* He knew that he had to do it. Warrants, dockets, Watch orders, signatures—that was what made the Watch a police force rather than just a bunch of fairly rough fellows with inquisitive habits. Paperwork: you had to have lots of it, and it had to be signed by him.

He signed the Arrests book, the Occurrences book, even the Lost Property book. Lost Property book! They never had one of those in the old days. If someone turned up complaining that they'd lost some small item, you just held Nobby Nobbs upside down and sorted through what dropped out.

But he didn't know two-thirds of the coppers he

---

*Vimes had got around to a Clean Desk policy. It was a Clean Floor strategy that eluded him at the moment.

employed now—not *know*, in the sense of knowing when they'd stand and when they'd run, knowing the little giveaways that'd tell him when they were lying or scared witless. It wasn't really his Watch anymore. It was the city's Watch. He just ran it.

He went through the Station Sergeant's reports, the Watch Officers' reports, the Sick reports, the Disciplinary reports, the Petty Cash reports—

"Duddle-dum-duddle-dum-duddle—"

Vimes slammed the Gooseberry down on the desk and picked up the small loaf of dwarf bread that for the last few years he'd used as a paperweight.

"Switch off or die," he growled.

"Now, I can see you're *slightly* upset," said the imp, looking up at the looming loaf, "but could I ask you to look at things from my point of view? This is my *job*. This is what I *am*. I am, therefore I think. And I think we could get along famously if you would only read the manu—please, no! I really could help you!"

Vimes hesitated in mid-thump, and then carefully put down the loaf.

"How?" he said.

"You've been adding up the numbers wrong," said the imp. "You don't always carry the tens."

"And how would you know that?" Vimes demanded.

"You mutter to yourself," said the imp.

"You *eavesdrop* on me?"

"It's my job! I can't switch my ears off! I have to listen! That's how I know about the appointments!"

Vimes picked up the Petty Cash report and glanced at the messy columns of figures. He prided himself on what he had, since infancy, called "sums."

Yes, he knew he plodded a bit, but he got there in the end.

"You think you could do better?" he said.

"Let me out and give me a pencil!" said the imp. Vimes shrugged. It had been a strange day, after all. He opened the little cage door.

The imp was a very pale green and translucent, little more than a creature made out of colored air, but it was able to grip the tiny pencil stub. It ran up and down the column of figures in the Petty Cash book and, Vimes was pleased to hear, it muttered to itself.

"It's out by three dollars and five pence," it reported after a few seconds.

"That's fine, then," said Vimes.

"But the money is not accounted for!"

"Oh yes it is," said Vimes. "It was stolen by Nobby Nobbs. It always is. He never steals more than four dollars fifty."

"Would you like me to make an appointment for a disciplinary interview?" said the imp hopefully.

"Of course not. I'm signing it off now. Er . . . thank you. Can you add up the other dockets?"

The imp beamed.

"Absolutely!"

Vimes left the imp scribbling happily and walked over to the window.

They don't acknowledge our law and they undermine our city. That's not just a bunch of deep-downers here to keep their fellow dwarfs on the straight seam. How far do those tunnels go? Dwarfs dig like crazy. But why here? What are they looking for? As sure as any hell you choose, there's no treasure trove under this city, no sleep-

ing dragon, no secret kingdom. There's just water and mud and darkness.

How far do they go? How much— hold on, we know this, we know this, don't we. We know about numbers and figures in today's Watch . . .

"Imp?" he said, turning around.

"Yes, Insert Name Here?"

"You see that big pile of paper in the corner?" said Vimes, pointing. "Somewhere in there are the gate guard reports for the past six months. Can you compare them with last week's? Can you compare the number of dunny wagons leaving the city?"

"**Dunny Wagon** not found in root dictionary. Searching slang dictionary . . . mip . . . mip . . . mip . . . **Dunny Wagon**, n.: cart for carrying night soil (see also *Honey Wagon, Treacle Wagon, Midnight Special, Gong Wagon, and variants*)," said the imp.

"That's right," said Vimes, who hadn't heard the Midnight Special one before. "Can you?"

"Ooh, yes!" said the imp. "Thank you for using the Dis-Organizer Mark five, the Gooseberry, the most advanced—"

"Yeah, don't mention it. Just look at the ones for the Hubwards Gate. That's closest to Treacle Street."

"Then I suggest you stand back, Insert Name Here," said the imp.

"Why?"

The imp leapt into the pile. There was some rustling noises, a couple of mice scampered out—and the pile exploded. Vimes backed away hurriedly as papers fountained into the air, borne aloft on a very pale green cloud.

Vimes had instigated record keeping at the gates not because he had a huge interest in the results, but because it kept the lads on their toes. It wasn't as if it was security duty. Ankh-Morpork was so wide open it was gaping. But the cart census was handy. It stopped watchmen falling asleep at their posts, and it gave them an excuse to be nosy.

You had to move soil. That was it. This was a city. If you were a long way from the river, the only way to do that was on a cart. Blast it, he thought, I should have asked the thing to see if there's been any increase in stone and timber loads, too. Once you've dug a hole in mud, you've got to keep it open—

The circling, swooping papers snapped back into piles. The green haze shrank with a faint *zzzzp* noise, and there was the little imp, ready to burst with pride.

"An extra one-point-one dunny carts a night over six months ago!" it announced. "Thank you, Insert Name Here! Cogito ergo sum, Insert Name Here. I exist, therefore I do sums!"

"Right, yes, thank you," said Vimes. Hmm. A bit more than one cart a night? They held a couple of tons, maximum. You couldn't make much of that. Maybe people living near that gate had been really ill lately. But . . . what would *he* do, in the dwarfs' position?

He damn well wouldn't send stuff out of the nearest gate, that's what. Ye gods, if they were tunneling in enough places, they could dump it *anywhere*.

"Imp, could you . . ." Vimes paused. "Look, don't you have some kind of a name?"

"Name, Insert Name Here?" said the imp, looking puzzled. "Oh, no. I am created by the dozen, Insert Name Here. A name would be a bit stupid, really."

"I'll call you Gooseberry, then. So . . . Gooseberry, can you give me the same figures for every city gate? And also the numbers of timber and stone carts?"

"It will take some time, Insert Name Here, but yes! I should love to!"

"And while you're about it, see if there were any reports of subsidence. Walls falling down, houses cracking, that sort of thing?"

"Certainly, Insert Name Here. You can rely on me, Insert Name Here!"

"Snap to it, then!"

"Yes, Insert Name Here! Thank you, Insert Name Here. I think much better outside the box, Insert Name Here!"

Zzzzp. Paper started to fly.

Well, who'd have thought it, Vimes wondered. Maybe the damned thing could be useful after all.

The speaking tube whistled. He unhooked it and said, "Vimes."

"I've got the evening edition of the *Times*, sir," said the distant voice of Sergeant Littlebottom. She sounded worried.

"Fine. Send it up."

"And there's a couple of people here who want to see you, sir." Now there was a guarded tone to her voice.

"And they can hear you?" said Vimes.

"That's right, sir. Trolls. They insist on seeing you personally. They say they have a message for you."

"Do they look like trouble?"

"Every inch, sir."

"I'm coming down."

Vimes hung up the tube. Trolls with a message. It was unlikely to be an invitation to a literary lunch.

"Er . . . Gooseberry?" he said.

Once again, the faint green blur coalesced into the beaming imp.

"Found the figures, Insert Name Here. Just working on them!" it said, and saluted.

"Good, but get back in the box, will you? We're going out."

"Certainly, Insert Name Here! Thank you for choosing the—"

Vimes pushed the box into his pocket, and went downstairs.

The main office included not only the duty officer's desk but also half a dozen smaller ones, where watchmen sat when they had to do the really tricky parts of police work, like punctuating a sentence correctly. A lot of rooms and corridors opened into it. A useful result of all this was that any action there attracted a lot of attention very quickly.

If the two trolls very conspicuously in the middle of the room had intended trouble, they'd picked a bad time. It was between shifts. Currently, they were trying without success to swagger whilst standing still, watched with deep suspicion by seven or eight officers of various shapes.

They'd brought it on themselves. They were *baaad* trolls. At least, they'd like everyone to think so. But they'd got it wrong. Vimes had seen bad trolls, and these didn't come close. They'd tried. Oh, they'd tried. Lichen covered their heads and shoulders. Clan graffiti adorned their bodies; one of them had even had his arm carved, which must have hurt, for that stone-cool troll look. Since wearing the traditional belt of human or dwarf skulls would have resulted in the wearer's heels leaving a groove all the way to the nearest nick, and monkey skulls left the wearer liable to ambush by dwarfs with no grounding in forensic anthropology, these trolls—

Vimes grinned. These boys had done the best they could with, oh dear, sheep and goat skulls. Well done, boys, that's really scary.

It was depressing. The old-time bad trolls didn't bother with all that stuff. They just beat you over the head with your own arm until you got the message.

"Well, gentlemen?" he said. "I'm Vimes."

The trolls exchanged glances through the mats of lichen, and one of them lost.

"Midder Chrysophrase he wanna see you," said Carved Arm sulkily.

"Is that so?" said Vimes.

"He wanna see you *now*," said the troll.

"Well, he knows where I live," said Vimes.

"Yeah. He does."

Three words, smacking into the silence like lead. It was the way the troll said them. A suicidal kind of way.

The silence was broken by the steely sound of bolts being shot home, followed by a click. The trolls turned. Sergeant Detritus was taking the key out of the lock of the Watch house's big, thick, double doors. Then he turned around and his heavy hands landed on the trolls' shoulders.

He sighed. "Boys," he said, "if dere was a Ph.D. in bein' fick, youse wouldn't be able to find a pencil."

The troll who'd uttered the not-very-veiled threat then made another mistake. It must have been terror that moved his arms, or dumb machismo. Surely no one with a functioning brain cell would have selected that moment to move their arms into what, for trolls, was the attack position.

Detritus's fist moved in a blur, and the crack, as it connected with the troll's skull, made the furniture rattle.

Vimes opened his mouth . . . and shut it again. Trollish was a very *physical* language. And you had to respect cultural traditions, didn't you? It wasn't only dwarfs who were allowed to have them, was it? Besides, you couldn't crack a troll's skull even with a hammer and chisel. *And he threatened your family*, his hind brain added. *He had it coming—*

There was a twinge of pain from the wound on his hand, echoed by the stab of a headache. Oh hells. And Igor said the stuff would work!

The stricken troll rocked for a second or two, and then went over forwards in one rigid movement.

Detritus walked across to Vimes, kicking the recumbent figure en passant.

"Sorry about dat, sir," he said, and his hand clanged on his helmet as he saluted. "Dey got no manners."

"All right, that's enough," said Vimes, and addressed the remaining, suddenly-very-alone messenger. "*Why* does Chrysophrase want to see me?"

"He wouldn't tell der Brothers Fick that, would he . . ." said Detritus, grinning horribly at the troll. There was no swagger left now.

"All I know is, it's about der killin' o' the *horug*," mumbled the troll, taking refuge in surliness. At the sound of the word the eyes of every watching dwarf narrowed further. It was a very bad word.

"Oh boy, oh boy, oh . . ." Detritus hesitated.

"Boy," said Vimes out of the corner of his mouth.

"—boy!" said Detritus triumphantly. "You are makin' friends like nobody's business today!"

"Where's the meeting?" said Vimes.

"Der Pork Futures Warehouse," said the troll. "You is to come alone . . ." he paused, awareness of his position dawning on him, and added, "if you don't mind."

"Go and tell your boss I might choose to wander that way, will you?" said Vimes. "Now get out of here. Let him out, Sergeant."

"An' take your rubbish home wid you," Detritus roared.

He slammed the doors behind the troll, bent under the weight of his fallen comrade.

"Okay," said Vimes, as tensions relaxed. "You heard the troll. A good citizen wants to help the Watch. I'll go and see what he's got to—"

His eye caught the front page of the *Times*, spread out on the desk. Oh hell, he thought wearily. There we are, at a time like this, with a troll officer holding a dwarf with his feet off the ground.

"It's a good picture of Detritus, sir," said Sergeant Littlebottom nervously.

"'The Long Arm of The Law,'" Vimes read aloud. "Is that supposed to be funny?"

"Probably it is to people who write headlines," said Cheery.

"Hamcrusher Murdered," Vimes read. "Watch Investigating."

"Where do they get this?" he said aloud. "Who tells them? Pretty soon I'll have to read the *Times* to find out what I'm doing today!" He flung the paper back on the desk. "Anything important I need to know about right now?"

"Sergeant Colon says there's been a robbery at the Royal—" Cheery began, but Vimes waved that away.

"More important than robberies, I mean," he said.

"Er . . . Another two officers have quit since I sent you that note, sir," said Cheery. "Corporal Ringfounder and Constable Schist at Chittling Street. Both say it's for, er, personal reasons, sir."

"Schist was a good officer," Detritus rumbled, shaking his head.

"Sounds like he decided to be a good troll instead," said Vimes. He was aware of a stirring behind him. He still had an audience. Oh well, time for *the* speech.

"I know it's hard for dwarf and troll officers right now," he said to the room at large. "I know that giving one of your own kind a tap with your truncheon because he's trying to kick you in the fork might feel like you're siding with the enemy. It's no fun for humans, either, but it's worse for you. The badge seems a bit heavy now, right? You see your people looking at you and wondering whose side you're on, yes? Well, you're on the side of the people, which is where the law ought to be. *All* the people, I mean, who're out there beyond the mob, who're fearful and puzzled and scared to go out at night. Now, funnily enough, the idiots who're out there right in front of you getting their self-defense in first are also the people, but since they don't seem to remember that, well, you're doing them a favor by cooling them off a bit. Hold on to that, and hold together. You think that you should stay home to make sure your ol' mum is okay? What good would you be against a mob? Together, we can stop things going that far. This'll go its course. I know we're all being run ragged, but right now I need everyone I can get, and in return there will be jam tomorrow and free beer, too. Maybe I'll even be a little blind when I'm signing the overtime dockets, who knows. Got it? But I want you all, whatever, *whoever* you are, to know this: I've got no patience with idiots who'll drag a grudge across five hundred miles and a thousand years. This is Ankh-Morpork. It's not Koom Valley. You *know* it's going to be a bad night tonight. Well, I'll be on duty. If you are, too, then I'll want to know that I can depend on you to watch my back as I'll watch yours. If I can't depend on you, I don't want to see you near me. Any questions?"

There was an embarrassed silence, as there always is on such occasions. Then a hand went up. It belonged to a dwarf.

"Is it true a troll killed the grag?" he asked. There was a murmuring from the watchmen, and he went on, a little less timorously, "Well, he *did* ask."

"Captain Carrot is investigating," said Vimes. "At the moment, we are still in the dark. But if indeed there has been a murder, then I *will* see that the murderer is brought to justice, no matter what size they are, what shape they are, who they are, or where they may be. You have my guarantee on that. My *personal* guarantee. Is that acceptable?"

The general change in the atmosphere indicated that it was so.

"Good," he said. "Now go out there and be coppers. Go on!"

The room emptied of all except those still laboring over the knotty problem of where they should put the comma.

"Er . . . permission t'speak freely, sir?" said Detritus, knuckling closer.

Vimes stared at him. When I first met you, you were chained to a wall like a watchdog and didn't speak much beyond a grunt, he thought. Truly, the leopard can change his shorts.

"Yes, of course," he said.

"You ain't serious, are you? You're not going runnin' after a coprolite like Chrysophrase, sir?"

"What's the worst he can do to me?"

"Rip off your head, grind you to mince, and make soup from your bones, sir," said Detritus promptly. "An' if you was a troll, he'd have all your teeth knocked out an' make cuff links out of 'em."

"Why'd he choose to do that now? Do you think he's looking for a war with us? That's not his way. He's hardly going to kill me by appointment, is he? *He* wants to talk to *me*. It's got to be to do with the case. He might know something. I don't dare *not go.* But I want you along. Scrounge up a squad, will you?"

A squad would be sensible, he admitted to himself. The streets were just too . . . nervous at the moment. He compromised with Detritus and a scratch band of whoever was doing nothing at the moment. That was one thing you could say about the Watch, it *was* representative. If you based your politics on what other people looked like, then you couldn't claim the Watch was on the side of any *shape*. That was worth hanging on to.

It seemed quieter outside, not so many people on the streets as usual. That wasn't a good sign. Ankh-Morpork could feel trouble ahead like spiders could feel tomorrow's rain.

What was this?

The creature swam through a mind. It had seen thousands of minds since the universe began, but there was something strange about this one.

It looked like a city. Ghostly, wavering buildings appeared through a drizzle of midnight rain. Of course, no two minds were alike . . .

The creature was old, although it would be more accurate to say that it had existed for a long time. When, at the start of all things, the primordial clouds of mind had collapsed into gods and demons and souls of all levels, it had been among those who had never drifted close to a major accretion. So it had entered the universe aimlessly, without task or affiliation, a scrap of being blowing free,

*fitting in wherever it could, a sort of complicated thought
looking for the right kind of mind. Currently—that is to
say, for the past ten thousand years, it had found work as
a superstition.*

*And now it was in this strange, dark city. There was
movement around it. The place was alive. And it rained.*

*For a moment, just then, it had sensed an open door,
a spasm of rage it could use. But just as it leapt to take
advantage, something invisible and strong had grabbed it
and flung it away.*

Strange.

With a flick of its tail, it disappeared into an alley.

The Pork Futures Warehouse was . . . one of those
things, the sort that you get in a city that has lived
with magic for too long. The occult reasoning, if
such it could be called, was this: pork was an important commodity in the city. Future pork, possibly even pork as yet unborn, was routinely traded by
the merchants. Therefore, it had to exist *somewhere*.
And the Pork Futures Warehouse came into existence, icy cold within as the pork drifted backwards
in time. It was a popular place for cold storage—and
for trolls who wanted to think quickly.

Even here, away from the more troubled areas of
the city, the people on the streets were . . . watchful.

And now they watched Vimes and his motley
squad pull up outside of the warehouse doors.

"I reckon at least one of us should go in wid you,"
Detritus rumbled, as protective as a mother hen.

"Chrysophrase won't be alone, you can bet on dat."
He unslung the Piecemaker, the crossbow he had
personally built from a converted siege weapon, the
multiple bolts of which tended to shatter in the air
from the sheer stress of acceleration. They could
remove a door not simply from its frame but also
from the world of objects bigger than a matchstick.
Its incredible inaccuracy was part of its charm. The
rest of the squad very quickly got behind him.

"Only you, then, Sergeant," said Vimes. "The
rest of you, come in only if you hear screaming. Me
screaming, that is." He hesitated, and then pulled
out the Gooseberry, which was still humming to
itself. "And no interruptions, understand?"

"Yes, Insert Name Here! Hmm hum hmm . . ."

Vimes pulled open the door. Dead, freezing air
poured out around him. Thick frost crackled under
his feet. Instantly, his breath twinkled in clouds.

He hated the Pork Futures Warehouse. The semi-
transparent slabs of yet-to-be-meat hanging in the
air, accumulating reality every day, made him shiver
for reasons that had nothing to do with temperature.
Sam Vimes considered crispy bacon to be a food
group in its own right, and the sight of it traveling
backwards in time turned his stomach the wrong way.

He took a few steps inside and looked around in
the dank, chilly grayness.

"Commander Vimes," he announced, feeling a bit
of a fool.

Here, away from the doors, freezing mist lay
knee-high on the floor. Two trolls waded through it
toward him. More lichen, he saw. More clan graffiti.
More sheep skulls.

"Leave weapons here," one rumbled.

"Baaa!" said Vimes, striding between them.

There was a click behind him, and the faint song of steel wires—under tension yet yearning to be free. Detritus had shouldered his bow.

"You can try takin' dis one off'f me if you like," he volunteered.

Vimes saw, further into the mist, a group of trolls. One or two of them looked like hired grunt. The others though . . . he sighed. All Detritus needed to do was fire that thing in this direction and quite a lot of the organized crime in the city would suddenly be very disorganized, as would be Vimes if he didn't hit the floor in time. But he couldn't allow that. There were rules here that went deeper than the law. Besides, a forty-foot hole in the warehouse wall would take some explaining.

Chrysophrase was sitting on a frost-crusted crate. You could always tell him in a crowd. He wore suits, when few trolls aspired to more than a few scraps of leather.

He even wore a tie, with a diamond pin. And today he had a fur coat around his shoulders. That had to be for show. Trolls *liked* low temperatures. They could think faster when their brains were cool. That's why the meeting had been called here. Right, Vimes thought, trying to stop his teeth from chattering, when it's *my* turn it's going to be in a sauna.

"Mr. Vimes! Good o' you to be comin'," said Chrysophrase jovially. "Dese gentlemen are all high-toned businessmen of my acquaintance. I 'spect you can put names to faces . . ."

"Yeah, the Breccia," said Vimes.

"Now den, Mr. Vimes, you know dat don't exist," said Chrysophrase innocently. "We just band togeder to furder troll interests in der city via many charitable concerns. You could say we are community leaders. Dere's no call for name-callin'."

Community leaders, Vimes thought. There'd been a lot of talk about community leaders lately, as in "community leaders appealed for calm," a phrase the *Times* used so often that the printers probably left it set in type. Vimes wondered who they were and how they were appointed, and, sometimes, if "appealing for calm" meant winking and saying "do not use those shiny new battle-axes in that cupboard over there . . . no, not that one, the other one." Hamcrusher had been a community leader.

"You said you wanted to talk to me alone," he said, nodding toward the shadowy figures. Some of them were hiding their faces.

"Dat is so. Oh, dese gennlemen behind me? Dey will be leaving us now," said Chrysophrase, waving a hand at them. "Dey're just here so' you understand dat one troll, dat is yours truly, is speakin' for der many. An,' at de same time, your good sergeant dere, my ol' frien' Detritus, is goin' outside for a smoke, would dat be der case? Dis conversation is between you an' me or it don't happen."

Vimes turned and nodded to Detritus. Reluctantly, with a scowl at Chrysophrase, the sergeant withdrew. So did the trolls. Boots crunched over the frost, and then doors slammed shut.

Vimes and Chrysophrase looked at each other in literally frozen silence.

"I can hear you teeth chattin'," said Chrysophrase.

"Dis place jus' right for troll, but for you it freezes der brass monkey, right? Dat why I bringed dis fur coat." He shrugged it off and held it out. "Dere jus' you and me here, okay?"

Pride was one thing; not being able to feel your fingers was another. Vimes wrapped himself in the fine, warm fur.

"Good. Can't talk to a man whose ears are froze, eh?" said Chrysophrase, pulling out a big cigar case. "Firstly, I am hearin' where one of my boys was disrespectful to you. I am hearin' how him suggestin' I am de kind of troll dat would get pers'nal, dat would raise a hand to your lovely lady an' your liddle boy who is growin' up so fine. Sometimes I am despairin' o' young trolls today. Dey show no respec'. Dey have no style. Dey lack finesse. If you are wanting a new rockery in your garden, just say der word."

"What? Just make sure I never clap eyes on him again," said Vimes shortly.

"Dat will not be a problem," said the troll. He indicated a small box, about a foot square, beside the crate. It was far too small to contain a *whole* troll.

Vimes tried to ignore it, but found this hard.

"Was that all you wanted to see me for?" he said, trying to stop his imagination playing its homemade horrors across his inner eyeballs.

"Smokin', Mr. Vimes?" Chrysophrase said, flipping open the case. "Der ones on der left is okay for humans. Finest kind."

"I've got my own," said Vimes, pulling out a battered packet. "What is this *about*? I'm a busy man."

Chrysophrase lit a silvery troll cigar and took a long pull. There was a smell like burning tin.

"Yeah, busy because dat ol' dwarf died," he said, not looking at Vimes.

"Well?"

"It was no troll done it," said Chrysophrase.

"How do you know?"

Now the troll looked directly at Vimes. "If it was, I would have foun' out by now. I bin askin' questions."

"So are we."

"I bin askin' questions more louder," said the troll. "I get lotsa answers. Sometimes I am gettin' answers to questions I ain't even asked yet."

I bet you are, Vimes thought. *I* have to obey rules.

"Why should you care who kills a dwarf?" he said.

"Mister Vimes! I am a honest citizen! It my public duty to care!" Chrysophrase watched Vimes's face to see how this was playing, and grinned. "All dis stoopid Koom Valley t'ing is bad for bidness. People are getting edgy, pokin' around, askin' questions. I am sittin' dere gettin' nervous. An' den I hear my ol' friend Mister Vimes is on der case and I am thinkin', dat Mister Vimes, he may be very insensitive to de nu-unces of troll culture sometimes, but der man is straight as a arrow and der are on him no flies. He will see where dis so-called troll left his club behind an' he is laughin' his head off, it is so see-through like glass! Some dwarf did it an' want to make de trolls look bad, Kew Eee Dee."

He sat back.

"What club?" said Vimes quietly.

"What's dat?"

"I haven't mentioned a club. There was nothing in the paper about a troll club."

"Dear Mister Vimes, dat's what der lawn ornaments is sayin'," said Chrysophrase.

"And dwarfs talk to you, do they?" said Vimes.

The troll looked thoughtfully at the roof, and blew out more smoke.

"Eventually," he said. "But dat's jus' detail. Jus' between you an' me, here an' now. We unnerstan' dese t'ings. It is clear as anyt'ing dat der crazy dwarfs had a fight, or der ol' dwarf died o' bein alive too long, or—"

"—or you asked him a few questions?"

"No callin' for dat, Mister Vimes. Dat club is nothin' but a red dried swimmin' thing. Der dwarfs put it dere."

"Or a troll did the murder, dropped his club, and ran," said Vimes. "Or he was clever, and thought 'No one would believe a troll would be so stupid as to leave his club, so if I *do* leave it, the dwarfs will get the blame.'"

"Hey, good job it so cold in here or I wouldn't be followin' you!" Chrysophrase laughed. "But den I ask, a troll gets into a nest o' dem lousy deepdowners and lays out jus' one? No way, Hose, eh! He'd whack as many of 'em as he could, thud, thud!"

He looked at Vimes's puzzlement and sighed.

"See, any troll gettin' in dere, he'd be a mad troll to start wid. You know how der kids are all wound up? People bin feeding dem dat honor an' glory an' destiny stuff, dat coprolite rots your brain faster'n Slab, faster even dan Slide. From what I am hearin', der dwarf got knocked off *for-rensic*, all slick an' quiet. We don't do dat, Mister Vimes. You played der game, you know it. Get a troll in der middle o' a load of dwarfs, he is like a fox in der . . . dem fings wi' wings, layin' dem egg fings . . ."

"Fox in a henhouse?"

"Dat's der—you know, fur, big ears—"

"Bunny?!"

"Right! Bash one dwarf an' sneak out? No troll'd stop at one, Mister Vimes. It's like you people an' peanuts. Der game got dat right."

"What's this game?"

"You never played Thud?" Chrysophrase looked surprised.

"Oh, *that*. I don't play games," said Vimes. "And on the subject of Slab, you *do* run the biggest pipeline. Just between you and me, here and now."

"Nah, I'm out o' dat whole thing," said Chrysophrase, waving his cigar dismissively. "You could say I am seein' der error o' my ways. From now on it's clean livin' straight down der middle. Property an' financial services, dat is der way forward."

"Glad to hear it."

"Besides, der kids are movin' in," Chrysophrase went on. "Sediment'ry trash. And dey cuts Slab w' bad sulfides an' cooks it up wi' ferric chloride an' crap like dat. You thought Slab was bad? You wait 'til you see Slide. Slab makes a troll go an' sit down to watch all der pretty colors, be no trouble to no one, nice and quiet. But Slide make him feel like him der biggest, strongest troll in der worl,' don't need sleep, don't need food. After a few weeks, don't need life. Dat ain't for me."

"Yes, why kill your customers?" said Vimes.

"Low blow, Mister Vimes, low blow. Nah, der new kids, half der time dey on Slide deyselves. Too much fightin,' too much of no respec'." He narrowed his eyes and leaned forward. "I know names and places."

"It's your duty as a good citizen to tell me, then," said Vimes. Ye gods, what does he think I am? But I *want* those names. Slide sounds nasty. Right now we need battle-crazy trolls like we need a hole in the head, which we'll probably end up getting.

"Can't tell you. Dat der problem," said Chrysophrase. "Dis ain't der time. You know what's happening out dere. If der stupid dwarfs want to fight, we'll need every troll. Dat's what I sayin.' I tellin' my people, give Vimes a chance. Be good citizens, not rockin' around der boat. People still listenin' to me an' my . . . associates. But not for much longer. I hope you on der case, Mister Vimes?"

"Captain Carrot is investigating right now," said Vimes.

Chrysophrase's eyes narrowed again.

"Carrot Ironfoundersson?" he said. "Der big dwarf? He a lovely boy, bright as a button, but to trolls dat won't look so good, I tell you flat."

"It doesn't look that good to dwarfs, if it comes to that," said Vimes. "But it's my Watch. I'll not be told who I put on what case."

"You trust him?" said Chrysophrase.

"Yes!"

"Okay, he a finker, he shiny. But . . . Ironfoundersson? Dwarf name. Dat a problem right dere. But der name Vimes . . . *dat* name means a lot. Can't be bribed, he once arrested der Patrician, not der sharpest knife in der drawer but honest like anything and he don't stop digging." Chrysophrase caught Vimes's expression. "Dat's what dey say. I wishin' Vimes was on dis case, 'cos him like me, bare-knuckle boy, he get at der truth soon enough. And to him I say: no troll did dat t'ing, not like dat."

Forget that he's talking street troll, Vimes told himself. That's just to seem like a good ol' troll. This is Chrysophrase. He beat out most of the old-style mobsters, who were pretty sharp players themselves, and he holds off the Thieves' Guild with one hand. And that's *without* sitting in a pile of snow. You *know* he's right. But . . . not the sharpest knife in the drawer? Thank you so very much!

But Captain Carrot was shiny, was he? Vimes's mind always looked for connections, and came up with: "Who is Mr. Shine?"

Chrysophrase was absolutely still, apart from the greenish smoke spiraling up from the cigar. Then, when he spoke, his air was uncharacteristically jovial.

"Him? Oh, a story for kids. Kinda like a troll legend from der far-off days o' long ahead," he said.*

"Like a folk hero?"

"Yeah, dat kinda t'ing. Kinda silly t'ing people talk about when times is tricky. Just a willie der wisp, not real. Dis is modern times."

And that seemed to be that.

Vimes stood up.

"All right, I've heard what you say," he said. "And now I've got a Watch to run."

Chrysophrase puffed his cigar and flicked the ash into the frost, where it sizzled.

"You going back to der Watch house by way o' Turn Again Lane?" he said.

---

*Troll lore says that living creatures actually move backwards through time. It's complicated.

"No, that's well out of—" Vimes stopped. There had been a hint of suggestion in the troll's voice.

"Give my regard to der ol' lady at next door to der cake shop," said the troll.

"Er . . . I will, will I?" said Vimes, nonplussed. "Sergeant!"

The door at the far end opened with a bang, and Detritus ran in, crossbow at the ready. Vimes, aware that one of the troll's few faults was an inability to understand all the implications of the term "safety catch," fought down a dreadful urge to dive for the ground.

"Time's comin' when we all got to know where we standin'," mused Chrysophrase, as if talking to the audience of ghostly pork. "An' who is standin' next to us."

As Vimes headed to the door, the troll added: "Give der coat to your lady, Mister Vimes. Wi' my compliments."

Vimes stopped dead, and looked down at the coat over his shoulders. It was of some silvery fur, beautifully warm, but not as warm as the rage rising within him. He'd nearly walked out wearing it. He'd come that close.

He shrugged it off and wrapped it into a ball. Quite probably several dozen small rare squeaky things had died to make this, but he could see to it that their deaths were not, in some small way, in vain.

He threw the bundle high in the air, yelled "Sergeant!" and threw himself on the floor. There was the instant slap of the bow, a sound as of a swarm of maddened bees, the *plinkplinkplink* of arrow fragments turning a circle of metal roof into a colander, and the smell of burnt hair.

Vimes got to his feet. What was falling around him was a kind of hairy snow.

He met Chrysophrase's gaze.

"Trying to bribe a Watch officer is a serious offense," he said.

The troll winked. "Honest like anyt'ing, I tell 'em. Nice to have dis little talk, Mister Vimes."

When they were well outside, Vimes pulled Detritus into an alley, insofar as it was possible to pull a troll anywhere.

"Okay, what do you know about Slide?" he said.

The troll's red eyes gleamed. "I bin hearin' rumors."

"Head to Treacle Mine Road and put a heavy squad together. Go to Turn Again Lane, behind the Scours. There's a wedding-cake maker up there, I think. You've got a nose for drugs. Poke it around, Sergeant."

"Right!" said Detritus. "You bin told somethin', sir?"

"Let's just say I think it's an earnest of good intent, shall we?" said Vimes.

"Dat's good, sir," said the troll. "Ernest who?"

"Er . . . someone we know wants to show us what a good citizen he is. Get to it, okay?"

Detritus slung his crossbow over his shoulder for ease of carriage and knuckled off at high speed. Vimes leaned against the wall. This was going to be a long day. And now he—

On the wall, just a little above head height, a troll had scored a rough sketch of a cut diamond.

You could tell troll graffiti easily—they did it with a fingernail and it was usually an inch deep in the masonry.

Next to the diamond was scored: SHINE.

"Ahem," said a small voice in his pocket. Vimes sighed, and pulled out the Gooseberry, while still staring at the word.

"Yes?"

"You said you didn't want to be interrupted . . ." said the imp defensively.

"Well? What have you got to say?"

"It's eleven minutes to six, Insert Name Here," said the imp meekly.

"Good grief! Why didn't you tell me!" Vimes looked aghast.

"Because you said you didn't want to be interrupted!" the imp quavered.

"Yes, but not—" Vimes stopped. Eleven minutes. He couldn't run it, not at this time of day. "Six o'clock is . . . *important*," he muttered.

"You didn't tell me that!" said the imp, holding its head in its hands. "You just said no interruptions! I'm really, really sorry—"

SHINE forgotten, Vimes looked around desperately at the nearby buildings. There wasn't much use for clacks towers down here, where the slaughterhouse district met the docks, but he spotted the big semaphore tower atop the dock superintendent's office.

"Get up there!" he ordered, opening the box. "Tell them you've come from me and this is priority one, right? They're to tell Pseudopolis Yard where I'm starting from! I'll cross the river on Misbegot

Bridge and head along Prouts! The officers at the Yard will know what this is all about! Go!"

The imp went from despair to enthusiasm in an instant. It saluted. "Yes indeed, sir. The Bluenose™ Integrated Messenger Service will not let you down, Insert Name Here. I shall interface right away!" It leapt down and became a disappearing blur of very pale green.

Vimes ran down to the dockside and began to race upriver, past the ships. The docks were always too crowded, and the road was an obstacle course of bales and ropes and piles of crates, with an argument every ten yards. But Vimes was a runner by nature, and knew all the ways to make progress in the city's crowded streets. He dodged and leapt, jinked and weaved, and, where necessary, barged. A rope tripped him up; he rolled upright. A stevedore bumped into him; Vimes laid him out with an uppercut and speeded up in case the man had chums around.

This was important . . .

A shiny, four-horse carriage swung out of Monkey Street, with two footmen clinging to the back of it. Vimes speeded up in a desperate burst, grabbed a handhold, pulled himself up between the astonished footmen, dragged himself across the swaying roof, and dropped down on the seat beside the young driver.

"City Watch," he announced, flashing his badge. "Keep going straight ahead!"

"But I'm supposed to turn left onto—" the young man began.

"And give it a touch of the whip, if you please," said Vimes, ignoring him. "This is important!"

"Oh, right! Death-defying high-speed chase, is it?" said the coachman, enthusiasm rising. "*Right!* I'm the boy for that! You've got your man right here, sir. D'you know, I can make this carriage go along for fifty yards on two wheels? Only old Miss Robinson won't let me. Right side or left side, just say the word! Hyah! Hyah!"

"Look, just—" Vimes began, as the whip cracked overhead.

"O'course, getting the horses to run along on two legs was the trick. Actually, it's more of a hop, you might say," the coachman went on, turning his hat around for minimum wind resistance. "Here, want to see my wheelie?"

"Not especially," said Vimes, staring ahead.

"The hooves don't 'arf raise sparks when I do me wheelie, I can tell you! Hyah!"

The scenery was blurring. Ahead was the cut-through leading to Two Pint Dock. It was normally covered by a swing bridge—

—normally.

It was swung now. Vimes could see the masts of a ship being warped out of the dock and into the river.

"Oh, don't you bother about that, sir," yelled the coachman beside him. "We'll go along the quay and jump it!"

"You can't jump a two-master with a four-horse carriage, man!"

"I bet you can if you aim between the masts, sir! Hyah! Hyah!"

Ahead of the coach, men were running for cover. Behind it, the footmen were seeking other employment. Vimes pushed the boy back into his seat, grabbed a handful of reins, put both feet against the brake lever, and *hauled.*

The wheels locked. The horses began to turn. The coach slid, the metal rims of the wheels sending up sparks and the throaty scream of metal. The horses turned some more. The coach began to swing, dragging the horses with it, whirling them out like fairground mounts. Their hooves made trails of fire across the cobblestones.

At this point, Vimes let go of everything, gripped the underside of the seat with one hand, held on to the rail with the other, shut his eyes, and waited for all the noise to die away.

Blessedly, it did. Only one little sound remained: a petulant banging on the coach roof, caused, probably, by a walking stick. A querulous, elderly female voice could be heard saying: "Johnny? Have you been driving *fast* again, young man?"

"A bootlegger's turn!" Johnny breathed, looking at a team of four steaming horses now facing back the way they'd come. "I am *impressed!*"

He turned to Vimes, who wasn't there.

The men moving the ship had dropped their ropes and run at the sight of coach and four spinning down the road toward them. The dock entrance was narrow. A man could easily scramble up a rope onto the deck, run across the ship, and let himself down on the cobbles on the other side. And this, a man had just done.

Speeding along, Vimes could see that Misbegot Bridge was going to be a struggle. An overloaded hay wagon had wedged itself between the rickety houses that lined the bridge, ripped out part of someone's upper story, and had shed some of its load in the process. There was a fight going on between the carter and the unimpressed owner of the new bungalow. Valuable seconds were spent struggling over and through the hay until he was hurrying through the backed-up traffic to the other end of the bridge. Ahead of him was the wide thoroughfare known as Prouts, full of vehicles and uphill all the way.

He wasn't going to make it. It must be gone five to six already. The thought of it, the thought of that little face—

"Mister Vimes!"

He turned. A mail coach had just pulled out onto the road behind him and was coming up at a trot. Carrot was sitting beside the driver and waving frantically at him.

"Get on the step, sir!" he yelled. "You don't have much time!"

Vimes started to run and, as the coach drew level, jumped onto the door's step and hung on.

"Isn't this the mail coach to Quirm?" he shouted, as the driver urged the horses into a canter.

"That's right, sir," said Carrot. "I explained it was a matter of extreme importance."

Vimes redoubled his grip. The mail coaches had good horses. The wheels, not very far away from him, were already a blur.

"How did you get here so quick?" he yelled.

"Shortcut through the Apothecary Gardens, sir!"

"What? That little walk by the river? That's never wide enough for a coach like this!"

"It was a bit of a squeeze, sir, yes. It got easier when the coach lamps scraped off."

Vimes took in the state of the coach's side. The paintwork was scored all along it.

"All right," he shouted, "tell the driver I'll meet the bills, of course! But it'll be wasted, Carrot. Park Lane'll be jam-packed at this time of day!"

"Don't worry, sir! I should hang on very tight if I were you, sir!" shouted Carrot, above the rising wind.

Vimes heard the whip crack. This was a *real* mail coach. Mailbags don't care if they're comfortable. He could feel the acceleration.

Park Lane would be coming up very soon. Vimes couldn't see much, because the wind of their flight was making his eyes water, but up ahead was one of the city's most fashionable traffic jams. It was bad enough at any time of day, but early evening was particularly horrible, owing to the Ankh-Morpork belief that right of way was the prerogative of the heaviest vehicle or the gobbiest driver. There were minor collisions all the time, which were inevitably followed by both vehicles blocking the junction while the drivers got down to discussing road-safety issues with reference to the first weapon they could get their hands on. And it was into this maelstrom of jostling horses, scurrying pedestrians, and cursing drivers that the mail coach was heading, apparently, at a full gallop.

He shut his eyes and then, hearing a change in the sound of the wheels, risked opening them again.

The coach flew across the junction. Vimes had a momentary glimpse of a huge line, fuming and shouting behind a couple of immovable troll officers, before they were spinning on down toward Scoone Avenue.

"You closed the road? You closed the road!" he yelled as they plunged on.

"And Kings Way, sir. Just in case," Carrot shouted down.

"You closed *two* major roads? Two whole damn roads? In the rush hour?"

"Yes, sir," said Carrot. "It was the only way."

Vimes hung on, speechless. Would *he* have dared to do that? But that was Carrot all over. There was a problem, and now it's gone. Admittedly, the whole city is probably solid with wagons by now, but that's a *new* problem.

He'd be home in time. Would a minute have mattered? No, probably not, although his young son appeared to have a very accurate internal clock. Possibly even two minutes would be okay. Three minutes, even. You could go to five, perhaps. But that was just it. If you could go to five minutes, then you'd go to ten, then half an hour, a couple of hours . . . and not see your son all evening. So that was that. Six o'clock, prompt. Every day. Read to Young Sam. No excuses. He'd promised himself that. *No excuses*. No excuses at all. Once you had a good excuse, you opened the door to bad excuses.

He had *nightmares* about being too late.

He had a lot of nightmares about Young Sam. They involved empty cots and darkness.

It had all been too . . . good. In a few short years, he, Sam Vimes, had gone up in the world like a balloon. He was a Duke, he commanded the Watch, he was powerful, he was married to a woman whose compassion, love, and understanding he knew a man such as he did not deserve, and he was as rich as Creosote. Fortune had rained its gravy, and he'd been the man with the big bowl. And it had all happened so *fast*.

And then Young Sam had come along. At first it had been fine. The baby was, well, a baby, all lolling head and burping and unfocused eyes, entirely the preserve of his mother. And then, one evening, his son had turned and looked directly at Vimes, with eyes that for his father outshone the lamps of the world, and fear had poured into Sam Vimes's life in a terrible wave. All this good fortune, all this fierce joy . . . it was wrong. Surely the universe could not allow this amount of happiness in one man, not without presenting a bill. Somewhere a big wave was cresting, and when it broke over his head it would wash everything away. Some days, he was sure he could hear its distant roar . . .

Shouting incoherent thanks, he leapt down as the coach slowed, flailed to stay upright, and skidded into his driveway. The front door was already opening when he raced toward it, scattering gravel, and there was Willikins holding up The Book. Vimes grabbed it and pounded up the stairs as, down in the city, the clocks began to mark various approximations of the hour of six o'clock.

Sybil had been adamant about not having a nursemaid. Vimes, for once, had been even more adamant that they got one, and a head cavern girl for the pedigree dragon pens outside. A body could only do so much, after all. He'd won. Purity, who seemed a decent type, had just finished settling Young Sam into his cot when Vimes staggered in. She gave him about one third of a curtsy before she caught his

pained expression and remembered last week's im-
promptu lecture on The Rights of Man, and then
she hurried out. It was important that no one else
was here. This moment in time was just for the Sams.

Young Sam pulled himself up against the cot's
rails, and said "Da!" The world went soft.

Vimes stroked his son's hair. It was funny, really.
He spent the day yelling and shouting and talking and bellowing . . . but here, in this quiet time
smelling (thanks to Purity) of soap, he never knew
what to say. He was tongue-tied in the presence of a
fourteen-month-old baby. All the things he thought
of saying, like "Who's Daddy's little boy, then?"
sounded horribly false, as though he'd got them
from a book. There was nothing to say nor, in this
soft pastel room, anything that needed to be said.

There was a grunt from under the cot. Dribble
the dragon was dozing there. Ancient, fireless, with
ragged wings and no teeth, he clambered up the
stairs every day and took up station under the cot.
No one knew why. He made little whistling noises
in his sleep.

The happy silence enveloped Vimes, but it
couldn't last. There was The Reading Of The Picture Book to be undertaken. That was the *meaning*
of six o'clock.

It was the same book, every day. The pages of said
book were rounded and soft where Young Sam had
chewed them, but to one person in this nursery this
was the book of books, the greatest story ever told.
Vimes didn't need to read it anymore. He knew it by
heart.

It was called "Where's My Cow?"

The un-identified complainant has lost their cow. That was the story, really.

Page one started promisingly:

> *Where's my cow?*
> *Is that my cow?*
> *It goes baa!*
> *It is a sheep!*
> *No, that's not my cow!*

Then the author began to get to grips with their material:

> *Where's my cow?*
> *Is that my cow?*
> *It goes naaaay!*
> *It is a horse!*
> *No, that's not my cow!*

At this point, the author had reached an agony of creation and was writing from the racked depths of their soul.

> *Where's my cow?*
> *Is that my cow?*
> *It goes HRUUUGH!*
> *It is a hippopotamus!*
> *No, that's not my cow!*

This was a good evening. Young Sam was already grinning widely and crowing along with the plot.

Eventually, the cow would be found. It was that much of a page-turner. Of course, some suspense was lent by the fact that all other animals were presented in some way that could have confused a kitten who perhaps had been raised in a darkened room. The horse was standing in front of a hat stand, as they so often did, and the hippo was eating at a trough against which was an upturned pitchfork. Seen from the wrong direction, the tableau might look for just one second like a cow . . .

Young Sam loved it, anyway. It must have been the most cuddled book in the world.

Nevertheless, it bothered Vimes, even though he'd got really good at the noises and would go up against any man in his rendition of the HRUUUGH! But is this a book for a city kid? When would *he* ever hear these noises? In the city, the only sound those animals would make was "sizzle." But the nursery was full of the conspiracy, with baa-lambs and teddy bears and fluffy ducklings everywhere he looked.

One evening, after a trying day, he'd tried the Vimes street version:

> *Where's my daddy?*
> *Is that my daddy?*
> *He goes "Bugrit! Millennium hand and shrimp!"*
> *He is Foul Ol' Ron!*
> *No, that's not my daddy!*

It had been going really well when Vimes heard a meaningful little cough from the doorway, wherein stood Sybil. Next day, Young Sam, with a child's unerring instinct for this sort of thing, said "Buglit!" to Purity. And that, although Sybil never raised the subject even when they were alone, was that. From then on Sam stuck rigidly to the authorized version.

He recited it tonight, while wind rattled the windows, and this little nursery world, with its pink-and-blue peace, its creatures who were ever so very soft and wooly and fluffy, seemed to enfold them both. On the nursery clock, a little wooly lamb rocked the seconds away.

When he not quite awoke, in twilight, with ragged strands of dark sleep filling his mind, Vimes stared in incomprehension at the room. Panic filled him. What was this place? Why were there all these grinning animals? What was lying on his foot? Who was this doing the asking, and why was he wrapped in a blue shawl with ducks on it?

Blessed recollection flowed in. Young Sam was fast asleep, with Vimes's helmet clutched like a teddy bear, and Dribble, always on the lookout for somewhere warm to slump, had rested his head on Vimes's boot. Already the leather was covered with goo.

Vimes carefully retrieved his helmet, gathered the shawl around him, and wandered down into the big front hall. He could see a light on under the door of the library, and so, still slightly muzzy, he pushed his way in.

Two watchmen stood up. Sybil turned in her chair by the fire. Vimes felt the ducks slither down his shoulders, slowly, and end up in a heap on the floor.

"I let you sleep, Sam," said Lady Sybil. "You didn't get in this morning until after three."

"Everyone's double-shifting, dear," said Sam, daring Carrot and Sally to even think about telling anyone they'd seen the boss wearing a blue shawl covered in ducks. "I've got to set a good example."

"I'm sure you intend to, Sam, but you *look* like a horrible warning," said Sybil. "When did you last eat?"

"I had a lettuce, tomato, and bacon sandwich, dear," he said, endeavoring by the tone of his voice to suggest that the bacon had been a mere condiment rather than a slab barely covered by the bread.

"I expect you jolly well did," said Sybil, rather more accurately conveying the fact that she didn't believe a word of it. "Captain Carrot has something to tell you. Now, you sit down and I'm going to see what's happened to dinner."

When she bustled out in the direction of the kitchens, Vimes turned to the watchmen and debated for a moment whether to give that sheepish little grin and eye-roll that between men means "Women, eh?" and decided not to, on the basis that the watchmen consisted of Lance Constable von Humpeding, who'd think he was a fool, and Captain Carrot, who wouldn't know what it meant.

He settled instead on "Well?"

"We did the best we could, sir," said Carrot. "I was right. That mine is a very unhappy place."

"Murder scenes usually are, yes."

"Actually, I don't think we found the murder scene, sir."

"Didn't you see the body?"

"Yes, sir. I think. Really, sir, you had to be there—"

"I don't think I can go through with this," Angua had hissed as she headed along Treacle Street again.

"What's wrong?" said Carrot. Angua jerked a thumb over her shoulder.

"Her! Vampires and werewolves: not good company!"

"But she's a Black Ribboner," Carrot protested mildly. "She doesn't—"

"She doesn't have to *do* anything! She just is! For one of us, being around a vampire is like the worst bad hair day you can imagine. And believe me, a werewolf knows what a *real* bad hair day is!"

"Is it the smell?" said Carrot.

"Well, that's not good, but it's more than that. They're so . . . poised. So perfect. I get near her and I feel . . . hairy. I can't help it, it goes back thousands of years! It's the image. Vampires are always so . . . cool, so in control, but werewolves are, well, shambling animals. Underdogs."

"But that's not true. A lot of Black Ribboners are totally neurotic, and you're so sleek and—"

"Not when I'm around vampires! They trigger off something! Look, stop trying to be logical about it, will you? I hate it when you get logical on me. Why didn't Mister Vimes hold out? All right, all *right*, I'm on top of it. But it's hard, that's all."

"I'm sure it's not easy for her, either—" Carrot began.

Angua gave him a Look. But that's him, she thought. He really *does* think like that. It's just that he doesn't know when saying something like that is a really bad idea. Not easy for her? When was it ever easy for me? At least *she* probably doesn't have to stash changes of clothes around the city! Okay, going cold bat can't be nice, but we get cold bat every month. And when do I ever rip out a throat? I hunt chickens! *And* I pay for them in advance. Does she suffer from PLT? I don't think so! Oh gods, and it's already well past Waxing Gibbous tonight. I can *feel* my hair growing! Bloody vampires! They make such a big thing about not being murderous bloodsuckers anymore. They get all the sympathy!

Even his!

All this flashed past in a second. She said: "Let's just get down there and get it done and get out, shall we?"

There was still a crowd hanging around near the entrance. Among them was Otto Chriek, who gave Carrot a little shrug.

There were still guards on duty, too, but it was clear that someone had been talking to them. They nodded to the squad when they arrived. One of them even opened the door, very politely.

Carrot beckoned the other watchmen closer.

"Everything we say will be overheard, understand?" he said. "Everything. So be careful. And remember—as far as they are concerned, you can't see in the dark."

He led the way inside, to where Helmclever stood, beaming and edgy.

"Welcome, Head Banger," said the dwarf.

"Er, if we are using Morkporkian, I would prefer Captain Carrot," said Carrot.

"As you wish, Smelter," said the dwarf. "The elevator awaits!"

As they descended, Carrot said, "What powers this, please?"

"A Device," said Helmclever, pride breaking out over his nervousness.

"Really? You have many Devices?" said Carrot.

"An axle and an average bar."

"An average bar? I've only ever heard of them."

"We are fortunate. I will be happy to show it to you. It is invaluable for food preparation," Helmclever gabbled. "And down below we have a number of cubes, of varying powers. Nothing may be withheld from the Smelter. I am ordered to show you everything you wish to see and tell you everything you wish to know."

"Thank you," said Carrot as the elevator stopped in blackness speckled with the corpse glow of vurms. "How large are your diggings here?"

"I cannot tell you that," said Helmclever quickly. "I do not know. Ah, here is Ardent. I will go back up—"

"No, Helmclever, remain with us, please," said a darker shadow in the gloom. "You should see this, too. Good day to you, Captain Carrot and—" Angua detected an element of distaste "—ladies. Please follow me. I am sorry for the lack of light. Perhaps your eyes will adapt. I will be happy to describe to you any object that you touch. Now I will lead you to the place where the dreadful occurrence . . . occurred."

Angua looked around as they were led along the tunnel, noting that Carrot had to walk with his knees slightly bent. *Head Banger, eh? Funny, you never mention that to the lads!*

Every dozen yards or so, Ardent would stop in front of a round door, invariably with the vurms clustered around it, and turn a wheel. The doors creaked when they opened, and they opened with a ponderousness that suggested they were heavy. Here and there in the tunnels were . . . things, mechanical things, hanging from the wall and clearly there with a purpose. Vurms glowed around them. She hadn't got a clue what the objects were for, but Carrot greeted them with enthusiastic glee, like a schoolboy.

"You have air bells and water boots, Mr. Ardent! I've only ever heard of them!"

"You were raised in the good rock of Copperhead, were you not, Captain? Mining in this wet plain is like digging tunnels in the sea."

"And the iron doors are quite watertight, are they?"

"Yes, indeed. Airtight, too."

"Remarkable! I should like to visit again, when this wretched business is over. A dwarf mine under the city! It's quite hard to believe!"

"I'm sure that could be arranged, Captain."

And that was Carrot at work. He could sound so innocent, so friendly, so . . . stupid, in a puppy-dog kind of way, and then he suddenly became this big block of steel and you walked right into it. By the smell of it, Sally was watching him with interest.

Be sensible, Angua told herself. Don't let the vampire get to you. Don't start believing you're stupid and hairy. Think clearly. You *do* have a brain.

Surely people could go mad, living in this murk? Angua found it easier to close her eyes. Down here, her nose worked better without distraction. Darkness helped. With her eyes shut, various faint colors danced across her brain. Without the stink of the damned vampire, though, she would have been able to pick up a lot more. The stench poisoned every sensation. *Hold on, don't think like that, you're just letting your mind do the thinking for you . . . hang on, that's wrong . . .*

There was a faint outline in the corner of the next chamber, which was quite large. It looked like . . . an outline. A chalk outline. A *glowing* chalk outline.

"I understand this is the approved method?" said Ardent. "You will be aware of night chalk, Captain? It is made of crushed vurm. The glow persists for about a day. On the floor here you will see, or rather, you will *feel* the club that dealt him his deathblow. Just under your hand, Captain. There is blood on it. I regret the darkness, but we kept the vurms out. They would have feasted, you understand."

Angua saw Carrot, outlined in his permanent smell of soap, feel his way across the space. His hand touched another metal door.

"Where does this go, sir?" he said, tapping it.

"To the outer chambers."

"Was it open at the time the troll attacked the grag?"

You really think a troll did? Angua wondered.

"I believe so," said Ardent.

"Then I would like it open now, please."

"I cannot agree to that request, Captain."

"I did not intend it to be a request, sir. After it has been opened, I will need to know who was in the mine at the time the troll broke in. I will need to speak to them, and to whoever discovered the body. *Hara'g, j'kargra.*"

For Angua, the smell of Ardent changed. Under all those layers, the dwarf was suddenly uncertain. He'd walked right into it. He hesitated for several seconds before replying.

"I will . . . endeavor to meet your reque—your requirements, Smelter," he said. "I will leave you now. Come, Helmclever."

"*Grz dava'j?*" said Carrot. "*K'zakra'j? D'j h'ragna ra'd'j!*"

Ardent stepped forward, uncertainty growing, and held out both hands, palms down. For a moment, until his sleeves slipped, Angua saw a faintly glowing symbol on his right wrist. Every deep-downer had a *draht* as unique evidence of identity, in a world of shrouded figures. She'd heard they were made by tattooing vurm blood under the skin. It sounded painful.

Carrot took his hands for a moment, and then let go.

"Thank you," he said, as if the dwarfish interlude had not taken place. The two dwarfs hurried away.

In the thick darkness, the watchmen were left alone.

"What was all that about?" said Angua.

"Just reassuring him," said Carrot cheerfully. He reached into a pocket. "Now we've arrived, let's have some light in here, shall we?"

Angua smelled his hand move vigorously across the wall once or twice, as if he was painting. There arose an aroma of . . . pork pie?

"Soon be brighter," he said.

"Captain Carrot, this wasn't where—" Sally began.

"All in good time, Lance Constable," said Carrot firmly. "For now, we just observe."

"But I must tell you—"

"*Later on*, lance constable," said Carrot a little louder. Vurms were flowing around the open door they'd arrived by, and across the stone. "By the way, er, Sally . . . will you be all right if we view the body?"

That's right, Angua thought, think of *her*. I've dealt with blood every day. Walk a mile in *my* nostrils!

"Old blood will not be a problem, sir," said Sally. "There's some in here. But there's—"

"I expect they've set up a morgue," said Carrot quickly. "The death rites are quite complex."

Morgue? A home away from home for you, my dear! snarled Angua's inner wolf.

The vurms were spreading out now, crawling across the wall with a purpose.

She crouched down, to bring her nose nearer to the floor. I can smell dwarfs, lots of dwarfs, Angua thought. Hard to smell trolls, especially underground. Blood on the club, like a flower. Dwarf smell on the club, but there's dwarf smell everywhere. I can smell— hang on, that's familiar . . .

The floor mostly smelled of slime and loam. Carrot's footprints showed up, and so did *hers*. There was a lot of dwarf smell, and she could still just make out the smell of their concern. This is where they found the body, then? But this patch of mud here, this was different. It had been trodden into the floor, but it smelled just like the heavy clay from up around Quarry Lane. Who lived in Quarry Lane? Most of the trolls in Ankh-Morpork.

A clue.

She smiled in the dwindling darkness. And the trouble with clues, as Mister Vimes always said, was that they were so easy to make. You could walk around with a pocket full of the bloody things.

The darkness was disappearing because the light was growing. Angua looked up.

There was a huge, bright symbol on the wall where Carrot had touched it. He dragged some meat across it, she thought. They've turned up for the feast . . .

Ardent came back in, with Helmclever trailing after him.

He got as far as: "The door here can be opened again but, alas, we—" and stopped.

They were happy vurms. By the standards of greeny-white glow, they were brilliant.

Behind Carrot there was now a gently glowing circle, with two diagonal lines slashed through it. Both dwarfs stared at it as if in shock.

"Well, let's take a look, shall we?" said Carrot, apparently oblivious to all this.

"—we, alas, the water . . . water . . . not *entirely* watertight . . . the other doors . . . the troll caused flooding . . ." Ardent murmured, not taking his eyes off the glow.

"But you say we can go through here, at least?" said Carrot politely, pointing to the sealed door.

"Er . . . yes. Yes. Certainly."

The steward hurried forward and produced a key. The wheel, unlocked, turned easily. Angua was acutely aware of how the muscles on Carrot's bare arms glistened and pumped as he pulled the metal door open.

Oh no, not *yet*, surely! She ought to have at least another day! It was the vampire, that's what it was, standing there looking so innocent. Bits of her body *wanted* her to become a wolf, right now, to defend herself . . .

There was a pillared room on the other side of the door. It smelled damp and unfinished. There were vurms on the ceiling, but the floor was muddy and squelched underfoot.

Angua could make out another dwarf door across the room, and there was one on either side as well.

"We take spoil to a heap on the waste ground outside," said Ardent. "We, er, believe the troll got in that way. It was an unpardonable oversight." He still sounded uneasy.

"And the troll was not seen?" said Carrot, kicking at the mud.

"No. These chambers are finished. The diggers are elsewhere, but they came as soon as they could. We believe the grag had come up here for solitude. To die at the random hand of an abomination!"

"Lucky for the troll, wasn't it, sir?" said Angua sharply. "He just *happened* to wander in and stumble across Hamcrusher?"

Carrot's boot struck something metallic. He kicked some more mud away.

"You've laid rails?" he said. "You must be shifting a lot of spoil, sir."

"Better to push than to carry," said Ardent. "Now, I have arranged for—"

"Hold on, what's this?" said Carrot. He squatted down and pulled at something pale. "It's a piece of bone, by the look of it. On a string."

"There are plenty of old bones," said Ardent. "Now, I—"

It came free with a *gloop*, and grinned at them in the sickly light.

"It doesn't look *very* old, sir," said Carrot.

Just one breath was enough for Angua.

"It's a sheep skull," she said. "About three months dead." Oh, *another* clue, she added to herself. Nice and convenient for us to find, too.

"Could have been dropped by the troll," said Carrot.

"A troll?" said Ardent, backing away.

It wasn't the reaction Angua had expected. Ardent had been nervous already, but now, under all those wrappings, he was on the verge of panic.

"You did say a troll had attacked the grag, sir?" said Carrot.

"But we never— I never saw that before! Why didn't we find it? Did it come back?"

"All the doors are sealed, sir," said Carrot patiently. "Aren't they?"

"But have we sealed it in here with us?" It was practically a shriek.

"You'd know, sir, wouldn't you?" said Carrot. "Trolls sort of, well, stand out."

"I must fetch guards!" said Ardent, backing away toward the single open door. "It could be anywhere!"

"Then you could be heading right toward it, *sir*," said Angua.

Ardent stopped dead for a moment, and then uttered a little whimper and ran into the dark, Helmclever on his heels.

"Well, how do we all think that went?" said Angua, with a horrible smile. "And what was that you said to him in dwarfish . . . 'You know I am a dwarf in the brotherhood of all dwarfs'?"

"Erm, 'With emphatic certainty you know me. I observe the rites of the dwarf. What/who am I? I am the Brothers united,'" said Sally carefully.

"Well done, lance constable!" said Carrot. "That was an excellent translation!"

"Yes, did you bite someone clever?" said Angua.

"I *am* a Black Ribboner, Sergeant," said Sally meekly. "And I'm naturally good at languages. While we're alone, Captain, can I mention something else?"

"Certainly," said Carrot, trying the wheel on one of the closed doors.

"I think a lot of things are wrong here, sir. There was something very strange about the way Ardent reacted to that skull. Why would he think the troll was still here, after all that time?"

"A troll getting into a dwarf mine can do a lot of damage before it's stopped," said Carrot.

"Ardent really wasn't expecting that skull, sir," said Sally, pressing on. "I heard his heart racing. It terrified him. Er . . . something more, sir. There's lots of city dwarfs here. Dozens. I can feel their hearts, too. There are six grags. Their hearts beat very slowly. And there are other dwarfs, too. Strange ones, and only a few of them. Maybe ten."

"That's useful to know, lance constable, thank you very much."

"Yes, I don't know how we managed before you

came," said Angua. She walked quickly over to the other side of the dank room so that they wouldn't see her face.

She needed fresh air, not the pervasive, clinging, old-root-cellar reek of this place. Her head was full of shouting. The Temperance League? "Not One Drop"? Did anyone believe that for one *minute*? But everyone wanted to fall for it, because vampires could be so *charming*. Of course they were! It was part of being a vampire! It was the only way to get people to stay the night in the dreadful castle! Everyone knew a leopard couldn't change his shorts! But no, stick on a stupid black ribbon and learn the words for "Lips that touch Ichor shall never touch Mine" and they fall for it every time. But werewolves? Well, they were just sad monsters, weren't they? Never mind that life was a daily struggle with the inner wolf, never mind that you had to force yourself to walk past every lamppost, never mind that in every petty argument you had to fight back the urge to settle it all with just one bite.

Never mind that, because everyone *knew* that a creature that was a wolf and a human combined was a kind of dog. They were *expected* to behave.

Part of her was shouting that this wasn't so, that this was just PLT and the known effects of a vampire's presence, but somehow, now, with the smells around her becoming so strong that they were approaching solidity, she did not want to listen. She wanted to smell the world, she was practically climbing into her own nose.

After all, that was why she was in the Watch, wasn't it? For her nose?

New smell, new smell . . .

Sharp blue-gray of lichen, the browns and purples of old carrion, undertones of wood and leather . . . even as a full wolf, she'd never tasted the air so forensically as this. Something else, sharp, chemical . . . The air was full of the smell of damp and dwarfs, but these little traces ran through it like a piccolo hornpipe through a requiem, and formed one thing . . .

"Troll," she croaked. "Troll. Troll with skull belt and head-locks. On Slab, or something like it! Troll!" Angua was almost barking at the far door now. "Open the door! This way!"

She was barely needing her eyes now, but there on the metal of the door, in charcoal, someone had drawn a circle with two diagonal lines through it.

Suddenly Carrot was by her side. At least he had the decency not to say "Are you sure?" as he rattled the big wheel. The door was locked.

"I don't think there's water behind this," he said.

"Oh, really?" Angua managed. "You know that was just . . . to keep us out!"

Carrot turned. Running toward them was a squad of dwarfs. They were heading for the door as though quite oblivious to the presence of the watchmen.

"*Don't* let them go through first!" said Angua through gritted teeth. "Trail is . . . faint!"

Carrot drew his sword with one hand and held up his badge with the other.

"City Watch!" he roared. "Lower your weapons, please! Thank you!"

The squad slowed, which meant that, in the nature of these things, those at the back piled into the hesitant ones in front.

"This is a crime scene!" Carrot announced. "I am still the smelter! Mr. Ardent, are you there? Do you have guards on the other side of this door?"

Ardent pushed through the throng of dwarfs.

"No, I believe not," he said. "Is the troll still behind it?"

Carrot glanced at Sally, who shrugged. Vampires had never developed the ability to listen for troll hearts. There was no point.

"Possibly, but I don't think so," said Carrot. "Please unlock it. We might yet find a trail!"

"Captain Carrot, you know that the safety of the mine must always come first!" said Ardent. "Of course you must give chase. But first we will open the door, and make certain there is no danger behind it. You must concede us that."

"Let them," hissed Angua. "It'll be a clearer scent. I'll be okay."

Carrot nodded, and whispered back: "Well done!"

Under her flesh, she felt her tail want to wag. She wanted to lick his face. It was the dog part of her doing the thinking. *You're a good dog. It was important to be a good dog.*

Carrot pulled her aside as a couple of dwarfs approached the door purposefully.

"But it's long gone," she murmured as two more dwarfs came up behind the first two. "The scent's twelve hours old, at least—"

"What are they doing?" said Carrot, half to himself. The two new dwarfs were covered from head to toe in leather, like Ardent, but wore chain mail over the top of it; their helmets were quite unadorned, but covered the whole face and head, with only a slit for the eyes. Each dwarf carried a large black pack on his back and held a lance in front of him.

"Oh no," said Carrot, "surely not here—"

At a word of command, the door was swung open, revealing only darkness beyond.

The lances spat flame, long yellow tongues of it, and the black dwarfs walked slowly along behind them. Smoke, heavy and greasy, filled the air.

Angua fainted.

Darkness.

Sam Vimes struggled up the hill, tired to the bone.

It was warm, warmer than he'd expected. Sweat stung his eyes. Water splashed under his feet and made his boots slip. And, ahead, up the slope, a child was screaming.

He knew he was shouting. He would hear the breath wheezing in his throat, could feel his lips moving, but he couldn't hear the words he was reciting over and over again.

The darkness felt like cold ink. Tendrils of it dragged at his mind and his body, slowing him down, dragging him back . . .

And now they came at him with flames—

Vimes blinked, and found himself staring at the fireplace. The flames flicked peacefully.

There was the swish of a dress as Sybil came back into the room, sat down, and picked up her darning.

He watched her dully. She was darning his socks.

They had maids in this place and *she* darned his *socks*. It wasn't as if they didn't have so much money that he could have a new pair of socks every day. But she'd picked up the idea that it was a wifely duty, and so she did it. It was comforting, in a strange sort of way. It was only a shame that she wasn't, in fact, any good at mending holes, so Sam ended up with sock heels that were huge welts of criss-crossing wool. He wore them anyway, and never mentioned it.

"A weapon that fires flame," he said slowly.

"Yes, sir," said Carrot.

"Dwarfs have weapons that fire flame."

"The deep-downers use them to explode pockets of mine gas," said Carrot. "I never expected to see them here!"

"It's a weapon if some bastard points it at me!" said Vimes. "How much gas did they expect to find in Ankh-Morpork?"

"Sir? Even the *river* catches fire in a hot summer!"

"Okay, okay. I'll grant you that," Vimes conceded unwillingly. "Make sure the word gets out, will you? Anyone seen above-ground with one of those things, we'll shoot first and there will be no *point* in asking questions afterwards. Good grief, that's all we need. Have you got anything *more* to tell me, Captain?"

"Well, afterwards we did get to see Hamcrusher's body," said Carrot. "What can I say? On his wrist was the *draht* that identifies him, and his skin was pale. There was a terrible wound on the back of his head. They say it's Hamcrusher. I can't prove it. What I can say is that he didn't die where they said he did, or when they said he did."

"Why?" said Vimes.

"Blood, sir," said Sally. "There should have been blood everywhere. I looked at the wound. What that club hit over the head was already a corpse, and he wasn't killed in that tunnel."

Vimes took several slow breaths. There was so much bad stuff here you needed to take it one horror at a time.

"I'm worried, Captain," he said. "Do you know why? It's because I've got a feeling that very soon I'm going to be asked to confirm that there's evidence that a troll did the deed. Which, my friend, will be like announcing the outbreak of war."

"You did ask us to investigate, sir," said Carrot.

"Yes, but I didn't expect you to come back with the wrong result! The whole thing stinks! That clay from Quarry Lane *was* planted, wasn't it?"

"It must have been. Trolls don't clean their feet much, but walking mud all the way? Not a chance."

"And they don't leave their clubs behind, either," growled Vimes. "So it's a setup, right? But it turns out there really *was* a troll! Was Angua *sure*?"

"Positive, sir," said Carrot. "We've always trusted her nose before. Sorry, sir, she had to go and get some fresh air. She was straining her senses as it was, and she got a lungful of that smoke."

"I can imagine," said Vimes. Hell's bells, he thought. We were right on the point where I could tell Vetinari that it looked like some kind of half-baked inside job faked to look as though a troll did it, and we find out there *was* a troll. Huh . . . so much for relying on the evidence.

Sally coughed politely. "Ardent was shocked and frightened when the captain found the skull, sir," she said. "It wasn't an act. I'm certain of it. He was near collapse with terror. So was Helmclever, the whole time."

"Thank you for that, lance constable," said Vimes gravely. "I suspect I shall feel the same way when I go out there with a megaphone and shout 'Hello, boys, welcome to the replay of Koom Valley! Hey, let's hold it right here in the city!'"

"I don't think you should actually put it like that, sir," said Carrot.

"Well, yes, I'll probably try to be a bit more subtle, since you mention it," said Vimes.

"And it'd be at least the sixteenth battle referred to as Koom Valley," Carrot went on, "or seventeen, if you include the one in Vilinus Pass, which was more of a fracas. Only three of them were in the original Koom Valley, the one immortalized in Rascal's painting. It's said to be quite accurate. Of course, it took him years."

"An amazing work," said Sybil, not looking up from her darning. "It used to belong to my family before we gave it to the museum, you know."

"Isn't progress a wonderful thing, Captain?" said Vimes, pouring as much sarcasm into his tone as possible, since Carrot was so bad at recognizing it. "When we have *our* Koom Valley, our friend Otto will be able to take a color iconograph of it in a fraction of a second. Wonderful. It's been a long time since this city was last burned to the ground."

He ought to be springing into action. Once upon a time, he would have done. But now, perhaps he should take these precious moments to work out what he should *do* before he sprang.

Vimes tried to think. Don't think of it all as one big bucket of snakes. Think of it as one snake at a time. Try to sort it out. Now, what needs to be done first?

Everything.

All right, try a different approach.

"What are these mine signs all about?" he said. "That Helmclever sort of drew one at me. I saw one on the wall, too. And you drew one."

"'The Following Dark,'" said Carrot. "Yes. It was scrawled all over the place."

"What does it mean?"

"Dread, sir," said Carrot earnestly. "A warning of terrible things to come."

"Well, if one of those little sods so much as surfaces with one of those flame weapons in his hand, that *will* be true. But . . . you mean they scrawl it on walls?"

Carrot nodded. "You have to understand about a dwarf mine, sir. It's a kind of—"

—emotional hothouse, was how Vimes understood it, although no dwarf would ever describe it that way. Humans would have gone insane living like that, cramped together, no real privacy, no real silence, seeing the same faces every day for years on end. And since there were a lot of pointy weapons around, it'd only be a matter of time before the ceilings dripped blood.

Dwarfs didn't go mad. They stayed thoughtful and somber and keen on their job. But they scrawled mine sign.

It was like an unofficial ballot, voting by graffiti, showing your views on what was going on. In the confines of a mine, any problem was everyone's problem, stress leapt from dwarf to dwarf like lightning. The signs grounded it. They were an outlet, a release, a way of showing what you felt without challenging anyone (because of all the pointy weapons).

The Following Dark: We await what follows with dread. Another translation might mean, in effect: Repent, ye sinners!

"There are hundreds of runes for darkness," said Carrot. "Some of them are part of ordinary dwarfish, of course, like the Long Dark. There's plenty like that. But some are . . ."

"Mystical?" Vimes suggested.

"Unbelievably mystical, sir. There's books and books about them. And the way dwarfs think about books and words and runes . . . well, you wouldn't believe it, sir. W— they think the world was *written*, sir. All words have enormous power. Destroying a book is worse than murder to a deep-downer."

"I've rather gathered that," said Blackboard Monitor Vimes.

"Some deep-downers believe that the dark signs are real," Carrot went on.

"Well, if you can see the writing on the wall—" Vimes began.

"Real like alive, sir," said Carrot earnestly. "Like they exist somewhere down in the dark under the world, and they cause themselves to be written. There's the Waiting Dark . . . that's the dark that fills a new hole. The Closing Dark . . . I don't know about that one, but there's an Opening Dark, too. The Breathing Dark, that's rare. The Calling Dark, very dangerous. The Speaking Dark, the Catching

Dark. The Secret Dark, I've seen that. They're all fine. But the Following Dark is a very bad sign. I used to hear the older dwarfs talking about that. They said it could make lamps go out, and much worse things. When people start drawing that sign, things have got very bad."

"This is all very interesting, but—"

"Everyone in the mine is nervous as heck, sir. Tense like wires. Angua said she could smell it, but so could I, sir. I grew up in a mine. When something is wrong, everyone catches it. On days like that, sir, my father used to stop all mining operations. You get too many accidents. Frankly, sir, the dwarfs are mad with worry. The Following Dark signs are everywhere. It's probably the miners they've hired since they came here. They feel that something is very wrong, but the only thing they can do about it is sign."

"Well, their top grag has been killed—"

"I can feel the atmosphere in a mine, sir. Any dwarf can. And that one is rancid with fear and dread and horrible confusion. And there's worse things in the Deeps than the Following Dark."

Vimes had a momentary vision of vengeful darkness rising through caves like a tide, faster than a man could run . . .

. . . which was stupid. You couldn't *see* dark.

Hold on, though . . . sometimes you could. Back in the old days, when he was on nights all the time, he'd known all the shades of darkness. And sometimes you got darkness so thick that you almost felt you had to push your way through it. Those were nights when horses were skittish, and dogs whined, and down in the slaughterhouse district the animals broke out of their pens. They were inexplicable, just like those nights that were quite light and silvery even though there was no moon in the sky.

He'd learned, then, not to use his little lantern. Light not only ruined your vision, it blinded you. You stared into the dark until it blinked. You stared it down.

"Captain, I'm getting a bit lost here," said Vimes. "I didn't grow up in a mine. Are these signs drawn up because dwarfs *think* bad things are going to happen and want to ward them off, or think the mine *deserves* the bad things happening, or because they *want* the bad things to happen?"

"Can be all three at once," said Carrot, wincing. "It can get really *intense* when a mine goes bad."

"Oh, good grief!"

"Oh, it can be awful, sir. Believe me. But no one would ever draw the worst of the signs and *want* it to happen. Just the drawing wouldn't be enough, anyway. You have to want it to happen with your very last breath."

"And which one is that?"

"Oh, you don't want to know, sir."

"No, I did ask," said Vimes.

"No. You really don't want to know, sir. Really."

Vimes was about to start yelling, but he stopped to think for a moment.

"Actually, no, I don't think I do," he agreed. "This is all about hysteria and mysticism. It's just weird folklore. Dwarfs believe it. I don't. So . . . how did you get the vurms to form that sign?"

"Easy, sir. You just smear the wall with a piece

of meat. That's a feast for vurms. I wanted to shake Ardent up a bit. Make him nervous, like you taught me. I wanted to show him I knew about signs. I am a dwarf, after all."

"Captain, this is probably not the time to break it to you, but—"

"Oh, I know people laugh, sir. A six-foot dwarf! But being a human just means being born to human parents. That's easy. Being a dwarf doesn't mean being born to dwarfs, though it's a good start. It's about certain things you do. Certain ceremonies. I've done them. So I'm a human *and* a dwarf. The deep-downers find it a bit hard to deal with that."

"It's mystic again, is it?" said Vimes wearily.

"Oh yes, sir." Carrot coughed. Vimes recognized that particular cough. It meant that bad news was on the captain's mind and he was wondering how to shape it to fit the available not-going-totally-postal space in Vimes's head.

"Out with it, Captain."

"Er . . . this little chap turned up," said Carrot, opening his hand. The Gooseberry imp sat up.

"I ran all the way, Insert Name Here," it said proudly.

"We spotted it jogging along the gutter," said Carrot. "It wasn't hard to see, glowing pale green like that."

Vimes pulled the Gooseberry box out of his pocket and put it on the floor. The imp climbed inside.

"Ooh, that feels so good," it said. "Don't talk to me about rats and cats!"

"They chased you? But you're a magical creature, aren't you?" said Vimes.

"They don't know that!" said the imp. "Now, what was it . . . oh, yes. You asked me about the night soil removal. Over the past three months the extra honey wagon load has averaged forty tons a night."

"Forty tons? That'd fill a big room! Why didn't we know about it?"

"You did, Insert Name Here!" said the imp proudly. "But they were leaving from every gate, you see, and probably no guard ever spotted more than one or two extra carts."

"Yes, but they turned in reports every night! Why didn't *we* spot it?"

There was an awkward pause.

The imp coughed. "Um . . . no one read the reports, Insert Name Here. They appear to be what we in the trade call write-only documents."

"Wasn't *anyone* supposed to be reading them?" Vimes demanded.

There was another thundering silence.

"I rather think you were, dear," said Sybil, paying attention to her darning.

"But I'm in charge!" Vimes protested.

"Yes, dear. That's the point, really."

"But I can't spend all my time shuffling bits of paper!"

"Then get someone else to do it, dear," said Sybil.

"Can I do that?" said Vimes.

"Yes, sir," said Carrot. "You're in charge."

Vimes looked at the imp, which gave him a willing grin.

"Can you go through *all* of my in-tray—"

". . . floor . . ." murmured Sybil.

"—and tell me what's important?"

"Happy to, Insert Name Here! Only one question, Insert Name Here. What *is* important?"

"Well, the fact that the honey wagons are carting a whole lot more muck out of the city is pretty damn important, don't you think?"

"I wouldn't know, Insert Name Here," said the imp. "I do not, in fact, think *as such*. But I surmise that, if I had drawn your attention to such a fact a month ago, you would have told me to stick my head up a duck's bottom."

"That's true," said Vimes, nodding. "I probably would. Captain Carrot?"

"Sir!" said Carrot, sitting up straight.

"What's the situation on the street?"

"Well, troll gangs have been wandering around the city all day. Dwarfs, too. Now a lot of the dwarfs are hanging around in the square, sir, and a fair number of trolls are congregating in the Plaza of Broken Moons."

"How many are we talking about here?" said Vimes.

"About a thousand, all told. They've been drinking, of course."

"Just in the mood for a fight, then."

"Yes, sir. Just drunk enough to be stupid but too sober to fall over," said Carrot.

"Interesting observation, Captain," said Vimes thoughtfully.

"Yes, sir. The word is that they'll start at nine. Arrangements have been made, I gather.

"Then I think before it gets dark there should be a load of coppers in the Cham, right between them, don't you?" said Vimes. "Get the word out to the Watch houses."

"I've done that, sir," said Carrot.

"And get some barricades sorted out."

"All arranged, sir."

"And call out the Specials?"

"I put the word out an hour ago, sir."

Vimes hesitated. "I've got to be there, Captain."

"We should have enough men, sir," said Carrot.

"But you won't have enough *commander*," said Vimes. "If Vetinari hauls me over the coals tomorrow because there was a major riot in the city center, I don't want to tell him I was having a quiet evening at home." He turned to his wife. "Sorry, Sybil."

Lady Sybil sighed. "I think I shall have to have a word with Havelock about the hours he makes you keep," she said. "It's not doing you any good, you know."

"It's the job, dear. Sorry."

"It's just as well I got the cook to make up a flask of soup, then."

"You did?"

"Of course. I *know* you, Sam. And there're some sandwiches in a bag. Captain Carrot, you are to make sure he eats the apple and the banana. Dr. Lawn says he must eat at least five pieces of fruit or vegetables every day!"

Vimes stared woodenly at Carrot and Sally, trying to project the warning that the first officer to crack a smile or even mention this to anyone, ever ever ever, would have a very hard time of it indeed.

"And, incidentally, tomato ketchup is not a vegetable," Sybil added. "Not even the dried stuff 'round the top of the bottle. Well, what are you all waiting around for?"

"There's something I didn't want to mention in front of her ladyship," said Carrot as they hurried down to the Yard. "Er . . . Hitherto is dead, sir."

"Who's Hitherto?"

"Lance Constable Horace Hitherto, sir? Got walloped on the back of the head last night? When we were at that meeting? When there was that, er, 'disturbance'? Got sent to the Free Hospital?"

"Oh, gods . . ." said Vimes. "It seems like a week ago. He'd only been with us a couple of months!"

"They said at the hospital his brain died, sir. I'm sure they did their best."

Did we do ours? Vimes wondered. But it was a bloody melee, and the cobblestone came out of nowhere. Could have hit me, could have hit Carrot. Hit the kid, instead. What'll I tell his parents? Killed in the line of duty? But his duty shouldn't have been to stop one lot of idiot citizens murdering another lot of idiot citizens.

It's all got out of hand. There aren't enough of us. And now there's a few less.

"I'll go and see his mum and dad tomor—" he began, and sluggish memory shifted at last. "Does— didn't he have a brother in the Watch?"

"Yessir," said Carrot. "Lance Constable Hector Hitherto, sir. They joined together. He's down at Chitterling Street."

"Then get hold of his sergeant and tell him Hector is *not* allowed on the street tonight, okay? I want him introduced to the joys of filing. In a cellar, if possible. And wearing a very thick helmet."

"I understand, sir," said Carrot.

"How's Angua?"

"I think she'll be fine after having a lie-down, sir. The mine really got to her."

"I'm really, really sorry about that—" Sally began.

"Not your fault, lance constable . . . Sally," said Vimes. "It was mine. I know about the vampire and werewolf thing, but I needed you both to be down there. It's just one of those decisions, okay? I suggest you take the evening off. No, that's an order. You've done very well on your first day. Off you go. Get your head down . . . or whatever."

They watched her out of sight before continuing down the street.

"She is very good, sir," said Carrot. "She picks things up fast."

"Yes, very fast. I can see she's going to be useful," said Vimes thoughtfully. "Doesn't that strike you as odd, Captain? Up she pops, just when we need her."

"She has been here for a couple of months, though," said Carrot. "And the League vouches for her."

"A couple of months is about the same time as Hamcrusher's been here, too," said Vimes. "And if you wanted to find things out, we're not a bad outfit to join. We're *official* prodnoses."

"Sir, you don't think—"

"Oh, I'm sure she's a Black Ribboner, but I don't think a vampire comes all the way from Uberwald to play the cello. Still, as you say, she does a good job."

Vimes stared at nothing for a moment and then said thoughtfully: "Doesn't one of our Specials work for the clacks company?"

"That'd be Andy Hancock, sir," said Carrot.

"Oh gods. You mean Two Swords?"

"That's him, sir. Very keen lad."

"Yes, I saw the dockets. *Normally* a training dummy lasts for months, Captain. You're not supposed to chop through three in half an hour!"

"He'll be down at the Yard now, sir. Do you want a word with him?" said Carrot.

"No. *You* have a word with him."

Vimes lowered his voice. So did Carrot. There was whispering. Then Carrot said: "Is that strictly legal, sir?"

"I don't see why not. Let's find out, shall we? We haven't had this little conversation, Captain."

"Understood, sir."

Ye gods, it *was* so much better when there was just four of us up against that bloody great dragon, Vimes thought as they walked on. Of course, we nearly got burned alive a few times, but at least it wasn't *complicated*. It was a damn great dragon. You could see it coming. It didn't get political on you.

It had started to rain a fine, invasive rain by the time they arrived at Pseudopolis Yard. Vimes had, with extreme reluctance, to hand it to Carrot. He certainly could organize. The place was bustling. Wagonloads of yellow and black barricades were being trundled out of the Old Lemonade Factory. Watchmen were pouring in from every street.

"I really pushed the boat out on this one, sir," said Carrot. "I thought it was important."

"Well done, Captain," said Vimes as they stood like islands in the flood. "But I think there is a little matter of forward planning you may have over-looked . . ."

"Really, sir? I thought I've covered everything," said Carrot, looking puzzled.

Vimes slapped him on the back.

"Probably not this one," he said. And added, but only to himself: Because *you*, Captain, are not a bas-tard.

Bewildered and aimless, the troll wanders through the world . . .

Brick's head really *gonged*. He didn't want to be doing dis, but he'd fallen into bad company. He often fell into bad company, he reflected, although some-times he had to look all day to find it, 'cos Brick was a loser's loser. A troll without a clan or a gang, and who is considered thick even by other trolls, has to take any bad company he can find. In this case, he'd met Totally Slag an' Hardcore an' Big Marble, an' it had been easier to fall in wi' dem dan decide not to, an' dey'd met up wi' *more* trolls an' now . . .

Look at it like dis, he thought as he trudged along, singin' gang songs a bit behind the beat, because he didn't know the words . . . all right, being in der middle of dis mob o' trolls ain't "lyin' low," dat is a fact. But Totally Slag had said the word wuz dat der Watch wuz *also* after der troll who'd been down dat mine, right? An,' if you fink about it, der best place to hide a troll, right, is in a big *bunch* of trolls. 'Cos the Watch'd be pokin' around in der cellars where der real mean trollz hung out, dey wouldn't be lookin' *here*. An' if dey did, an' were puttin' der finger on him, den all dese brother trolls would help him out.

He wasn't too certain about that last bit, in his heart of hearts. His possibly negative IQ, complete absence of street cred, and, above all, his permanent inclination to snort, suck, swallow, or bite anything that promised to make his brain sparkle, meant that he had been turned down even by the Tenth Egg Street Can't-Fink-Of-A-Name Gang, rumored to be so dense that one of their members was a lump of concrete on a piece of string. No, it would be hard to imagine any troll caring much what happened to Brick. But right now dey were brothers, and der only game in town.

He nudged the skull-necklaced, graffiti-ornamented, lichen-covered, huge club–dragging troll marching stoically alongside him.

"Resplect, bro!" he said, clenching a scabby fist.

"Whyn't you go and *ghuhg* yourself, Brick, you little piece of coprolite . . ." the troll muttered.

"Right off!" said Brick cheerfully.

The main office was packed, but Vimes fought his way through by shoving and shouting until he reached the duty desk, which was under siege.

"It looks worse than it is, sir!" shouted Cheery over

the din. "Detritus and Constable Bluejohn are in the Cham right now, along with all three golem officers! We've started getting the line in place! Both the mobs are too busy getting themselves worked up!"

"Good work, Sergeant!"

Cheery leaned down and lowered her voice. Vimes had to hang on to the tall desk to stop himself being carried away by the throng.

"Fred Colon's signing up the Specials in the Old Lemonade Factory, sir. And Mr. de Worde of the *Times* is looking for you."

"Sorry, Sergeant, didn't catch that last bit!" said Vimes loudly. "The lemonade factory, right? Okay!"

He turned around and almost tripped over Mr. A. E. Pessimal, who was holding a neat clipboard.

"Ah, Your Grace, there's just a *few* small matters I'd like to discuss with you," said the gleaming little man.

Vimes's mouth dropped open.

"And you think this is a good time, do you?" he managed as he was jostled by an officer carrying a bundle of swords.

"Well, yes, I've turned up a number of little financial and procedural problems," said A. E. Pessimal calmly, "and I think it's vitally important that I understand exactly what—"

Vimes, grinning horribly, grabbed him by the shoulder.

"Yes! *Right!* Absolutely!" he shouted. "My dear Mr. Pessimal, what *have* I been thinking of? You *should* understand! Come with me, please!"

He half-dragged the bewildered man out through the back door, lifted him out of the way of a trundling cart as he negotiated the crowded yard, and hustled him into the old factory yard, where the Specials were being kitted up.

Technically, they were the citizen's militia, but, as Fred Colon had remarked, it was "better to have them in here pissing themselves than outside pissing on you." The Special constables were men—mostly—who could be coppers in times of dire need but were generally disqualified from formal Watch membership by reason of shape, profession, age, or, sometimes, brain.

A lot of the professionals didn't like them, but Vimes had lately taken the view that when push came to shove it was better to have your fellow citizens shoving alongside you and, that being the case, you might as well teach them how to hold a sword right, lest the arm they clumsily removed was yours.

Vimes pulled A. E. Pessimal through the press of bodies until he found Fred Colon, who was handing out one-size-doesn't-fit-anybody helmets.

"New man for you, Fred," he said loudly. "Mr. A. E. Pessimal, plain A. E. if he ever makes friends. He's the government inspector. Kit him out, full fig, and don't forget the riot shield. A. E. here wants to *understand* coppering, so he's kindly volunteered to be an acting constable on the barricades with us." Over the top of A. E. Pessimal's head he gave Fred a big wink.

"Oh, er, *right*," said Fred, and his face, in the flickering light of the flares, acquired the innocent smile of one about to make someone's life a little pot of bubbling dread. He leaned over the trestle table.

"Know how to use a sword, Acting Constable Pessimal?" he said, and dropped a helmet on the man's head, where it spun.

"Well, I didn't exactly—" the inspector began as a very elderly sword was shoved across the planks, followed by a heavy truncheon.

"A shield, then? Any good with a shield?" said Fred, pushing a large such item after the sword.

"Actually, I didn't mean—" said A. E. Pessimal, trying to hold both the sword and the truncheon and dropping both, and then the sword and the truncheon and the shield and dropping all three.

"Any good at running a hundred yards in ten seconds? In this?" Fred went on. A ragged chain-mail coat dropped slowly off the table like a parcel of snakes and landed on A. E. Pessimal's bright little shoes.

"Uh, I don't think—"

"Standing still and going to the toilet really, really quickly?" said Fred. "Oh well, you'll learn soon enough."

Vimes turned the man around, picked up thirty-five pounds of rust-eaten chain mail, and dropped it into his arms, causing A. E. Pessimal to bend double. "I'll introduce you to some of the citizens who will be fighting alongside you tonight, shall I?" he said as the little man hobbled after him. "This is Willikins, my butler. No sharpened pennies in your cap tonight, Willikins?"

"No, sir," said Willikins, staring at the struggling A. E. Pessimal.

"Glad to hear it. This is Acting Constable Pessimal, Willikins." Vimes winked.

"Honored to meet you, Acting Constable, sir,"

said Willikins gravely. "Now that sir is with us I am sure the miscreants will just melt away. Has sir by any chance gone sir-on-one with a troll before? No? A little advice, sir. The important thing is to get in front of them and dodge the first blow. They always leave themselves open and sir may then step smartly forward and select sir's target of choice."

"Er, what if . . . if I'm not in front of one when it tries to hit me?" A. E. Pessimal said, hypnotized by the description and dropping the sword again. "What if it is, in fact, behind me?"

"Ah, well, I am afraid that in that case sir has to go back and start all over again, sir."

"And . . . er . . . how do I do that?"

"Being born is traditionally the first step, sir," said Willikins, shaking his head.

Vimes gave him a nod, and moved the trembling Pessimal on through the chattering crowd, while the fine rain fell and the mists rose and the torches flickered.

"Good evening, sir!" said a cheerful voice, and there, yes, was Special Constable Hancock, an amiable bearded man with an amiable smile and more cutlery about his person than was good for Vimes's mental health. That was the trouble with some of the Specials. They really got into it. They bought their own gear, and it was always better than Watch issue. Some of them clanged even more than dwarfs, with patent handcuffs and complicated night-sticks and comfy padded helmets and pencils that wrote under-water and, in the case of Special Constable Hancock, two curved Agatean swords strapped across his back. Those who'd dared to venture into the training yard when he was using them said they looked rather impressive. Vimes had heard that an Agatean ninja could give a fly a shave and a haircut in mid-flight, but this didn't make him feel any better.

"Oh, hello . . . Andy," he said. "I think—"

"Captain Carrot's had a word with me," said Special Constable Hancock, giving him a huge wink. "I'll see to it!"

"Oh, good," said Vimes, horribly aware that he'd put himself in a tricky position vis-à-vis suggesting that maybe one sword might be enough. The man was going to do them a favor, after all. "Er . . . You'll be up against the trolls, at least to start with," he said. "Just remember that there's our people around you, will you? Remember Special Constable Piggle, eh?"

"But, in fairness, it was a clean cut, sir!" said Hancock. "Igor said he'd never done such an easy reattachment!"

"Nevertheless, it's truncheons only tonight, Andy, unless I give any other order, okay?"

"Understood, Commander Vimes. I've just got a new truncheon, as a matter of fact."

Some sixth sense made Vimes say: "Oh, really? May I see?"

"Right here, sir." Hancock pulled out what looked to Vimes like *two* truncheons, joined together with a length of chain.

"They're Agatean *numknuts*, sir. No sharp edges at all."

Vimes gave them an experimental swing and hit his own elbow. He handed them back quickly. "Rather you than me, lad. Still, I suppose they'll make a troll stop and think."

Mr. Pessimal was staring in horror, not least because wayward wood had just missed him.

"Oh, this is Mr. Pessimal, Andy," said Vimes. "He's finding out how we do things. Mr. Hancock is one of our . . . keenest Special Constables, Mr. Pessimal."

"Nice to met you, Mr. Pessimal!" said Hancock. "If you need any weapons catalogs, I'm your man!"

Vimes moved on quickly, just in case the man drew those swords again, and ran up against a slightly more reassuring figure.

"And here we have Mr. Boggis," he said. "*Good* to see you. Mr. Boggis is president of the Guild of Thieves, Mr. Pessimal."

Mr. Boggis saluted proudly. He had accepted a chain-mail jacket from Fred, but no power in the world would have parted him from his brown bowler hat. Any power nevertheless inclined to try would in any case have to contend with the narrow-eyed, stony-jawed men on either side of him, who had eschewed any weapons or armor. One of them was cleaning his fingernails with a cutthroat razor. In a strange but very *definite* way, they looked much more dangerous even than Special Constable Hancock.

"And also Vinnie 'No Ears' Ludd and Harry 'Can't Remember His Nickname' Jones, I see," Vimes went on. "You've brought your *bodyguards*, Mr. Boggis?"

"Vinnie and Harry like to get out in the fresh air, Mister Vimes," said Mr. Boggis. "And I see you've got your *own* bodyguard, then?" He beamed down on A. E. Pessimal and then grinned at Vimes. "You have to watch them little bantam fighters, Mister Vimes, they can have the nose off your face quicker'n wink. I can tell a killing covey when I see one, eh? Best of luck to you, Mr. Pessimal!"

Vimes bustled the astonished man away before Mr. Boggis was killed on the spot by the God of Overacting, and almost walked into the one Special who could be guaranteed not to talk too much.

"And here, Mr. Pessimal, here we have the University Librarian," he said, "Good man in a melee, eh?"

"But that— that's not a man! That's an orangutan, *Pongo Pongo*, native of BhangBhangduc and nearby islands!"

"Ook!" said the Librarian, patting A. E. Pessimal on the head and handing him a banana skin.

"Well done, A. E.!" said Vimes. "Not many people get that right!"

And so Vimes dragged the inspector back through the crowd of damp, armored men, introducing him right and left. Then he pushed him into a corner and, to faint stunned protestations, dragged the mail shirt over his head.

"You stick close behind me, Mr. Pessimal," he said as the man tried to move. "It could get a bit sticky later on. The trolls are up in the plaza and the dwarfs are down in the square, and both of 'em are drinking up enough courage to have a good scrap. That's why we'll be lining up in the Cham, right between 'em, the thin brown streak, haha. The dwarfs favor battle-axes, the trolls go in for clubs. Our weapon of first resort will be our truncheons, and our weapon of last resort is our feet. That is to say, we'll run like hell."

"But, but, you have *swords*!" A. E. Pessimal managed.

"*We* have swords, Acting Constable. Yes, that is a fact, but poking holes in citizens is Watch brutality, and we don't want any of that now, do we? Let's get going, I wouldn't like you to miss *anything*."

He harried the man again, out into the street and the stream of watchmen heading for the Cham. Apart from them, the street was empty. Ankh-Morpork people had an instinct for staying indoors when there were too many battle-axes and spiky clubs out there.

The Cham was simply a very, very wide road, once intended for ceremonial parades, a hangover from the days when the city had much to be ceremonious about. Drizzle filled it now and did not do much more than wet the pavements and reflect the light of the flares along the barricades.

Barricades . . . well, that's what they were called on the Watch inventory. Ha! Lengths of wood painted in black and yellow stripes and mounted on trestles were not *barricades*, not to anyone who'd been behind a real one, which was built of rubbish and furniture and barrels and fear and bowel-knotting defiance. No, these simple things were the physical symbol of an idea. It was a line in the sand. It said: thus far, and no further. It said, this is where the law is. Step over this line and you've gone *beyond* the law. Step over this line, with your massive axes and huge morning-stars and heavy, *heavy* spiky clubs, and we few, we happy few who stand here with our wooden truncheons, we'll . . . we'll . . .

. . . Well, you just better *not* step over the line, okay?

The yellow-and-black edges of the Law had been

set about twelve feet apart, giving plenty of room for two lines of watchmen standing back-to-back, facing outwards.

Vimes dragged Mr. Pessimal into the center of the Cham, between the lines, and let him go.

"Any questions?" he said as latecomers jostled past them to take up their positions.

The little man stared toward the distant plaza, where the trolls had lit a big fire, and then turned to look the other way, at the square, where the dwarfs had lit *several* fires. There was the sound of distant singing.

"Oh, yes, we'll get the singing first. At this point, it's all about getting the blood pounding, you see," Vimes added helpfully. "Songs about heroes, great victories, killing your enemies and drinking out of their warm skulls, that sort of thing."

"And then, er, they'll attack us?" said A. E. Pessimal.

"Well, not as such," Vimes conceded. "They'll try to attack the other bunch, and we're in the way."

"They won't go around, perhaps?" said A. E. Pessimal hopefully.

"I doubt it. They won't be in the mood for narrow alleys. They'll be thinking in straight lines. Charge and yell, they'll say, that's the way."

"Ah, there's the university over there!" said A. E. Pessimal, as if noticing the huge bulk of Unseen University for the very first time. "Surely the wizards could—"

"—magic their weapons out of their hands, possibly leaving them with all their fingers? Magic them into the cells? Turn them all into ferrets? And what then, Mr. Pessimal?" Vimes lit a cigar, cupping the match in his hand so that the flame made his face glow briefly. "Shall we follow where magic leads us? Wave a wand, eh, to find out who's guilty, and what of? *Magic* men good? The innocent would have nothing to fear, d'you think? I wouldn't bet tuppence, Mr. Pessimal. Magic's a little bit alive, a little bit tricky. Just when you think you've got it by the throat, it bites you in the arse. No magic in my Watch, Mr. Pessimal. We use good, old-fashioned policing."

"But there are *lots* of them, Commander."

"About a thousand altogether, I reckon," said Vimes placidly. "Plus who knows how many more out there who'll whale in if we let it get out of hand. This is just the hotheads and the gangs right now."

"B-but can't you just, er, leave them to it?"

"*No*, Mr. Pessimal, because that'd be what we in the Watch call 'complete and utter bloody chaos,' and it will not stop, and it will get bigger very quickly. We have to finish it right now, so—"

There was a thud from the direction of the plaza. It was loud enough to echo around the buildings.

"What was that?" A. E. Pessimal said, looking around hurriedly.

"Oh, that was to be expected," said Vimes.

Pessimal relaxed very slightly.

"It was?"

"Yes, it's the *gahanka*, the troll war beat," said Vimes. "They say that within ten minutes of hearing it, you're dead." Behind Pessimal, Detritus grinned, the torchlight turning his diamond teeth into rubies.

"Is that true?"

"I shouldn't think so," said Vimes. "And now

please excuse me for a while, Acting Constable Pessimal, I'll leave you in the good hands of Sergeant Detritus while I talk to my men. Stiffen their sinews, that sort of thing."

He moved away quickly. He told himself he shouldn't be doing this to the inspector, who was just a clerk in the wrong place and probably wasn't a bad man. The trouble was, the trolls up in the plaza probably weren't bad trolls, and the dwarfs down in the square probably weren't bad dwarfs, either. People who probably weren't bad could kill you.

The troll beat boomed around the city as Vimes reached Fred Colon.

"I see they're giving us the ol' *gahanka* then, Mister Vimes," said the sergeant, with nervous cheerfulness.

"Yep. They'll be charging pretty soon, I expect." Vimes screwed up his eyes, trying to see figures around the distant glow. Trolls didn't charge fast, but when they charged, it was like a wall getting nearer. Extending a hand and shouting "Halt" in a firm, authoritative voice probably would not be sufficient.

"You thinking about *another* barricade, Mister Vimes?" said Fred.

"Hmm?" said Vimes, dismissing the mental picture of himself laminated to the street.

"Barricades, sir," Colon prompted. "More'n thirty years ago?"

Vimes gave a curt nod. Oh yes, he remembered the Glorious Revolution. It hadn't really been a revolution, and had been glorious only if you thought an early grave was glorious. Men had died there, too, because of other men who, bar one or two, probably weren't bad . . .

"Yes," he said. "And it seems like only yesterday." Every day, he thought, it seems like only yesterday.

"Remember ol' Sergeant Keel? He pulled off a few tricks that night!" Sergeant Colon's voice, like A. E. Pessimal's, had a curiously hopeful tone.

Vimes nodded.

"I suppose you wouldn't have one or two up your sleeve, too, sir?" Fred went on, the hope now naked and unashamed.

"You know me, Fred, always willing to learn," said Vimes vaguely. He strolled on, nodding to watchmen he knew, slapping others on the back, and trying not to get trapped in anyone's gaze. Every face was in some way a reflection of the face of Fred Colon. He could practically *see* their thoughts, while the thud of five hundred clubs hitting the stone in unison banged on the eardrums like a hammer.

You have got it sorted, haven't you, Mister Vimes? We're not really going to be stuck here like the meat in a sandwich, right? It's a trick, yes? It is *a trick, isn't it? Sir?*

I hope it is, Vimes thought. But, one way or another, the Watch has to be here. That's the bloody truth of it.

Something had changed in the rhythm of the *ga-hanka*. You had to be listening, but some of the clubs were hitting the ground just ahead or just after the beat. *Ah.*

He reached Cheery and Carrot, who were staring at the distant fires of the dwarfs.

"We think we might be getting a result, sir," said Carrot.

"I damn well hope so! What's happening with the dwarfs?"

"No so much singing, sir," Cheery reported.

"Glad to hear it."

"We *could* handle them, though, couldn't we, sir?" said Carrot. "With the golem officers on our side, too? If it came to it?"

Of course we couldn't, Vimes's mind supplied, not if they mean it. What we could is die valiantly. I've seen men die valiantly. There's no future in it.

"I don't want it to come to it, Captain—" Vimes stopped. A deeper shadow had moved among the shadows.

"What's the password?" he said quickly.

The shadowy figure, who was cloaked and hooded, hesitated.

"Pathword? Excthuthe me, I've got it written down thomewhere—" it began.

"Okay, Igor, come on in," said Carrot.

"How did you know it wath me, thur?" said Igor, ducking under the barricade.

"Your aftershave," said Vimes, winking at the captain. "How did it go?"

"Jutht as you thaid, thur," said Igor, pushing his hood back. "Inthidentally, thur, I have thcrubbed the thlab well and my couthin Igor ith thtanding by to lend a hand. In cathe of any little acthidenth, thur . . ."

"Thank you for thinking of that, Igor," said Vimes, as if Igors ever thought of anything else. "I hope it won't be needed."

He looked up and down the Cham. The rain was falling harder now. Just once, the copper's friend had turned up when he really needed it. Rain tended to dampen martial enthusiasm.

"Anyone seen Nobby?" he said.

A voice from the shadows said, "Here, Mister Vimes! Been here five minutes!"

"Why didn't you sing out, then?"

"Couldn't remember the password, sir! I thought I'd wait 'til I heard Igor say it!"

"Oh, come on in. Did it work?"

"Better'n you'd imagine, sir!" said Nobby, rain pouring down his cloak.

Vimes stood back. "Okay, lads, then this is *it*. Carrot and Cheery, you head for the dwarfs, me and Detritus will take the trolls. You know the drill. Lines to advance slowly, and no edged weapons. I repeat, *no* edged weapons until it's that or die. Let's do this like coppers, okay? On the signal!"

He hurried back up the line of barricades as fast as the stir ran along the ranks of the watchmen.

Detritus was waiting stoically. He grunted when Vimes arrived.

"Clubs have jus' about stopped, sir," he reported.

"I heard, Sergeant." Vimes took off his oiled leather cloak and hung it on the barricade. He needed his arms free.

"By the way, how did it go in Turn Again Lane?" he said, stretching and breathing deeply.

"Oh, wonnerful, sir," said Detritus happily. "Six alchemists an' fifty pound o' fresh Slide. In an' out, quick an' sweet, all banged up in the Tanty."

"Didn't know what hit 'em, eh?" said Vimes.

Detritus looked mildly offended at this. "Oh no, sir," he said. "I made sure they knew *I* hit 'em."

And then Vimes spotted Mr. Pessimal, still where he had left him, his face a pale disc in the shadows. Well, enough of that game. Maybe the little tit would have learned something, standing here in the rain, waiting to be caught between a couple of screaming mobs. Maybe he'd had time to wonder what it was like to spend your life going through moments like that. A bit harder than pushing paper, eh?

"If I was you, I'd just wait here, Mr. Pessimal," he said as kindly as he could manage. "This might be a bit rough in parts."

"No, Commander," said A. E. Pessimal, looking up.

"What?"

"I have been paying attention to what has been said, and intend to face the foe, Commander," said A. E. Pessimal.

"Now see here, Mr. Pessi . . . er, see here, A. E.," said Vimes, putting his hand on the little man's shoulder. He stopped. A. E. Pessimal was trembling so much that his chain mail was faintly jingling. Vimes persevered. "Look, go on home, eh? This isn't where you belong." He patted the shoulder a few times, totally nonplussed.

"Commander Vimes!" snapped the inspector.

"Er, yes?"

A. E. Pessimal turned up to Vimes a face wetter than the drizzle rightly accounted for.

"I am an acting constable, am I not?"

"Well, yes, I know I *said* that, but I did not expect you to take it *seriously* . . ."

"I am a serious man, Commander Vimes. And there is no place I would rather be now than here!"

Acting Constable Pessimal said, his teeth chattering. "And no time I'd rather be here than now! Let's *do* this, shall we?"

Vimes looked at Detritus, who shrugged his massive shoulders. Something was happening here, in the mind of a little man whose back he could probably break with one hand.

"Oh, well, if you say so," he said hopelessly. "You heard the inspector, Sergeant Detritus. Let's *do* this, shall we?"

The troll nodded, and turned to face the distant troll encampment. He cupped his hands and bellowed a string of trollish, which bounced off the buildings.

"Something we can all understand, perhaps?" said Vimes as the echoes died away.

A. E. Pessimal stepped forward, taking a deep breath.

"C'mon if you think you're hard enough!" he screamed wildly.

Vimes coughed. "Thank you, Mr. Pessimal," he said weakly. "I imagine that should do it."

The moon was somewhere beyond the clouds, but Angua didn't need to see it. Carrot once had a special watch made for her birthday. It was a little moon that turned right around, black side and white side, every twenty-eight days. It must have cost him a lot of money, and Angua now wore it on her collar, the one item of clothing that she could wear all month around. She couldn't bring herself to tell him she didn't need it. You *knew* what was happening.

It was hard to know much else right now, because she was thinking with her nose. That was the problem with the wolf times; the nose took charge.

Currently, Angua was searching the alleys around Treacle Street, spiraling out from the dwarf mine. She prowled onwards in a world of color; smells overlaid one another, drifting and persisting. The nose was also the only organ that could see backwards in time.

She'd already visited the spoil heap on the waste ground. There was the smell of troll there. It had got out that way, but there was no point in following a trail that cold. Hundreds of street trolls wore lichen and skulls these days. But the foul, oily stuff, that was a smell that was clinging to her memory. The little devils must have some other ways in, right? And you had to move the air around in a mine, right? So some trace of that oil would find its way out along with the air. It probably wouldn't be strong, but she didn't need it to be. A trace of it was all she needed. It would be more than enough.

As she padded through the alleys, and leapt walls into midnight yards, she kept clenched in her jaws the little leather bag that was a friend to any thinking werewolf, such a creature being defined as one who remembers that your clothes don't magically follow you. The bag held a lightweight silk dress and a large bottle of mouthwash, which Angua considered to be the greatest invention of the last hundred years.

She found what she was looking for behind Broad

Way: it stood out against the familiar organic smells of the city as a tiny black ribbon of stench that left zigzags in the air as breezes and the passage of carts had dragged it this way and that.

She began to move with more care. This wasn't an area like Treacle Street; people with money lived here, and they often spent that money on big dogs and DISPROPORTIONATE RESPONSE signs in their driveways. As it was, she heard the rattle of chains and the occasional whine as she slunk along. She hated being attacked by large, ferocious dogs. It always left a mess and the mouthwash was afterwards never strong enough.

The thread of stink was floating through the railings of Empirical Crescent, one of the city's great architectural semiprecious gems. It was always hard to find people prepared to live there, however, despite the general desirable nature of the area. Tenants seldom stayed for more than a few months before moving hurriedly, sometimes leaving all their possessions behind.*

---

*Empirical Crescent was just off Park Lane, in what was generally a high-rent district. The rents would have been higher still were it not for the continued existence of Empirical Crescent itself, which, despite the best efforts of the Ankh-Morpork Historical Preservation Society, had still not been pulled down.

This was because it had been built by Bergholt Stuttley Johnson, better known to history as Bloody Stupid Johnson, a man who combined in one frail body such enthusiasm, self-delusion, and *creative* lack of talent that he was, in many respects, one of the great heroes of architecture. Only Bloody Stupid Johnson could have invented the thirteen-inch foot and a triangle with three right angles in it. Only Bloody Stupid Johnson could have twisted common matter through dimensions it was not supposed to go. And only Bloody Stupid Johnson could have done all this by accident.

His highly original multidimensional approach to geometry was responsible for Empirical Crescent. On the outside it was a normal terraced crescent of the period, built of honey-colored stone with the

She sailed over the railing with silence and ease and landed on all fours on what had once been gravel path. Residents in the crescent seldom did much gardening, since even if you planted bulbs you could never be sure whose garden they'd come up in.

Angua followed her nose to a patch of rampant thistles. Some molding bricks in a circle marked what must have been an old well.

The oily stink was heavy here, but there was a fresher, far more complex smell that raised the hairs on Angua's neck.

There was a vampire down there.

Someone had pulled away the weeds and debris, including the inevitable rotting mattress and decomposing armchair.* Sally? What was she doing here?

Angua pulled a brick out of the rotted edging and let it drop. Instead of a splash, there was a clear, wooden thump.

Oh well. She went back to human to get down; claws were fine, but some things were better done by monkeys. The sides were, of course, slimy, but so many bricks had fallen out over the years that the descent turned out to be easier than she'd expected. And it was only about sixty feet deep, built in the days when it was widely believed that any water that supported so many little whiskery swimming things *must* be healthy.

---

occasional pillar or cherub nailed on. Inside, the front door of No. 1 opened into the back bedroom of No. 15, the ground-floor front window of No. 3 showed the view appropriate to the second floor of No. 9, and smoke from the dining-room fireplace of No. 2 came out of the chimney of No. 19.

*But it was okay to throw your rubbish into the garden, because it might not be your garden you were throwing it into.

There were fresh planks in the bottom. Someone—and surely it could only have been the dwarfs—had broken into the well down here, and laid a couple of planks across it. They had dug this far, and stopped. Why? Because they'd reached the well?

There was dirty water, or water-like liquid, just under the planks. The tunnel was a bit wider here, and dwarfs had been here—she sniffed—a day ago, no more. Yes. Dwarfs had been here, had fished around, and had then all left at once. They hadn't even bothered to tidy up. She could smell it like a picture.

She crept forward, the tunnels mapping themselves in her nostrils. They weren't nicely finished, like the tunnels Ardent moved in. They were rougher, with lots of zigzags and blind alleys. Rough planks and balks of timber held back the fetid mud of the plains, which was nevertheless oozing through everywhere. These tunnels weren't built to last; they were there for a quick and definitely dirty job, and all they had to do was survive until it was done.

So . . . the diggers had been looking for something, but weren't sure where it was until they were within, what, about twenty feet of it, when they'd . . . smelled it? Detected it? The last stretch to the well was dead straight. By then, they knew where they were going.

Angua crept on, almost bending double to clear the low ceiling until she gave up and went back to wolf. The tunnel straightened out, with the occasional side passage that she ignored, although they smelled long. The vampire smell was still an annoying theme in the nasal symphony, and it came close to drowning the reek of foul water oozing from the walls. Here and there, vurms had colonized the ceiling. So had bats. They stirred.

And then there was another scent as she passed a tunnel opening. It was quite faint, but it was unmistakably the whiff of corruption. A fresh death . . .

Three fresh deaths. At the end of a short side tunnel were the bodies of two, no, three dwarfs, half-buried in mud. They *glowed*. Vurms had no teeth, Carrot had told her. They waited until the prospective meal became runny of its own accord. And, while they waited for the biggest stroke of luck ever to have come their way, they celebrated. Down here, in a world far away from the streets, the dwarfs would dissolve in light.

Angua sniffed.

Make that *very* fresh—

"They found something," said a voice behind her. "And then it killed them."

Angua leapt.

The leap wasn't intentional. Her hindbrain arranged it all by itself. The front brain, the bit that knew that sergeants should not attempt to disembowel lance constables without provocation, tried to stop the leap in mid-air, but by then simple ballistics were in charge. All she managed was a mid-air twist, and struck the soft wall with her shoulder.

Wings fluttered a little way off, and there was a

drawn-out organic sound, a sound that conveyed the idea that a slaughterhouse man was having some difficulty with a tricky bit of gristle.

"You know, Sergeant," said the voice of Sally, as if nothing had happened, "you werewolves have it easy. You stay one thing and you don't have any problems with body mass. Do you know how many bats I have to become for my body weight? More than a hundred and fifty, that's how many. And there's always one, isn't there, that gets lost or flies the wrong way? You can't think straight unless you get your bats together. And I'm not even going to touch on the subject of reassimilation. It's like the biggest sneeze you can think of. *Backwards.*"

There was no point in modesty, not down here in the dark. Angua forced herself to change back, every brain cell piling in to outvote tooth and claw. Anger helped.

"Why the hell are you here?" she said, when she had a mouth that worked.

"I'm off duty," said Sally, stepping forward. "I thought I'd see what I could find." She was totally naked.

"You couldn't have been so lucky!" Angua growled.

"Oh, I don't have your *nose*, Sergeant," said Sally, with a sweet smile. "But I was using a hundred and fifty pretty good flying ones, and they can cover a lot of ground."

"I thought vampires could rematerialize their clothes," said Angua accusingly. "Otto Chriek can!"

"Females can't. We don't know why. It's probably part of the whole underwired-nightdress business. That's where you score again, of course. When you're in one hundred and fifty bat bodies, it's quite hard to remember to keep two of them carrying a pair of pants." Sally looked up at the ceiling, and sighed. "Look, I can see where this is going. It's going to be about Captain Carrot, isn't it . . ."

"I saw the way you were smiling at him!"

"I'm sorry! We can be very personable! It's a vampire thing!"

"You were so keen to impress him, eh!"

"And you aren't? He's the kind of man anyone would want to impress!"

They watched each other warily.

"He *is* mine, you know," said Angua, feeling the nascent claws strain under her fingernails.

"You're his, you mean!" said Sally. "You know it works like that. You trail after him!"

"I'm sorry! It's a werewolf thing!" Angua yelled.

"Hold it!" Sally thrust both hands in front of her in a gesture of peace. "There's something we'd better sort before this goes any further!"

"Yeah?"

"Yes. We're both wearing nothing, we're standing in what, you may have noticed, is increasingly turning into mud, and we're squaring up to fight. Okay. But there's something missing, yes?"

"And that is . . . ?"

"A paying audience? We could make a *fortune*." Sally winked. "Or we could do the job we came here to do."

Angua forced her body to relax. *She* should have been saying that. She was the sergeant, wasn't she?

"All right, all right," she said. "We're both here,

okay? Let's leave it at that. Were you saying that these dwarfs were killed by some . . . *thing* from the well?"

"Possibly. But if they were, it used an axe," said Sally. "Take a look. Scrape some of the mud away. It's been oozing over them since I arrived. That's probably why you missed it," she added generously.

Angua hauled one dwarf out of the shining slime.

"I see," she said, letting the body fall back. "This one hasn't been dead two days. Not much effort made to hide them, I see."

"Why bother? They've stopped pumping out these tunnels, the props look pretty temporary, the mud's coming back. Besides, who'd be stupid enough to come down here?"

A piece of wall slithered down, with a sticky, organic, cow-pat sort of noise. Little plops and trickles filled the tunnel. Ankh-Morpork's underworld was stealthily reclaiming its own.

Angua closed her eyes and concentrated. The slime reek, the vampire's smell, and the water that was now ankle-deep all jostled for attention, but this was competition time. She couldn't let a vampire take the lead. That would be so . . . *traditional.*

"There were other dwarfs," she murmured. "Two— no, three . . . er, four more. I'm getting . . . the black oil. Distant blood. Down the tunnel." She stood up so sharply that she nearly hit her head on the tunnel roof. "C'mon!"

"It's getting a bit unsafe—"

"We could solve this! Come *on*! *You* can't be afraid of dying!"

Angua plunged away.

"And you think spending a few thousand years buried in sludge is likely to be fun?" shouted Sally, but she was talking only to dripping mud and fetid air. She hesitated a moment, groaned, and followed Angua.

Further along the main tunnel there were more passages branching off. On either side, rivers of mud, like cool lava, were already flowing out of them. Sally splashed past something that looked like a huge copper trumpet, turning gently on the current.

The tunnel was better built here than the ones nearer the well. And there, at the end of it, was a pale light, and Angua, crouched by one of the big, round dwarf doors. Sally paid her no attention. She barely glanced at the dwarf slumped with his back against the bottom of the door.

Instead, she stared at the symbol scrawled large on the metal. It was big and crude, and might be a round, staring eye with a tail, and it gleamed with the greeny-white glow of vurms.

"He wrote it in his blood," said Angua, without looking up. "They left him for dead, but he was only dying, you see. He managed to make it to here, but the killers had shut the door. He scratched at it, smell here, and he's worn away his fingernails. Then he made that sign in his own warm blood and sat here, holding the wound shut, watching the vurms turn up. I'd say he's been dead for eighteen hours or so. Hmm?"

"I think we should get out of here right now," said Sally, backing away. "Do you know what that sign means?"

"I know it's mine sign, that's all. Do *you* know what it means?"

"No, but I know it's one of the *really* bad ones. It's not good seeing it here. What are you doing with that body?" Sally backed away further.

"Trying to find out who he was," said Angua, searching the dwarf's clothing. "It's the sort of thing we do in the Watch. We don't stand around getting worried about drawings on the wall. What's the problem?"

"Right now?" said the vampire. "He's . . . oozing a bit . . ."

"If I can stand it, so can you. You see a lot of blood in this job. Don't attempt to drink it, that's my advice," said Angua, still rummaging. "Ah . . . he's got a rune necklace. And . . ." she pulled a hand out of the dead dwarf's jerkin, "can't make this out very well, but I can smell ink, so it may be a letter. Okay. Let's get out of here." She stood up. "Did you hear me?"

"The sign was written by someone dying," said Sally, still keeping her distance.

"Well?"

"It's probably a curse."

"So? We didn't kill him," said Angua, getting to her feet with some difficulty.

They looked down at the liquid mud now rising to their knees.

"Do you think it cares?" said Sally matter-of-factly.

"No, but I think there may be another way out in that last tunnel we passed," said Angua, looking back along the tunnel.

She pointed. Scuttling along with blind determination, a line of vurms marched along the dripping roof almost as fast as the mud flowed down below. They were heading into the side tunnel in a glowing stream.

Sally shrugged. "It's worth a try, yes?"

They left, and the sound of their splashing soon died away.

Slowly the mud rose, rustling in the gloom. The trail of vurms gradually disappeared overhead. The vurms that made the sign remained though, because such a feast as this was worth dying for.

Their glow winked out, one insect at a time.

The darkness beneath the world caressed the sign, which flamed red and died.

Darkness remained.

On this day in 1802, the painter Methodia Rascal tried putting the thing under a heap of old sacks, in case it woke up the Chicken, and finished the last troll, using his smallest brush to paint the eyeballs.

It was five a.m. Rain rustled out the sky, not hard, but with a gentle persistence.

In Sator Square, and in the Plaza of Broken Moons, it hissed on the white ash of the bonfires, occasionally exposing the orange glow, which would briefly sizzle and spit.

A family of gnolls were sniffing around, each one dragging his or her little cart. A few officers were keeping an eye on them. Gnolls weren't choosy about what they collected, provided it didn't actually struggle, and even then there were rumors.

But they were tolerated. Nothing cleaned up the place like a gnoll.

From here, they looked like little trolls, each with a huge compost heap on its back. That represented everything it owned, and mostly what it owned was rotten.

Sam Vimes winced at the pain in his side. Just his luck. Two coppers injured in the entire damn affair, and he had to be one of them? Igor had done his best, but broken ribs were broken ribs, and it'd be a week or two before the suspicious green ointment made much difference. His hand twinged in sympathy with them, too.

Still, he enjoyed a bit of a warm glow about the whole thing. They *had* used good, old-fashioned policing, and since good, old-fashioned policemen are invariably outnumbered, he'd employed the good, old-fashioned police methods of cunning, deceit, and any damn weapon you could lay your hands on.

It had hardly been a fight at all. The dwarfs had mostly been sitting and singing gloomy songs, because they fell over when they tried to stand up, or had tried to stand up and were now lying down and snoring. The trolls were, on the other hand, mostly upright, but went over when you pushed them. One or two, a little clearer in the head than the others, had put up a ponderous and laughable fight but had fallen to that most old-fashioned of police methods: the well-placed boot. Well, most of them had. Vimes shifted to ease the aching in his side; he should have seen that one coming.

But all's well that ends well, eh? No deaths at all, and just to put a little cherry on the morning cake, he had in his hand an early-morning edition of the *Times*, in which a leading article deplored the gangs stalking the city and wondered if the Watch was "up to the job" of cleaning up the streets.

Well, yes, I think we are, you pompous twerp. Vimes struck a match on a plinth and lit a cigar in recognition of a petty but darkly satisfying triumph. Gods knew they needed one. The Watch had taken a pounding over the whole damn Koom Valley thing, and it was good to hand the lads something to be proud of for a change. All in all, it was definitely a Result—

He stared at the plinth. He didn't remember what statue had once been there. It celebrated generations of graffiti artists now.

A piece of troll graffiti adorned it now, obliterating everything done by the artists who used mere paint. He read:

MR. SHINE!

HIM DIAMOND!

Mine sign, city scrawl, he thought. Thing go bad, and people are moved to write on the walls . . .

"Commander!"

He turned. Captain Carrot, armor gleaming, was hurrying toward him, his face, as usual, radiating an expression of a hundred percent pure Keen.

"I thought I told everyone not on prisoner duty to get some sleep, Captain?" said Vimes.

"Just clearing up a few things, sir," said Carrot. "Lord Vetinari sent a message down to the Yard. He wants a report. I thought I'd better tell you, sir."

"I was just thinking, Captain," said Vimes expansively. "Should we put up a little plaque? Something simple? It could say something like BATTLE OF KOOM VALLEY NOT FOUGHT HERE, GRUNE THE 5TH, YEAR OF THE PRAWN. Could we get them to do a bloody stamp? What do you think?"

"I think you need to get some sleep yourself, Commander," said Carrot. "And technically, it isn't Koom Valley until Saturday."

"Of course, monuments to battles that didn't take place might be stretching things a bit, but a stamp—"

"Lady Sybil really worries about you, sir." Carrot broadcast concern.

The fizz in Vimes's head subsided. As if awakened by the reference to Sybil, the debtors of his body queued up to wave their overdue IOUs: feet—dead tired and in need of a bath; stomach—gurgling; ribs—on fire; back—aching; brain—drunk on its own poisons. Bath, sleep, eat . . . good ideas. But still must do things . . .

"How's our Mr. Pessimal?" he said.

"Igor's fixed him up, sir. He's a bit amazed at all the fuss. Now, I know I can't order you to go and see his lordship—"

"No, you can't, because I am a *commander*, Captain," said Vimes, still fuzzily intoxicated on exhaustion.

"—but *he* can and he *has*, sir. And your coach will

be waiting for you outside the palace when you come out. That's *Lady Sybil's* orders, sir," said Carrot, appealing to higher authority.

Vimes looked up at the ugly bulk of the palace. Suddenly, clean sheets seemed such a sweet idea.

"Can't face him like this," he murmured.

"I had a word with Secretary Drumknott, sir. Hot water, a razor, and a big cup of coffee will be waiting in the palace."

"You thought of everything, Carrot . . ."

"I hope so, sir. Now off you—"

"But I thought of *something*, eh?" said Vimes, swaying cheerfully. "Better dead drunk than just dead, eh?"

"It was a classic ruse, sir," said Carrot reassuringly. "One for the history books. Now, off you go, sir. I'm going to have a look for Angua. She hasn't slept in her bed."

"But at this time of the month—"

"I know, sir. She hasn't slept in her basket, either."

In a dank cellar that once was an attic and was now half-full of mud, the vurms poured out of a small hole where wooden planks had long since worn away.

A fist punched up. Soggy timber split and crumbled.

Angua pulled herself up into this new darkness, then reached down to help Sally, who said: "Well, here's another fine mess."

"Let's hope so," said Angua. "I think we need to go up at least one more level. There's an archway here. Come on."

There had been too many dead ends, forgotten stinking rooms and false hopes, and altogether too much slime.

After a while, the smell became almost tangible, and then it managed to become just another part of the darkness. The women wandered and scrambled from one dripping, fetid room to another, testing the muddy walls for hidden doors, searching for even a pinprick of light in the ceilings hanging with interesting but horrible growths.

Now they heard music. Five minutes wading and slithering brought them to a blocked-in doorway, but since it had been filled by the more modern Ankh-Morpork mortar of sand, horse dung, and vegetable peelings, several bricks had already fallen out. Sally removed most of the rest with one punch.

"Sorry about that," she said. "It's a vampire thing."

The cellar behind the demolished wall had some barrels in it, and looked as though it was regularly used. There was a proper door, too. Rather dull, repetitive music filtered down from between the boards. There was a trapdoor in them.

"O-kay," said Angua. "There's people up there, I can smell them—"

"I count fifty-seven hearts beating," said Sally. Angua gave her a Look.

"You know, that's one particular talent I'd keep to myself, if I was you," she said.

"Sorry, Sergeant."

"It's not the sort of thing people want to hear," Angua went on. "I mean, I personally am quite capable of crushing a man's skull in my jaws, but I don't go around telling everyone."

"I shall make a note of it, Sergeant," said Sally, with a meekness that was quite possibly feigned.

"Good. Now . . . what do we look like? Swamp monsters?"

"Yes, Sergeant. Your hair looks dreadful. Just like a great lump of green slime."

"Green?"

"I'm afraid so."

"And my emergency dress is back down there somewhere," said Angua. "It's past dawn, too. Can you, er, go bats now?"

"In daylight? One hundred and fifty disoriented bits of me? No! But you could get out as a wolf, couldn't you?"

"I'd kind of prefer not to be a slime monster coming through the floor, if it's all the same to you," said Angua.

"Yes, I can see that. It does not pay to advertise." Sally flicked away a lump of nameless ooze. "Ugh, this stuff is *foul*."

"So, the best we can hope for is that when we make a run for it, no one will recognize us," said Angua, pulling a lump of wobbly green stuff from her hair. "At least we—oh, no . . ."

"What's wrong?" said Sally.

"Nobby Nobbs! He's up there! I can *smell* him!" She pointed urgently at the boards overhead.

"You mean Corporal Nobbs? The little . . . man with the spots?" said Sally.

"We're not under a Watch house, are we?" said Angua, looking around in panic.

"I don't think so. Someone's dancing, by the sound of it. But look, how can you smell one human in the middle of all . . . this?"

"It never leaves you, believe me." The smell of old cabbage, acne ointment, and nonmalignant skin disease became transmuted, in Corporal Nobbs, into a strange odor that lay across the nose like a saw blade on a harp. It wasn't *bad*, as such, but it was like its host: strange, ubiquitous, and hellishly difficult to forget.

"Well, he's a fellow officer, isn't he? Won't he help us?" said Sally.

"We are *naked*, Lance Constable!"

"Only technically. This mud really sticks."

"I mean *underneath* the mud!" said Angua.

"Yes, but if we had clothes on we'd be naked underneath *them*, too!" Sally pointed out.

"This is not the time for logic! This is the time for not seeing Nobby grinning at me!"

"But he's seen you when you're wolf-shaped, hasn't he?" said Sally.

"So?" snapped Angua.

"Well, technically you're naked then, aren't you?"

"*Never tell him that!*"

Nobby Nobbs, a shadow in the warm red gloom, nudged Sergeant Colon.

"You don't have to keep your eyes shut, Sarge,"

he said. "It's all legit. It's an artistic celebration of the female body, Tawneee says. Anyway, she's got clothes on."

"Two tassels and a folded hanky is not clothes, Nobby," said Fred, sinking down in his seat. The Pink PussyCat Club! Now, fair's fair, he'd been in the army and Watch, and you couldn't spend all that time in uniform without seeing a thing or two—or three, now he came to recollect—and it was true, as Nobby had pointed out, that the ballerinas down at the opera house didn't leave a lot to the imagination, at least not to Nobby's, but when all was said and done, ballet had to be Art, even though it was a bit short on plinths and urns, on account of being expensive to look at, and moreover, ballerinas didn't whizz around upside down. And the worst of it was, he'd already spotted two people he knew in the audience. Fortunately they hadn't seen him, which was to say that whenever he'd sneaked a glance their way, they were looking in completely the opposite direction.

"Now this bit is really hard," whispered Nobby conversationally.

"Er . . . is it?" Fred Colon closed his eyes again.

"Oh, yes. It's the Triple Corkscrew—"

"Look, don't the management object to you coming in here?" Fred managed, shifting even further down in his seat.

"Oh, no. They like having a watchman in," said Nobby, still watching the stage. "They say it makes people behave. Anyway, I only come in so's I can walk Betty home."

"Betty being—?"

"Tawneee's actually only her pole name," Nobby said. "She says no one would be interested in an exotic dancer with a name like Betty. She says it sounds like she'd be better with a bowl of cake mixture."

Colon shut his eyes, trying to banish a mental conjunction of the bronzed lithe figure on stage and a bowl of cake mixture.

"I think I could do with a breath of fresh air," he groaned.

"Oh, not yet, Sarge. Broccolee's on next. She can touch the back of her head with her foot, you know—"

"I don't believe that!" said Fred Colon.

"She can, Sarge, I've seen—"

"I don't believe there's a dancer called Broccoli!"

"Well, she did used to be called Candi, Sarge, but then she heard that broccoli is better for you—"

"Corporal Nobbs!"

The sound appeared to be coming from under the table.

Nobby stared at Fred Colon, and then looked down.

"Yes?" he ventured, with caution.

"This is Sergeant Angua," said the floor.

"Oh?" said Nobby.

"What is this place?" the voice continued.

"The Pink PussyCat Club, Sergeant," said Nobby obediently.

"Oh, gods." There was some conversation down below, and then the voice said: "Are there *women* up there?"

"Yes, Sergeant. Er . . . what are you doing down there, Sarge?"

"Giving you orders, Nobby," said the voice from below. "*Are* there women up there?"

"Yes, Sarge. Lots."

"Good. Please ask one to come down into the beer cellar. We'll need a couple of buckets of warm water and some towels, got that?"

Nobby was aware that the musicians had stopped playing and Tawneee had paused in mid–drop-and-split. Everyone was listening to the talking floor.

"Yes, Sergeant," said Nobby. "I've got it."

"And some clean clothes. And . . ." There was subterranean whispering ". . . make that several buckets of water. And a scrubbing brush. And a comb. And another comb. And more towels. Oh, and two pairs of shoes, size six and . . . four and a half? Really? Okay. And is Fred Colon with you, or is that a stupid question?"

Fred cleared his throat.

"I'm here, Sergeant," he reported. "But I only came along to—"

"Good. I want to borrow a set of your stripes. I've got a bad feeling about the next few hours and I don't want *anyone* to forget I'm a sergeant. Got that, the pair of you?"

"*It's full moon*," Fred whispered to Nobby, as one man to another, and then he said aloud: "Yes, Sergeant. This may take a while—"

"No! It won't. Because you've got a werewolf and a vampire down here, understand? I'm having a really bad hair day and she's got a toothache! We come up in ten minutes looking human or we come up anyway! What?" There was more whispering. "Why a beetroot? Why in gods' names is a girly show likely to contain a beetroot? What? Okay. Will an apple do? Nobby, Lance Constable von Humpeding needs an apple, urgently. Or something else that she can bite. Now, jump to it!"

Coffee was only a way of stealing time that should by rights belong to your slightly older self. Vimes drank two cups, and had a wash and at least an attempt at a shave, which made him feel quite human if he ignored the sensation that parts of his head were stuffed with warm cotton wool. At last, deciding that he felt as good as he was going to, and could probably handle quite long questions, he was ushered into the Oblong Office of the Patrician of Ankh-Morpork.

"Ah, Commander," said Lord Vetinari, looking up after a considered interval and pushing aside some paperwork. "Thank you for coming. It seems that congratulations are in order. So I am told."

"And why's that, sir?" said Vimes, putting on his special, blank, talking-to-Vetinari face.

"Come now, Vimes. Yesterday it looked as if we would be having a species war right in the middle of the city, and suddenly we are not. Those gangs were quite fearsome, I gather."

"Most of 'em were asleep or squabbling among themselves by the time we arrived, sir. We just had to tidy them away," Vimes volunteered.

"Yes indeed," said Vetinari. "It was quite astonishing, really. Do sit down, by the way. It really is not necessary for you to stand in front of me like a corporal on a charge."

"Don't know what you mean, sir," said Vimes, collapsing gratefully into a chair.

"You don't? I was referring, Vimes, to the speed with which both parties managed to incapacitate themselves with strong liquor at the same time . . . ?"

"I wouldn't know anything about that, sir." That was an automatic reaction; it made life simpler.

"No? It appears, Vimes, that while steeling themselves for the fracas to come, both the trolls and the dwarfs came into possession of what I assume they thought was beer . . . ?"

"They had been on the pi— been drinking all day, sir," Vimes pointed out.

"Indeed, Vimes, and possibly that is why the dwarf contingent were less than cautious in drinking copiously from beer that had been considerably . . . fortified? Areas of Sator Square, I gather, still smell faintly of *apples*, Vimes. One could come to believe, therefore, that what they were drinking was, in fact, a mixture of strong beer and scumble, which is, as you know, distilled from apples—"

"Uh, mostly apples, sir," said Vimes helpfully.

"Quite. The cocktail is known as Fluff, I believe. As to the trolls, one might speculate that it would be very hard to find anything to make their beer even more dangerous than it palpably is, but I wonder if you have heard, Vimes, that an admixture of various metallic salts produces a drink known as *luglarr*, or 'Big Hammer'?"

"Can't say I do, sir."

"Vimes, some of the flagstones in the plaza have actually been etched by the stuff!"

"Sorry about that, sir."

Vetinari drummed his fingers on the table.

"What would you do if I asked you an outright question, Vimes?"

"I'd tell you a downright lie, sir."

"Then I will not do so," said Vetinari, smiling faintly.

"Thank you, sir. Nor will I."

"Where are your prisoners?"

"We spread them around the Watch house yards," said Vimes. "As they wake up, we hose 'em clean, take their names, give 'em a receipt for their weapon and a hot drink, and push 'em out into the street."

"Their weapons are culturally very important to them, Vimes," said Vetinari.

"Yeah, sir, I know. I myself have a strong cultural bias against getting my brains bashed in and my knees cut off," said Vimes, stifling a yawn and wincing as his ribs objected.

"Indeed. Were there any casualties in the battle?"

"None that won't heal." Vimes grimaced. "I have to report that Mr. A. E. Pessimal sustained a broken arm and multiple bruises, though."

Vetinari actually looked taken aback.

"The inspector? What was he doing?"

"Er . . . attacking a troll, sir."

"I'm sorry? *Mr. A. E. Pessimal* attacked a *troll*?"

"Yessir."

"A. E. Pessimal?" Vetinari repeated.

"That's the man, sir."

"A *whole* troll?"

"Yessir. With his teeth, sir."

"Mr. A. E. *Pessimal*? You are sure? Small man? Very clean shoes?"

"Yessir."

Vetinari grabbed a helpful question from the gathering throng.

"*Why?*"

Vimes coughed. "Well, sir . . ."

. . . The troll mob was a tableau. Trolls stood or sat or lay where they had been when the Big Hammer had struck. There *were* a few slow imbibers who put up a bit of a fight, and one who had stuck with a bottle of looted sherry put up a spirited last-drop stand until golem Constable Dorfl picked him up bodily and bounced him on his head.

Vimes walked through it all, as the squad dragged or rolled slumbering trolls into neat lines to await the wagons. And then—

The day was not improving for Brick. He'd drunk a beer. Well, maybe more'n one. Where was der harm in dat?

And now, dere, right in front of him, wearing one o' dem helmets an' everyting, was, yeah, could be a dwarf, insofar as the fizzing, sizzling pathways of his brain were capable of deciding anything at all. What der hell, they decided, it wasn't a troll and dat was what it was all about, right? An' here was his club, right here in his han'—

Instinct caused Vimes to turn as a troll opened

red eyes, blinked, and began to swing a club. Too slowly, too slowly in the suddenly frozen time, he tried to dive away, and he felt the club smash into his side and lift him, lift him up and tip him onto the ground. He could hear shouting as the troll lumbered forward, club raised again to make Vimes at one with the bedrock.

Brick became aware that he was being attacked. He stopped what he was doing and, with sparks going fwizzle! *in his brain, looked down his right knee. Some little gnome or somethin' was attacking him wi' a blunt sword and kickin' an' screamin' like a mad t'ing. He put it down to the drink, like der feelin' that his ears were givin' off flames, an' brushed der fing away with a flip of his hand.*

Vimes, helpless, saw A. E. Pessimal tumble across the plaza, and watched the troll turn back to the clubbing at hand. But Detritus, arriving behind it now, pulled it around with one shovel-sized hand and *here* came the Detritus fist, like the wrath of gods.

For Brick, everything went dar—

"You wish me to believe," said Lord Vetinari, "that Mr. A. E. Pessimal *single-handedly* attacked a troll?"

"Both hands, sir," said Vimes. "And feet, too. And tried to bite it, we think."

"Isn't that certain death?" said Vetinari.

"That didn't seem to worry him, sir."

Vimes had last seen A. E. Pessimal being bandaged by Igor and smiling in a semiconscious way. Watchmen were dropping in all the time to say things like "Hi, big man!" and slap him on the back. The world had turned for A. E. Pessimal.

"Might I inquire, Vimes, why one of my most conscientious and most decidedly *civilian* clerks was in a position to do this?"

Vimes shifted uncomfortably. "He was inspecting. Learning all about us, sir."

He gave Vetinari a look that said: If you take this any further, I will have to lie.

Vetinari returned one that said: I know.

"You yourself are not too badly injured?" the Patrician said aloud.

"Just a few scratches, sir," said Vimes.

Vetinari gave him a look that said: Broken ribs, I'm certain of it.

Vimes returned one that said: Nothing.

Vetinari wandered over to the window and stared down at the waking city. He didn't speak for some time, and then let out a sigh.

"Such a shame, I think, that so many of them were born here," he said.

Vimes stuck with saying nothing. It generally sufficed.

"Perhaps I should have taken action against that wretched dwarf," Vetinari went on.

"Yes, sir."

"You think so? A wise ruler thinks twice before directing violence against someone because he does not approve of what they say."

Once again, Vimes did not comment. He himself directed violence daily and with a certain amount of enthusiasm against people, because he didn't approve of them saying things like "Give me all your money" or "What are you going to do about it, copper?" But perhaps rulers had to think differently. Instead, he said: "Someone else didn't, sir."

"Thank you for that, Vimes," said the Patrician, turning around sharply. "And have you found out who they *are* yet?"

"Investigations are continuing, sir. Last night's affair got in the way."

"Is there any evidence that it *was* a troll?"

"There is . . . puzzling evidence, sir. We are . . . assembling a jigsaw, you might say." Except that we haven't got any of the edges and it'd help if we had the lid of the box, he added to himself. And, because Vetinari's face bore a hungry look, Vimes continued aloud: "If you're expecting me to pull a magic rabbit out of my helmet, sir, it'll be a cooked one. The dwarfs are *certain* it was a troll. There's a thousand years of history telling them. They don't *need* proof. And the trolls don't think it was a troll but probably wish it was. This isn't about a murder, sir. Something inside 'em's gone click, and it's time for all good men— well, you know what I mean— to fight Koom Valley all over again. Something else is going on in that mine, I know it. Something bigger than murder. All those tunnels . . . what are they for? All those lies . . . I can smell lies, and the place is full of them."

"Much hangs on this, Vimes," said Vetinari. "It's bigger than you know. I have this morning had a clacks from Rhys Rhysson, the Low King. All politicians have their enemies, of course. There are, shall we say, factions that disagree with him, his policy toward us, his conciliatory approaches to the troll

clans, his stance on the whole wretched *Ha'ak* thing
. . . And now there are stories about a troll killing a
grag and, yes, rumors that the Watch has threatened
the dwarfs . . ."

Vetinari held up a pale hand as Vimes opened his
mouth to protest.

"We need to know the *truth*, Vimes. Commander
Sam Vimes's truth. It may count for more than you
think. In the Plains, certainly, and much further.
People know about you, Commander. Descendant of
a watchman who believed that if a corrupted court
will not behead an evil king, then the watchman
should do it himself—"

"It was only *one* king," Vimes protested. "It wasn't
a habit!"

"Sam Vimes once arrested *me* for treason," said
Vetinari calmly. "And Sam Vimes once arrested a
dragon. Sam Vimes stopped a war between nations
by arresting *two* high commands. He's an arresting
fellow, Sam Vimes. Sam Vimes killed a werewolf
with his bare hands, and carries law with him, like
a lamp—"

"Where did all that come from?"

"Watchmen across half the continent will say that
Sam Vimes is as straight as an arrow, can't be corrupted, won't be turned, never took a bribe. *Listen*
to me. If Rhys falls, the next Low King will *not* be
one who is prepared to talk to the trolls. Can I make
it simple for you? Those clans whose leaders have
been dealing with Rhys will in all likelihood feel
they have been made fools of, overthrow said leaders, and replace them with trolls too belligerent and
stupid to *be* fools. And there *will* be a war, Vimes.

It'll come here. It won't be a gang crumble such as you thwarted last night. We won't be able to hold fast or stand aloof. Because we have our own fools, Vimes, as I'm sure you know, who'll insist we pick sides. Koom Valley will be everywhere. Find me a murderer, Vimes. Hound them down and bring them into the daylight. Troll or dwarf or human, it doesn't matter. Then at least we shall have the truth, and can make use of it. It is rumor and uncertainty that are our enemies now. The Low King's throne trembles, Vimes, and thus do the foundations of the world."

Vetinari paused, and carefully squared up the paperwork in front of him, as if he now felt he'd gone too far.

"However, obviously I do not wish to put you under any kind of pressure," he finished.

In Vimes's confused, lukewarm brain, one word bobbed to the surface.

"Crumble?" he said.

Lord Vetinari's secretary leaned down and whispered into his master's ear.

"Ah, I believe I meant 'rumble,'" said Vetinari brightly.

Vimes was still trying to cope with the international news digest.

"All this over one murder?" he said, trying to stifle a yawn.

"No, Vimes. You said it yourself: all this over thousands of years of tension and politics and power struggles. In recent years, things have gone in certain ways, causing power to shift. There are those who would like it to shift back, even if it returns on a tide of blood. Who cares about one dwarf? But if his death can be turned into a *casus belli*—" here Lord Vetinari looked at Vimes's sleepy eyes and went on, "—that is, a reason for war, then suddenly he is the most important dwarf in the world. When did you last get some proper sleep, Vimes?"

Vimes muttered something about "not long ago."

"Go and have some more. And then find me the murderer. Quickly. Good day to you."

Not just thrones trembling, Vimes managed to think. Your chair is wobbling a bit, too. Pretty soon some people will be saying: Who let all these dwarfs in here? They undermine our city and they don't obey our laws. And the trolls? We used to chain 'em up like guard dogs, and now they're allowed to walk around threatening real people!

They'd be gathering now, the plotters, the people who chatted quietly in the corner at parties, the people who know how to fashion opinions into knives. Last night's little fray had been turned into a joke that had probably dismayed the party people, but you couldn't do it twice. Once things began to spread, once a few humans had been killed, you wouldn't need to talk behind closed doors anymore. The mob would scream on your behalf.

They undermine our city and they don't obey our laws . . .

He climbed in the coach on legs that were only marginally under his control, muttered an instruction to head for Pseudopolis Yard, and fell asleep.

It was still nighttime in the city of endless rain. It was never not nighttime. No sun rose here.

The creature lay coiled in its alley.

Something was seriously wrong. It had expected resistance. There was always resistance, and it always overcame it. But even now, when the invisible bustle of the city had slowed, there was no way in. Time and again it'd be sure that it had found a point of control, some tide of rage it could use, and time and again it'd be slammed back here, into this dark alley where the gutters overflowed.

This was not the usual kind of mind. The creature struggled. But no mind had ever beaten it yet. There was always a way . . .

Through the ruin of the world the troll staggers . . .

Brick lurched out of Dolly Sisters Watch house, clutching his head with one hand and, in the other, holding the bag that contained as many of his teeth as Detritus been able to find. The sergeant had been very decent about dat, Brick thought. Detritus had also explained to him exactly what would have happened to him had his second blow hit the human, graphically indicating that finding Brick's teeth would have been secondary to finding a head to put them in.

He'd gone on to say, though, that there might be a place in the Watch for any troll who could still stand up after a head full of Big Hammer, and maybe Brick might like to conduct his future behavior with an eye to this.

So, Brick thought, insofar as the term could be applied to any brain activity within two days of Big Hammer, der future was looking so bright dat he had to walk along wid his eyes almost shut, although dat was probably der Big Hammer again.

But—

He'd heard the other trolls talking. And the watchmen, too. All dis stuff about a troll killing a dwarf down in dat new mine. Now, Brick was still certain he hadn't killed no dwarf, even after half an ounce of Scrape. He'd gone over and over it in what currently remained of his mind. Trouble was, der Watch had all dese tricks dese days, dey could tell what a guy had for dinner just by looking at his plate. An' he'd lost a skull down dere, too, he was sure o' dat. Like, dey could jus' *sniff* it and know it was him! Except it *wasn't* him, right? 'Cos dey said der troll dropped his club, an' Brick still had his club, 'cos he hit dat top watchman wi' it, so maybe that was what dey called an Ally By? Yes? Despite the cerebral gurgling noise of the Big Hammer draining away from his higher brain functions, Brick suspected that it wasn't. An' anyway, if dey lookin' for a troll what done der deed, and dey find out I was dere, lost a skull an' everytin' an' I say, okay, I was dere but I never walloped no dwarf, de'll say, ho yus, pull der other one, it is havin' bells on.

Right here, and right now, Brick was feeling a very lonely troll.

Dere was nothin' for it. Dere was only one person who could help him w' dis one. It was too much t'inkin' for one troll.

Slinking through alleys, pressed against walls,

keeping his head down, avoiding every living creature, Brick sought out Mr. Shine.

Angua decided to go straight to Pseudopolis Yard rather than a closer Watch house. That was HQ, after all, and besides, she always kept a spare uniform in her locker.

What was annoying was that Sally walked so easily in six-inch heels. That was vampires for you. *She* had taken hers off and was carrying them; it was that or turn an ankle. The Pink PussyCat Club had a fairly limited choice of footwear. There wasn't much to choose from in the way of clothing, either, if by clothing you meant something that actually made an attempt to cover anything.

Angua had been rather surprised that the stage wardrobe had included a female Watch outfit, but with skimpy papier-mâché armor and a skirt that was much too short to be any protection. Tawneee had explained, rather carefully, that men sometimes liked to see a pretty girl in armor. To Angua, who'd found that men she was apprehending never looked very pleased to see *her*, this was food for thought.

She'd settled for a sequined gold dress, which just didn't work. Sally had picked something simple and cut to the thigh, in blue, which, of course, had become stunning the moment she'd put it on. She looked *fabulous*.

So when Angua strode into the main office, slamming the big doors back, and there was a derisory wolf-whistle, the unwise watchman found himself being pushed backwards until he was slammed against the wall. He felt two sharp points pressed against his neck as Angua growled, "You *want* a wolf, do you? Say, 'No, Sergeant Angua.'"

"No, Sergeant Angua!"

"You don't? I was probably mistaken then, was I?" The points pressed a little harder. In the man's mind, steely talons were about to pierce his jugular.

"Couldn't say for sure, Sergeant Angua!"

"My nerves are a tad stretched right now!" Angua howled.

"Hadn't noticed, Sergeant Angua!"

"We're all a little bit on edge at the moment, wouldn't you say!"

"That's ever so true, Sergeant Angua!"

Angua let the man's boot reach the ground. She put two black, shiny, and noticeably *pointed* heels into his unresisting hands.

"Could you do me a really big favor, please, and take these back up to the Pink PussyCat Club?" she said sweetly. "They belong to someone called Sherilee, I think. Thank you."

She turned and looked over to the duty desk, where Carrot was watching her with his mouth open. Well aware of the stir she was causing, she walked up to the desk past an audience of shocked faces and threw a muddy necklace down onto the open Incident Book.

"Four dwarfs murdered by other dwarfs, down in the Long Dark," she said. "I'll bet my nose on it. That belonged to one of them. He'd also got this." A muddy envelope was dropped by the necklace. "It's pretty slimy, but you can read it. Mister Vimes is going to go postal." She looked up into the blue eyes of Carrot. "Where is he?"

"Sleeping on a mattress in his office," said Carrot, and shrugged. "Lady Sybil knew he wouldn't go home, so she got Willikins to make up a bed down here. Are you two all right?"

"Fine, sir," said Sally.

"I was getting very worried—" Carrot began.

"Four dead dwarfs, Captain," said Angua. "City dwarfs. That's what you should be worrying about. Three half-buried, this one crawled away."

Carrot picked up the necklace and read the runes.

"Lars Legstrong," he said. "I think I know the family. Are you sure he was murdered?"

"Throat cut. It'd be hard to call it suicide. But he took some time to die. He made it to one of their damn doors, which they'd locked shut, and scrawled one of their signs on it in his own blood. Then he sat down and waited to die in the dark. In the damn dark, Carrot! They were working dwarfs! They had shovels and wheelbarrows! They were down there doing a job, and when they weren't needed anymore they got the chop! Hacked down and left for the mud! He might even still have been alive down there when Mister Vimes and I went in. Behind their bloody thick door, dying by inches. And do you know what *this* means?"

She pulled a folded piece of card out of her bodice and passed it over.

"A drinks menu?" said Carrot.

"Open it," snapped Angua. "I'm sorry it's written in lipstick, it was all we could find."

Carrot flipped it open. "Another dark symbol?" he said. "I don't think I know this one."

There were other dwarf officers in the office. Carrot held up the symbol.

"Does anyone here know what this means?"

A few helmeted heads shook, and a few dwarfs backed away, but a deep voice from the doorway said: "Yes, Captain Carrot. I suspect I do. Does it look like an eye with a tail?"

"Yes . . . er . . . sir?" said Carrot, staring. A shadow moved.

"It was drawn in the dark? By a dying dwarf? In his own blood? It is the Summoning Dark, Captain, and it will be *moving*. Good morning to you. I am Mr. Shine."

Carrot's jaw dropped as the watchmen turned to look at the newcomer. He loomed in the doorway, almost as broad as he was tall, in a black cloak and hood that hid any possible feature.

"*The* Mr. Shine?" he said.

"Regrettably so, Captain, and can I charge you to see that no one in this room leaves for a few minutes after I do? I like to keep my movements . . . private."

"I didn't think you were real, sir!"

"Believe me, young man, I wish it were possible to keep you in that happy state," said the hooded figure. "However, my hand is forced."

Mr. Shine stepped forward, pulling a rangy figure into the room. It was a troll, whose look of sullen defiance did not quite manage to conceal knee-knocking terror.

"This is Brick, Captain. I deliver him back into

the *personal* custody of your Sergeant Detritus. He has information of use to you. I have heard his story. I believe him. You must move fast. The Summoning Dark may already have found a champion. What else . . . oh yes, be sure not to keep that symbol in a dark place. Keep light around it at all times. And now, if you will excuse the theatricals—"

The black robe twitched. Hard, white, *blinding* light filled the room for a second. When it had gone, so had Mr. Shine. All that was left was a large, round stone on the stained floor.

Carrot blinked, and then pulled himself together.

"All right, you heard," he said to the suddenly animated room at large. "No one is to follow Mr. Shine, understood?"

"Follow *him*, Captain?" said a dwarf. "We're not mad, you know!"

"Dat's right," said a troll. "Dey say he can reach inside o' you an' stop your heart!"

"Mr. Shine?" said Angua. "Is he what they've been writing about on the walls?"

"It looks like that," said Carrot shortly. "And he said we don't have much time. Mr. . . . Brick, was it?"

While Chrysophrase's trolls had contrived to swagger while standing still, Brick just managed to huddle all alone. You usually need two to huddle, but here was a troll trying to hide behind himself. No one could hide behind Brick; for a troll, he was stick-thin to the point of knobbliness. His lichen was cheap and matted, not the real thing at all, probably the stuff they made up out of broccoli stalks in the back alleys of Quarry Lane. His belt of skulls was a disgrace; some of them were clearly the papier-mâché kind that could be bought from any joke shop. One had a red nose.

He looked around nervously, and there was a thud as his club dropped from his fingers.

"I'm in deep copro, right?" he said.

"Certainly we need to talk to you," said Carrot. "Do you want a lawyer?"

"No, I ate already."

"You *eat* lawyers?" said Carrot.

Brick gave him an empty stare until sufficient brain had been mustered.

"What d'y'call dem fings, dey kinda crumble when you eat dem?" he ventured.

Carrot looked at Detritus and Angua, to see if there was going to be any help there.

"*Could* be lawyers," he conceded.

"Dey go soggy if you dips 'em in somfing," said Brick, as if undertaking a forensic examination.

"More likely to be biscuits, then?" Carrot suggested.

"Could be. Inna packet wi' all paper on. Yeah, biscuits."

"What I meant," said Carrot, "was when we talk to you, do you want someone to be on your side?"

"Yes please. Everyone," said Brick promptly. To be the center of attention in a room full of watchmen was his worst nightmare. No, hold on, what about dat time when he had dat bad Slab wot had bin cut wi' ammonium nitrate? Whooo! Good-bye lobes! Yep! Den dis was his second worst nightmar— no, come to fink of it, dere was dis time when he had dat stuff wot Hardcore jacked off'f One-Eyed Goddam, whee, yes! Who knows where *dat* has bin! All dem dancin' teef! So dis was his— hey, wait, remember dat time you got lunched on Scrape an' your arms flew away? Okay, dat was bad, so maybe *dis* was his . . . wait, wait, of course, can't be forgetting der day when you got baked on Sliver and blew powdered zinc up you nose an' thought you'd thrown up your feet? Aargh, here come dat time again when you'd, aargh no, when you'd, aargh—

Brick had got as far as his nineteenth worst nightmare before Carrot's voice cut through the snakes.

"Mr. Brick?"

"Er . . . is dat still me?" said Brick nervously. He could really, really do some Slab right now . . .

"Generally your advocate is one person," said Carrot. "We're going to have to ask you some difficult questions. You're allowed to have someone to help you. Perhaps you have a friend we could fetch?"

Brick pondered this. The only people he could think of in this context were Totally Slag and Big Marble, although more correctly they fell into the category of "people dat don't fro fings at me much and let me glom a bit o' Slab sometimes." Right now, these did not seem ideal qualifications.

He pointed to Sergeant Detritus.

"Him," he said. "He helped me find my teef."

"I'm not sure a serving officer is—" Carrot began.

"I'll volunteer for the role, Captain," said a little voice. Carrot peered over the edge of the desk.

"Mr. Pessimal? I don't think you should be out of bed."

"Uh . . . I am, in fact, acting lance constable, Captain," said A. E. Pessimal, politely yet firmly. He was on crutches.

"Oh? Er . . . right," said Carrot. "But, I still think you shouldn't be out of bed."

"Nevertheless, justice must be served," said A. E. Pessimal.

Brick bent down and peered closely at the inspector. "It's dat gnome from last night," he said. "Don't want him!"

"You can't think of *anyone*?" said Carrot.

Brick thought again, and at last brightened up.

"Yeah, I can," he said. "Easy. Someone to help me answer der questions, right."

"That's right."

"Well, easy peas. If you can fetch that dwarf I saw down in dat new dwarf mine last night, he'd help me."

The room went deadly quiet.

"And why would he do that?" said Carrot carefully.

"He could tell you why he was hitting dat other dwarf onna head," said Brick. "I mean, *I* don't know. But I 'spect he won't wanna come on account of me bein' a troll, so I'll stick with the sergeant, if it's all der same to you."

"I think this is going too far, Captain!" said A. E. Pessimal.

In the silence that followed this, Carrot's voice sounded very loud.

"I think this, Mr. Pessimal, is the point where we wake up Commander Vimes."

There was an old military saying that Fred Colon used to describe total bewilderment and confusion. An individual in that state, according to Fred, "couldn't tell if it was arsehole or breakfast time."

This had always puzzled Vimes. He wondered what research had been done. Even now, with his mouth tasting of warmed-over yesterday and everything curiously sharp in his vision, he thought he'd be able to tell the difference. Only one was likely to include a cup of coffee, for a start.

He had one now, ergo, it was breakfast time. Actually, it was near lunchtime, but that would have to do.

The troll known to everyone else and occasionally to himself as Brick was seated in one of the big troll cells, but in deference to the fact that no one could decide if he was a prisoner or not, the door had been left unlocked. The understanding was that, provided he didn't try to leave, no one would stop him leaving. Brick was engulfing his third bowl of mineral-rich mud that, to a troll, was nourishing soup.

"What *is* Scrape?" Vimes said, leaning back in the room's one spare chair and staring at Brick as a zoologist might eye a fascinating but highly unpredictable new species. He'd put the large round stone from the mysterious Mr. Shine on the table by the bowl, to see if it got any reaction, but the troll paid it no attention.

"Scrape? You don't see it much dese days now dat Slab's so damn cheap," rumbled Detritus, who was watching his new find with a proprietorial air, like a mother hen watching a chick who was about to leave the nest. "It what you 'scrape up,' see? It few bits o' drain-grade Slab boiled up in a tin wi' alcohol and pigeon droppins. It what der street trolls make when dey is short o' cash an' . . . what is it dey's short of, Brick?"

The moving spoon paused. "Dey is short o' self-respec', Sergeant," he said, as one might who'd had the lesson shouted into his ear for twenty minutes.

"By Io, he got it!" said Detritus, slapping the skinny Brick on the back so hard that the young troll dropped his spoon into the steaming gloop. "But dis lad has promised me all dat is behind him and he is damn straight now, on account o' havin' joined my One-Step Program! Ain't dat so, Brick? No more Slab, Scrape, Slice, Slide, Slunkie, Slurp, or Sliver for *dis* boy, right?"

"Yes, Sergeant," said Brick obediently.

"Sergeant, why do the names of all troll drugs start with *s*?" said Vimes.

"Ah, it make dem easier to remember, sir," said Detritus, nodding sagely.

"Ah, of course. I hadn't spotted that," said Vimes. "Has Sergeant Detritus explained to you why he calls it a one-step program, Brick?"

"Er . . . 'cos he won't let me put a foot wrong, sir?" said Brick, as if reading it off a card.

"An' Brick here's got something else to say to you, haven't you, Brick?" said the maternal Detritus. "Go on, tell Mister Vimes."

Brick looked down at the table. "Sorry I tried to kill you, Mister Vimes," he whispered.

"Well, we'll see about that, shall we?" said Vimes, for something better to say. "By the way, I think you meant Mister Vimes, and I prefer it if only people who've fought alongside me call me *Mister* Vimes."

"Well, technic'ly Brick *has* fought—" Detritus began, but Vimes put down his coffee mug firmly. His ribs were aching.

"No, 'in front of' is not the same thing as 'alongside,' Sergeant," he said. "It really isn't."

"Not really his fault, sir, it was more a case o' mistaken iden-tity," Detritus protested.

"You mean he didn't know who I was?" said Vimes. "That didn't seem to—"

"Nosir. He didn't know who *he* was, sir. He thought he was a bunch o' lights and fireworks. Trust me, sir, I reckon I can make something o' this one. Please? Sir, he was out o' his brain on Big Hammer and still he was walkin' about!"

Vimes stared at Detritus a moment, and then looked back at Brick.

"Mr. Brick, tell me how you got into the mine, will you?" he said.

"I told the other polisman—" Brick began.

"Now you tell Mister Vimes!" growled Detritus. "Right now!"

It took a little while, with pauses for bits of Brick's mind to shunt into position, but Vimes assembled it like this:

The wretched Brick had been cooking up Scrape with some fellow gutter trolls in an old warehouse in the maze of streets behind Park Lane, had blundered down into the cellar looking for a cool place to watch the display, and the floor had given way under him. By the sound of it, he'd fallen a long way, but to judge by the troll's natural state, he probably floated down like a butterfly. He'd ended up in a tunnel, "like a mine, y'know, wi' all wood holdin' der roof up," and had wandered along it in the hope that it led back to the surface or something to eat.

He didn't start to worry until he came out into a far grander tunnel, and the words "dwarfs" finally reached a bit of his brain with nothing to do but listen.

A troll in a dwarf mine goes on the rampage. It was one of those givens, like a bull in a china shop. But Brick seemed refreshingly free of hatred toward anyone. Provided the world supplied enough things beginning with *s* to make his head go "bzzz!," and the city had no shortage of these, he didn't much care about what else it did. Brick, down in the gutter, had even dropped below that horizon. No wonder Chrysophrase's shakedown hadn't corralled him. Brick was something you stepped over.

It might even have occurred to Brick, standing there in the dark with the sound of dwarf voices in the distance, to be afraid. And then he'd seen, through a big round doorway, one dwarf hold up another and hit it over the head. It was cave-gloomy, but trolls had good night vision, and there were always the vurms. The troll hadn't made out details and was not particularly interested in seeing any. Who cared what dwarfs did to one another? So long as they didn't do it to him, he didn't see a problem. But when the dwarf that had done the bashing started to shout, *then* there was a problem, large as life.

A big metal door right by him had slammed open and hit him in the face. When he peered out from behind it, it was to see several armed dwarfs running past. They weren't interested in what might be behind the door, not yet. They were doing what people do, which is run toward the source of the shouting. Brick, on the other hand, was only interested in getting as far away from the shouting as possible, and, right here, was an open door. He took it and ran, not stopping until he was out in the fresh night air.

There had been no pursuit. Vimes wasn't surprised. You needed a special kind of mind to be a guard. It was one that was prepared to be in a body that stood and looked at nothing very much for hours on end. Such a mind did not command high wages. Such a mind, too, would not be likely to start a search by looking in the tunnel it just arrived by. It would not be the sharpest knife in the drawer.

And so, aimlessly, without intent, malice, or even curiosity, a wandering troll had wandered into a dwarf mine, spotted a murder through a drug-addled perception, and wandered out again. Who could plan for anything like that? Where was the logic? Where was the sense?

Vimes looked at the watery, fried-egg eyes, the emaciated frame, the thin dribble of gods-knew-what from a crusted nostril. Brick wasn't telling lies. Brick had enough trouble dealing with things that *weren't* made up.

"Tell Mister Vimes about the big *wukwuk*," Detritus prompted.

"Oh, yeah," said Brick. "Dere was dis big *wukwuk* in der cave."

"I think I'm missing a vital point here," said Vimes.

"A *wukwuk* is what you make wi' charcoal an' niter an' Slab," said the sergeant. "All rolled up in paper, like a cigar, you know? He said it was—"

"We call dem *wukwuks* 'cos dey looks like . . . you know, a wukwuk," said Brick, with an embarrassed grin.

"Yes, I'm getting the picture," said Vimes wearily. "And did you try to smoke it?"

"Nosir. It was *big*," said Brick. "All rolled up in their cave, jus' by the manky ol' tunnel I fell into."

Vimes tried to fit this into his thinking, and left it out for now. So . . . a dwarf did it? Right. And right now he believed Brick, although a bucket of frogs would make a better witness. No sense in pushing him further right now, anyway

"Okay," he said. He reached down and came up with the mysterious stone that had been left on the floor of the office. It was about eight inches across, but curiously light. "Tell me about Mr. Shine, Brick. Friend of yours?"

"Mr. Shine is everywhere!" said Brick fervently. "Him diamond!"

"Well, half an hour ago he was in this building," said Vimes. "Detritus?"

"Sir?" said the sergeant, a guilty look spreading across his face.

"What do *you* know about Mr. Shine?" said Vimes.

"Er . . . he a bit like a troll god . . ." Detritus muttered.

"Don't get many gods in here, as a rule," said Vimes. "Someone's pinched the secret of fire, have you seen my golden apple? It's amazing how often we don't get that sort of thing in the crime book. He's a troll, is he?"

"Kinda like a . . . a king," said Detritus, as if every word was being dragged from him.

"I thought trolls didn't have kings these days," said Vimes. "I thought every clan ruled itself."

"Right, right," said Detritus. "Look, Mister Vimes, he Mr. Shine, okay? We don't talk about him much." The troll's expression was a mixture of misery and defiance. Vimes decided to go for a weaker target.

"Where did you find him, Brick? I just want to—"

"He came callin' to help you!" snarled Detritus. "What you doin,' Mister Vimes? Why you go on askin' questions? Wi' the dwarfs you have pussy feet, must not upset 'em, oh no, but what you do if dey was trolls, eh? Kick down der door, no problem! Mr. Shine bring you Brick, give you good advice, an' you talk like he bein' a bad troll! I'm hearin' now where Captain Carrot, he tellin' the dwarfs he the Two Brothers. You fink that make me happy? We know dat lyin' ol' dwarf lie, yes! We groan at it lyin,' yes! You want to see Mr. Shine, you show humble, you show respec,' yes!"

This is Koom Valley again, thought Vimes. He'd never seen Detritus this angry, at least at him. The troll was just *there*, reliable and dependable. At Koom Valley, two tribes had met, and no one blinked.

"I apologize," he said, blinking. "I didn't know. No offense was meant."

"Right!" said Detritus, his huge hand thumping on the table.

The spoon jumped out of Brick's empty soup bowl. The mysterious rock ball rolled across the table, with an inevitable little trundling noise, and cracked open on the floor.

Vimes looked down at two neat halves.

"It's full of crystals," he said. Then he looked closer. There was a piece of paper in one broken, glittering hemisphere.

He picked it up and read: Pointer & Pickles, Crystals, Minerals & Tumbling Supplies, No. 3 Tenth Egg Street, Ankh-Morpork.

Vimes put this down carefully, and picked up the two pieces of the stone. He pushed them together, and they fitted with the merest hairline crack. There was no sign that any glue had ever been used.

He looked up at Detritus.

"Did you know that was going to happen?" he said.

"No," said the troll. "But I fink Mr. Shine did."

"He's given me his address, Sergeant."

"Yeah. So maybe he want you to visit," Detritus conceded. "Dat is a honor, all right. You don't find Mr. Shine, Mr. Shine find you."

"How did he find *you*, Mr. Brick?" said Vimes.

Brick gave Detritus a panicky look. The sergeant shrugged.

"He pick me up one day. Gimme food," Brick mumbled. "He show me where to come for more. He tole me t'keep off'f the stuff, too. But . . ."

"Yes . . . ?" Vimes prompted.

Brick waved a pair of scarred, knobbly arms in a gesture that said, far more coherently than *he* could, that there was the whole universe on one side and Brick on the other, and what could anyone do against odds like that?

And so, he'd been handed over to Detritus, Vimes thought. That evened the odds somewhat.

He stood up, and nodded to Detritus.

"Should I take anything, Sergeant?"

The troll thought about this. "No," he said, "but maybe dere's some finkin' you could leave behind."

I should be in charge of the mine raid, thought Vimes. We might be starting a war, after all, so I'm sure people would like to think that someone high up was there when it happened. So, why do I think it's more important that I see the mysterious Mr. Shine?

Captain Carrot had been busy. The city dwarfs liked him. So he'd done what Vimes could not have done, or at least have done well, which was take a muddy dwarf necklace to a dwarf home down in New Cobblers and explain to two dwarf parents how it had been found. Things had happened quite fast after that, and one other reason for the speed was that the mine was shut. Guards and workers and dwarfs seeking guidance on the path of dwarfdom had turned up, to be met with locked doors. Money was owing, and dwarfs got very *definite* about things like that. A lot of the huge body of dwarf lore was about contracts. You were supposed to get *paid*.

No more politics, Vimes told himself. Someone killed four of *our* dwarfs, not some crazy rabble-rouser, and left them down there in the dark. I don't care who they are, they're going to be dragged into the light. It's the law. All the way to the bottom, all the way to the top.

But it's going to be done by dwarfs. Dwarfs will go to that well, and dig out that mud again, and bring up the proof.

He walked into the main office. Carrot was there, along with half a dozen dwarf officers. They looked grim.

"All set?" said Vimes.

"Yes, sir. We'll meet the others at Empirical Crescent."

"You've got enough diggers?"

"All dwarfs are diggers, sir," said Carrot solemnly. "There's timber on the way, and winching gear, too. Some of the miners joining us helped dig that tunnel, sir. They knew those lads. They're a bit bewildered and angry."

"I'll bet. They believe us, then, do they?" said Vimes.

"Er . . . more or less, sir. If the bodies aren't there, though, we're going to have some explaining to do."

"Very true. Didn't your lads know *what* they were digging for?"

"No, sir. They just got orders from the dark dwarfs. And different squads dug in different directions. A long way in different directions. As far as Money Trap Lane and Ettercap Street, they think."

"That's a big slice of the city!"

"Yessir. But there was something odd."

"Do go on, Captain," said Vimes. "We're good at odd."

"Every so often everyone had to stop work, and the foreign dwarfs listened at the walls with a big, er, thing, like an ear trumpet. Sally found something like that when she was down there."

"They were listening? In soggy mud? Listening for what? Singing worms?"

"The dwarfs don't know, sir. Trapped miners, they thought. I suppose it makes sense. A lot of the digging is through old stonework, so I suppose it's possible that other miners could be trapped somewhere that's got air."

"Not to last for weeks, though, surely? And why dig in different directions?"

"It's a puzzle, sir, there's no doubt about it. But we'll get to the bottom of it soon enough. Everyone's very keen."

"Good. But play down the Watch side, will you? This is a bunch of concerned citizens trying to find their loved ones after a reported mining disaster, okay? The watchmen are just helping them out."

"You mean 'remember I'm a dwarf,' sir?"

"Thank you for that, Carrot. Yes, exactly," said Vimes. "And now I'm off to see a legend with a name like a can of polish."

As he went out, he noticed the Summoning Dark symbol. The PussyCat Club drinks menu had been put with some care on a shelf by the window, where it got maximum light. It glowed. Maybe this was because Frosted Hot Lips Rose had been designed to be seen across a crowded bar in poor light, but it seemed to float above the oh-so-funny sticky cocktail names like Just Sex, Pussy Galore, and No Brainer, making them look faded and unreal.

Someone—several ones, by the look of it—had lit candles in front of it, for when night came.

It mustn't be kept in the dark, Vimes thought. I wish I wasn't.

Pointer and Pickles was dusty. Dust was the keynote of the shop. Vimes must have passed it a thousand times; it was that kind of shop, the kind you walked past. Dust and dead flies filled the little window, which nevertheless offered dim views of large lumps of rock, covered with dust, beyond.

The bell over the door gave a dusty jangle as Vimes entered the gloomy interior. The noise died away, and there was a definite feeling that this marked the end of the entertainment for today.

Then a distant shuffling was born in the heavy silence. It turned out to belong to a very old woman who appeared, at first sight, to be as dusty as the rocks she, presumably, sold. Vimes had his doubts even about that. Shops like this one often looked upon the selling of merchandise as, in some way, a betrayal of a sacred trust. As if to underline this, she was carrying a club with a nail in it.

When she was close enough for conversation, Vimes said: "I've come here to—"

"Do you believe in the healing power of crystals, young man?" snapped the woman, raising the club threateningly.

"What? What healing power?" said Vimes.

The old woman gave him a cracked smile, and dropped the club.

"Good," she said. "We like our customers to take

their geology seriously. We've got some trollite in this week."

"Good, but, in fact, I—"

"It's the only mineral that travels backwards in time, you know."

"I'm here to see Mr. Shine," Vimes managed.

"Mr. who?" said the old woman, putting a hand to her ear.

"Mr. Shine?" said Vimes, confidence already draining out of him.

"Never heard of him, dear."

"He, er, gave me this," said Vimes, showing her the two pieces of stone egg.

"Amethyst geode, very nice specimen, I'll give you seven dollars," said the old woman.

"Are you, er, Pickles or Pointer?" said Vimes, as a last resort.

"I'm Miss Pickles, dear. Miss Point—"

She stopped. Her expression changed, became slightly younger and considerably more alert.

"And I'm Miss Pointer, dear," she said. "Don't worry about Pickles, she just runs the body when I've got other things to do. Are you Commander Vimes?"

Vimes stared. "Are you telling me you're two people? With one body?"

"Yes, dear. It's supposed to be an illness, but all I can say is we've always got along well. I've never told her about Mr. Shine. Can't be too careful. Come this way, do."

She led the way through the dusty crystals and slabs into the back of the shop, where there was a wide corridor lined with shelves. Crystals of all sizes sparkled down at him.

"Of course, trolls have always been of interest to geologists, being made of metamorphorical rock," said Miss Pointer/Miss Pickles conversationally. "You're not a rock hound yourself, Commander?"

"I've had the occasional stone thrown at me," said Vimes. "I've never bothered to check what kind it was."

"Ha. Such a shame we're on loam here," said the woman as the sound of quiet voices drew nearer. She opened a door and stood aside. "I rent them the room," she said. "Do go in."

Vimes looked at the top few treads of a flight of stairs, heading down. Oh goody, he thought. We're going underground again. But there was warm light coming up, and the voices were louder.

The cellar was large and cool. There were tables everywhere, with a couple of people at each one, bent over a checkered board. A games room? The players were dwarfs, trolls, and humans, but what they had in common was concentration. Unconcerned faces glanced toward Vimes, who had paused, halfway down the stairs, and then looked back to the game at hand.

Vimes continued down to floor level. This had to be important, right? Mr. Shine had wanted him to see it. People—men, trolls, dwarfs—playing games. Occasionally, a couple of players would look up at each other, share a glance, and shake hands. Then one of them would go off to a new table.

"What do you notice, Mister Vimes?" said a deep voice behind him. Vimes forced himself to turn slowly.

The figure sitting in the shadows beside the stairway was shrouded entirely in black. He looked a good head taller than Vimes.

"They're all young?" he ventured, and added: "Mr. Shine?"

"Exactly! More youngsters tend to come along in the evenings, too. Do take a seat, sir."

"Why have I come to see you, Mr. Shine?" said Vimes, sitting down.

"Because you want to find out why you have come to see me," said the dark figure. "Because you're wandering in the dark. Because Mister Vimes, with his badge and his truncheon, is full of rage. More full than usual. Take care of that rage, Mister Vimes."

Mystic, thought Vimes. "I like to see whom I'm talking to," he said. "What are you?"

"You would not see me if I removed this hood," said Mr. Shine. "As for *what* I am, I'll ask you this: would it be true to say that Captain Carrot, while very happy to be a Watch officer, is the rightful king of Ankh-Morpork?"

"I have trouble with the term 'rightful,'" said Vimes.

"So I understand. It may well be that this is one reason why he hasn't yet chosen to declare himself," said Mr. Shine. "But no matter. Well, I am the rightful—excuse me—and indisputable king of the trolls."

"Really?" said Vimes. It wasn't much of a reply, but his options at this point were limited.

"Yes. And when I say 'indisputable,' I mean what I say, Mister Vimes. Hidden human kings have to resort to magic swords or legendary feats to reclaim their birthright. I do not. I just have to *be*. You are aware of the concept of metamorphorical rock?"

"You mean the way trolls look like certain types of rock?"

"Indeed. Schist, Mica, Shale, and so on. Even Brick, poor young Brick. No one knows why this is, and they have expended thousands of words in saying so. Oh, to hell with it, as you would say. You deserve a glimpse. Protect your eyes. I, Mister Vimes—"

A black-robed arm was extended, a black-velvet glove removed. Vimes shut his eyes in time, but the inside of his lids blazed red.

"—am diamond," said Mr. Shine.

The glare faded a little. Vimes risked opening his eyes a bit, and made out a hand, every flexing finger sparkling like a prism. The players glanced up, but they'd seen this before.

"Frost forms quite quickly," said Mr. Shine. When Vimes dared to peek, the hand glittered like the heart of winter.

"You're hiding out from jewelers?" he managed, taken aback.

"Hah! In fact, this city is indeed a very good place for people who don't wish to be seen, Mister Vimes. I have friends here. And I have talents. You'd find me quite hard to see if I wished to be unseen. I am also, frankly, intelligent, and intelligent all the time. I don't need the Pork Futures Warehouse. I can regulate the temperature of my brain by reflecting all heat. Diamond trolls are very rare, and when we do appear, kingship is our destiny."

Vimes waited. Mr. Shine, who was now pulling

his glove back on, appeared to have an agenda. The wisest thing was to let him talk until it all made sense.

"And do you know what happens when we become kings?" said Mr. Shine, now safely shrouded once more.

"Koom Valley?" Vimes suggested.

"Well done. The trolls unite, and we have the same tired old war, followed by centuries of skirmishing. That is the sad, stupid history of the trolls and the dwarfs. And this time, Ankh-Morpork will be caught up in it. You know that the troll and dwarf population here has grown enormously under Vetinari."

"All right, but if you're king, can't you just make peace?"

"Just like that? It'll need much more than that." The hood of the robe shook sadly. "You really know very little about us, Mister Vimes. You see us down on the plains, shambling around, *talkin' like dis*. You don't know about the history chant, or the Long Dance, or stone music. You see the hunched troll dragging his club. That's what the dwarfs did for us, long ago. They turned us, in your minds, into sad, brainless monsters."

"Don't look at me when you say that," said Vimes. "Detritus is one of my best officers!"

There was silence. The Mr. Shine said: "Shall I tell you what I think the dwarfs were looking for, Mister Vimes? Something of theirs. It is a thing that talks. And they found it, and I think what it had to say directly caused five deaths. I believe I know how to find the secret of Koom Valley. In a few weeks, everyone will be able to. But by then, I think, it will be too late. You must solve it, too, before the war sweeps up all of us."

"How do you know all this?" said Vimes.

"Because I'm magical," said the voice from the hood.

"Oh, well, if that's the way you're—" Vimes began.

"Patience, Commander," said Mr. Shine. "I just . . . simplified. Accept, instead, that I am very . . . smart. I have an analytical mind. I've studied the histories and lore of my hereditary enemy. I have friends who are dwarfs. Quite knowledgeable dwarfs. Quite . . . powerful dwarfs, who wish for an end to this stupid feud as much as I do. And I have a love of games and puzzles. The *Codex* was not a terrible challenge."

"If it's going to help me find the murderers of those dwarfs in the mine then you should tell me what you know!"

"Why trust what I say? I am a troll, I'm partisan, I might wish to direct your thoughts down the wrong path."

"Maybe you've already!" said Vimes hotly. He knew he was making a fool of himself; it only made him angrier.

"Good, that's the spirit!" said Mr. Shine. "Test all that I've told you! Where would we be if Commander Vimes relied on magic, eh? No, the secret of Koom Valley must be found by observation and questioning and facts, facts, facts. Possibly I'm helping you find them a little quicker than you might otherwise do. You just have to think about what you know, Commander. And, in the meantime, shall we play a little game?"

Mr. Shine picked up a box by his chair and up-ended it over the table.

"This is Thud, Mister Vimes," he said, as little stone figures bounced over the board. "Dwarfs versus trolls. Eight trolls and thirty-two dwarfs, forever fighting their little battles on a cardboard Koom Valley." He began to place the pieces, black-gloved hands moving with un-trollish speed.

Vimes pushed back his chair. "Nice to meet you, Mr. Shine, but all you are giving me is riddles and—"

"Sit *down*, Commander." The quiet voice had a schoolteacher harmonic to it that folded Vimes's legs under him. "Good," said Mr. Shine. "Eight trolls, thirty-two dwarfs. Dwarfs always start. A dwarf is small and fast and can run as many squares as possible in any direction. A troll—because we're stupid and drag our clubs, as everyone knows—can only move *one* square in any direction. There are other types of moving, but what do you see so far?"

Vimes tried to concentrate. It was hard. This was a game, it wasn't *real*. Besides, the answer was so obvious that it couldn't be the right one.

"It *looks* like the dwarfs must win every time," he ventured.

"Ah, natural suspicion, I *like* that. In fact, among the best players, the bias is slightly in favor of the trolls," said Mr. Shine. "This is largely because a troll can, in the right circumstances, do a *lot* of damage. How are your ribs, by the way?"

"All the better for you asking," said Vimes sourly. He'd forgotten them for twenty blessed minutes; now they ached again.

"Good. I'm glad Brick has found Detritus. He has

a good brain if he can be persuaded to stop frying it every half an hour. Back to our game . . . advantages to either side do not matter, in fact, because a complete game consists of *two* battles. In one, you must play the dwarfs. In the other, you must play the trolls. As you may expect, dwarfs find it easy to play the dwarf side, which needs a strategy and mode of attack that comes easy to a dwarf. Something similar applies to the trolls. But to *win*, you must play both sides. You must, in fact, be able to think like your ancient enemy. A really skilled player—well, take a look, Commander. Look toward the back of the room, where my friend Phyllite is playing against Nils Mousehammer."

Vimes turned.

"What am I looking for?" he said.

"Whatever you see."

"Well, that troll over there is wearing what looks like a large dwarf helmet . . ."

"Yes, one of the dwarf players made it for him. And he speaks quite passable dwarfish."

"He's drinking out of a horn, like the dwarfs do . . ."

"He had to have one made in metal! Troll beer would melt ordinary horn. Nils can sing quite a lot of the troll history chant. Look at Gabbro, over there. Good troll boy, but he knows all there is to know about dwarf battle bread. In fact, I believe that's a boomerang croissant on the table next to him. Purely for ceremonial purposes, of course. Commander?"

"Hmm?" said Vimes, turning his head. "What?" A slightly built dwarf at one of the tables was watching him with interest, as though he was some kind of fascinating monster.

Mr. Shine chuckled. "To study the enemy, you have to get under his skin. When you're under his skin, you start to see the world through his eyes. Gabbro is so good at playing from the dwarf viewpoint that his troll game is suffering, and he wants to go to Copperhead to learn from some of the dwarf thudmeisters there. I hope he does; they'll teach him how to play like a troll. None of these lads here were out getting fighting drunk last night. And thus we wear down mountains. Water dripping on a stone, dissolving and removing. Changing the shape of the world, one drop at a time. Water dripping on a stone, Commander. Water flowing underground, bubbling up in unexpected places."

"I think you're going to need a bit more of a gush," said Vimes. "I don't think a bunch of people playing games is going to break down a mountain anytime soon."

"It depends on where the drops fall," said Mr. Shine. "In time, they may wash away a valley, at least. You should ask yourself: why was I so keen to get into that mine?"

"Because there had been a murder!"

"And that was the only reason?" said the shrouded Mr. Shine.

"Of course!"

"And everyone knows what gossips dwarfs are," said Mr. Shine. "Well, I am sure you will do your best, Commander. I hope you find the murderer before the Dark catches up with them."

"Mr. Shine, some of my officers have lit candles around that damn symbol!"

"Good thinking, I'd say."

"So you really believe that it's some kind of a threat? How come you know so much about dwarf signs, anyway?"

"I have studied them. I accept the fact of their existence. Some of your officers believe. Most dwarfs do, somewhere in their gnarly little souls. I respect that. You can take a dwarf out of the Dark, but you can't take the Dark out of a dwarf. Those symbols are very old. They have real power. Who knows what old evil lurks in the deep darkness under the mountains? There's no darkness like it."

"You can take the mickey out of a copper, too," said Vimes.

"Ah, Mister Vimes, you have had a busy day. So much happening, so little time to think. Take time to reflect on all you know, sir. I am a reflecting kind of person."

"Commander Vimes?" The voice came from Miss Pointer/Miss Pickles, halfway up the stairs. "There is a big troll asking after you."

"What a shame," said Mr. Shine. "That will be Sergeant Detritus. Not good news, I suspect. If I had to guess, I'd say that the trolls have sent around the *taka-taka*. You must go, Mister Vimes. I'll be seeing you again."

"I don't think I'll see you," said Vimes. He stood up, and then hesitated.

"One question, right? And no funny answers, if you don't mind," he said. "Tell me why you helped

Brick. Why should you care about a slushed-out gutter troll?"

"Why should you care about some dead dwarfs?" said Mr. Shine.

"Because someone has to!"

"Exactly! Good-bye, Mr. Vimes."

Vimes hurried up the stairs and followed Miss Pointer/Miss Pickles out into the shop. Detritus was standing among the mineral specimens, looking uncomfortable, like a man in a morgue.

"What's happening?" said Vimes.

Detritus shifted uneasily.

"Sorry, Mister Vimes, but I was der only one dat knew where—" he began.

"Yes, okay. Is this about the *taka-taka*?"

"How did you know about dat, sir?"

"I don't. What *is* the *taka-taka*?"

"It der famous war club of der trolls," said Detritus. Vimes, with the image of the peace club of the trolls downstairs still in his mind, couldn't stop himself.

"You mean you subscribe and get a different war every month?" he said. But that sort of thing was wasted on Detritus. He treated humor as some human aberration that had to be overcome by talking slowly and patiently.

"No, sir. When der *taka-taka* is sent around the clans, it a summoning to war," he said.

"Oh damn. Koom Valley?"

"Yes, sir. An' I'm hearing dat der Low King and der Uberwald dwarfs is already on der way to Koom Valley, too. Der street is full of it."

"Er . . . bingle bingle bingle . . . ?" said a small and very nervous voice.

Vimes pulled out the Gooseberry and stared at it. At a time like this . . .

"Well?" he said.

"It's twenty-nine minutes past five, Insert Name Here," said the imp nervously.

"So?"

"On foot, at this time of day, you will need to leave now to be home at six o'clock," said the imp.

"Der Patrician want to see you and dere's clackses arrivin' and everythin'," said Detritus insistently.

Vimes continued to stare at the imp, which looked embarrassed.

"I'm going home," he said, and started walking. Dark clouds were rolling in overhead, heralding another summer storm.

"Dey've foun' der three dwarfs near der well, sir," said Detritus, lumbering after him. "Looks like it was other dwarfs what killed 'em, sure enough. The ol' grags have gone. Captain Carrot's put guards on every exit he can find . . ."

But they dig, Vimes thought. Who knows where all the tunnels go?

". . . and he wants permission to break open der big iron doors in Treacle Street," Detritus went on. "Dey can get at the last dwarf dat way."

"What are the dwarfs saying about it?" said Vimes, over his shoulder. "The living ones, I mean?"

"A lot of dem saw the dead dwarfs brought up," said Detritus. "I fink most of dem would hand him der crowbar."

Let's hear it for the mob, Vimes thought. Grab it

by its sentimental heart. Besides, the storm is beginning. Why worry about an extra raindrop?

"Okay," he said. "Tell him this. I *know* Otto will be there with his damn picture box, so when that door is wrenched open, it's going to be dwarfs doing it, okay? A picture full of dwarfs?"

"Right, sir!"

"How is young Brick? Will he swear a statement? Does he *understand* about that?"

"I reckon he could, sir."

"In front of dwarfs?"

"He will if I ask him, sir," said Detritus. "Dat I can promise."

"Good. And get someone to put out a message on the clacks, to every city watch and village constable between here and the mountains. Tell them to look out for a party of dark dwarfs. They've got what they came for and they're doing a runner, I know it."

"You want they should try to stop 'em?" the sergeant asked.

"No! No one should try it! Say they've got weapons that shoot fire! Just let me know where they're headed!"

"I'll tell dem dat, sir."

And I'm going home, Vimes repeated to himself. Everyone wants something from Vimes, even though I'm not the sharpest knife in the drawer. Hell, I'm probably a spoon. Well, I'm going to be Vimes, and Vimes reads *Where's My Cow?* to Young Sam at six o'clock. With the noises done right.

He went home at a brisk walk, using all the little shortcuts, his mind sloshing backwards and forwards like thin soup, his ribs nudging him occasionally to say yes, they were still here and twinging. He arrived at the door just as Willikins was opening it.

"I shall tell her ladyship you are back, sir," he called out as Vimes hurried up the stairs. "She is mucking out the dragon pens."

Young Sam was standing up in his cot, watching the door. Vimes's day went soft and pink.

The chair was littered with the favored toys of the hour—a rag ball, a little hoop, a wooly snake with one button eye. Vimes pushed them onto the rug, sat down, and took off his helmet. Then he took off his damp boots. You didn't need to heat a room after Sam Vimes had taken his boots off. On the wall, the nursery clock ticked, and with every tick and tock a little sheep jumped back and forth over a fence.

Sam unfolded the rather chewed, rather soggy book.

"Where's my cow?" he announced, and Young Sam chuckled. Rain rattled on the window.

> *Where's my cow?*
> *Is that my cow?*

. . . A "thing" that talks, he thought as his mouth and eyes took over the task at hand. I'm going to have to find out about that. Why'd it make dwarfs want to kill one another?

> *It goes baa!*
> *It is a sheep!*

. . . Why did we go into that mine? Because we heard there'd been a murder, that's why!

No, that's not my cow!

. . . Everyone knows that dwarfs gossip. It was stupid to tell them to keep it from us!

That's the deep-downers for you, they think they just have to say a thing and it's true!

Where's my cow?

. . . Water dripping on a stone.

Is that my cow?

Where did I see one of those Thud boards recently?

It goes naaaay!

Oh, yes, Helmclever. He was very worried, wasn't he?

It is a horse!

He had a board. He said he was a keen player.

No, that's not my cow!

That was a dwarf under pressure if ever I saw one; he looked as if he was dying to tell me something . . .

Where's my cow?

That look in his eyes . . .

Is that my cow?

I was so *angry*. Don't tell the Watch? What did they expect? You'd have thought he would have known . . .

It goes HRUUUGH!

He *knew* I'd go postal!

It is a hippopotamus!

He wanted me to be angry!

No, that's not my cow!

He damn well *wanted* me to be angry!

Vimes snorted and crowed his way through the rest of the zoo, missing out not one bark or squeak, and tucked up his son with a kiss.

There was the sound of tinkling glass from downstairs. Oh, someone's dropped a glass, said his front brain. But his back brain, which had steered him safely through these mean streets for more than fifty years, whispered: Like hell they did!

Purity would be up in her room. Cook had the evening off. Sybil was out feeding the dragons. That left Willikins. Butlers didn't drop things.

From below, there was a quiet "ugh," and then the thud of something hitting meat.

And Vimes's sword was on the hook at the other end of the hall, because Sybil didn't like him wearing it in the house.

As quietly as possible, he sought around for something, anything, that could be turned into a weapon. Regrettably, they had, when choosing toys for Young Sam, completely neglected the whole area of hard things with sharp edges. Bunnies, chickies, and piggies there were in plenty, but—ah! Vimes spotted something that would do, and wrenched it free.

Moving soundlessly on thick, over-darned socks, he crept down the stairs.

The door to the wine cellar was open. Vimes didn't drink these days, but guests did, and Willikins, in accordance with some butlerian duty to generations only just or as yet unborn, cared for it and bought the occasional promising vintage. Was there the crackle of glass being trodden on? Okay, did the stairs creak? He'd find out.

He reached the vaulted, damp cellar, and stepped carefully out of the light filtering down from the hall.

Now he could smell it . . . the faint reek of black oil.

The little bastards! And they could see in the dark, too, right?

He reached into his pocket and fumbled for his matches, while his heart thudded in his ears. His fingers closed over a match, he took a deep breath—

One hand grasped his wrist, and, as he swung madly at the darkness with the hind leg of a rocking horse, this, too, was wrested from him. Instinctively, he kicked out, and there was a grunt. His arms were released, and from somewhere near the floor, the voice of Willikins, rather strained, said: "Excuse me, sir, I appear to have walked into your foot."

"Willikins? What the hell's been happening?"

"Some dwarfish gentlemen called while you were upstairs, sir," said the butler, unfolding slowly. "Through the cellar wall, in fact. I regret to say that I found it necessary to deal somewhat strictly with them. I fear one might be dead."

Vimes peered around. "*Might* be dead? Is he still breathing?"

"I do not know, sir." Willikins applied a match, with great care, to a stub of candle. "I heard him gurgling, but he appears to have stopped. I'm sorry to say that they came upon me when I was leaving the ice store, and I was forced to defend myself with the first thing that came to hand."

"Which was . . . ?"

"The ice knife, sir," said Willikins levelly. He held up eighteen inches of sharp, serrated steel, designed to slice ice into convenient blocks. "The other gentleman I have lodged on a meat hook, sir."

"You didn't—" Vimes began, horrified.

"Only through his clothing, sir. I am sorry to have laid hands on you, but I feared the wretched oil might have been inflammable. I hope I got all of them. I would like to take this opportunity to apologize for the mess—"

But Vimes was gone and already halfway up the cellar steps. In the hall, his heart stopped.

A short dark figure was at the top of the stairs and disappearing into the nursery.

The broad, stately staircase soared in front of him, a stairway to the top of the sky. He ran up it, hearing himself screaming—

"I'll kill I'll killyoukillyoukillyoukillkillkill I'll kill you kill I'llkill you—" The terrible fury choked him, the rage and dreadful fear set his lungs on fire, and

still the stairs unrolled. There was no end to them. They climbed forever, while he was falling backwards, into hell. But hell buoyed him up, gave wings to his rage, lifted him, sent him back . . .

And then, his breath now nothing more than one long, profane scream, he reached the top step—

The dwarf came out of the nursery doorway, backwards and fast. He hit the railings and crashed through them onto the floor below. Vimes ran on, sliding on the polished wood, skidding as he swung into the nursery, dreading the sight of—

—Young Sam, sleeping peacefully. On the wall, the little lamb rocked the night away.

Sam Vimes picked up his son, wrapped in his blue blanket, and sagged to his knees. He hadn't drawn breath all the way up the stairs, and now his body cashed its checks, sucking in air and redemption in huge, racking sobs. Tears boiled out of him, shaking him wretchedly . . .

Through the running, wet blur, he saw something on the floor. There, on the rug, was the rag ball, the hoop, and the wooly snake, lying where they'd fallen.

The ball had rolled, more or less, into the middle of the hoop. The snake lay half-uncoiled, its head resting on the edge of the circle.

Together, in this weak nursery light, they looked at first glance like a big eye with a tail.

"Sir? Is everything all right?"

Vimes looked up and focused on the red face of Willikins, out of breath.

"Er . . . yeah . . . what? . . . yeah . . . fine . . . thanks," he managed, summoning his scattered senses. "Fine, Willikins. Thank you."

"One must've got past me in the dark—"

"Huh? Yeah, very remiss of you, then," said Vimes, getting to his feet but still clutching his son to him. "I'd just *bet* most butlers 'round here would have taken out all three with one swipe of their polishing cloth, right?"

"Are you all right, sir? Because—"

"But *you* went to the Shamlegger School of Butlering!" Vimes giggled. His knees were trembling. Part of him knew what this was all about. After the terror came that drunken feeling, when you were still alive and suddenly everything was funny. "I *mean*, other butlers just know how to cut people dead with a look, but *you*, Willikins, you know how to cut them dead with—"

"Listen, sir! He's got outside, sir!" said Willikins urgently. "So is Lady Sybil!"

Vimes's grin froze.

"Shall I take the young man, sir?" Willikins said, reaching.

Vimes backed away. A troll with a crowbar and a tub of grease would not have wrested his son from him.

"No! But give me that knife! And go and make sure Purity is all right!"

Clutching Young Sam to him, he ran back downstairs, across the hall, and out into the garden. It was stupid, stupid, stupid. He told himself that later. But right now Sam Vimes was thinking only in primary colors. It had been hard, hard, to go into the nursery in the face of the images that thronged his imagination. He was not going to go through that ever again. And the rage flowed back, easily, under control now. Smooth like a river of fire. He'd find them all, all of them, and they would *burn* . . .

The main dragon shed could only be reached now by dodging around three big cast-iron flame-deflector shields, put in place two months ago; dragon breeding was not a hobby for sissies or people who minded having to repaint the whole side of the house occasionally. There were big iron doors at either end; Vimes headed toward one at random, ran into the dragon shed, and bolted the door behind him.

It was always warm in there, because the dragons burped all the time; it was that or explode, which occasionally did happen. And there was Sybil, in full dragon-keeping gear, walking calmly between the pens with a bucket in each hand, and behind her the doors at the other end were opening, and there was a short, dark figure, and there was a rod with a little pilot flame on the end, and—

"Look out! Behind you!" Vimes yelled.

His wife stared at him, turned around, dropped the buckets, and started to shout something.

And then the flame blossomed. It hit Sybil in the chest, splashed across the pens, and went out abruptly. The dwarf looked down and began to thump the pipe desperately.

The pillar of flame that was Lady Sybil said, in an authoritative voice that brooked no disobeying:

"Lie down, Sam. Right now." And Sybil dropped to the sandy floor as, all down the lines of pens, dragon heads rose on long dragon necks.

Their nostrils were flaring. They were breathing in.

They'd been challenged. They'd been offended. And they'd just had their supper.

"*Good* boys," said Sybil, from the floor.

Twenty-six streams of answering dragon fire rose to the occasion. Vimes, lying on the floor so that his body shielded Young Sam, felt the hairs crisp on the back of his neck.

This wasn't the smoky red of the dwarf fire; this was something only a dragon's stomach could cook up. The flames were practically invisible. At least one of them must have hit the dwarf's weapon, because there was an explosion and something went through the roof. The dragon pens were built like a fireworks factory: the walls were very thick, and the roof was as thin as possible, to provide a faster exit to heaven.

When the noise had died to an excited hiccuping, Vimes risked looking up. Sybil was also getting to her feet, a little clumsily, because of all the special clothing every dragon breeder wore.*

The iron of the far doors glowed around the black outline of a dwarf. A little way in front of them, two iron boots were cooling from white heat in a puddle of molten sand.

Metal went *plink*.

Lady Sybil reached up with heavy-gloved hands, patted out some patches of burning oil on her leather apron, and lifted off her helmet. It landed on the sand with a thud.

"Oh, Sam . . ." she said softly.

"Are you all right? Young Sam is fine. We've got to get out of here!"

---

*That is to say, every dragon breeder not currently occupying a small artistic urn.

"Oh, Sam . . ."

"Sybil, I need you to take him!" Vimes said, speaking slowly and clearly to get through the shock. "There could be others out there!"

Lady Sybil's eyes focused.

"Give him to me," she ordered. "And *you* take Raja!"

Vimes looked where she was indicating. A young dragon with floppy ears and an expression of mildly concussed good humor blinked at him. He was a Golden Wouter, a breed with a flame so strong that one of them had once been used by thieves to melt their way into a bank vault.

Vimes picked him up carefully, and still winced. Ye gods, the ache in his hand had gone all the way to the elbow . . .

"Coal him up," Sybil commanded.

Good old Sybil, he told himself as he fed anthracite into Raja's eager gullet. Her female forebears had valiantly backed up their husbands as distant embassies were besieged, had given birth on a camel back or in the shade of a stricken elephant, had handed around little gold-wrapped chocolates while trolls were trying to break into the compound, or had merely stayed at home and nursed such bits of husbands and sons that made it back from endless little wars. The result was a species of woman who, when duty called, turned into solid steel.

Vimes flinched as Raja burped.

"That was a dwarf, wasn't it?" said Sybil, cradling Young Sam. "One of those deep-down ones you see about?"

"Yes."

"Why did it try to kill me?"

When people are trying to kill you, it means you're doing something right. It was a rule Sam had lived by. But this . . . even a real stone killer like Chrysophrase wouldn't have tried something like this. It was insane. *They will burn. They will burn . . .*

"I think they're frightened of what I'm going to find out," said Vimes. "I think it's all gone wrong for them, and they want to stop me."

Could they have been that stupid? he wondered. A dead wife? A dead child? Could they think that would mean *for one moment* that I'd stop? As it is, when I catch up with whoever ordered this, *and I will*, I hope there's someone there to hold me back.

They will burn for what they did.

"Oh, Sam . . ." murmured Sybil, the iron mask falling for a moment.

"I'm sorry. I never expected this," said Vimes. He put the dragon down and held her carefully, almost fearfully. The rage had been so strong; he felt he might grow spikes, or snap into shards. And the headache was coming back, like a lump of lead nailed just over his eyes.

"Whatever happened to all that, you know, hi-ho, hi-ho, and being kind to poor lost orphans in the forest, Sam?" Sybil whispered.

"Willikins is in the house," he said. "Purity is as well."

"Let's go and find them, then," said Sybil. She grinned, a little damply. "I wish you wouldn't bring your work home with you, Sam."

"This time it followed me," said Vimes grimly. "But I intend to tidy it up, believe me."

They shall bur— no! They shall be hunted down to any hole they hide in and brought back to face justice. Unless (oh please!) they resist arrest . . .

Purity was standing in the hall, alongside Willikins. She was holding a trophy Klatchian sword, without much conviction. The butler had augmented his weaponry with a couple of meat cleavers, which he hefted with a certain worrying expertise.

"My gods, man, you're covered in blood!" Sybil burst out.

"Yes, Your Ladyship," said Willikins smoothly. "May I say in mitigation that it is not, in fact, mine."

"There was a dwarf in the dragon house," said Vimes. "Any sign of any others?"

"No, sir. The ones in the cellar had an apparatus for projecting fire, sir."

"The dwarf we saw had one too," said Vimes, adding: "It didn't do him any good."

"Indeed, sir? I apprised myself of its use, sir, and tested my understanding by firing it down the tunnel they had arrived by until it ran out of igniferous juice, sir. Just in case there were more. It is for this reason, I suspect, that the shrubbery at Number Five is on fire."

Vimes hadn't met Willikins when they were both young. The Cockbill Street Roaring Lads had a treaty with Shamlegger Street, thus allowing them to ignore that flank while they concentrated on stopping the territorial aggression of the Pigsty Hill Dead Marmoset Gang. He was *glad* he hadn't fetched up against young Willikins.

"They must have come up for air there," he said. "The Jeffersons are on holiday."

"Well, if they're not ready for that sort of thing, they shouldn't be growing rhododendrons," said Sybil matter-of-factly. "What now, Sam?"

"We're staying the night at Pseudopolis Yard," said Vimes. "Don't argue."

"Ramkins have never run away from *anything*," Sybil declared.

"Vimeses have run like hell all the time," said Vimes, too diplomatic to mention the aforesaid ancestors who came home in pieces. "That means you fight where *you* want to fight. We're all going to go and get the coach, and we're all going down to the Yard. When we're there, I'll send people back to pick up our stuff. Just for one night, all right?"

"What would you like me to do with the visitors, sir?" said Willikins, with a sidelong glance at Lady Sybil. "One is indeed dead, I am afraid. If you recall, I must have stabbed him with the ice knife I happened to be innocently holding, having been cutting ice for the kitchen," he added, poker-faced.

"Put him on the roof of the coach," said Vimes.

"The other one also appears to be dead, sir. I'd swear he was fine when I tied him up, sir, because he was cursing me in their lingo."

"You didn't tie him up too hard, did—" Vimes began, and gave up on it. If Willikins wanted someone dead, he wouldn't have taken a prisoner. It must have been a surprise, breaking into a cellar and meeting something like Willikins. Anyway, to hell with them.

"Just . . . died?" he said.

"Yes, sir. Do dwarfs naturally salivate green?"

"What?"

"There is green around his mouth, sir. Could be a clue, in my opinion."

"All right, put him on the roof of the coach, too. Let's go, shall we?"

Vimes had to insist that Sybil traveled on the inside. Usually, she got her own way and he was happy to give it to her, but the unspoken agreement was that when he *really* insisted, she listened. It's a married couple thing.

Vimes rode beside Willikins, and got him to stop halfway down the hill where a man was selling the evening edition of the *Times*, still damp from the press.

The picture on the front page was of a mob of dwarfs. They were pulling open one of the mine's big, round metal doors; it was hanging off its hinges. In the middle of the group, hands gripping the edge of the frame and muscles bulging, was Captain Carrot. Gleaming, with his shirt off.

Vimes grunted happily, folded up the paper, and lit a cheroot. The shaking in his legs was barely noticeable now, the fires of that terrible rage banked but still glowing.

"A Free Press, Willikins. You just can't beat it," he said.

"I've often heard you remark as much, sir," said Willikins.

The entity slithered through the rainy streets. Confounded again! It was getting through, it knew it! It was being

heard! And yet every time it tried to follow the words, it was thrown back. Bars had blocked its way, doors that had been open locked themselves as it approached. And what was this? Some kind of low-class soldier! By now it would have had berserkers biting their shields in half!

That was not the main problem, though. It was being watched. And that had never *happened before.*

There was a crowd of dwarfs milling around outside the Yard. They did not look belligerent—that is to say, any more than a species the members of which, by custom and practice, wear a big heavy helmet, mail, iron boots, and carry an axe all the time can fail to look belligerent—but they did look lost and bewildered and unsure why they were there.

Vimes got Willikins to drive in through the coach arch and take the bodies of the attackers down to Igor, who knew about things like people dying with green mouths.

Sybil, Purity, and Young Sam were hustled away to a clean office. Interesting thing, Vimes thought as he watched Cheery and a group of dwarf officers fuss over the child: even now—in fact, especially now, given the way the tension had made everyone revert to old certainties—he wasn't sure how many female dwarf officers he had. It was a brave female dwarf who advertised the fact, in a society where the wearing of even a decent, floor-length leather-and-chain-mail dress instead of leggings positioned you on the moral map at the far side of Tawneee and her hardworking coworkers at the PussyCat Club. But introduce a gurgling kid into the room, and you could spot them instantly, for all their fearsome clang and beards you could lose a rat in.

Carrot pushed his way through the crowd and saluted.

"A lot's been happening, sir!"

"My word, has it?" said Vimes, with manic brightness.

"Yessir. Everyone was pretty . . . angry when we brought the dead dwarfs up, and what with one thing and another, opening the big door in Treacle Street was pretty popular. All the deep-downers have gone, except one—"

"That'd be Helmclever," said Vimes, heading for his office.

Carrot looked surprised. "That's right, sir. He's in a cell. I'd like you to have a look at him, if you don't mind. He was crying and moaning and trembling in a corner, with lit candles all 'round him."

"More candles? Afraid of the dark?" Vimes suggested.

"Could be, sir. Igor says the trouble's in his head."

"Don't let Igor try to give him a new one!" said Vimes quickly. "I'll go down there as soon as I can."

"I've tried talking to him, but he just looks blank, sir. How did you know he was the one we found?"

"I've got some edges and some bits that are an interesting shape," said Vimes, sitting down at his desk. When Carrot looked blank, he went on: "Of the jigsaw puzzle, Captain. But there are lots of bits of sky. However, I think I might be nearly there, because I think I've been handed a corner. What talks underground?"

"Sir?"

"You know, the dwarfs were listening for something underground? You wondered if someone was trapped, right? But is there . . . I don't know . . . something dwarf-made that talks?"

Carrot's brow wrinkled.

"You're not talking about a *cube*, are you, sir?"

"I don't know. Am I? You tell me!"

"The deep-downers have some in their mine, sir, but I'm sure there's none buried here. They're generally found in hard rocks. Anyway, you wouldn't listen for one. I've never heard of them talking when they are found. Some dwarfs have spent years learning how to use just one of them!"

"Good! Now: What Is A Cube?" said Vimes, glancing at his in-tray. Oh, good. There weren't any memos from A. E. Pessimal.

"It's, um . . . it's like a book, sir. Which talks. A bit like your Gooseberry, I suppose. Most of them contain interpretations of dwarf lore by ancient lawmasters. It's very old . . . magic, I suppose."

"Suppose?" said Vimes.

"Well, technomantic Devices look like things that are *built*, you know, out of—"

"Captain, you've lost me again. What are Devices and why do you pronounce the capital *D*?"

"Cubes are a type of Device, sir. No one knows who made them or for what original purpose. They might be older than the world. They've been found in volcanoes and the deepest rocks. The deep-downers have most of them. They come in all sorts of—"

"Hold on, you mean that when they're dug up, there's dwarf voices from millions of years ago? Surely dwarfs haven't been—"

"No, sir. Dwarfs put them on later. I'm not too well up on this. I think when they're first found, they mostly have natural noises, like moving water or birdsong or rocks moving, that sort of thing. The grags found out how to get rid of those to make room for words, I think. I did hear about one that was the sounds of a forest. Ten million years of sounds, in a cube less than two inches across."

"And they're valuable, these things?"

"Unbelievably valuable, especially the cubes. Worth mining through a mountain of granite, as we say . . . er, that's a dwarf 'we,' not a copper 'we,' sir."

"So, digging through a few thousand of tons of Ankh-Morpork muck would be worth it, then?"

"For a cube? Yes! Is that what all this is about? But how would it get here? The average dwarf might never see one in his whole life. Only grags and great chieftains use them! And why would it be talking? All dwarf ones can only be brought to life by a key word!"

"Search me. What do they look like? Apart from being cubical, I assume?"

"I've only ever seen a few, sir. They're, oh, up to six inches on a side, look like old bronze, and they glitter."

"Green and blue?" said Vimes sharply.

"Yes, sir! They had a few in the mine in Treacle Street."

"I think I saw them," said Vimes. "And I think they've got one more. Voices from the past, eh? How come I've never heard of them before?"

Carrot hesitated. "You're a very busy man, sir. You can't know everything."

Vimes detected just a soupçon of a smidgen of a reproach there.

"Are you saying I'm a man of narrow horizons, Captain?"

"Oh no, sir. You're interested in *every* aspect of police work and criminology."

Sometimes it was impossible to read Captain Carrot's face. Vimes didn't bother to try.

"I'm missing something," he said. "But this is about Koom Valley, I know it. Look, what *is* the secret of Koom Valley?"

"I don't know, sir. I don't think there is one. I suppose the big secret would be which side attacked first. You know, sir, both sides say they were ambushed by the other side."

"Does that sound very *interesting* to you?" said Vimes. "Would it matter much now?"

"Who started it all? I should say so, sir!" said Carrot.

"But I thought they'd been scrapping since time began?"

"Yes. But Koom Valley was the first *official* one, sir."

"Who won?" said Vimes.

"Sir?"

"It's not a difficult question, is it? Who won the first Battle of Koom Valley?"

"I suppose you could say it was rained off, sir," said Carrot.

"They stopped a grudge match like that because of a bit of rain?"

"For a *lot* of rain, sir. A thunderstorm just sat there in the mountains above it. There were flash floods, full of boulders. The fighters were knocked off their feet and washed away, some were struck by lightning—"

"It quite ruined the whole day," said Vimes. "All right, Captain, do we have any idea where the bastards have gone?"

"They had an escape tunnel—"

"I bet they did!"

"—and collapsed it after them. I've got men digging—"

"Stand them down. They could be in a safe house, they could have got out in a cart, hell, they could all be wearing helmets and chain mail and passing for city dwarfs. Enough of that. We've been running people ragged. Let them go for now. I think we'll be able to find them again."

"Yes, sir. The grags left so fast, sir, that they left some other Devices. I have secured them for the city. They must have been very frightened. They just took the cubes and ran. Are you all right, sir? You look a bit flustered."

"Actually, Captain, I feel inexplicably cheerful. Would you like to hear how *my* day went?"

The showers in the Watch house were the talk of the city. Vimes had paid for them himself, after Vetinari made an acidic comment about the cost. They were a bit primitive and were really no more than watering-can heads connected to a couple of water tanks on the next floor, but after a night in Ankh-Morpork's underworld, the thought of being really clean was very attractive. Even so, Angua hesitated.

"This is *wonderful*," said Sally, turning gently under a spray. "What's wrong?"

"Look, I'm just dealing with it, all right?" snapped Angua, standing just beyond the spray. "It's full moon, okay? The wolf is a bit strong."

Sally stopped scrubbing.

"Oh, I *see*," she said. "Is it the whole B.A.T.H. thing?"

"You just *had* to say that, didn't you," said Angua, and forced herself to step onto the tiles.

"Well, what do you do normally?" said Sally, handing her the soap.

"Cold water, and pretend it's rain. Don't you dare laugh! Change of subject, right now!"

"All right. What did you think of Nobby's girl-friend?" said Sally.

"Tawneee? Friendly. Good-looking . . ."

"Try perfect physical beauty? Astonishing pro-portions? A walking classic?"

"Well . . . yes. Pretty much," Angua conceded.

"And all that is Nobby Nobbs's *girlfriend*?"

"She seems to think so."

"You're not telling me she *deserves* Nobby?" said Sally.

"Look, Verity Pushpram doesn't deserve Nobby, and she's got a weird squint, arms like a stevedore, and cooks shellfish for a living," said Angua. "That's how things are."

"Is she his old girlfriend?"

"He used to say so. As far as I know, the physical side of the relationship consisted of her hitting him with a wet fish whenever he went near her."

Angua squeezed the last of the slime out of her hair. It was tough stuff to loose. As it was, some of it was fighting not to go down the plug hole.

That was enough. She didn't like to spend too much time in the S.H.O.W.E.R. Another six or so sessions, and the smell would have quite gone away. The important thing now was to remember to use a towel and not to shake herself dry.

"You think I went down there to impress Captain Carrot, don't you," said Sally, behind her.

Angua stopped, her head wrapped in toweling. Oh well, it was going to happen sooner or later . . .

"No," she said.

"Your heartbeat says otherwise," Sally said meekly. "Don't worry. I wouldn't have a chance. His heart beats faster every time he looks at you, and yours skips a beat every time you see him."

Okay, then, this is it, said the wolf who was never far away, this is where we sort it out, claw against fang . . . *No!* Don't listen to the wolf! But it would help, wouldn't it, if this stupid bitch stopped listening to the bat . . .

"Stay out of people's hearts," she growled.

"I can't. You can't switch off your nose, can you? Can you?"

The moment of the wolf had passed. Angua relaxed a little. His heart beat faster, did it?

"No," she said. "I can't."

"Has he ever seen you without your uniform?"

Ye gods, thought Angua, and headed for her clothes.

"Well . . . of course . . ." she mumbled.

"I meant wearing something else. Like— a dress?" Sally went on. "Come *on*. Every copper spends *some* time out of uniform. That's how you *know* you're off duty."

"But it's pretty much a 24/8 job for us," said Angua. "There's always—"

"You mean it is for him, because he likes it that way, and so you go along with it?" said the vampire, and that one got through all Angua's defenses.

"It's my life! Why should I listen to advice from a vampire?"

"Because you're a werewolf," said Sally. "Only a vampire would dare to give it, right? You don't have to be at his heel all the time."

"Look, I've been through all this, understand? It's a werewolf thing. We are what we are!"

"I'm not. You don't get the black ribbon just for signing the pledge, you know. And it doesn't mean you stop craving blood. You just don't do anything about it. At least you can go out at night and chase chickens."

There was a stony silence. Then Angua said: "You know about the chickens?"

"Yes."

"I pay for them, you know."

"I'm sure you do."

"And it's not as though it's every night."

"I'm sure it isn't. Look, do you know there are people out there who will *volunteer* to be a vampire's . . . dinner companion? Providing it's all done with style? And *we* are considered weird?" She sniffed. "By the way, what did you wash your hair in?"

"Willard Brothers 'Good Girl!' Flea Shampoo," said Angua. "It brings out the gloss," she added defensively. "Look, I want to get this clear, right? Just because we spent hours wading around under the city, and, okay, maybe saved each other's lives once or twice, it does not mean we're friends, okay? We just happened to . . . be there at the same time!"

"You *do* need some time off," said Sally. "I was going to buy a drink for Tawneee anyway, to say thanks, and Cheery wants to tag along. How about it? We've been stood down for now. Time out for a little fun?"

Angua struggled with a seething snake's nest of emotions. Tawneee *had* been very kind, and far more helpful than you might expect from someone wearing six inches of heel and four square inches of clothing.

"Come *on*," said Sally encouragingly. "I don't know about you, but it's going to take a bit of effort to get the taste of that mud out of my mouth."

"Oh, all *right*! But this *doesn't* mean we're bonding!"

"Fine. Fine."

"I'm not a bondage kind of person," Angua added.

"Yes, yes," said Sally. "I can see that."

Vimes sat and stared at his notebook. He'd got "talking cube" written down and circled.

Out of the corner of his ear, he could hear the

sounds of the City Watch rising from below: the bustle in the yard of the Old Lemonade Factory, where the Specials were assembling again, just in case; the rattle of the hurry-up wagon; the general murmur of voices coming up through the floor . . .

After some thinking, he wrote "old well" and circled that, too.

He'd scrumped plums in the gardens of Empirical Crescent with all the other kids. Half the houses were empty, and no one cared much. Yes, there had been a well, but it had long been full up to the top with garbage, even then. Grass was growing on the top. They only found the bricks because they looked for them.

So, let's say that anything buried right at the bottom, where the dwarfs had headed, had been dumped, oh, more than fifty, sixty years ago . . .

You seldom saw a dwarf in Ankh-Morpork even forty years ago, and they weren't anything like rich or powerful enough to own a cube. They were hard workers, seeking—just possibly—a better life. So, what *human* would throw away a talking box worth a mountain of gold? He'd have to be bloody mad—

Vimes sat rigidly, staring at the scrawls on the page. In the distance, Detritus was barking a command at someone.

He felt like a man crossing a river on stepping-stones. He was nearly halfway across, but the next stone was just a bit too far and could only be reached with serious groinal stress. Nevertheless, his foot was waving in the air, and it was that or a soaking . . .

He wrote: "Rascal." Then he circled the word several times, the pencil biting into the cheap paper.

Rascal must have been to Koom Valley. Let's say he found a cube there, who knows how. Just lying there? Anyway, he brings it home. He paints his picture and goes mad, but somewhere along, the cube starts talking to him.

Vimes wrote "SPECIAL WORD?" He drew a circle around it so hard that his pencil broke.

Maybe he can't find the word for "stop talking"? Anyway, he chucks it down a well . . .

He tried to write "Did Rascal ever live in Empirical Crescent?," and then gave up and tried to remember it.

Anyway . . . then he dies and, afterwards, this damn book is written. It doesn't sell many copies, but recently it's republished and . . . ah, but *now* there're lots of dwarfs in the city. Some of them read it, and something tells them that the secret is in this cube. They want to find out where it is. How? Damn. Doesn't the book say the secret of Koom Valley is in the painting? Okay. Maybe he . . . somehow painted some kind of code into the painting to say where the cube was? But so what? What was so bad to hear that you killed the poor devils who heard it?

I think I'm looking at this wrong. It's not my cow. It's a sheep with a pitchfork. Unfortunately, it goes *quack*.

He was getting lost now, going all over the place, but he'd got a toe on the opposite stone and he felt he made some progress. But to what, exactly?

I mean, what would *really* happen if there was real proof that, say, the dwarfs ambushed the trolls? Nothing that isn't happening already, that's what. You can always find an excuse that your side will accept, and who cares what the enemy thinks? In the real world, it wouldn't make any difference.

There was a very faint knock at the door, the sort that you use if you secretly hope it won't be answered. Vimes sprang from his chair and pulled it open.

A. E. Pessimal stood there.

"Ah, A. E.," said Vimes, going back to his desk and laying down his pencil. "Come on in. What can I do for you? How's the arm?"

"Er . . . could you spare a moment of your time, Your Grace?"

Your Grace, thought Vimes. Well, he hadn't the heart to object, this time.

He sat down again. A. E. Pessimal was still wearing the chain-mail shirt with the Specials badge on it. He didn't look very shiny. Brick's swipe had bowled him across the plaza like a ball.

"Er . . ." A. E. Pessimal began.

"You'll have to start as a lance constable, but a man of your talents ought to make it to sergeant within a year. And you can have your own office," said Vimes.

A. E. Pessimal shut his eyes. "How did you know?" he breathed.

"You attacked a boozed-up troll with your teeth," said Vimes. "'*There's* a man born for the badge,' I thought to myself."

And that's what you've always wanted, right? But you were always too small, too weak, too shy to be a watchman. I can buy big and strong anywhere. Right now I need a man who knows how to hold a pencil without breaking it.

"You'll be my adjutant," he went on. "You'll handle all my paperwork. You'll read the reports, you'll try to figure out what's important. And so you can learn what *is* important, you'll have to do at least two patrols a week."

A tear was running down A. E. Pessimal's cheek. "Thank you, Your Grace," he said hoarsely.

If A. E. Pessimal had enough chest to stick out, it would be sticking.

"Of course, you'll need to finish your report on the Watch first," Vimes added. "That is a matter between you and his lordship. And now, if you will excuse me, I really must get on. I look forward to seeing you working for me, Lance Constable Pessimal."

"Thank you, Your Grace!"

"Oh, and you won't call me 'Your Grace,'" said Vimes. He thought for a moment, and decided that the man had earned this, all in one go, and added: "'Mister Vimes' will do."

And so we make progress, he said to himself, after A. E. Pessimal had floated away. And his lordship won't like it, so, as far as I can see, there's no downside. *Quis custodiet ipsos custodes*, er, *qui custodes custodient?* Was that right for "Who watches the watcher that watches the watchmen?"? Probably not. Still . . . your move, my lord.

He was just puzzling over his notebook again when the door opened without an introductory knock.

Sybil entered, with a plate.

"You're not eating enough, Sam," she announced. "And the canteen here is a disgrace. It's all grease and garbage!"

"That's what the men like, I'm afraid," said Vimes guiltily.

"I've cleaned out the tar in the tea urn, at least," Sybil went on, with satisfaction.

"You cleaned out the tea urn?" said Vimes in a hollow voice. It was like being told that someone had wiped the patina off a fine old work of art.

"Yes, it was like tar in there. There really wasn't much proper food in the store, but I managed to make you a bacon, lettuce, and tomato sandwich."

"Thank you, dear." Vimes cautiously lifted a corner of the bread with his broken pencil. There seemed to be too much lettuce, which was to say, there was some lettuce.

"There's a lot of dwarfs come to see you, Sam," said Sibyl, as if this was preying on her mind.

Vimes stood up so fast that his chair fell over.

"Is Young Sam all right?" he said.

"Yes, Sam. They're city dwarfs. You know them all, I think. They say they want to talk to you about—"

But Vimes was already clattering down the stairs, drawing his sword as he did so.

The dwarfs were clustered nervously by the duty sergeant's desk. They had that opulence of metal-work, sleekness of beard, and thickness of girth that marked them out as dwarfs who were doing very well for themselves, or who had been right up until now.

Vimes appeared in front of them like a whirlwind of wrath.

You scum, you rat-sucking little worm-eaters! You heads-down little scurriers in the dark! What did you bring to my city? What were you thinking? Did you want the deep-downers here? Did you dare deplore what Ham-crusher said, all that bile and ancient lies? Or did you say, "Well, I don't agree with him, of course, but he's got a point"? Did you say, "Oh, he goes too far, but it's about time somebody said it"? And now have you come here to wring your hands and say how dreadful, it was nothing to do with you? Who were the dwarfs in the mobs, then? Aren't you community leaders? Were you leading them? And why are you here now, you ugly, sniveling grubbers? Is it possible, is it possible, that now, after that bastard's bodyguards tried to kill my family, you're here to complain? Have I broken some code, trodden on some ancient toe? To hell with it. To hell with you.

He could feel the words straining, fighting to get out, and the effort of restraining them filled his stomach with acid and made his temples throb. Just one whine, he thought. Just one pompous moan. Go on.

"Well?" he demanded, rubbing his aching hand.

The dwarfs had perceptibly moved backwards. Vimes wondered if they'd read his thoughts; they'd echoed in his brain loudly enough.

A dwarf cleared his throat. "Commander Vimes—" he began.

"You're Pors Stronginthearm, aren't you?" Vimes demanded. "One half of Burleigh & Stronginthearm? You make crossbows."

"Yes, Commander, and—"

"Remove your weapons! All of them! All of you!" Vimes snapped.

The room fell silent. Out of the corner of his eye, Vimes saw a couple of dwarf officers, who had at least been pretending to be engaged in paperwork, rising from their seats.

He was being dangerously stupid, part of him

knew, but right now he wanted to hurt a dwarf and he wasn't allowed to do it with steel. Most of the battle stuff they wore was simply for clang in any case, but a dwarf would sooner drop his drawers than put aside his axe. And these were serious city dwarfs, with seats in the guilds and everything. Ye gods, he *was* going too far.

He managed to grunt: "All right, keep your battle-axes. Leave everything else at the desk. You'll get a receipt."

For a moment, quite a long moment, he thought, no, he *hoped* they would refuse. But one of them, somewhere in the group, said: "I think we must do this for the commander. These are difficult times. We must learn to fit them."

Vimes went up to his office, hearing the clinks and clangs behind him, and landed so violently in his chair that this time a wheel snapped off. The receipt was a nasty touch. He was quite pleased with it.

On his desk, on a little stand that Sybil had made for it, was his official baton of office. It was, in fact, the same size as the ordinary coppers' truncheons, but turned out of rosewood and silver instead of lignum vitae or oak. It still had plenty of weight, though. Certainly enough to leave the words Protecter of thee Kinge's Piece printed back to front on a dwarf skull.

The dwarfs were ushered in, looking slightly less heavy.

Just one word, Vimes thought as the acid swirled. One damn word. Go on. Just *breathe* wrong.

"Very well, what can I do for you?" he said.

"Uh, I'm sure you know all of us," Pors began, trying to smile.

"Probably. The dwarf next to you is Grabpot Thundergust, who has just launched the new Ladies' Secrets range of perfumes and cosmetics. My wife uses your stuff all the time."

Thundergust, in traditional chain mail, a three-horned helmet, and with an enormous axe strapped across his back, gave Vimes an embarrassed nod. Vimes's gaze moved on.

"And you are Setha Ironcrust, proprietor of the chain of bakeries of the same name, and you are surely Gimlet Gimlet, owner of two famous dwarf delicatessens and the newly opened Yo Rat! in Attic Bee Street." Vimes looked around the office, dwarf after dwarf, until he got back to the front row and a dwarf of fairly modest dress by dwarf standards, who had been watching him intently. Vimes had a good memory for faces, and had seen this one recently, but couldn't place it. Perhaps it had been behind a well-flung halfbrick . . .

"You, I *don't* think I know," he said.

"Oh, we haven't exactly been introduced, Commander," said the dwarf cheerfully. "But I'm very interested in the theory of games."

. . . or Mr. Shine's Thud Academy? Vimes thought. The dwarf's voice sounded like the one that had, he'd admit it, been of diplomatic help downstairs. He wore a simple, plain, round helmet, a plain leather shirt with some basic mail on it, and his beard was clipped to something tidier than the general dwarf-ish gorse-bush effect. Compared to the other dwarfs, this one looked . . . streamlined. Vimes couldn't even see an axe.

"Indeed?" he said. "Well, in fact, I don't play 'em, so what's your name?"

"Bashfull Bashfullsson, Commander. *Grag* Bashfullsson."

Quietly, Vimes picked up his truncheon and rolled it in his fingers.

"Not underground, then?" he said.

"Some of us move on, sir. Some of us think that darkness isn't a depth, it's a state of mind."

"That's nice of you," said Vimes. *Oh, friendly and forward-looking, are we now? Where were you yesterday? But now I've got all the aces! Those bastards murdered four city dwarfs! They broke into my home, tried to kill my wife! And now they've had it away on their toes! Wherever they've gone, they're going dow— coming up!*

He put the truncheon back on its stand. "As I said, what can I do for you . . . gentlemen?"

He got the sense that they were all turning, physically or mentally, to Bashfullsson. *I see,* he thought, it seems that what we have here is a dozen monkeys and one organ grinder, eh?

"How can we help *you*, Commander?" said the grag.

Vimes stared. *You could have stopped them, that's how you could have helped. Don't give me those somber faces. Maybe you didn't say "yes" but you sure as hell didn't say "no!" loud enough. I owe you not one damned thing. Don't come to me for your bloody absolution.*

"Right now? By going out into the street, walking up to the biggest troll you can see, and shaking him warmly by the hand, maybe?" said Vimes. "Or just going out into the street. Quite frankly, I'm busy, gentlemen, and the middle of a horse race is not the time to be mending fences."

"They'll be heading for the mountains," said Bashfullsson. "They'll steer clear of Uberwald and Lancre. They won't be sure of meeting friends there. That means going into the mountains via Llamedos. Lots of caves there."

Vimes shrugged.

"We can see you're annoyed, Mister Vimes," said Stronginthearm. "But we—"

"I've got two dead assassins in the morgue," said Vimes. "One of 'em died of poison. What do you know about that? And I'm *Commander* Vimes, thank you."

"It's said they take a slow poison before they go on an important mission," said Bashfullsson.

"No turning back, eh?" said Vimes. "Well, that's interesting. But it's the living that concern me right now." He stood up. "I have to go and see a dwarf in the cells who does not want to talk to me."

"Ah, yes. That would be Helmclever," said Bashfullsson. "He was born here, Commander, but went off to study in the mountains more than three months ago, against his parents' wishes. I'm sure he never intended anything like this. He was trying to find himself."

"Well, he can start looking in my cells," said Vimes crisply.

"May I be there when you question him?" said the grag.

"Why?"

"Well, for one thing, it may prevent rumors that he was mistreated."

"Or start them?" said Vimes. Who watches the watchmen? he asked himself. Me!

Bashfullsson gave him a cool look. "It could . . . calm the situation, sir."

"I don't habitually beat up prisoners, if that's what you're suggesting," said Vimes.

"And I am sure you would not wish to do so to-night."

Vimes opened his mouth to shout the grag out of the building, and stopped.

Because the cheeky little sod had got it right slap-bang on the money. Vimes had been on the edge since leaving the house. He'd felt a tingling across his skin, and a tightness in his gut, and a sharp, nasty little headache. Someone was going to pay for all this . . . this . . . this *thisness*, and it didn't need to be a screwed-up bit player like Helmclever.

And he was not certain, not certain at all, what he'd do if the prisoner gave him any lip or tried to be smart. Beating people up in little rooms . . . he knew where that led. And if you did it for a good reason, you'd do it for a bad one. You couldn't say "we're the good guys" and do bad-guy things. Sometimes the watching watchman inside every good copper's head could use an extra pair of eyes.

Justice had to be *seen* to be done, so he'd see it done up good and proper.

"Gentlemen," he said, keeping his eye on the grag but talking to the room at large, "I know all of you, you all know me. You're all respected dwarfs with a stake in this city. I want you to vouch for Mr. Bash-fullsson, because I've never met him before in my life. Come on, Gimlet, I've known you for years, what do you say?"

"They killed my son," said Ironcrust.

A knife dropped into Vimes's head. It slipped down his windpipe, sliced his heart, cut through his stomach, and disappeared. Where the rage had been, there was a chill.

"I'm sorry, Commander," said Bashfullsson quietly. "It's true. I don't think Gunder Ironcrust was interested in the politics, you understand. He just took a job at the mine because he wanted to feel like a real dwarf and work with a shovel for a few days."

"They left him to the mud," said Ironcrust, in a voice that was eerily without emotion. "Any help you need, we will give. Any help. But when you find them, kill them all."

Vimes could think of nothing more to say than "*I will catch them.*" He *didn't* say: Kill them? No. Not if they surrender, not if they don't come at me armed. I know where that leads.

"Then we will leave and let you get about your business," said Stronginthearm. "Grag Bashfullsson is known to us, indeed. A little modern, perhaps. A little young. Not the kind of grag we grew up with, but . . . yes, we'd vouch for him. Good night, Commander."

Vimes stared at his desk as they filed out. When he looked up, the grag was still there, with a patient little smile.

"You don't look like a grag. You look like just another dwarf," said Vimes. "Why haven't I heard of you?"

"Because you are a policeman, perhaps?" said Bashfullsson meekly.

"Okay, I take the point. But you're not a deep-downer?"

Bashfullsson shrugged. "I can think deep thoughts. I was born here, Commander, just like Helmclever. I don't believe I need a mountain over my head in order to be a dwarf."

Vimes nodded. A local lad, not some mountain graybeard. Got a quick brain, too. No wonder the leaders like him. "All right, Mr. Bashfullsson, you can tag along," he said. "But it's on two conditions, okay? Condition one: you've got five minutes to lay your hands on a Thud set. I think you can do that."

"I think I can, too," said the dwarf, smiling faintly. "And the other condition?"

"How long will it take you to teach me to play?" said Vimes.

"You? You've never played it at all?"

"No. A certain troll showed me the game a little while ago, but I've never played games since I grew up. I used to be good at tiddley-rats* when I was a nipper, though."

"Well, a few hours should be—" Bashfullsson began.

"We don't have time," said Vimes. "You've got ten minutes."

---

*A famous Ankh-Morpork gutter sport, second only to dead-rat conkers. Turd races in the gutter appear to have died out, despite an attempt to take them upmarket with the name Poosticks.

The drinking had started in The Bucket, in Gleam Street. This was the coppers' pub. Mr. Cheese, the owner, understood about coppers. They liked to drink somewhere where they wouldn't see anything that reminded them they were a copper. Fun was not encouraged.

It was Tawneee who suggested that they move to Thank Gods It's Open.

Angua wasn't really in the mood, but she hadn't the heart to say no. The plain fact was that while Tawneee had a body that every other woman should hate her for, she compounded the insult by actually being very likable. This was because she had the self-esteem of a caterpillar and, as you found out after any kind of conversation with her, about the same amount of brain. Perhaps it all balanced out, perhaps some kindly god had said to her: "Sorry, kid, you are going to be thicker than a yard of lard, but the good news is, that's not going to matter."

And she had a stomach made of iron, too. Angua found herself wondering how many hopeful men had died trying to drink her under the table. Alcohol didn't seem to go to her brain at all. Maybe it couldn't find it. But she was pleasant, easygoing company, if you avoided allusion, irony, sarcasm, repartee, satire, and words longer than "chicken."

Angua was tetchy because she was dying for a beer, but the young man behind the bar thought that "a pint of Winkles" was the name of a cocktail. Given the drinks on offer, perhaps this was not surprising.

"What?" said Angua, reading the menu, "is a Screaming Orgasm?"

"Ah," said Sally, "looks like we got to you just in time, girl!"

"No," sighed Angua as the others laughed; that was *such* a vampire response. "I mean what's it *made* of?"

"Almonté, Wahlulu, Bearhuggers Whiskey Cream, and vodka," said Tawneee, who knew the recipe for every cocktail ever made.

"And how does it work?" said Cheery, craning to see over the top of the bar.

Sally ordered four, and turned back to Tawneee.

"So . . . you and Nobby Nobbs, eh?" she said. "How about that?" Three sets of ears flared.

The other thing you got used to in the presence of Tawneee was silence. Everywhere she went, went quiet. Oh, and the stares. The silent stares. And sometimes, in the shadows, a sigh. There were *goddesses* who'd kill to look like Tawneee.

"He's nice," said Tawneee. "He makes me laugh and he keeps his hands to himself."

Three faces locked in expressions of concentrated thought. In Angua's case, one was: This is Nobby we're talking about. There are *so* many questions that we are *not* going to ask.

"Has he shown you the tricks he can do with his spots?" she said.

"Yes. I thought I'd widdle myself! He's so funny!"

Angua stared into her drink. Cheery coughed. Sally studied the menu.

"And he's very dependable," said Tawneee. And, as if dimly aware that this was still not sufficient, she added sadly: "If you must know, he's the first boy who's *ever* asked me out."

Sally and Angua breathed out together. Light

dawned. Ah, *that* was the problem. And this one's a
baaaad case.

"I mean, my hair's all over the place, my legs are
too long, and I know my bosom is far too—" Tawneee went on, but Sally had raised a quietening hand.

"First point, Tawneee—"

"My real name's Betty," said Tawneee, blowing
a nose so exquisite that the greatest sculptor in the
world would have wept to carve it. It went *blort*.

"First point, then . . . Betty," Sally managed,
struggling to use the name, "is that no woman under
forty-five—"

"Fifty," Angua corrected.

"Right, fifty . . . no woman under fifty uses the
word 'bosom' to name anything connected to her.
You just don't do it."

"I didn't know that," Tawneee sniffed.

"It's a fact," said Angua. And, oh dear, how to
begin to explain the jerk syndrome? To someone
like Tawneee, on whom the name Betty stuck like
rocks to a ceiling? This wasn't just a *case* of the jerk
syndrome, this was *it*, the quintessential, classic,
pure platonic example that should be stuffed and
mounted and preserved as a teaching aid for students
in the centuries to come. And she was *happy* with
Nobby!

"What I've got to tell you now is . . ." she began,
and faded in the face of the task, "is . . . look, shall
we have another drink? What's the next cocktail on
the menu?"

Cheery peered at it.

"Pink, Big and Wobbly," she announced.

"Classy! We'll have four!"

Fred Colon peered through the bars. He was, on the whole, a pretty good jailer; he always had a pot of tea on the go, he was, as a general rule, amiably disposed to most people, he was too slow to be easily fooled, and he kept the cell keys in a tin box in the bottom drawer on his desk, a long way out of reach of any stick, hand, dog, cunningly thrown belt, or trained Klatchian monkey spider.*

He was a bit worried about this dwarf. You got all sorts in jail, and they often yelled a bit, but with this one he didn't know what was worse, the sobbing or the silence. He'd put one candlestick on a stool by the bars, too, because the dwarf carried on alarmingly if there wasn't enough light.

He stirred the tea reflectively and handed the mug to Nobby.

"We've got a rum 'un here, I reckon," he said. "A dwarf that's scared of the dark? Not right in the head, then. Wouldn't touch his tea and biscuit. What do you think?"

"I think I'll have his biscuit," said Nobby, reaching over to the plate.

"Why're you down here, anyway?" said Fred. "I'm surprised you ain't out there a-ogling of young women."

"Tawneee's going out boozing with the girls tonight," said Nobby.

"Ah, you want to warn her about that sort of thing,"

---

*Making Fred Colon possibly unique in the annals of jail history.

said Fred Colon. "You know what it's like in the center when the pubs and clubs empty. There's throwin' up and yellin' and unladylike behavior and takin' their vests off and I don't know what. 'S called . . ." he scratched his head ". . . minge drinking."

"She's only gone out with Angua and Sally and Cheery, Sarge," said Nobby, taking another biscuit.

"Ooo, you wanna watch that, Nobby. Women gangin' up on man—" Fred paused. "A vampire and a werewolf out on the razzle? Take my tip, lad, stay indoors tonight. And if they start behaving in—"

He stopped as the sound of Sam Vimes's voice came down the spiral stone steps, followed closely by its owner.

"So, I've got to stop them forming a block, right?"

"If you're playing the troll side, yes," said a new voice. "A tight group of dwarfs is bad news for trolls."

"Trolls shove, dwarfs throw?"

"Right."

"And the central rock, no one can jump that, right?" said Vimes.

"Yes."

"I still think the dwarfs have it all their own way."

"We shall see. The important thing—"

Vimes stopped when he saw Nobby and Colon.

"Okay, lads, I'll talk to the prisoner now," he said. "How is he?"

Fred indicated the hunched figure on the narrow bunk in the corner cell.

"Captain Carrot tried talking to him for nearly half an hour, and you know he's got a way with people," he said. "Didn't get as much as a sentence out of him. I read him his rights but don't ask *me* if he understood 'em. He didn't want his tea and biscuit, at any rate. That's rights 5 and 5b," he added, looking Bashfullsson up and down. "He gets right 5c only if we've got Teatime Assortment."

"Can he walk?" said Vimes.

"He sort of shuffles, sir."

"Fetch him out, then," said Vimes, and, seeing Fred's inquiring look at Bashfullsson, he went on: "This gentleman is here to make sure we don't use the rubber truncheon, Sergeant."

"Didn't know we had one, Mister Vimes," said Fred.

"We haven't," said Vimes. "No point in hitting 'em with something that bounces, eh?" he added, looking at Bashfullsson, who smiled, once again, his strange little smile.

One candle burned on the table. For some reason, Fred had seen fit to put another one on a stool near the one occupied cell.

"Isn't it a bit dark in here, Fred?" said Vimes as he pushed aside the debris of mugs and old newspapers that covered most of the table.

"Yessir. The dwarfs came and nicked some of our candles to put 'round their heathe—that nasty sign," said Fred, with a nervous look at Bashfullsson. "Sorry, sir."

"I don't know why we can't just burn it," grumbled Vimes, setting out the Thud board.

"That would be dangerous, now that the Summoning Dark is in the world," said Bashfullsson.

"You believe in that stuff?" said Vimes.

"Believe? No," said the grag. "I just know it exists.

The troll pieces go all 'round the central stone, sir," he added helpfully.

Populating the board with its little warriors took some time, but so did the arrival of Helmclever. With Fred Colon steering him gently by a shoulder, he walked like someone in a dream, his eyes turned up so that they mostly showed the whites. His iron boots scraped on the flagstones.

Fred pushed him gently into a chair and put the second candle beside him. Like magic, the dwarf's eyes focused on the little stone armies to the exclusion of everything else in the jail.

"We're playing a game, Mr. Helmclever," said Vimes quietly. "And you can choose your side."

Helmclever reached out with a trembling hand and touched a piece. A troll. A dwarf had chosen to play as the trolls. Vimes gave the hovering Bashfullsson a questioning glance, and got another smile in return.

Okay, you got as many of the little sods as possible in a defensive huddle, right? Vimes's hand hesitated, and shifted a dwarf across the board. The click as he placed it was echoed by the one made by the movement of Helmclever's next troll. The dwarf looked sleepy, but his hand had moved with snake speed.

"Who killed the four mining dwarfs, Helmclever?" said Vimes softly. "Who killed the boys from the city?"

Dull eyes looked at him, and then, meaningfully, at the board. Vimes moved a dwarf at random.

"The dark soldiers," Helmclever whispered as a little troll clicked smartly into place.

"Who ordered it?" Again the look, again a dwarf placed at random followed by a troll that was moved so fast that the two pieces seemed to hit the board together.

"Grag Hamcrusher ordered it."

"Why?" Click/click.

"They had heard it speaking."

"What was it that spoke? Was it a cube?" Click/click.

"Yes. It was dug up. It said it spoke with the voice of B'hrian Bloodaxe."

Vimes heard a gasp from Bashfullsson, and caught Fred Colon's eye. He jerked his head toward the cell-block door, and mouthed a couple of words.

"Wasn't he a famous dwarf king?" said Vimes. Click/click.

"Yes. He commanded the dwarfs at Koom Valley," said Helmclever.

"And what did this voice say?" said Vimes. Click/click. And a third click from behind Vimes as Fred Colon locked the door and stood in front of it, looking impassive.

"I do not know. Ardent said it was about the battle. He said it was lies."

"Who killed Grag Hamcrusher?" Click/click.

"I do not know. Ardent called me to the meeting and said there was terrible fighting among the grags. Ardent said one of them killed him in the dark, with a mining hammer, but none knew who. They were all struggling together."

All dressed alike, Vimes thought. Just shapes, if you can't see their wrists . . .

"Why did they want to kill him?" Click/click.

"They had to stop him destroying the words! He was screaming and hitting the cube with the hammer!"

"There are . . . sensitive areas on a cube, and it is possible that if they are touched in the wrong order, all the sound will vanish," whispered Bashfullsson.

"I should think the hammer would do the trick whatever it hit!" said Vimes, turning his head.

"No, Commander. Devices are immensely tough."

"They must be!"

Vimes turned back to Helmclever.

"It's wrong to destroy lies, but it's okay to kill the miners?" he said. Click.

He heard the hiss of Bashfullsson's intake of breath. Well, yes, perhaps that could have been better put. There was no answering move. Helmclever hung his head.

"It was *wrong* to kill the miners," he whispered. "And why not destroy lies? But it is wrong to think these thoughts, so I . . . I said nothing. The old grags were angry and upset and confused, so Ardent took charge. He said one dwarf killing another underground, everyone knew that was no business of humans. He said he could make it all right. He said everyone must listen to him. He told the dark guards to take the body to the new outer chamber. And . . . he told me to fetch my club . . ."

Vimes glanced at Bashfullsson and mouthed the word "Club?" He got an emphatic nod in return.

Helmclever sat hunched in silence, and then raised one hand slowly and moved a troll. Click.

Click/click. Click/click. Click/click. Vimes tried to spare a few brain cells for the game while his

mind raced and tried to piece the random information spilling out of Helmclever.

So . . . It all starts when they come here looking
for this magic cube, which can speak . . .

"Why did they come to the city? How did they
know the cube was here?" Click/click.

"When I went to begin my training, I took a copy
of the *Codex*. Arden confiscated it, but then they
called me to a meeting and said it was very important and they would honor me by letting me go with
them to the city. Ardent told me it was a great opportunity. Grag Hamcrusher had a mission, he said."

"They hadn't even known about the painting?"

"They lived under a mountain. They believe that
humans are not real. But Ardent is smart. He said
there were always rumors that something had come
out of Koom Valley."

I bet he *is* smart, Vimes thought. So they come
here, do a little light pastoral work and rabble-
rousing, and search for the cube in a very dwarfish
way. They find it. But the poor bastards who were
doing the digging hear what it's got to say. Well,
everyone knows dwarfs gossip, so the dark guards
make sure these four don't have a chance to.

Click/click. Click/click.

Then friend Hamcrusher doesn't like what he
hears, either. He wants to destroy this thing. In the
struggle in the dark, one of the other grags does
the world a favor and fetches him a crack on the nog-
gin. But, whoops, big mistake, because the mob is
going to miss him and his jolly urging to wholesale
troll slaughter. You know how dwarfs gossip, and you
can't kill 'em all. So while it's still just us together in

the dark, we need a plan! Forward, Mr. Ardent, who says "I know! We'll take the corpse out to a tunnel that a troll just might have got into, and bash its head in with a club. A troll did it. What right-thinking dwarf could possibly believe anything else?"

Click/click.

"Why the candles?" said Vimes. "The old grags had been sitting in brilliant candlelight when I saw them." Click/click.

"The grags ordered it," Helmclever whispered. "They feared what might come for them in darkness."

"And what was it that might come?" Click . . .

Helmclever's hand stopped in mid-air. For several seconds, nothing moved in the little circle of yellow light except the candle flames themselves; in the darkness beyond, the shadows craned to hear.

"I . . . cannot say," whispered the dwarf. Click. Click/click . . . click . . . click.

Vimes glared at the board. Where'd that troll come from? Helmclever had wiped three dwarfs off the board in one go!

"Ardent said there's always a troll. A troll got into the mine," said Helmclever. "The grags said yes, that must have been it."

"But they knew the truth!" Click/click . . . click . . . click. Three more dwarfs gone, just like that . . .

"Truth is what a grag says it is," said Helmclever. "The sunlight world is a bad dream anyway. Ardent said no one was to speak about it. He said I was to tell all the guards . . . about the troll."

Blame it on a troll, Vimes thought. For a dwarf, that came naturally. A big troll did it and ran away.

This isn't just a can of worms, it's a nest of bloody vipers!

He stared at the board. Bloody hell. I'm running into a wall here. What am I left with? Brick saw a dwarf hitting another dwarf, but that wasn't the murder—that was Ardent or someone giving Hamcrusher's dead body that distinctive, bashed-by-a-troll look. I'm not actually certain that's a major crime. The *murder* was done in the dark by one of six dwarfs, and the other five might not even know who did it! Okay, maybe I can say they conspired to conceal a crime . . . hold on . . .

"But it wasn't Ardent who said that the *Watch* should not be told," he said. "That was you, wasn't it? Did you *want* me to be angry, Mr. Helmclever?" He moved a dwarf. Click.

Helmclever looked down.

Since no answer was forthcoming, Vimes captured the wandering troll and placed it beside the board.

"I did not think you would come." Helmclever's voice was barely audible. "Hamcrusher was . . . I think . . . I didn't . . . Ardent said you wouldn't worry, because the grag was such a danger. He said the grag had ordered the miners to be killed, and so now it was ended. But I thought it . . . I . . . it wasn't right. Things were wrong! I heard you were full of pride. I had to get you . . . interested. He . . . he . . ."

"You thought I wouldn't be? A troll is accused of murdering a dwarf, at a time like this, and I *wouldn't* be interested?" said Vimes.

"Ardent said that you would not be, because no

humans were involved. He said you would not care what happens to dwarfs."

"He ought to get out in the fresh air more!"

Helmclever's eyes and nose were running now, and dripping on the board. A storm stops the battle, Vimes thought. Then the dwarf lifted his head and wailed. "It was the club the troll Mr. Shine gave me for winning five games in a row," he wailed. "He was my friend! He said I was as good as a troll, so I should have a club! I told Ardent it was a war trophy! But he took it and bashed that poor dead body!"

Water dripping on a stone, Vimes thought. And it depends on where the drops fall, right, Mr. Shine? What good has it done this poor devil? He wasn't in the right job to have doubt enter his life!

"All right, Mr. Helmclever, thank you for this," he said, sitting back. "There is just one thing, though. Do you know who sent those dwarfs to my house?"

"What dwarfs?"

Vimes stared into the weeping, red-rimmed eyes. Their owner was either telling the truth or the stage had missed a major talent.

"They came to attack me and my family," he said.

"I . . . did hear Ardent talking to the captain of the guard," Helmclever murmured. "Something about . . . a warning . . ."

"*A warning?* Do you call—" Vimes began and stopped when he saw Bashfullsson shaking his head. Right. Right. No point in taking it out on this one. He's had all the stuffing knocked out of him in any case.

"They are very frightened now," Helmclever said.

"They don't understand the city. They don't understand why trolls are allowed here. They don't understand people who don't . . . understand them. They fear you. They fear everything, now."

"Where have they gone?"

"I don't know. Ardent said they would have gone now anyway, because they've got the cube and the painting," said Helmclever. "He said the painting will show where there are more lies, and those can be destroyed. But they fear most of all the Summoning Dark, Commander. They can feel it coming for them."

"It's only a drawing," said Vimes. "I don't believe in it."

"I do," said Helmclever calmly. "It is in this room. How does it come? It comes in darkness and in vengeance and in disguise."

Vimes felt his skin twitch. Nobby looked around the grimy stone walls. Bashfullsson sat bolt upright in his chair. Even Fred Colon shifted uneasily.

This is just mystic stuff, Vimes told himself. It's not even human mystic stuff. I don't belive in it. So why does it feel a bit chilly in here?

He coughed. "Well, once it knows they've gone, I expect it'll head out after them."

"And it will come for me," said Helmclever in the same calm voice. He folded his hands in front of him.

"Why? You didn't kill anybody," said Vimes.

"You don't understand! They . . . they . . . when they killed the miners, one was not all the way dead, and, and, and we could hear him hammering on the door with his fists, and I stood in the tunnel and listened to him die and I *wished* him dead so that the noise would stop, but, but, but when it did, it went on in my head, and I could, I could, I could have turned the wheel but I was afraid of the dark guards who have no souls, and because of that the darkness will take mine . . ."

The little voice died away.

There was a nervous cough from Nobby.

"Well, thank you again," said Vimes. Good grief, they really messed up his head, poor little sod.

And I've got nothing, he thought. I might get Ardent on a charge of falsifying evidence. I can't put Brick in the witness box, because I'll simply be proving that there *was* a troll in the mine. All I've got is young Helmclever here, who's clearly unfit to testify.

He turned to Bashfullsson, and shrugged. "I think I'd like to keep our friend here tonight, for his own good. I can't imagine there's anywhere else for him to go. The statement he made is, of course, covered by . . ."

Now *his* voice trailed off as his memory nudged him. He turned back in his chair to glare at the sorrowful Helmclever.

"What painting?" he said.

"The painting of the Battle of Koom Valley by Methodia Rascal," said the dwarf, not looking up. "It's very big. They stole it from the museum."

"What?" said Fred Colon, who was making tea in the corner. "It was them?"

"What? *You* know about this, Fred?" Vimes demanded.

"We, yes, Mister Vimes, we did a report—"

"Koom Valley, Koom Valley, Koom Valley!"

roared Vimes, slapping his hand down on the table so hard that the candlesticks jumped into the air. "A report? What the hell good's a report? Have I got time these days to read reports? Why doesn't someone *tell* me these thi—"

One candlestick rolled on to the floor and went out. Vimes grabbed for the other as it reached the edge of the table, but it spun away from his fingers and landed wick-first on the flagstones.

Darkness fell like an axe.

Helmclever groaned. It was a heartfelt, soul-creaking groan, like a death rattle from a living mouth.

"*Nobby!*" screamed Vimes. "*Light a godsdamn match right now and that's a godsdamn order!*"

There was a frantic scrabbling in the dark, and then a matchhead was a sudden supernova.

"Well, bring it here, man!" he shouted to Nobby. "Get those candles lit!"

Helmclever was still staring at the table, where the ill-tempered thump had scattered the remains of the game.

Vimes glanced down at the game board as the candle flames grew.

If you were the kind to see things, you'd say that the trolls and dwarfs had fallen in a rough circle around the central rock, while a few more dwarfs had rolled away in a line. You'd say, in fact, that from above, they formed the shape of a round eye. With a tail.

Helmclever gave a little sigh and slipped sideways onto the floor.

Vimes stood up to help him, and then remembered just in time about politics. He forced himself to back away, hands in the air.

"Mr. Bashfullsson?" he said. "I can't touch him. Please?"

The grag nodded, and knelt down by the dwarf.

"No pulse, no heartbeat," he announced after a few seconds. "I'm sorry, Commander."

"Then it looks as though I'm now in your hands," said Vimes.

"Indeed. In the hands of a dwarf," said the grag, standing up. "Commander Vimes, I will swear that Helmclever was treated with nothing but concern and courtesy while I was here. And perhaps with more kindness from you than a dwarf might have a right to expect. His death is not on your hands. The Summoning Dark called him. Dwarfs will understand."

"Well, I don't! Why'd it kill him? What did the poor bugger do?"

"I think it's more true to say that the *fear* of the Summoning Dark killed him," said the grag. "He left a miner trapped, heard his cries in the dark, and did nothing. To all dwarfs, that is a terrible crime."

"As bad as wiping away a word?" said Vimes sourly. He felt more shaken up than he'd care to admit. He shouldn't have slapped the table like that, but he'd been so *angry*. Now his hand hurt more than ever.

"Some would say it is far worse. His own guilt and fear killed Helmclever. It's as if he had his own Summoning Dark in his head," said Bashfullsson. "In a way, perhaps, we all have, Commander. Or something similar."

"You know, your religion really messes people up," said Vimes.

"Not in comparison to what they do to one another," said Bashfullsson, calmly folding the dead dwarf's hands across his chest. "And it is not a religion, Commander. Tak wrote the World and the Laws, and then He left us. He does not require that we think of Him, only that we think."

He stood up. "I shall explain the situation to my fellows, Commander. Incidentally, I would ask you to take me with you to Koom Valley."

"Did I say I was going to Koom Valley?" said Vimes.

"All right," said the grag calmly. "Let's say, then, that *should* the mood take you to go to Koom Valley, you will take me? I know the place, I know the history, I even know quite a lot about mine sign, especially the Major Darknesses. I may be useful."

"You demand all that just for telling the truth?" said Vimes.

"As a matter of fact, no. *J'ds hasfak 'ds*: 'I bargain with no axe in my hand.' I will tell the truth whatever you decide," said Bashfullsson. "However, since you are not going to Koom Valley, Commander, I will not press you. It was only an idle thought."

Fun. What is it good for?

It's not pleasure, joy, delight, enjoyment, or glee. It's a hollow, cruel, vicious little bastard, a word for something sought with a hilarious couple of wobbly antennae on your head and the words I WANT IT! on your shirt, and it tends to leave you waking up with your face stuck to the street.

Somehow, Angua had acquired a magenta feather boa. It wasn't her. It wasn't anyone. It had just turned up. The sheer fakery of it made her more gloomy. Something was nagging at the back of her mind, and it annoyed her that she didn't know what it was.

They had ended up in Biers, as she knew they would. It was the undead bar, although it tolerated anyone who wasn't too normal.

It certainly tolerated Tawneee. She just didn't get it, did she? The reason why men never talked to her? The trouble was, thought Angua, that Nobby wasn't actually a bad . . . person. As such. As far as she knew, he'd always been faithful to Miss Pushpram, which was to say that when it came to being hit with a fish and then pelted with clams, he never thought of any other girl but her. He actually had quite a romantic soul, but it was encased in what could only be called . . . Nobby Nobbs.

Sally had accompanied Tawneee to the ladies', which was always wise in Biers. Now Angua was staring at yet another cocktail menu, painted on a board above the bar, in a very shaky script, by Igor.*

He'd done his best to flow with the zeitgeist, or would have done if he'd known what the word meant, but had totally failed to grasp the subtleties of the modern cocktail bar, so that the drinks on offer included:

---

*Who wasn't *an* Igor, but was merely called one. It was best not to have fun with him on this subject, and especially not to ask him to sew your head back on.

HAVIN YOU TEEF SMASHED IN BY A BIG STINKY FIST
HEAD NAILED TO THE DOOR
KICK INNA FORK
LIKE BIG LUMP OF STEEL HAMMER FRU YOU EARS
NECK BOLT

Actually, the Neck Bolt wasn't too bad, Angua had to admit.

"'S'cuse me," said Cheery, teetering on a bar stool, "but what was all that about Tawneee? I could see you and Sally nodding to each other!"

"That? Oh, it's the jerk syndrome." Angua remembered who she was talking to, and added: "Er . . . dwarfs probably don't have that. It means . . . sometimes a woman is so beautiful that any man with half a brain isn't going to *think* of asking her out, okay? Because it's *obvious* that she's far too grand for the likes of him. Are you with me?"

"I think so."

"Well, that's Tawneee. And, for the purposes of this explanation, Nobby has not got half a brain. He's so used to women saying no when he asks them out that he's not afraid of being blown off. So he asks her, because he figures, why not? And *she*, who by now thinks there's something wrong with her, is so grateful she says okay."

"But she *likes* him."

"I know. That's where it all gets strange."

"It's much simpler for dwarfs," said Cheery.

"I expect it is."

"But probably not as much fun," said Cheery, looking crestfallen.

Tawneee was returning. Angua ordered three

Neck Bolts while Cheery hopefully negotiated for a Screaming Orgasm.* And then, with occasional assistance from Sally, Angua explained to Tawneee the facts of . . . well . . . *everything*.

It took some while. You had to keep changing the shape of sentences to get them to fit into the currently available space in Tawneee's brain. Angua clung to the idea, though, that the girl couldn't be *that* stupid. She worked in a strip club, didn't she?

"I mean, why do you think men pay to watch you onstage?" she asked.

"Because I'm very good," said Tawneee promptly. "When I was ten, I got the Dancer of the Year Award in Miss Deviante's ballet and tap class."

"Tap-dancing?" said Sally, grinning. "Hey, why don't you try that onstage?"

Angua closed her mind to the image of Tawneee tap-dancing. The club would probably burn to the ground.

"Er . . . let me try this another way . . ." she said. "And I'm telling you this as another woma— female . . ."

Tawneee listened intently, and even the way in which she looked puzzled was unfair to the rest of her sex.

When Angua had finished, she watched the angelic expression hopefully.

"So what you're saying, right," said Tawneee, "is that walking out with Nobby is like going into a big posh restaurant and only eating the bread roll?"

"Exactly!" said Angua. "You've got it!"

---

*Patience is a key virtue among dwarfs.

"But I never really *meet* men. Granny told me not to act like a floozy."

"And you don't think that working at—" Angua began, but Sally cut in.

"Sometimes you need to flooze regularly," she said. "Haven't you ever just gone into a bar and had a drink with a man?"

"No."

"Right," said Sally. She drained her glass. "I don't like these Neck Bolts. Let's go somewhere else and . . ." she paused, "open your mind to poshibiliteesh."

It was odd, having Sybil in Pseudopolis Yard. It had been one of the Ramkin family homes before she'd given it to the Watch. She'd been a girl there. It had been her home.

Some apprehension of this crept into the chipped and stained souls of the watchmen. Men not known for the elegance of their manners found themselves automatically wiping their feet as they came in, and respectfully removing their helmets.

They spoke differently, too, slowly and hesitantly, anxiously scanning the sentence ahead for expletives to delete. Someone even found a broom and swept up, or at least moved the dirt to a less obvious place.

Upstairs, in what had been up until then the cash office, Young Sam slept peacefully in a makeshift bed. One day, Vimes hoped, he would be able to tell him that on one special night he'd been guarded by four troll watchmen. They'd been off duty but volunteered to come in for this, and were just *itching* for some dwarfs to try anything. Sam hoped the boy would be impressed; the most other kids could hope for was angels.

Vimes had commandeered the canteen, because it had a big enough table. He'd spread out a map of the city. A lot of the rest of the planking was occupied by pages from the *Koom Valley Codex*.

This wasn't a game, this was a puzzle. A sort of, yes, jigsaw puzzle. And he ought to be able to do it, he reasoned, because he already had nearly all the corners.

"Ettercap Street, Money Trap Lane, Crybaby Alley, Scuttlebutt Court, the Jeebies, Pellicool Steps," he said. "Tunnels everywhere! They were lucky to find it after only three or four. Mr. Rascal must have had lodgings in half the streets in the area. Including Empirical Crescent!"

"But hwhy?" said Sir Reynold Stitched. "I mean, hwhy dig tunnels everyhwhere?"

"Tell him, Carrot," said Vimes, drawing a line across the city.

Carrot cleared his throat. "Because they were dwarfs, sir, and deep-downers at that," he said. "It wouldn't occur to them *not* to dig. And mostly it'd be just a matter of clearing out buried rooms, in any case. That's a stroll, to a dwarf. And they were laying rails, so they could take the spoil out anywhere they wanted."

"Yes, but sureleah—" Sir Reynold began.

"They were listening out for something talking at the bottom of an old well," said Vimes, still bending over the map. "What chance that'd still be visible?

And people can get a bit iffy when a bunch of dwarfs turn up and start digging holes in the garden."

"It'd be very slow, sureleah?"

"Well, yes, sir. But it would be in the dark, under their control, and secret," said Carrot. "They could go anywhere they wanted. They could zigzag around if they weren't certain, they could home in with their listening tube, and they'd never have to speak to a human or see daylight. Dark, controllable, and *secret*."

"Deep-downers in a nutshell," said Vimes.

"This is very exciting!" said Sir Reynold. "And they dug into the cellars of my museum?"

"Over to you, Fred," said Vimes, carefully drawing a line across the map.

"Er, right," said Fred Colon. "Er . . . Nobby an' me found out where only a couple of hours ago," he said, thinking it wisest not to add "after Mister Vimes yelled at us and made us tell him every last detail and then sent us back and told us what to look for." What he *did* add was: "They were pretty clever, sir. The mortar even looked dirty. I bet you're saying to yourself, ahah, sir?"

"I am?" said Sir Reynold, bewildered. "I hwould normalleah say 'my goodness.'"

"I expect you're saying to yourself, ahah, how were they able to build up the wall again after they'd got the muriel out, sir, and we reckon—"

"hWell, I imagine one dwarf stayed behind to make good, lay low, as you hwould say, and hwandered out in the morning," said Sir Reynold. "There hwere people going in and out all the time. hWe hwere looking for a big painting, after all, not a person."

"Yessir. We reckon one dwarf stayed behind to

make good, lay low, and wandered out in the morning. There were people going in and out all the time. You were looking for a big painting, after all, not a person," said Fred Colon. He'd been very pleased to come up with that theory, so he was going to say it out loud no matter what.

Vimes tapped the map. "And here, Sir Reynold, is where a troll called Brick fell through another cellar floor into their tunnel," he said. "He also told us he saw something in the main mine, which sounds very much like the Rascal."

"But, alas, you have not found it," said Sir Reynold.

"I'm sorry, sir. It's probably long gone out of the city."

"But hwhy?" said the curator. "They could have studied it in the museum! hWe're very interactive these days!"

"*Interactive?*" said Vimes. "What do you mean?"

"hWell, people can . . . look at the pictures as much as they hwant," said Sir Reynold. He sounded a little annoyed. People shouldn't ask that kind of question.

"And the pictures do what, exactly?"

"Er . . . hang there, Commander," said Sir Reynold. "Of course."

"So what you mean is, people can come and look at the pictures, and the pictures, for their part, are looked at?"

"Rather like that, yes," said the curator. He thought for a moment, aware that this probably wasn't sufficient, and added: "But *dynamicaleah.*"

"You mean the people are *moved* by the pictures, sir?" said Carrot.

"Yes!" said Sir Reynold, with huge relief. "hWell

done! That's just hwhat happens. And hwe've had the Rascal on public display for years. hWe even have a stepladder, in case people hwant to examine the mountains. Sometimes people come in hwith a bee in their bonnet that one of the hwarriors is pointing to some bareleah visible cave or something. Frankleah, if there hwas some secret, *I* hwould have found it by now. There hwas no *point* to the theft!"

"Unless someone *had* found the secret and didn't want anyone else to find it," said Vimes.

"That hwould be rather a coincidence, hwouldn't it, Commander? It's not that anything has just changed recentleah. Mr. Rascal didn't turn up and paint another mountain! And, although I hate to say this, just destroying the painting hwould have been enough."

Vimes walked around the table. All the bits, he thought, I must have all the bits by now.

Let's start with this legend of a dwarf turning up, nearly dead, weeks after the battle, babbling about treasure.

All right, then it might have been this talking cube thing, Vimes thought. He survived the battle, hid out somewhere, and he's got this thing and it's *important*. He's got to get it somewhere safe . . . no, maybe he's got to get people to *listen* to it. And, of course, he doesn't take it with him, 'cos there's still likely to be trolls wandering the area and right now they'll be in a mood to club first and try to think up some questions later. He needs some bodyguards.

He gets as far as some humans, but when he's leading them back to the place where it's hidden, he finally dies.

Forward two thousand years. Would a cube last that long? Hell, they bob up in molten lava!

So it's lying there. Methodia Rascal comes along, looking for . . . a nice view, or something, and he looks down and there it is? Well, I'll have to accept that he did, because he found it and got it talking, who knows how. But he couldn't *stop* it. He drops it down the well. The dwarfs find it. They listen to the box, but hate what they hear. They hate it so much that Hamcrusher has four miners killed just because they heard it, too. So why the painting? It shows what the box is talking about? Where the box is? If you've got the box in your hand, isn't that *it*?

Anyway, who says it was the voice of Bloodaxe doing the speaking? It could be anybody. Why would you believe what it said?

He was aware of Sir Reynold talking to Carrot . . .

". . . said to your sergeant Colon here, the painting is set several miles from hwhere the actual battle hwas fought. It's in entireleah the hwrong part of Koom Valley! That's just about the one thing both sides are agreed on!"

"So why did he set it there?" said Vimes, staring at the table as if hoping to draw a clue from it by willpower alone.

"Who knows? It's all Koom Valley. There are about two hundred and fifty square miles of the place. I imagine he just chose somewhere that looked dramatic."

"Would you chaps like a cup of tea?" said Lady Sybil, from the door. "I felt a bit at a loose end, so I made a pot. And you should be getting your head down, Sam."

Sam Vimes looked panicky, a figure of authority caught once again in a domestic situation.

"Oh, Lady Sybil, they took the Rascal!" said Sir Reynold. "I know it belonged to your family!"

"My grandfather said it was just a damn nuisance," said Sybil. "He used to let me unroll it on the floor of the ballroom. I used to name all the dwarfs. We looked for the secret, because he said there was hidden treasure, and the painting showed you where it was. Of course, we never found it, but it kept me quiet on rainy afternoons."

"Oh, it hwasn't great art," said Sir Reynold. "And the man hwas *quite* mad, of course. But somehow it spoke to people."

"I wish it'd say something to me," said Vimes. "You really don't need to make tea for people, dear. One of the officers—"

"Nonsense! We must be hospitable," said Sybil.

"Of course, people *tried* to copeah it," said the curator, accepting a cup. "Oh dear, they hwere terrible! A painting fifteah feet long and ten feet deep is really *quite* impossible to copy hwith any kind of accuraceah—"

"Not if you lay it out on the ballroom floor and get a man to make you a pantograph," said Sybil, pouring tea. "This teapot is really a disgrace, Sam. Worse than the urn. Doesn't *anyone* ever clean it out?"

She looked up at their faces.

"Did I say something wrong?" she said.

"You made a copy of the Rascal?" said Sir Reynold.

"Oh, yes. The whole thing, on a scale of one to five," said Sybil. "When I was fourteen. It was a school project. We were doing dwarf history, you see, and, well, since we owned that painting, it was too good to miss. You know what a pantograph is, don't you? It's a very simple way of making larger or smaller copies of a painting, using geometry, some wooden levers, and a sharp pencil. Actually, I did it as five panels ten feet square, that's full-size, to make sure I got all the detail, and then I did the one-fifth scale version to display it as poor Mr. Rascal wanted it displayed. I got full marks from Miss Turpitude. She was our math teacher, you know, she wore her hair in a bun with a pair of compasses and a ruler stuck in it? She used to say that a girl who knew how to use a set square and protractor would go a long way in life."

"What a shame you no longer have it!" said Sir Reynold.

"Why should you say that, Sir Reynold?" said Sybil. "I'm sure I've still got it somewhere. I had it hanging up from the ceiling of my room for some time. Let me think . . . did we take it with us when we moved? I'm sure—" She looked up brightly. "Ah, yes. Have you even been up to the attics here, Sam?"

"No!" said Vimes.

"Now's the time, then."

"I've never been on a girls' night out before," said Cheery as they walked, a little uncertainly, through the nighttime city. "Was that last bit supposed to happen?"

"What bit was that?" said Sally.

"The bit where the bar was set on fire."

"Not *usually*," said Angua.

"I've never seen men *fight* over a woman before," Cheery went on.

"Yeah, that was something, wasn't it?" said Sally. They'd dropped Tawneee off at her home. She'd been in quite a thoughtful frame of mind.

"And all she did was smile at a man," said Cheery.

"Yes," said Angua. She was trying to concentrate on walking.

"It'd be a bit of a shame for Nobby if she lets that go to her head, though," said Cheery.

Save me from talkative druks . . . drinks . . . *drunks*, Angua thought. She said: "Yes, but what about Miss Pushpram? She's thrown some quite expensive fish at Nobby over the years."

"We've struck a blow for womanhood," Sally declared loudly. "Shoes, men, coffins . . . never accept the first one you see."

"Oh, *shoes*," said Cheery. "I can talk about *shoes*. Has anyone seen the new Yan Rockhammer solid-copper slingbacks?"

"Er . . . we don't go to a metalworker for our footwear, dear," said Sally. "Oh . . . I think I'm going to be sick . . ."

"Serves you right for drinking . . . vine," said Angua maliciously.

"Oh ha ha," said the vampire, from the shadows. "I'm perfectly fine with *sarcastic pause* 'vine,' thank you! What I *shouldn't* have drunk was sticky drinks with names made up by people with less sense of humor than, uh, excuse me . . . oh, noooo . . ."

"Are you all right?" said Cheery.

"I've just thrown up a small, hilarious, paper umbrella . . ."

"Oh dear."

"And a sparkler . . ."

"Is that you, Sergeant Angua?" said a voice in the gloom. A lantern was opened, and lit the approaching face of Constable Visit. As he approached, she could just make out the thick wad of pamphlets under his other arm.

"Hello, Washpot," she said. "What's up?"

". . . looks like a twist of lemon . . ." said a damp voice from the shadows.

"Mister Vimes sent me to search the dens of iniquity and low places of sin for you," said Visit.

"And the literature?" said Angua. "By the way, the words 'nothing personal' could have so easily been added to that last sentence."

"Since I was having to tour the temples of vice, Sergeant, I thought I could do Om's holy work at the same time," said Visit, whose indefatigable evangelical zeal triumphed over all adversity.* Sometimes whole bars full of people would lie down on the floor with the lights out when they heard he was coming down the street.

There were sounds of retching from the darkness.

"'Woe unto those who abuseth the vine,'" said Constable Visit. He caught the expression on Angua's face and added "no offense meant."

"We've been through all that," moaned Sally.

---

*They say there's one in every police station. Constable Visit-The-Ungodly-With-Explanatory-Pamphlets was enough for two.

"What does he want, Washpot?" said Angua.

"It's about Koom Valley again. He wants you back at the Yard."

"But we were stood down!" Sally complained.

"Sorry," said Visit cheerfully, "I reckon you've been stood up again."

"The story of my life," said Cheery.

"Oh, well, I suppose we'd better go," said Angua, trying to disguise her relief.

"When I say 'the story of my life,' obviously I don't mean the *whole* story," mumbled Cheery, apparently to herself, as she trailed behind them into a world blessedly without fun.

The Ramkins never threw anything away. There was something worrying about their attics, and it wasn't just that they had a faint aroma of long-dead pigeons.

The Ramkins *labeled* things. Vimes had been into the big attics in Scoone Avenue to fetch down the rocking horse and the cot and a whole box of elderly but much-loved soft toys smelling of mothballs. Nothing that might ever be useful again was thrown away. It was carefully labeled and put in the attic.

Brushing aside cobwebs with one hand and holding up a lantern with the other, Sybil led the way past boxes of MEN'S BOOTS, VARIOUS; RISIBLE PUPPETS, STRING & GLOVE; MODEL THEATER AND SCENERY. Maybe that was the reason for their wealth: they had bought things that were built to last, and now they seldom had to buy anything at all. Except food, of course, and even then Vimes would not have been surprised to see boxes labeled APPLE CORES, VARIOUS, or LEFTOVERS, NEED EATING UP.*

"Ah, here we are," said Sybil, lifting aside a bundle of fencing foils and lacrosse sticks. She pulled a long, thick tube out into the light.

"I didn't color it in, of course," she said as it was manhandled back to the stairs. "That would have taken forever."

Getting the heavy bundle down to the canteen took some effort and a certain amount of shoving, but eventually it was lifted onto the table and the crackling scroll removed.

While Sir Reynold unrolled the big ten-foot squares and enthused, Vimes pulled out the small-scale copy that Sybil had created. It was just small enough to fit on the table; he weighed down one end with a crusted mug and put a saltcellar on the other.

Methodia's notes made sad reading. Difficult reading, too, because a lot of them were half-burned, and in any case Rascal's handwriting was what might have been achieved by a spider on a trampoline during an earthquake.

The man was clearly as mad as a spoon, writing notes that he wanted to keep secret from the Chicken; sometimes he'd stop writing in mid-note if he thought the Chicken was watching. Apparently,

---

*That was a phrase of Sybil's that got to him. She'd announce at lunch, "we must have the pork tonight, it needs eating up." Vimes never had an actual problem with this, because he'd been raised to eat what was put in front of him, and do it quickly, too, before someone else snatched it away. He was just puzzled at the suggestion that he was there to do the food a favor.

he was a very sad sight to see until he picked up a brush, whereupon he would work quite quietly and with a strange glow to his features. And that was his life: one huge oblong of canvas. Methodia Rascal: born, painted famous picture, thought he was a chicken, died.

Given that the man couldn't touch bottom with a long stick, how could you make sense out of anything he wrote? The only note that seemed concise, if horrible, was the one generally accepted as his last, since it was found under his slumped body. It read:

Awk! Awk! It comes! IT COMES!

He'd choked on a throatful of feathers. And on the canvas, the last of the paint was still drying.

Vimes's eye was caught by the message numbered, arbitrarily, #39:

I thought it was a guiding omen, but it screams in the night.

An omen of what? And what about #143?

The dark, in the dark, like a star in chains.

Vimes had made a note of that one. He'd made a note of many others, too. But the worst thing about them—or the best, if you were keen on mysteries—was that they could mean *anything*. You could pick your own theory. The man was half-starved and in mortal dread of a chicken that lived in his head. You might as well try to make sense of raindrops.

Vimes pushed them aside and stared at the careful

pencil drawing. Even at this size, it was confusing. Up front, faces were so large that you could see the pores on a dwarf's nose. In the distance, Sybil had meticulously copied figures that were a quarter of an inch high.

Axes and clubs were being waved, spears were being pointed, there were charges and counter-charges and single combats. Across the whole length of the picture, dwarfs and trolls were locked in ferocious battle, hacking and smashing—

He thought: Who's missing?

"Sir Reynold, could you help me?" he said quietly, lest the nascent thought turn tail and run.

"Yes, Commander?" said the curator, hurrying over. "Doesn't Ladeah Sybil do the most *exquisite*—"

"She's very good, yes," said Vimes. "Tell me . . . how did Rascal *know* all this stuff?"

"There were many dwarf songs about it, and some troll stories. Oh, and some humans hwitnessed it."

"So Rascal could have read about it?"

"Oh, yes. Apart from the fact that he put it in the wrong part of the valley, he'd got it down quite accurately."

Vimes didn't take his gaze off the paper battle.

"Does anyone know why he put it in the wrong place, then?" he said.

"There are several theories. One is that he hwas deceived by the fact that the dead dwarfs hwere cremated at that end of the valley, but after the storm that hwas hwhere many of the bodies ended up. There was also a great deal of dead hwood for bonfires. But *I* believe he chose that end because the view is so much better. The mountains are so dramatic."

Vimes sat down, staring at the sketch, willing it to yield its secret.

Everyone will know the secret in a few weeks, Mr. Shine had said. Why?

"Sir Reynold, was anything going to happen to the painting in the next couple of weeks?" he said.

"Oh, yes," said the curator. "Hwe hwould have installed it in its new room."

"Anything special about that?"

"I did tell your sergeant, Commander," said the curator a little reproachfully. "It is circular. Rascal always intended it to be seen in the round, as it hwere. So that the viewer could be there."

And I'm nearly there, too, Vimes thought.

"I think the cube told the dwarfs something about Koom Valley," he said, in a faraway voice, because he felt as though he was already in the valley. "It told them that the place where it was found was important. Even Rascal thought it was important. They needed a map, and Rascal painted one, even if he didn't know it. Fred?"

"Yessir?"

"The dwarfs weren't bothered about damaging the bottom of the painting because it doesn't contain anything important. It's just people. People move around."

"But, hwith respect, Commander, so do all those boulders," said Sir Reynold.

"They don't matter. No matter how much the valley has changed, this picture will work," said Vimes. The glow of understanding lit his brain.

"But even the rivers moved over the years, and any amount of boulders have rolled down from the mountains," said Sir Reynold. "I'm told the area looks nothing like that now."

"Even so," said Vimes, in the same dreamy voice, "this map will work for thousands of years. It doesn't mark a rock or a hollow or a cave, it just marks a spot. I can pinpoint it. That is, if I had a pin."

"I have one!" Sir Reynold said triumphantly, reaching to his lapel. "I spotted it in the street yesterday, and of course hwe all know the old saying: 'See a pin and pick it up, and all day long—'"

"Yes, thank you," said Vimes, taking it. He walked to the end of the table and picked up one end of the painting, and dragged it back down the length of the table, the heavy paper flapping after him.

He pinned the two ends together, held up the circle he had made, and lowered it over his head.

"The truth is in the mountains," he said. "For years you've been looking at a line of mountains. It's really a circle of mountains."

"But I knew that!" said Sir Reynold.

"In a way, sir, but you probably didn't *understand* it until now, yes? Rascal was standing somewhere *important*."

"hWell, yes. But it hwas a cave, Commander. He specifically mentions a cave. That's hwhy people have searched along the valley hwalls. The painting's set right in the middle, near the river."

"Then there's something we still don't know!" said Vimes, annoyed that a big moment had so quickly become a small one. "I'll find out what it is when I get there!"

There. He'd said it. But he'd known that he was going to go, known for . . . how long? It seemed like forever, but had it seemed like forever yesterday? This afternoon? He could see the place in his mind's eye. Vimes at Koom Valley! He could practically taste the air! He could hear the roaring of the river, which ran as cold as ice!

"Sam—" Sybil began.

"No, this has got to be sorted out," Vimes said quickly. "I don't care about the stupid secret! Those deep-downers murdered our dwarfs, remember? *They* think the painting is a map they can use, and that's why they're going there. I've got to go after them."

"Look, Sam, if—" Sybil tried.

"We can't afford a war between the trolls and the dwarfs, dear. That business the other night was just a dumb gang fight. A real war in Ankh-Morpork would wreck the place! And somehow it's all tied up with this!"

"I agree! I want to come, too!" Sybil screamed.

"Besides, I'll be perfectly safe if— what?" Vimes gaped at his wife while his mental gears ripped into reverse. "No, it's too dangerous!"

"Sam Vimes, I've dreamed of visiting Koom Valley all my life, so don't you think for one moment you're gallivanting off to see it and leave me at home!"

"I don't gallivant! I've never gallivanted. I don't know *how* to vant! I don't even have a galli! But there's going to be a war there soon!"

"Then I shall tell them we're not involved!" said Sybil calmly.

"That won't work!"

"Then it won't work in Ankh-Morpork, either," said Sybil, with the air of some player cunningly knocking out four dwarfs in one go. "Sam, you *know* you're going to lose this. There's no point in arguing. Besides, I speak dwarfish. We'll take Young Sam, too."

"No!"

"So that's all sorted, then," said Sybil, apparently struck by sudden deafness. "If you want to catch up with the dwarfs, I suggest *we* leave as soon as possible."

Sir Reynold turned to her with his mouth open.

"But, Ladeah Sybil, armies are already massing there. It's no place for a ladeah!"

Vimes winced. Sybil had made up her mind. This was going to be like watching that dwarf being flamed by dragons, all over again.

Lady Sybil's bosom, which she was allowed to have, expanded as she took a deep breath; it seemed to lift her slightly off the ground.

"Sir Reynold," she said, with a side order of ice. "In the Year of the Louse, my great-grandmother once cooked, *personally*, a full dinner for eighteen in a military redoubt that was entirely surrounded by bloodthirsty Klatchians, *and* she felt able to include sorbet and nuts. My grandmother, in the Year of the Quiet Monkey, defended our embassy in Pseudopolis against a mob, with no assistance but that offered by a gardener, a trained parrot, and a pan of hot cooking fat. My late aunt, when our coach was once held up at bowpoint by two desperate highwaymen, gave them such a talking-to that they actually ran away crying for their mothers, Sir Reynold, their *mothers*. We are no strangers to danger, Sir Reynold. May I also remind you that quite probably half the dwarfs who fought at Koom Valley *were* ladies? No one told *them* to stay at home!"

So that's settled, then, thought Vimes. We— damn!

"Captain?" he said. "Send someone to find that dwarf Grag Bashfullsson, will you? Tell him Commander Vimes presents his compliments and will indeed be leaving first thing in the morning."

"Er . . . right, sir. Will do," said Carrot.

How did he know I'd be going? Vimes wondered. I suppose it was inevitable? But he could have hung us out to dry if he'd said we'd mistreated that dwarf. And he's one of Mr. Shine's pupils, I'll bet on it. Good idea to keep an eye on him, perhaps . . .

When *did* Lord Vetinari sleep? Presumably, the man must get his head down at some point, Vimes had reasoned. Everyone slept. Catnaps could get you by for a while, but sooner or later you need a solid eight hours, right?

It was almost midnight, and there was Vetinari at his desk, fresh as a daisy and chilly as morning dew.

"Are you sure about this, Vimes?"

"Carrot can look after things. They've quietened down, anyway. I think most of the serious troublemakers have headed for Koom Valley."

"A good reason, one might say, for you not to go. Vimes, I have . . . agents for this sort of thing."

"But you wanted me to hunt them down, sir!" Vimes protested.

"In Koom Valley? At this time? Taking a force there now could have far-reaching consequences, Vimes!"

"Good! You told me to drag them into the light! As far as they're concerned, *I* am far-reaching consequences!"

"Well, certainly," said Vetinari, after staring at Vimes for longer than was comfortable. "And when you have boldly reached so far, you will need friends. I shall make sure the Low King is at least aware of your presence."

"Don't worry, he'll find out soon enough," growled Vimes. "Oh, yes."

"I have no doubt he will. He has his agents in our city, just as I have in his. So I will do him the courtesy of telling him formally what he will in any case know. That is called *politics*, Vimes. It is a thing we try to do in the government."

"But . . . spies? I thought we were chums with the Low King!"

"Of course we are," said Vetinari. "And the more we know about each other, the friendlier we shall remain. We'd hardly bother to spy on our enemies. What would be the point? Is Lady Sybil happy to let you go?"

"She's coming with me. She insists."

"Is that safe?"

"Is here safe?" said Vimes, shrugging. "We had dwarfs coming up through the damn floor! Don't worry, she and Young Sam will be kept out of harm's way. I'll take Fred and Nobby. And I want to take Angua, Sally, Detritus, and Cheery, too. Multi-species, sir. That always helps the politics."

"And the Summoning Dark? What about *that*, Vimes? Oh, *don't* look at me like that. It's common talk among the dwarfs. One of the dying dwarfs put a curse on everyone who was in the mine, I'm told."

"I wouldn't know about that, sir," said Vimes, resorting to the wooden expression that so often saw him through. "It's mystic. We don't do mystic in the Watch."

"It's not a joke, Vimes. It's very old magic, I understand. So old, indeed, that most dwarfs have forgotten that it *is* magic. And it's powerful. It will be tracking them."

"I'll just look out for a big floaty eye with a tail, then, shall I?" said Vimes. "That should make it easy."

"Vimes, I *know* you must be aware that the symbol is not the thing itself," said the Patrician.

"Yessir. I know. But magic has no place in coppering. We don't use it to find culprits. We don't use it to get confessions. Because you can't trust the bloody stuff, sir. It's got a mind of its own. If there's a curse chasing these bastards, well, that's its business. But if I reach 'em first, *sir*, then they'll be my prisoners and it'll have to get past me."

"Vimes, Archchancellor Ridcully tells me he believes it may be a quasidemonic entity that is untold millions of years old!"

"I've said my piece, sir," said Vimes, staring at a point just above Lord Vetinari's head. "And it is my duty to catch up with these people. I believe they may be able to help me with my inquiries."

"But you have no evidence, Vimes. And you are going to need very solid evidence."

"Right. So I want to bring them back here, eyeballs

on a string or not. Them and their damn guards. So's I can inquire. Someone will tell me something."

"And it'll also be to your personal satisfaction?" said Vetinari sharply.

"Is this a trick question, sir?"

"Well done, well done," said Vetinari softly. "Lady Sybil is a remarkable woman, Vimes."

"Yessir. She is."

Vimes left.

After a while, Vetinari's chief clerk, Drumknott, entered the room on velvet feet and placed a cup of tea in front of Vetinari.

"Thank you, Drumknott. You were listening?"

"Yes, sir. The Commander seemed very forth-right."

"They invaded his home, Drumknott."

"Quite, sir."

Vetinari leaned back, and stared at the ceiling.

"Tell me, Drumknott, are you a betting man at all?"

"I have been known to have the occasional 'little flutter,' sir."

"Given, then, a contest between an invisible and very powerful quasidemonic *thing* of pure vengeance on the one hand, and the commander on the other, where would you wager, say . . . one dollar?"

"I wouldn't, sir. That looks like one that would go to the judges."

"Yes," said Vetinari, staring thoughtfully at the closed door. "Yes, *indeed.*"

I don't use magic, thought Vimes, walking through the rain toward Unseen University. But, sometimes, I tell lies.

He avoided the main entrance and headed as circumspectly as possible for Wizards' Passage, where, halfway down, university access for all was available via several loose bricks. Generations of rascally drunk student wizards had used them to get back in late at night. Later on, they'd become very important and powerful wizards, with full beards and fuller stomachs, but had never lifted a finger to have the wall repaired. It was, after all, Traditional. Nor was it usually patrolled by the Lobsters,* who believed in Tradition even more than the wizards.

On this occasion, though, one was lurking in the shadows, and jumped when Vimes tapped him on the shoulder. "Oh, it's you Commander Vimes, sir. It's me, sir, Wiggleigh, sir. The archchancellor is waiting for you in the gardener's hut, sir. Follow me, sir. Mum's the word, eh, sir?"

Vimes trailed after Wiggleigh across the dark, squelchy lawns. Oddly, though, he didn't feel so tired now. Days and days of bad sleep and he felt quite fresh, in a fuzzy sort of way. It was the smell of the chase, that's what it was. He'd pay for it later.

Wiggleigh, looking both ways with a conspiratorial air that would have attracted instant attention had anyone been watching, opened the door of the garden shed.

---

*The university porters, or bledlows, who doubled, with rather more enthusiasm, as its under-proctors, a private police force. They commanded their nickname for being thick-shelled, liable to turn red when hot, and having the smallest brain for their size of any known creature.

There was a large figure waiting inside.

"Commander!" it bellowed happily. "What larks, eh? *Very* cloak-and-dagger!"

Only heavy rain could possibly muffle the voice of Archchancellor Ridcully when he was feeling cheerful.

"Could you keep it down a bit, Archchancellor?" said Vimes, shutting the door quickly.

"Sorry! I mean, sorry," said the wizard. "Do take a seat. The compost sacks are quite acceptable. Well, er . . . how may I help you, Sam?"

"Can we agree for now that you can't?" said Vimes.

"Intriguing. Do continue," said Ridcully, leaning closer.

"You know I won't have magic used in the Watch," Vimes went on. As he sat down in the semidarkness, a coiled-up hosepipe ambushed him from above, as they do, and he had to wrestle it to the shed floor.

"I do, sir, and I respect you for it, although there are those that think you are a damn silly fool."

"Well . . ." Vimes said, trying to put "damn silly fool" behind him, "the fact is, I must get to Koom Valley very fast. Er . . . very fast indeed."

"One might say—*magically* fast?" said Ridcully.

"As it were," said Vimes, fidgeting. He really hated having to do this. And what *had* he sat on?

"Mmm," said Ridcully. "But without, I imagine, any significant hocus-pocus? You appear uncomfortable, sir!"

Vimes triumphantly held up a large onion. "Sorry," he said, tossing it aside. "No, definitely no pocus. Possibly a little hocus. I just need an edge. They've got a day's start on me."

"I see. You will be traveling alone?"

"No, there will have to be eleven of us. Two coaches."

"My word! And disappearing in a puff of smoke to reappear elsewhere is—"

"Out of the question. I just need—"

"An edge," said the wizard. "Yes. Something magical in its cause but not in its effect. Nothing too obvious."

"And no chance of anyone being turned into a frog or anything like that," said Vimes quickly.

"Of course," said Ridcully. He clapped his hands together. "Well, Commander, I'm afraid we can't help you. Meddling in things like this is not what wizarding is all about!" He lowered his voice and went on: "We will *particularly* not be able to help you if you have the coaches, empty, around the back in, oh, call it about an hour?"

"Oh? Er . . . right," said Vimes, trying to catch up. "You're not going to make them fly or anything, are you?"

"We're not going to do anything, Commander!" said Ridcully jovially, slapping him on the back. "I thought that was agreed! And I think also that you should leave now, although, of course, you have, in fact, not been here. And neither have I. I say, this spying business is pretty clever, eh?"

When Vimes was gone, Mustrum Ridcully sat back, lit his pipe, and, as an afterthought, used the last of the match to light the candle lantern on the potting table. The gardener could get pretty acerbic if people messed about with his shed, so perhaps he ought to tidy up a bit—

He stared at the floor, where a tumbled hosepipe and a fallen onion made what looked, at a casual glance, like a large eyeball with a tail.

The rain cooled Vimes down. It had cooled down the streets, too. You have to be really keen to riot in the rain. Besides, news of last night had got around. No one was *sure*, of course, and such were the effects of Fluff and Big Hammer that a large if elementary school of thought had been left uncertain about what really happened. They woke up feeling bad, right? *Something* must have happened. And tonight the rain was setting in, so maybe it was better to stay in the pub.

He walked through the wet, whispering darkness, mind ablaze.

How fast could those dwarfs travel? Some of them sounded pretty old. But they'd be *tough* and old. Even so, the roads in that direction were none too good, and a body could only stand so much shaking.

And Sybil was taking Young Sam. That was stupid, except that it . . . wasn't stupid, not after dwarfs had broken into your home. Home was where you had to feel safe. If you didn't feel safe, it wasn't home. Against all common sense, he agreed with Sybil. Home was where they were together. She'd already sent off an urgent clacks to some old chum of hers who lived near the valley; she seemed to think it was going to be some kind of family outing.

There was a group of dwarfs hanging around on a

corner, heavily armed. Maybe the bars were all full, or maybe they needed cooling down, too. No law against hanging around, right?

Wrong, growled Vimes as he drew nearer. Come along, boys. Say something wrong. Lay hold of a weapon. Move slightly. Breathe loudly. Give me something that could be stretched to "in self-defense." It'd be my word against yours, and believe me, lads, I'm unlikely to leave you capable of saying a single damn *thing*.

The dwarfs took one clear look at the approaching vision, haloed in torchlight and mist, and took to their heels.

Right!

The entity known as the Summoning Dark sped through streets of eternal night, past misty buildings of memory that wavered at its passage. It was getting there, it was getting there. It was having to change the habits of millennia, but it was finding ways in, even if they were no bigger than keyholes. It had never had to work this hard before, never had to move this fast. It was . . . exhilarating.

But always, when it paused by some grating or unguarded chimney, it heard the pursuit. It was slow, but it never stopped following. Sooner or later, it would catch up.

Grag Bashfullsson lodged in a subdivided cellar in Cheap Street. The rent wasn't much, but he had to admit that neither was the accommodation: he could lie on his very narrow bed and touch all four walls or, rather, three walls and a heavy curtain that separated his little space from that of the family of nineteen dwarfs that occupied the rest of the cellar. But meals were included, and they respected his privacy. It was something, to have a grag as a lodger, even if this one seemed rather young and showed his face. It still impressed the neighbors.

On the other side of the curtain, children were squabbling, a baby was crying, and there was the smell of rat-and-cabbage casserole. Someone was sharpening an axe. And someone else was snoring. For a dwarf in Ankh-Morpork, solitude was something that you had to cultivate on the inside.

Books and papers filled the space that wasn't bed. Bashfullsson's desk was a board laid across his knees. He was reading a battered book, its cover cracked and moldy, and the runes passing under his eye said: "It has no strength in this world. To fulfill any purpose, the Dark must find a champion, a living creature it can bend to its will . . ."

Bashfullsson sighed. He'd read the phrase a dozen times, hoping he could make it mean something other than the obvious. He copied the words into his notebook anyway. Then he put the notebook in his satchel, swung the satchel onto his back, went and paid Toin Footstamper two weeks' rent in advance, and stepped out into the rain.

Vimes didn't remember going to sleep. He didn't re-member sleeping. He surfaced from darkness when Carrot shook him awake.

"The coaches are in the yard, Mister Vimes!"

"Fwisup?" murmured Vimes, blinking in the light.

"I've told people to load them up, sir, but—"

"But what?" Vimes sat up.

"I think you'd better come and see, sir."

When Vimes stepped out into the damp dawn, two coaches were indeed standing in the yard. Detritus was idly watching the loading, while leaning on the Piecemaker.

Carrot hurried over when he saw the commander.

"It's the wizards, sir," he said. "They've done something."

The coaches looked normal enough to Vimes, and he said so.

"Oh, they *look* fine," said Carrot. He reached down and put his hand on the doorsill, and added: "But they *do* this."

He lifted the laden coach over his head.

"You shouldn't be able to do that," said Vimes.

"That's right, sir," said Carrot, lowering the coach gently onto the cobbles. "It doesn't get any heavier with people inside, either. And if you come over here, sir, they've done something to the horses, too."

"Any idea *what* they've done, Captain?"

"None whatsoever, sir. The coaches were just outside the university. Haddock and I drove them down here. Very light, of course. It's the harnesses that are worrying me. See here, sir."

"I see the leather's very thick," said Vimes. "And what're all these copper knobs? Something magical?"

"Could be, sir. Something happens at thirteen miles an hour. I don't know what." Carrot patted the side of the coach, which slid away.

"The thing is, sir, I don't know how much of an edge this gives you."

"What? Surely a weightless coach would—"

"Oh, it'll help, sir, especially on the inclines. But horses can only go so fast for so long, sir, and once they've got the coach moving, it's a rolling weight and not so much of a problem."

"Thirteen miles an hour," Vimes mused. "Hmm. That's pretty fast."

"Well, the mail coaches are getting nine or ten miles an hour average on many runs now," said Carrot. "But the roads will get a lot worse when you get near Koom Valley."

"You don't think it'll take wing, do you?"

"I think the wizards would have said so if it was going to do something like that, sir. But it's funny you should mention it, because there's seven broomsticks nailed underneath each coach."

"What? Why don't they just float out of the yard?"

"Magic, sir. I think they just compensate for the weight."

"Good grief, yes. Why didn't I think of that?" said

Vimes sourly. "And that's why I don't like magic, Captain. 'cos it's *magic*. You can't ask questions, it's magic. It doesn't explain anything, it's magic. You don't know where it comes from, it's magic! That's what I don't like about magic, it does everything by magic!"

"That's the significant factor, sir, there's no doubt about it," said Carrot. "I'll just see to the last of the packing, if you'll excuse me . . ."

Vimes glared at the coaches. He probably shouldn't have brought in the wizards, but where was the choice? Oh, they could probably have sent Sam Vimes all that way in a puff of smoke and the blink of an eye, but who'd actually arrive there, and who'd come back? How would he know if it was him? He was certain that people were not supposed to disappear like that.

Sam Vimes had always been, by nature, a pedestrian. That's why he was also going to take Willikins, who knew how to drive. He'd also demonstrated to Vimes his ability to throw a common fish knife so hard that it was quite difficult to pull out of the wall. At times like this, Vimes liked to see a skill like that in a butler—

"'S'cuse me, sir," said Detritus, behind him. "Could I have a word, pers'nal?"

"Yes. Of course," said Vimes.

"I, er, hope what I said yesterday inna cells wasn't goin' too—"

"Can't remember a word of it," said Vimes.

Detritus look relieved. "Thank you, sir. Er . . . I want to take young Brick with us, sir. He's got no kin here, doesn't even know what clan he is. He'll only get messed up again if I take my eye off'f him. An' he's never seen der mountains. Never been ouside der city, even!"

There was a pleading look in the troll's eyes. Vimes recollected that his marriage to Ruby was happy but childless.

"Well, we don't seem to have a weight problem," he said. "All right. But you're to keep an eye on him, okay?"

The troll beamed. "Yessir! I'll see you don't regret it, sir!"

"Breakfast, Sam!" called Sybil, from the doorway. A nasty suspicion gripped Vimes, and he hurried over to the other coach, where Carrot was strapping on the last bag.

"Who packed the food? Did Sybil pack the food?" he said.

"I think so, sir."

"Was there . . . fruit?" said Vimes, probing the horror.

"I believe so, sir. Quite a lot. And vegetables."

"*Some* bacon, surely?" Vimes was nearly begging. "Very good for a long journey, bacon. It travels well."

"I think it's staying at home today," said Carrot. "I have to tell you, sir, that Lady Sybil has found out about the bacon sandwich arrangement. She said to tell you the game was up, sir."

"I *am* the commander around here, you know," said Vimes, with as much hauteur as he could muster on an empty stomach.

"Yes, sir. But Lady Sybil has a very quiet way of being firm, sir."

"She *has*, hasn't she," said Vimes as they strolled

toward the building. "I'm a very lucky man, you know," he added, just in case Carrot may have got the wrong impression.

"Yes, sir. You are indeed."

"Captain!"

They turned. Someone was hurrying through the gate. He had two swords strapped to his back.

"Ah, Special Constable Hancock," said Carrot, stepping forward. "Do you have something for me?"

"Er . . . yes, Captain." Hancock looked nervously at Vimes.

"This *is* official business, Andy," said Vimes reassuringly.

"Not much to give you, sir. But I asked around, and a young lady sent at least two self-coded droppers to Bonk in the last week. That means it goes to the main tower there and gets handed over to whoever turns up with the right authorization. We don't have to know who they are."

"Well done," said Carrot. "Any description?"

"Young lady with short hair is the best I could get. Signed the message 'Aicalas.'"

Vimes burst out laughing. "Well, that's about it. Thank you, Special Constable Hancock, very much."

"Crime and the clacks is going to be a growing problem," said Carrot sadly, when they were alone again.

"Quite likely, Captain," said Vimes. "But here and now we know that our Sally is not being straight with us."

"We can't be *certain* it's her, sir," said Carrot.

"Oh no?" said Vimes happily. "This quite cheers me up. It's one of the lesser-known failings of the vampire. No one knows why they do it. It goes with having big windows and easily torn curtains. A sort of undeath wish, you might say. However clever they are, they can't resist thinking that no one will recognize their name if they spell it *backwards*. Let's go."

Vimes turned back to head into the building, and noticed a small, neat figure standing patiently by the door. It had the look of someone who was quite happy to wait. He sighed. I bargain without an axe in my hand, eh?

"Breakfast, Mr. Bashfullsson?" he said.

"This is all rather fun," said Sybil an hour later as the coaches headed out of the city. "Do you remember when we last went on holiday, Sam?"

"That wasn't really a holiday," said Vimes. Above them, Young Sam swung back and forth in a little hammock, cooing.

"Well, it was very interesting, all the same," said Sybil.

"Yes, dear. Werewolves tried to eat me."

Vimes sat back. The coach was comfortably upholstered and well sprung. At the moment, while it threaded through the traffic, the magical loss of weight was hardly noticeable. Would it mean anything? How fast could a bunch of old dwarfs travel? If they really had taken a big wagon, the coaches would catch them tomorrow, when the mountains were still a distant prospect. In the meantime, at least he could get some rest.

He pulled out a battered volume titled *Walking in the Koom Valley*, by Eric Wheelbrace, a man who apparently had walked on just about everything bigger than a sheep track in the Near Ramtops.*

It had a sketch map, the only actual map of the valley Vimes had seen. Eric wasn't a half-bad sketch artist.

Koom Valley was . . . well, Koom Valley was basically a drain, that's what it was; nearly thirty miles of soft limestone rock edged by mountains of harder rock, so what you had would have been a canyon if it wasn't so wide. One end was almost on the snowline, the other merged into the plains.

It was said that even clouds kept away from the desolation that was Koom Valley. Maybe they did, but that didn't matter. The valley got the water anyway, from meltwater and the hundreds of waterfalls that poured over its walls from the mountains that cupped it. One of those falls, the Tears of the King, was half a mile high.

The Koom River didn't just rise in this valley. It leapt and danced in this valley. By the time it was halfway down this valley, it was a crisscrossing of thundering waters, forever merging and parting. They carried and hurled great rocks, and played with whole fallen trees from the dripping forests colonizing the scree that had built up against the

---

*And even then had been belaboring mountain goats on apparently sheer cliff faces and, while pebbles slid and bounced around him, was clearly accusing them of obstructing his right to roam. Eric believed very firmly that the Land Belonged To The People, and also that he was more The People than anyone else was. Eric went everywhere with a map encased in waterproof material, on a string around his neck. Such people are not to be trifled with.

walls. They gurgled into holes and rose again, miles away, as fountains. They had no mapable course—a good storm higher up in the mountains could bring house-sized rocks and half a stricken woodland down in the flood, blocking the sinkholes and piling up dams. Some of these could survive for years, becoming little islands in the leaping waters, growing little forests and little meadows and colonies of big birds. Then some key rock would be shifted by a random river, and within an hour, it would all be gone.

Nothing that couldn't fly lived in the valley, at least for long. The dwarfs had tried to tame it, back before the first battle. It hadn't worked. Hundreds of trolls and dwarfs had been swept up in the famous flood, and many had never been found again. Koom Valley had taken them all into its sinkholes and chambers and caverns, and had kept them.

There were places in the valley where a man could drop a colored cork into a swirling sinkhole and wait for more than twenty minutes before it bobbed up on a fountain less than a dozen yards away.

Eric himself had seen this trick done by a guide, Vimes read, who'd demanded half a dollar for the demonstration. Oh yes, people visited the valley, human sightseers, poets and artists looking for inspiration in the ragged, uncompromising wilderness. And there were human guides who'd take them up there, for a hefty price. For a few extra dollars, they'd tell the history of the place. They'd tell you how the wind in the rocks, and the roaring of the waters, carried the sounds of ancient battle, continuing in death. They'd say, maybe all those trolls and dwarfs the valley took are still fighting, down there in the dark maze of caves and thundering torrents.

One admitted to Eric that when he was a boy, during a cool summer when the meltwaters were pretty low, he'd roped down into one of the sinkholes (because, like all such stories, the history of Koom Valley wouldn't have been complete without rumors of vast treasures swept down into the dark) and had himself heard, above the sound of the water, battle noises and the shouting of dwarfs, no sir, honestly sir, it chilled my blood so it did, sir, why, thank you very much, sir . . .

Vimes sat up in his seat.

Was that true? If that man had gone a little further, would he have found the little talking cube that Methodia Rascal had been unlucky enough to take home? Eric had dismissed it as an attempt to scrounge another dollar, and probably it was, but— no, the cube would surely have been long gone by then. Even so. It was an intriguing thought.

The driver's hatch slid back.

"Outside the city, sir, clear road ahead," Willikins reported.

"Thank you." Vimes stretched, and looked across at Sybil. "Well, this is where we find out. Hang on to Young Sam."

"I'm sure Mustrum wouldn't do anything dangerous, Sam," said Sybil.

"I don't know about that," said Vimes, opening the door. "I'm sure he wouldn't *mean* to."

He swung himself out and hauled himself on the roof of the coach, with a helping hand from Detritus.

The coach was moving well. The sun was shining. On either side of the highway, the cabbage fields lent their gentle perfume to the air.

Vimes settled down beside the butler.

"Okay," he said. "Everyone holding on to something? Good. Let 'em go!"

Willikins cracked the whip. There was a mild jolt as the horses stretched, and Vimes felt the coach speed up.

And that seemed to be it. He'd expected something a little more impressive. They were gradually going faster, yes, but that in itself didn't seem very magical.

"I reckon about twelve miles an hour now, sir," said Willikins. "That's pretty good. They're running well without—"

Something was happening to the harnesses. The copper discs were sparking.

"Look at der cabbages, sir!" Detritus shouted.

On either side of the road, cabbages were bursting into flames and rocketing out of the ground. And still the horses went faster.

"It's about power!" yelled Vimes, above the wind. "We're running on cabbages! And the—"

He stopped. The rear two horses were rising gently in the air. As he stared, the lead pair rose, too.

He risked turning in his seat. The other coach was keeping up with them; he could clearly see Fred Colon's pink face, staring ahead in rigid terror.

When Vimes turned back to look ahead, all four horses were off the ground.

And there was a fifth horse, larger than the other four, and transparent. It was visible only because of the dust and the occasional glint of light off an invisible flank; it was, in fact, what you got if you took away a horse but left the movement of a horse, the speed of a horse, the . . . spirit of a horse, that part of a horse which came alive in the rushing of the wind. The part of a horse that was, in fact, Horse.

There was hardly any sound now. Perhaps sound was unable to keep up.

"Sir?" said Willikins quietly.

"Yes?" said Vimes, his eyes streaming.

"It took us less than a minute to go that last mile. I timed us between milestones, sir."

"Sixty miles in an hour? Don't be daft, man! A coach can't go that fast!"

"Just as you say, sir."

A milestone flashed past. Out of the corner of his ear, Willikins heard Vimes counting under his breath until, before very long, another stone fell away behind them.

"Wizards, eh?" said Vimes weakly, staring ahead again.

"Indeed, sir," said Willikins. "May I suggest that once we are through Quirm, we head straight across the grass country?"

"The roads up there are pretty bad, you know," said Vimes.

"So I believe, sir. However, that will not, in fact, matter," said the butler, not taking his eyes off the unrolling road ahead.

"Why not? If we try to go at speed over those rough—"

"I was referring obliquely, sir, to the fact that we are not precisely touching the ground anymore."

Vimes, clinging with care to the rail, looked over the side. The wheels were turning idly. The road, just below them, was a blur. Ahead of them, the spirit of the horse galloped serenely onwards.

"There's plenty of coaching inns around Quirm," he said. "We could, er, stop for lunch?"

"Late breakfast, sir! Mail coach ahead, sir! Hold tight!"

A tiny square block on the road ahead was getting bigger quite fast. Willikins twitched on the reins, Vimes had a momentary vision of rearing horses, and the mail coach was a dwindling dot, soon hidden by the smoke of flaming brassicas.

"Dem milestones is goin' past real fast now," Detritus observed in a conversational tone of voice. Behind him, Brick lay flat on the roof of the coach with his eyes shut tight, having never before been in a world where the sky went all the way to the ground; there were brass rails around the top of the coach, and he was leaving fingerprints in them.

"Could we try braking?" said Vimes. "Look out! Haycart!"

"That only stops the wheels spinning, sir!" yelled Willikins as the cart went by with a *whoom* and fell back into the distance.

"Try pulling on the reins a little!"

"At this speed, sir?"

Vimes slid back the hatch behind him. Sybil had Young Sam on her knee, and was pulling a wooly jumper over his head.

"Is everything all right, dear?" he ventured.

She looked up and smiled. "Lovely, smooth ride, Sam. Aren't we going rather fast, though?"

"Er . . . could you please sit with your back to the horses?" said Sam. "And hold on tight to Young Sam? It might be a bit . . . bumpy."

He watched her shift seats. Then he shut the hatch, and yelled to Willikins.

"Now!"

Nothing seemed to happen. In Vimes's mind, the milestones were already going *zip* . . . *zip* as they flashed past.

Then the flying world slowed, while in the fields on either side hundreds of burning cabbages leapt toward the sky, trailing oily smoke. The horse of light and air disappeared, and the real horses dropped gently to the road, going from floating statues to beasts in full gallop without a stumble.

He heard a brief scream as the rear coach tore past and swerved into a field full of cauliflowers, where, eventually, it squelched to a flatulent halt. And then there was stillness, except for the occasional thud of a falling cabbage. Detritus was comforting Brick, who'd not picked a good day to go cold turkey; it was turning out to be frozen roc.

A skylark, safely above cabbage range, sang in the blue sky. Below, except for the whimpering of Brick, all was silent.

Absentmindedly, Vimes pulled a half-cooked leaf off his helmet and flicked it away.

"Well, that was fun," he said, his voice a little distant.

He got down carefully and opened the coach door.

"Everyone all right in here?" he said.

"Yes. Why have we stopped?" said Sybil.

"We ran out of . . . er, well, we just ran out," said

Vimes. "I'd better go and check that everyone else is all right . . ."

The milestone nearby proclaimed that it was but two miles to Quirm. Vimes fished out the Gooseberry as a red-hot cabbage smacked into the road behind him.

"Good morning!" he said brightly to the surprised imp. "What is the time, please?"

"Er . . . nine minutes to eight, Insert Name Here," said the imp.

"So that would mean a speed slightly above one mile a minute," mused Vimes. "Very good."

Moving like a sleepwalker, he walked into the field on the other side of the road and followed the trail of stricken, steaming greens until he reached the other coach. People were climbing out of it.

"Everyone okay?" he said. "Breakfast today will be boiled cabbage, baked cabbage, fried cabbage—" he stepped smartly aside as a steaming cauliflower hit the ground and exploded "—and Cauliflower Surprise. Where's Fred?"

"Looking for somewhere to throw up," said Angua.

"Good man. We'll take a minute or two to rest here, I think."

With that, Sam Vimes walked back to the milestone, sat down next to it, put his arms around it, and held on tight until he felt better.

You could catch up with the dwarfs long before they're near Koom Valley. Good grief, at the speed we did earlier

*you'd have to watch out in case you smash into the back of
them!*

Vimes's thoughts nagged at him as Willikins drove
the coach, at a very sedate speed, out of Quirm and
then, on a clear stretch of road, unleashed the hidden
horsepower until they were bowling along at forty
miles every hour. That seemed quite fast enough.

*No one was hurt, after all. You could get to Koom
Valley by nightfall!*

Yes, but that was not the plan.

Okay, he thought, but what was the plan, exactly?
Well, it helped that Sybil knew more or less everybody, or at least everybody who was female, of a certain age, and who had been to the Quirm College
for Young Ladies at the same time as Sybil. There
appeared to be hundreds of them. They all seemed
to have names like Bunny or Bubbles, they kept in
touch meticulously, they'd all married influential or
powerful men, they all hugged one another when
they met, and went on about the good old days in
Form 3b or whatever, and if they acted together,
they could probably run the world or, it occurred to
Vimes, might already be doing so.

They were Ladies Who Organize.

Vimes did his best, but he could never keep track
of them. A web of correspondence held them all together, and he marveled at Sybil's ability to be concerned over the problems of a child, whom she'd
never met, of a woman she hadn't seen in twenty-five
years. It was a female thing.

So they would be staying in the town near the foot
of the valley, with a lady currently known only as
Bunty, whose husband was the local magistrate. Ac-

cording to Sybil, he had his own police force. Vimes translated this, in the privacy of his head, as "he's got his own gang of thuggish, toothless, evil-smelling thief-takers" since that was what you generally got in these little towns. Still, they might be useful.

Beyond that . . . there was no plan. He intended to find the dwarfs and capture and drag as many as possible back to Ankh-Morpork. But that was an intention, not a plan. It was a firm intention, though. Five people had been murdered. You couldn't just turn your back on that. He'd drag 'em back and lock them up and throw everything at 'em and see what stuck. He doubted if they had many friends now. Of course, it'd get political, it always did, but at least people would *know* that he'd done all he could, and it was the best he could do. With any luck, it would stop anyone else getting funny ideas.

And then there was the damn Secret, but it occurred to him that if he *did* find it, and it simply was proof that the dwarfs ambushed the trolls or the trolls ambushed the dwarfs or they both ambushed each other at the same time, well, he might as well drop it down a hole. It really wouldn't change anything. And it was unlikely to be a pot of gold; people didn't take a lot of money onto battlefields, because there wasn't very much to spend it on.

Anyway, it had been a good start. They'd clawed some time, hadn't they? They could keep up a cracking pace and change horses at every staging inn, couldn't they? Why was he trying to persuade himself? It made *sense* to slow down. It was *dangerous* to go fast.

"If we keep up this pace, we might get there the

day after tomorrow, right?" he said to Willikins as they rattled on between stands of young maize.

"If you say so, sir," said Willikins. Vimes noted the hint of diplomacy.

"You don't think so?" he said. "Come on, you can speak your mind!"

"Well, sir, those dwarfs want to get there fast, d'you think?" said Willikins.

"I expect so. I don't think they want to hang around. So?"

"So I'm just puzzled that you think they'll be using the road, sir. They could use broomsticks, couldn't they?"

"I suppose so," Vimes conceded. "But the archchancellor would have told me if they'd done that, surely."

"Begging your pardon, sir, but what business would it be of his? They wouldn't have to bother the gentlemen at the university. Everyone knows the best broomsticks are made by the dwarfs, up at Copperhead."

The coach rolled on.

After a while, Vimes inquired, in the voice of one who has been thinking deeply: "They'd have to travel at night, though. They'd be spotted otherwise."

"Very true, sir," said Willikins, staring ahead.

There was more thoughtful silence.

"Do you think this thing could jump fences?" said Vimes.

"I'm game to give it a try, sir," said Willikins. "I think the wizards put some thought into all this."

"And how fast do you think it could go, for the sake of argument?" said Vimes.

"Dunno, sir. But I've got a feeling it might be pretty fast. A hundred miles in an hour, maybe?"

"You really think so? That means we could be halfway there in a couple of hours!"

"Well, you did say you wanted to get there fast, sir," said Willikins.

This time, the silence went on longer, before Vimes said: "All right, stop somewhere. I want to make sure that everyone knows what we're going to do."

"Happy to do that, sir," said Willikins. "It'll give me a chance to tie my hat on."

What Vimes remembered most of all about that journey—and there was so much of it he wanted to forget—was the silence. And the *softness*.

Oh, he could feel the wind in his face, but it was only a breeze, even when the ground was a flat green blur. The air was shaping itself around them. When Vimes experimentally held up a piece of paper a foot above his head, it blew away in an instant.

The corn exploded, too. As the coach approached, the green shoots grew out of the ground as if dragged, and then burst like fireworks.

The corn belt was giving way to cattle country, when Willikins said: "You know, sir, this thing steers itself. Watch."

He lowered the reins as a patch of woodland approached. The scream had hardly formed in Vimes's throat before the coach curved around the woodland and then swung delicately back onto its original course.

"Don't do that again, please!" said Vimes.

"All right, sir, but it's steering itself. I don't think I could *make* it run into anything."

"Don't try!" Vimes said quickly. "And I swear I saw a cow explode back there! Keep us away from towns and people, will you?"

Behind the coach, turnips and rocks leapt into the air and bounced away in the opposite direction. Vimes hoped they wouldn't get into trouble about that.*

The other thing that Vimes noticed was the landscape ahead was strangely bluish, while behind them it had a relatively red tint. He didn't like to point this out, though, in case it sounded strange.

They had to stop twice to get directions, and were twenty miles from Koom Valley at half past five. There was a coaching inn. They sat out in its yard. No one spoke much. Apart from the speed-hungry Willikins, the only people not shaken by the journey were Sybil and Young Sam, who seemed quite happy, and Detritus, who had watched the world skim past with every sign of enjoyment. Brick was still face-down on the coach roof, holding tight.

"Ten hours," said Fred Colon. "And that included lunch and stoppin' to be sick. I can't believe it . . ."

"I don't fink people are s'posed to go this fast," Nobby moaned. "I fink my brain's still back home."

"Well, if we're going to have to wait for it to catch up, Nobby, I'll buy a house here, shall I?" said Fred.

Nerves were frayed, brains were jogging behind

---

*But as it happened, it was all blamed on people from another world, so that was all right.

. . . this is why I don't like magic, thought Vimes. But we're here, and it's amazing how the inn's beer helped recovery.

"We might even be able to have a quick look at Koom Valley before it gets dark," he ventured, to general groaning.

"No, Sam! Everyone needs a meal and a rest!" said Sybil. "Let's go into town like proper people, nice and slowly, and everyone will be fresh for tomorrow."

"Lady Sybil is right, Commander," said Bashfullsson. "I wouldn't advise going up to the valley at night, even at this time of the year. It's so easy to get lost."

"In a valley?" said Vimes.

"Oh yes, sir," Cheery chimed in. "You'll see why, sir. And mostly, if you get lost, you die."

On the sedate journey into town, and because it was six o'clock, Vimes read *Where's My Cow?* to Young Sam. In fact, it became a communal effort. Cheery obliged by handling the chicken noises, an area in which Vimes felt he was somewhat lacking, and Detritus delivered a HRUUUGH! that rattled the windows. Grag Bashfullsson, against all expectation, managed a very passable pig. To Young Sam, watching with eyes like saucers, it was indeed the Show Of The Year.

Bunty was surprised to see them so soon, but Ladies Who Organize are seldom thrown by guests arriving unexpectedly early.

It turned out Bunty was Berenice Waynesbury, née Mousefather, which must have come as a relief, with a daughter who was married and lived just outside Quirm and a son who'd had to go to Fourecks in a hurry over a *complete* misunderstanding but was now into sheep in a big way and she hoped Sybil and of course His Grace would be able to stay until Saturday because she'd invited simply *everybody* and wasn't Young Sam simply *adorable* . . . and so on, right up to "—and we've cleaned out one of the stables for your trolls," said with a happy smile.

Before Sybil or Vimes could say a word, Detritus had removed his helmet and bowed.

"T'ank you very much, missus," he said gravely, "you know, sometimes people forget to clean dem out first. It's dem little touches dat mean a lot."

"Why, thank you," said Bunty. "How charming. I've, er, never seen a troll wearing clothing before . . ."

"I can take dem off if you like," said Detritus. At which point, Sybil took Bunty gently by the arm and said: "Let me introduce you to everybody else . . ."

Mr. Waynesbury, the magistrate, wasn't the venal pocket-liner Vimes had expected. He was thin, tall, and didn't say a great deal, and spent his time at home in a study filled with law books, pipes, and fishing tackle; he dispensed justice in the mornings, fished during the afternoon, and charitably forgave Vimes for his total lack of interest in dry flies.

The local town of Ham-on-Koom made a good living off the river. When the Koom hit the plains, it widened and slowed and was more full of fish than a tin of sardines. Marshes spread out on either side, too, with deep and hidden lakes that were the home and feeding ground of innumerable birds.

Oh . . . and there were the skulls, too.

"I am the coroner as well," he told Vimes as he unlocked a cupboard in his desk. "We get a few bones washed down here every spring. Mostly tourists, of course. They really will not take advice, alas. But sometimes we get things that are of more . . . historical interest." He put a dwarf skull on the leather desktop.

"About a hundred years old," he said. "From the last big battle, a hundred years ago. We get the occasional piece of armor, too. We put it all in the charnel house, and occasionally the dwarfs or the trolls come with a cart to sort through it and carry it away. They take it very seriously."

"Any treasure?" said Vimes.

"Hah. Not that I get told about. But I'd hear about it if there was anything big." The magistrate sighed. "Every year people come to search for it. Sometimes they are lucky."

"They find gold?"

"No, but they get back alive. The others? They wash up out of the caves, in the fullness of time." He selected a pipe from a rack on his desk and began to fill it. "I'm amazed that anyone feels it necessary to take weapons up the valley. It'll kill you on a whim. Will you take one of my lads, Commander?"

"I have my own guide," said Vimes, and then added, "But thank you."

Mr. Waynsbury puffed his pipe.

"As you wish, of course," he said. "I shall watch the river, in any case."

Angua and Sally had been put in the same bedroom. Angua tried to feel good about that. The woman wasn't to know. Anyway, it was nice to get between clean sheets, even if the room had a slightly musty smell. More must, less vampire, she thought; look on the bright side.

In the darkness, she opened one eye.

Someone had moved silently across the room. They'd made no noise but, nevertheless, their passage had stirred the air and changed the texture of the subtle night sounds.

They were at the window now. It was bolted shut, and a faint noise was probably the bolt being slipped back.

It was easy to tell when the window itself was opened; new scents flooded in.

There was a creak that possibly only a werewolf would have heard, followed by a sudden rustling of many leathery wings. *Little* leathery wings.

Angua shut her eye again. The little minx! Maybe Sally just didn't care anymore? No point in trying to follow her, though. She debated the wisdom of shutting the window and bolting the door, just to see what excuses Sally came up with, but dismissed it. No good telling Mister Vimes yet, either, what could she prove? It'd all be put down to the were-wolf/vampire thing . . .

And now Koom Valley stretched away ahead of Vimes, and he could see why he hadn't made plans. You couldn't make plans for Koom Valley. It'd laugh at them. It would push them away, like it pushed away roads.

"Of course, you're seeing it at its best at this time of year," said Cheery.

"By 'best' you mean—?" Vimes prompted.

"Well, it's not actually trying to murder us, sir. And there's the birds. And when the sun's right, you get some wonderful rainbows."

There were *lots* of birds. Insects bred like mad in the wide, shallow pools and dams that littered the floor of the valley in late spring. Most of them would be dry by the late summer, but for now Koom Valley was a smorgasbord of things that went *bzz!* And the birds had come up from the plains to feast on all of it. Vimes wasn't good at birds, but they mostly looked like swallows, millions of them. There were nests on the nearest cliff, a good half mile away, and Vimes could hear the chattering from here. And where trees and rocks had piled up in dams, saplings and green plants had sprouted.

Below the narrow track the party had taken, water gushed from half a dozen caves and joined together for one wild waterfall into the plain.

"It's all so . . . so alive," said Angua. "I was expecting just barren rock."

"Dat's what it like up at der battle place," said Detritus, spray glistening on his skin. "My dad took me up dere when we were comin' to der city. He showed me dis kind o' rocky place, hit me on der head, and said, 'Remember.'"

"Remember what?" said Sally.

"He didn't say. So I just, you know, gen'rally remembered."

I didn't expect this, Vimes thought. It's so . . . chaotic. Oh, well, let's get clear of the cliff wall, at least. All these bloody great boulders must have got here from somewhere.

"I can smell smoke," Angua announced after a while as they made their way unsteadily across the debris-strewn track.

"Campfires from up the valley," said Cheery. "Early arrivals, I expect."

"You mean people queue up for a place in the battle?" said Vimes. "Watch this boulder, it's slippery."

"Oh, yes. The fighting doesn't start until Koom Valley Day. That's tomorrow."

"Damn, I lost track. Will it affect us down here?"

Bashfullsson coughed politely. "I don't think so, Commander. This area is too dangerous to fight in."

"Well, yes, I can see it would be terrible if anyone got hurt," said Vimes, climbing over a long heap of rotting timber. "That would spoil the day for everyone."

Historical Re-creation, he thought glumly as they picked their way across, under, over, or through the boulders and insect-buzzing heaps of splintered timber, with streamlets running everywhere. Only we do it with people dressing up and running around with blunt weapons, and people selling hot dogs, and the girls all miserable because they can only dress up as wenches, wenching being the only job available to women in the olden days.

But the dwarfs and the trolls . . . they fight it again,

for real. Like, perhaps, if they fight it enough times, they'll get it right?

Now there was a hole in the track in front of him, half-blocked with the winter's debris, but still managing to swallow a whole streamlet. It poured, foaming, into the depths. There was a booming noise, far below. When he knelt down and touched the water, it was so cold it stung.

"Yes, watch out for sinkholes, Commander," said Bashfullsson. "This is limestone. Water wears it away quite quickly. We'll probably see some much bigger ones. Often they're hidden by rotting debris. Watch where you tread."

"Don't they get blocked up?"

"Oh, yes, sir. You've seen the size of the rocks that roll down here."

"It must be like a giant game of billiards!"

"Something like that, I expect," said Bashfullsson carefully.

After ten minutes, Vimes sat down on a log, pulled off his helmet, took out a big red handkerchief, and wiped his forehead.

"It's getting hotter," he said. "And everywhere in this bloody place looks the same— ow!"

He slapped at his wrist.

"The midges can be a bit extreme, sir," Cheery volunteered. "It's said that when they bite extra-hard, there's a storm coming."

They both looked up at the mountains. There was a yellow haze at the far end of the valley, and clouds between the peaks.

"Oh, *good*," said Vimes. "Because it feels like that bite went to the bone."

"I wouldn't worry too much, Commander," said Cheery. "The big Koom Valley storm was a once-in-a-lifetime occurrence."

"It certainly was a lifetime if you were caught in it," said Vimes. "This damn place is getting to me, I don't mind admitting it."

By now, the rest of the squad had caught up. Sally and Detritus were visibly suffering from the heat. The vampire sat down in the shade of a big rock without saying anything. Brick lay down by the icy stream and stuck his head in it.

"I'm afraid I'm not much help here, sir," said Angua. "I can smell dwarf, but that's about it. There's just too much damn water everywhere!"

"Maybe we won't need your nose," said Vimes. He unslung the tube that contained Sybil's sketch, unrolled the drawing, and pinned the ends together.

"Give me a hand with this, will you, Cheery?" he said. "Everyone else, get some rest. And don't laugh."

He lowered the circlet of mountains over his head. There was a cough from Angua, which he pretended to ignore.

"Okay," said Vimes, turning the stiff paper to get the mountains lined up just above their penciled outlines. "That's Copperhead over there, and Cori Celesti over *there* . . . and they line up pretty well against the drawing. We're practically on top of it already!"

"Not really, Commander," said Bashfullsson behind him. "They're both almost four hundred miles away. They'd look pretty much the same from anywhere in this part of the valley. You need to look at the nearer peaks."

Vimes turned.

"Okay. What's that one that looks really steep on the left-hand side?"

"That is The King, sir," said Cheery. "He's about ten miles away."

"Really? He looks closer . . ."

Vimes found the mountain on the drawing. "And that small one over there?" he said. "The one with two peaks?"

"I don't know the name, sir, but I can see the one you mean."

"They're too small and too close together . . ." Vimes muttered.

"Then walk toward them, sir. Mind where you're putting your feet. Only tread on bare rock. Keep off piles of debris. The grag is right. It could be over an old sinkhole and you might drop right through."

"O-kay. About halfway between them is that funny-shaped little outcrop. I'll head directly for it. *You* watch where I'm putting my feet, too, will you?"

Trying to keep the paper level, stumbling on rocks, splashing through ice rivulets, Vimes walked the lonesome valley . . .

"Damn and blast!"

"Sir?"

Vimes peered over the top of his ring of paper. "I've lost The King. That damn great ridge of boulders is in the way. Hold on . . . I can see that mountain with the chunk taken out of it . . ."

It looked so simple. It *would* have been simple if Koom Valley had been flat and not littered with rubbish like the ten-pin bowling alley of the gods. In some places, they had to backtrack, because a wall of tangled, stinking, gnat-infested timber blocked the way. Or the barrier was a wall of rocks the length of a street. Or a wide, mist-filled, thundering cauldron of white water that elsewhere would have a name like The Devil's Cauldron but here was nameless, because this was Koom Valley and for Koom Valley there just weren't enough devils and they didn't have enough cauldrons.

And the flies stung, and the sun shone, and the rotting wood and damp air and lack of wind created a sticky, swamp-like miasma that seemed to weaken the muscles.

No wonder they fought at the other end of the valley, Vimes thought. There was air and wind up there. At least you'd be comfortable.

Sometimes they'd come out into a clear stretch that looked quite like the scene that Methodia Rascal had painted, but the nearby mountains didn't quite match up, and it was off again into the maze. You had to detour, and then detour around the detour.

At last, Vimes sat down on a bleached, crumbling log and put the paper aside.

"We must've missed it," he said, panting. "Or Rascal didn't get the mountains quite right. Or maybe even a slice of mountain fell off in the last hundred years. It could have happened. We could be twenty feet away from whatever it is we're looking for and still miss it." He slapped a gnat off his wrist.

"Cheer up, sir, I think we're fairly close," said Cheery.

"Why? What makes you think that?" said Vimes, wiping his brow.

"Because I think you may be sitting on the painting, sir. It's very dirty, but that looks like rolled-up canvas to me."

Vimes stood up quickly, and inspected the log. One corner of what he'd taken to be yellow-gray bark peeled back to reveal paint on the other side.

"And those timbers over there—" Cheery began but stopped, because Vimes had raised a finger to his lips.

There were, indeed, some long, thin pine saplings lying nearby, stripped of all branches. They would have gone unnoticed if it wasn't for the presence of the rolled-up painting.

They did just what we did, Vimes thought. It was probably easier, if they had enough dwarfs to hold up the painting; the mountains would be properly colored, not just pencil lines, and it would be more accurate on the bigger canvas. They could take their time, too. They thought they were well ahead of me. All they were worried about was some bloody mystic symbol.

He drew his sword and beckoned Cheery to follow him.

There's not just dark dwarfs here, then, he thought, creeping around the nearby rocks. They wouldn't have stood out here in daylight. So let's see how many stayed on guard . . .

None, as it turned out. It was something of an anticlimax. Beyond the rocks was the spot that X would have marked, if there had been an X.

They must have been really confident, Vimes realized. By the look of it, they'd moved tons of rock and stricken timber, and there were the crowbars to prove it.

Right now would be a really good time for Angua and the others to catch us up, he decided.

In front of them was a hole about six feet wide. A steel bar had been laid across it, bedded into two freshly chiseled grooves, and from the bar a stout rope disappeared into the depths. From far below came the thunder of dark waters.

"Mr. Rascal must've been a brave man to stand here," said Vimes.

"I expect it was a plugged hole a hundred years ago," said Cheery.

"I'll tell you what," said Vimes, kicking a pebble into the dark. "Pretend I'm a city man who doesn't know a bloody thing about caves, why don't you?"

"It's what you get when a hole gets blocked, sir," said Cheery patiently. "Mr. Rascal probably just had to climb down onto a plug of debris."

This is the place.

So . . . this is where he found the talking cube, Vimes thought. Ignoring Cheery's protests, because he was the commander around here, he swung down onto the rope and lowered himself a few feet.

There, tucked under the lip of the hole, a stubby piece of iron was rusted into the rock. A few links of equally rusted chain hung from it.

It sang in its chains . . .

"There was a note about the thing being in chains," he said. "Well, there's some chain here, and what could be the stub of a knife!"

"Dwarf steel, sir!" said Cheery reproachfully. "It does last."

"It could last all that time?"

"Oh yes. I expect the sink became a fountain for a while since Rascal's day, and forced the blockage out. That sort of thing happens all the time in Koom Va— er, what are you doing, sir?"

Vimes was staring down into the darkness. Below, unseen, dark waters churned. So . . . the messenger climbed up this hole, he thought. Where to hide the cube safely?

There could be trolls up above. But a fighting dwarf would have a dagger, certainly, and they love chains. Yes . . . here would be a good place. And he'd be back soon, anyway . . .

"Old men climbed down this?" he said, staring down the rope into the dark.

"Old dwarfs, sir. Yes. We're strong for our size. You're not going down, are you, sir?"

There's a side tunnel down there . . .

"There must be a side tunnel down there," said Vimes. Thunder rumbled, far up in the mountains.

"But the others will be here soon, sir! Aren't you rushing things?"

Don't wait for them . . .

"No. Tell them to follow me. Look, we've lost time. I can't hang around all day."

Cheery hesitated, and then pulled something out of a pouch on her belt.

"Then at least take these, sir," she said. He grabbed the little package as it fell. It was surprisingly heavy.

"Waxed matches, sir, they don't get wet. And the wrapping will burn like a torch for at least four minutes. There's a small loaf of dwarf bread, too."

"Well . . . thank you," said Vimes to the worried

round shadow against the yellow sky. "Look, I'll see if there's any light down there, and if there isn't, I'll come straight back. I'm not *that* daft."

He let himself slide on down the rope. There was a knot every couple of feet. The air was winter-cold after the heat of the valley. Fine spray came up from below.

There *was* a tunnel, well above the cauldron. He could make himself believe there was light in the distance, too. Well, he wasn't stupid. He needed to—

Let go . . .

His hands loosened their grip. He didn't even have time to swear before the water closed over him.

Vimes opened his eyes. After a while, moving his arm slowly, because of the pain, he found his face and checked that his eyelids were, indeed, open.

What bits of his body weren't aching? He checked. No, there seemed to be none. His ribs were carrying the melody of pain, but knees, elbows, and head were all adding trills and arpeggios. Every time he shifted to ease the agony, it moved somewhere else. His head ached as if someone was hammering on his eyeballs.

He groaned, and coughed up water.

Gritty sand was under him. He could hear the rush of water somewhere nearby, but the sand under him was merely damp. And that didn't seem right.

He risked turning over, a process that extracted a considerable amount of groan.

He could remember the icy water. There had been no question of swimming. All he'd been able to do was roll himself into a ball as the water threw and scraped and banged him through the bagatelle board of Koom Valley. He'd gone over an underground waterfall once, he was sure, and had managed to suck in a breath before being whisked onward. And then there was depth, and pressure, and his life started to unroll before his eyes, and his last thought had been please, please, can we skip the bit with Mavis Trouncer . . .

And now he was here on an invisible beach, totally out of the water? But this place surely didn't have tides!

So someone was somewhere in the blackness, watching him. That was it. They'd pulled him out and now they were watching him . . .

He opened his eyes again. Some of the pain was gone, leaving stiffness as payment. He had a feeling that time had passed. The darkness pressed in on all sides, thick as velvet.

He rolled back with more groans, and this time managed to push himself onto his hands and knees.

"Who's there?" he mumbled, and, very carefully, got to his feet.

Being upright seemed to shake his brain into gear again.

"Anyone there?" The darkness swallowed the sound. Anyway, what would he have done if something had said "Yes!"

He drew his sword and held it out in front of him as he shuffled forward. After a dozen steps, it clinked against rock.

"Matches," he mumbled. "Got matches!"

He found the wax bundle and, working his clammy fingers slowly, drew out one match. Scraping the wax off the head with his thumb, he struck it against the stone.

The glare hurt his eyes. Look, quick! Flowing water, smooth sand, hand- and footprints coming out of the water, one set only? Yes. Walls looked dry, small cave, darkness over there, way out . . .

Vimes limped toward the oval entrance as quick as he could while the match spat and fizzed in his hand.

There was a bigger cave here, so big that the blackness in it seemed to suck all the light from the match, which scorched his fingers and died.

The heavy darkness closed in again, like curtains, and now he knew what the dwarfs meant. This wasn't the darkness of a hood, or a cellar, or even of their shallow little mine. He was a long way below the ground here, and the weight of all that darkness bore down on him.

Now and again, a drop of water went *plink* into some unseen pool.

Vimes staggered onwards. He knew he was bleeding. He *didn't* know why he was walking, but he did know that he had to.

Maybe he'd find daylight. Maybe he'd find a log that had been washed in here, and float his way out. He wasn't going to die, not down here in the dark, a long way from home.

A lot of water was dripping in this cavern. A lot of it was going down his neck right now, but there were *plinks* on every side. Hah, water trickling down your neck and odd noises in the shadows . . . well, that's when we find out if we've got a real copper, right? But there were no shadows here. It wasn't light enough.

Perhaps that poor sod of a dwarf had wandered through here. But *he* found a way out. Maybe he knew the way, maybe he had a rope, maybe he was young and limber . . . and so he'd got out, dying on his feet, and tucked away the treasure, out of the way, and then went down the valley, walking through his grave. That's how it could take people. He remembered Mrs. Oldsburton, who went mad after her baby died, cleaning everything in the house, every cup, wall, ceiling, and spoon, not seeing anybody or hearing anything, just working all day and all night. Something in the head went click, and you found something to do, anything, to stop yourself thinking.

Best to stop thinking that the way out the dwarf had found had been the one Vimes had dropped in by, and he had no idea where that was now.

Maybe he could simply jump back in the water, knowing what he was doing this time, and maybe he'd make it all the way down to the river before the turbulent currents battered him to death. Maybe he—

Why the hell had he let go of that rope? It had been like that little voice that whispers "Jump" when you're at a cliff edge, or "Touch the fire." You didn't listen, of course. At least most people didn't, most of the time. Well, a voice had said "Let go," and he had . . .

He shuffled on, aching and bleeding, while the dark curled its tail around him.

"He'll be back soon, you know," said Sybil. "Even if it's at the very last minute."

Out in the hall, a big grandfather clock had just stopped chiming half past five.

"I'm sure he will," said Bunty. They were bathing Young Sam.

"He's *never* late," Sybil went on. "He says if you're late for a good reason you'll be late for a bad one. And it's only half past five, anyway."

"Plenty of time," Bunty agreed.

"Fred and Nobby did take the horses up to the valley, didn't they?" said Sybil.

"*Yes*, Sybil. You watched them go," said Bunty. She looked over Sybil's head to the gaunt figure of her husband, who was standing in the hall doorway. He shrugged hopelessly.

"Only the other day, he was running up the stairs as the clocks were striking six," Sybil said, calmly soaping Young Sam with a sponge shaped like a teddy bear. "The very last second. You wait and see."

He wanted to sleep. He'd never felt this tired before. Vimes slumped to his knees, and then fell sideways onto the sand.

When he forced his eyes open, he saw pale stars above him, and had, once again, the sensation that there was someone else present.

He turned his head, wincing at the stab of pain, and saw a small but brightly lit folding chair on the sand. A robed figure was reclining in it, reading a book. A scythe was stuck in the sand beside it.

A white, skeletal hand turned a page.

"You'll be Death, then?" said Vimes, after a while.

AH, MISTER VIMES, ASTUTE AS EVER. GOT IT IN ONE, said Death, shutting the book on his finger to keep the place.

"I've seen you before."

I HAVE WALKED WITH YOU MANY TIMES, MISTER VIMES.

"And this is *it*, is it?"

HAS IT NEVER STRUCK YOU THAT THE CONCEPT OF A WRITTEN NARRATIVE IS SOMEWHAT STRANGE? said Death.

Vimes could tell when people were trying to avoid something they really didn't want to say, and it was happening here.

"Is it?" he insisted. "Is this it? This time I die?"

COULD BE.

"Could be? What sort of answer is that?" said Vimes.

A VERY ACCURATE ONE. YOU SEE, YOU ARE HAVING A NEAR-DEATH EXPERIENCE, WHICH INESCAPABLY MEANS THAT I MUST UNDERGO A NEAR-*VIMES* EXPERIENCE. DON'T MIND ME. CARRY ON WITH WHATEVER YOU WERE DOING. I HAVE A BOOK.

Vimes rolled over onto his stomach, gritted his teeth, and pushed himself onto his hands and knees again. He managed a few yards before slumping back down.

He heard the sound of a chair being moved.

"Shouldn't you be somewhere else?" he said.

I AM, said Death, sitting down again.

"But you're here!"

As WELL. Death turned a page and, for a person without breath, managed a pretty good sigh. IT APPEARS THAT THE BUTLER DID IT.

"Did what?"

IT IS A MADE-UP STORY. VERY STRANGE. ALL ONE NEED DO IS TURN TO THE LAST PAGE AND THE ANSWER IS THERE. WHAT, THEREFORE, IS THE POINT OF DELIBERATELY NOT KNOWING?

It sounded like gibberish to Vimes, so he ignored it. Some of the aches were gone, although his head still hammered. There was an empty feeling everywhere. He just wanted to sleep.

"Is that clock right?"

"I'm afraid it is, Sybil."

"I'll just go outside and wait for him, then. I'll have the book ready," said Lady Sybil. "He won't let anything stop him, you know."

"I'm sure he won't," said Bunty.

"Although things can be very treacherous in the lower valley at this time of—" her husband began, and was fried into silence by his wife's stare.

It was six minutes to six.

"Ob oggle oog soggle!"

It was a very little, watery sound, and it came from somewhere in Vimes's trousers. After a few moments, enough time to recollect that he had both hands and trousers, he reached down and, after a struggle, freed the Gooseberry from his pocket. The case was battered, and the imp, when Vimes had got the flap open, was quite pale.

"Ob ogle soggle!"

Vimes stared at it. It was a talking box. It meant something.

"Woggle soggle lob!"

Slowly, Vimes tipped the box up. Water poured out of it.

"You weren't listening! I was shouting and you weren't listening!" the imp whined. "It's five minutes to six! Read to Young Sam!"

Vimes dropped the protesting box on his chest and stared up at the pale stars.

"Mus' read to Young Sam," he murmured, and shut his eyes.

They snapped open again.

"Got t'read to Young Sam!"

The stars were moving. It wasn't the sky! How could it be the sky? This was a bloody cave, wasn't it?

He rolled over and got to his feet in one movement. There were more stars now, drifting along the walls. The vurms were moving with a purpose. Overhead, they had become a glowing river.

Although they were flickering a little, the lights were also coming back on in Vimes's head. He peered into what was now no longer blackness but merely gloom, and gloom was like daylight after the darkness that had gone before.

"... got to read to Young Sam ..." he whispered, to a cavern of giant stalactites and stalagmites, all gleaming with water, "... to read to Young Sam ..."

Stumbling and sliding through shallow pools, running across the occasional patch of white sand, Vimes followed the lights.

Sybil tried not to look at the worried faces of her host and hostess as she crossed their hall. She glared at the grandfather clock. The minute hand was nearly on the 12, and trembling.

She threw open the front door. There was no Sam there, and no one galloping down the road.

The clock struck the hour. She heard someone step quietly beside her.

"Would you like me to read to the young man, madam?" said Willikins. "Perhaps a man's voice would—"

"No, I'll go up," said Sybil quietly. "You wait here for my husband. He won't be long," she added firmly.

"Yes, madam."

"He'll probably be quite rushed."

"I shall usher him up without delay, madam."

"He *will* be here, you know!"

"Yes, madam."

"*He will walk through walls!*"

Sybil climbed the stairs as the chimes ended. The clock was a *wrong* clock. Of course it was!

Young Sam had been installed in the old nursery of the house, a rather somber place full of grays and browns. There was a truly frightening rocking horse, all teeth and mad glass eyes.

The boy was standing up in his cot. He was smiling, but the smile faded into puzzlement as Sybil pulled up a chair and sat down next to him.

"Daddy has asked Mummy to read to you tonight, Sam," she announced brightly. "Won't that be fun!"

Her heart did not sink. It could not. It was already as low as any heart could go. But it curled up and whimpered as she watched the little boy stare at her, at the door, at her again, and then throw back his head and scream.

Vimes, half limping and half running, tripped and fell into a shallow pool.

He found he'd stumbled over a dwarf. A dead one. Very dead. So dead, in fact, that the dripping water had built a small stalagmite on him, and with a film of milky stone had cemented him to the rock against which he sat.

". . . got to read to Young Sam," Vimes told the shadowy helmet, earnestly.

A little way away, on the sand, was a dwarf's battle-axe. What was going on in Vimes's mind was not exactly coherent thought, but he could hear faint noises up ahead and an instinct older than thought decided there was no such thing as too much cutting power.

He picked it up. It was covered with no more

than a thin coat of rust. There were other humps and mounds on the cavern floor, which, now that he came to look at them, might all be—

No time! Read book!

At the end of the cavern, the ground sloped up, and had been made treacherous by the dripping water. It fought back, but the axe helped. One problem at a time. Climb hill! Read book!

And then the screaming started. His son, screaming.

It filled his mind.

They will burn . . .

A staircase floated in his vision, reaching endlessly upwards into darkness. The screaming came from up there.

Feet slithered. The axe bit into the milky stone. Weeping and cursing, sliding at every step, Vimes struggled to the top of the slope.

A new, huge cave spread out below. It was busy with dwarfs. It looked like a mine.

There were four of them, only a few feet away from Vimes, whose vision was full of rocking lambs. They stared at this sudden, bloody, swaying apparition, which was dreamily waving a sword in one hand and an axe in the other.

They had axes, too. But the thing glared at them and asked:

"Where's . . . My . . . Cow?"

They backed away.

"Is that my cow?" the creature demanded, stepping forward unsteadily. It shook its head sadly.

"It goes Baaaa!" it wept. "It is . . . a sheep . . ."

Then it fell to its knees, clenched its teeth, turned

its face upwards, like a man tortured beyond his wits, beseeching the gods of fortune and the tempest, and screamed:

"No! That! Is!! Not!!! My!!! Cow!!!!!"

The words echoed around the cavern *and broke through mere rock, so great was the force behind them, melted mere mountains, screamed across the miles . . .*

And in the somber nursery, Young Sam stopped crying and looked around, suddenly happy but puzzled, and said, to his despairing mother's surprise: "Co!"

The dwarfs backed away down the slope. Overhead, the vurms were still pouring in, outlining the invader against their green-white glow.

"Where's my cow? Is that my cow?" it demanded, following them.

In every part of the cavern, dwarfs had stopped work. There was hesitancy in the air. This was only one man, after all, and the thought in many minds was: What is someone else going to do about this? It had not yet progressed to: What am *I* going to do about this? Besides, where was the cow? There were cows down here?

"It goes Naaaaay. It is a horse! That is not my cow!"

Dwarfs looked at one another. Where was the horse, then? Did you hear a horse? Who else is down here?

The four guards had retreated to the cavern for advice and reorientation. There was a number of deep-downers there, clustered in frantic conversation and watching the approaching man.

In Vimes's strobing vision, there were fluffy bunnies, too, and quacky ducks . . .

He had dropped to his knees again, and was staring at the ground and crying.

Half a dozen shrouded dark guards stepped out from the group. One of them carried ahead of him a flame weapon, and advanced on the figure cautiously. The flame of its little pilot light was the brightest thing in the cave.

The figure looked up, the light reflected red in its eyes, and growled: "Is that my cow?"

Then it threw the axe overarm, full at the guard. It struck the flame weapon, which exploded.

"It goes HRUUUGH!"

"Hg!" said Young Sam, as his mother hugged him and stared blankly at the wall.

Burning oil fountained across the dark. Some of it splashed on Vimes's arm. He slapped at it. There was pain, intense pain, but he knew this only in the same way that he knew the moon existed. It was there, but it was a long way off and didn't affect him very much.

"That's not my cow!" he said, standing up.

He strode on now, over the burning oil, through red-edged smoke, past the dwarfs rolling desperately on the ground to put out the flames. He seemed to be looking for something.

Two more guards ran at him. Without appearing to notice them, Vimes crouched and whirled the sword around in a circle. A little lamb rocked in front of his eyes.

A dwarf with greater presence of mind than the others had found a crossbow and was taking aim when he had to stop to brush away the bats streaming past him. He raised the bow again, looked around at a noise like two slabs of meat being slapped together, and was picked up and thrown across the cave by a naked young woman. An astonished miner swung his axe at the smiling girl, who vanished in a cloud of bats.

There was a lot of yelling going on. Vimes paid it no attention. Dwarfs were running through the smoke. He merely slapped them aside. He had found what he was seeking.

"Is that my cow? It goes Mooooo!"

Picking up another fallen axe, Vimes started to run.

"Yes! That's my cow!"

The grags were behind a ring of guards, in a frantic huddle, but Vimes's eyes were on fire, and there were flames streaming from his helmet. A dwarf holding a flamethrower threw it down and fled.

"Hooray, hooray, it's a wonderful day, for I have found my cow!"

. . . and perhaps that, it was said later, was what did it. Against the berserker, there is no defense. They had sworn to fight to the death, but not to *this* death. The slowest four guards went down to the axe and the sword, the others scattered and ran.

And now Vimes paused in front of the cowering old dwarfs, raising the weapons over his head—

And halted, rocking like a statue.

Night, forever. But within it, a city, shadowy and only real in certain ways.

The entity cowered in its alley, where the mist was rising. This could not have happened!

Yet it had. The streets had filled with . . . things. Animals! Birds! Changing shape! Screaming and yelling! And, above it all, higher than the rooftops, a lamb rocking back and forth in great slow motions, thundering over the cobbles . . .

And then bars had come down, slamming down, and the entity had been thrown back.

But it had been so close! It had saved the creature, it was getting through, it was beginning to have control . . . and now this . . .

In the darkness of the inner city, above the rustle of the never-ending rain, it heard the sound of boots approaching.

A shape appeared in the mist.

It drew nearer.

Water cascaded off a metal helmet and an oiled leather cloak as the figure stopped and, entirely unconcerned, cupped its hand in front of its face and lit a cigar.

Then the match was dropped on the cobbles, where it hissed out, and the figure said: "What are you?"

The entity stirred, like an old fish in a deep pool. It was too tired to flee.

"I am the Summoning Dark." It was not, in fact, a sound, but had it been, it would have been a hiss. "Who are you?"

"I am the Watchman."

"They would have killed his family!" The darkness lunged, and met resistance. "Think of the deaths they have caused! Who are you to stop me?"

"He created me. Quis custodiet ipsos custodes? Who watches the watchmen? Me. I watch him. Always. You will not force him to murder for you."

"What kind of human creates his own policeman?"

"One who fears the dark."

"And so he should," said the entity, with satisfaction.

"Indeed. But I think you misunderstand. I am not here to keep darkness out. I'm here to keep it in." There was a clink of metal as the shadowy watchman lifted a dark lantern and opened its little door. Orange light cut through the blackness. *"Call me . . . the Guarding Dark. Imagine how strong I must be."*

The Summoning Dark backed desperately into the alley, but the light followed it, burning it.

"And now," said the watchman, *"get out of town."*

—and went down as a werewolf landed on his back.

Angua drooled. The hair along her spine stood out like a saw blade. Her lips curled back like a wave. Her growl was from the back of a haunted cave. All together, these told the brain of anything monkey-shaped that movement meant death. And that stillness, while it also meant death, didn't mean immediate, *this actual second*, death, and was therefore the smart-monkey option.

Vimes didn't move. The growl knotted his muscles. Terror was in control.

I salute you, said a thought that was not his, and he felt the sudden absence of something whose presence he had not noticed before. In the blackness behind his eyes, some dark fin swished and vanished.

He heard a whimper, and the weight on him disappeared. He rolled over and saw, fading in the middle of the air, a crude drawing of an eye with a tail. It dwindled into nothing, and the all-enveloping darkness slowly gave way to flames and the light of the vurms. Blood had been spilled; they were pouring down the walls. He felt . . .

A certain amount of time passed. Vimes jerked awake.

"I read it for him!" he said, mostly to reassure himself.

"You did, sir," said the voice of Angua, behind him. "Very clearly, too. We were more than two hundred yards away. Well done, sir. We thought you ought to have a rest."

"What *have* I done well?" said Vimes, trying to sit up. The movement filled his world with pain, but he managed a brief glimpse before slumping back.

There was a lot of smoke in the cave, but there were actual torches flickering here and there. And a great many dwarfs, some distance away, some sitting down, some standing around in groups.

"Why are there so many dwarfs here, Sergeant?" he asked, looking up at the cavern roof. "That is, why are there so many dwarfs here that aren't actually trying to kill us?"

"They're from the Low King, sir. We're their prisoners . . . sort of . . . er . . . but not exactly . . ."

"Of Rhys? Bugger that!" said Vimes, trying to get to his feet again. "I saved his bloody life once!" He managed to get upright, but then the world pivoted around him, and he would have fallen if Angua hadn't caught him and lowered him onto a rock. Well, at least he was sitting up now . . .

"Not *exactly* prisoners," Angua said. "We can't go anywhere. But since we wouldn't know where to go even if we could go anywhere, it's all a bit moot. Sorry I'm only in a shift, sir, you know how it is. The dwarfs have promised to fetch my gear. Er . . . it's all gone political, sir. The dwarf in command seems a decent sort but he's way out of his depth, so he's sticking with what he knows, sir. And, er, he doesn't know a lot. Do you remember *anything* about what happened? You've been out for a good twenty minutes."

"Yes. There were . . . wooly lambs . . ." Vimes's voice trailed into silence for a while. Somehow, what he'd just said took the ring of veracity and dropped it in a deep, deep hole. "There weren't wooly lambs, right?" he asked hopelessly.

"I didn't see any," said Angua carefully. "I did see a striding, screaming, vengeful maniac, sir. But in a good way," she added.

The internal Vimes looked at memories he didn't remember from the first time around.

"I—" he began.

"Everything's . . . sort of fine, sir," said Angua quickly. "But come and see this. Bashfullsson said you ought to see everything."

"Bashfullsson . . . he's the know-it-all dwarf, right?" he said.

"Ah, it's all coming back, sir," said Angua. "Good. He was a bit worried about that."

Vimes was steadier on his feet now, but his right arm hurt like hell, and all the other pains that the day had accumulated were coming back and waving. Angua carefully led him through puddles and across rocks as slippery as wet marble until they reached a stalagmite. It was about eight feet high.

It was a troll. It wasn't a rock shaped like a troll, it was a troll. They only got stonier when they died,

Vimes knew, but the lines of this one had been softened by the milky rock dripped on the troll's head.

"But now look at this, sir," said Angua, leading him on. "They were destroying them . . ."

There was another stalagmite, lying on its side in a pool. It had been smashed off at the base. And it was . . . a dwarf.

Dwarfs crumble after death, just like humans, but all the armor, mail, chains, and heavy leather mean there's no great change to the eye of the casual observer. The flowing rock had covered it all in a glistening shroud.

Vimes straightened up and looked across the cavern. Shapes loomed in the gloom, all the way to the near wall, where the drip of ages had formed a perfect ivory waterfall, frozen in time.

"There are more?"

"About twenty, sir. Half of them had been smashed before you . . . arrived. Look at this one over here, sir. You can just make them out. They're sitting back-to-back, sir."

Vimes stared at the figures under the glaze, and shook his head. A dwarf and a troll, together, cemented in rock.

"Is there anything to eat?" he said. It wasn't the most awe-inspired thing to say, but it came from the stomach, with feeling.

"Our rations got lost in the excitement, sir. But the dwarfs will share theirs. They aren't unfriendly, sir. Just cautious."

"Share? They have dwarf bread?"

"I'm afraid so, sir."

"I thought it was illegal to give that to prisoners.

I think I'll wait, thanks. And now, Sergeant, you can tell me about the excitement."

It hadn't exactly been an ambush; the dwarfs just caught up with them. Their captain had been given rather wide orders to follow Vimes and his party, and there had been a certain chilliness when he found that the party included two trolls. This was still Koom Valley, after all. Vimes felt a pang of sympathy for him; he'd had a simple job to do, and suddenly it was full of politics. Been there, done that, bought the singlet, thought Vimes.

Fortunately, Grag Bashfullsson had a way with words. Since they were all going the same way—

And it had been a long way. The fleeing dwarfs had brought down the ceiling not far from the entrance tunnel, and a journey that had taken Vimes a few minutes had taken the pursuers the best part of a day, even with Sally scouting ahead. Angua spoke of caves even bigger than this, of vast waterfalls in the dark. Vimes said, yes, he knew.

Then the words of *Where's My Cow?* had boomed under Koom Valley, shaking the rock of ages and making the stalactites hum in sympathy, and the rest had been a matter of running . . .

"I can remember reading to Young Sam," said Vimes slowly. "But there were these . . . strange pictures in my head." He stopped. All that anger, all that red-hot rage, had flowed out of him in a torrent, without thought. "I killed those damn soldiers . . ."

"Most of them, sir," said Angua cheerfully. "And there's a couple of miners who got in the way who'll be aching for months."

It *was* all coming back to Vimes now. He wished it wasn't. There was always a part of the human brain that objected to fighting dwarfs. They were child-sized. Oh, they were also at least as strong as a human, and more resilient, and would take any advantage in a fight, and if you were lucky, you learned to overcome that prejudice *before* you were hacked off at the knees, but it was always there . . .

"I remember those old dwarfs," he said. "They were cowering like little maggots. I wanted to smash them . . ."

"You resisted for almost four seconds, sir, and then I brought you down," said Angua.

"And that was a good thing, was it?" said Vimes.

"Oh, yes. It's why you're still here, Commander," said Bashfullsson, appearing from behind a stalagmite. "I'm glad to see you up and about again. This is a historical day! And you still have a soul, it appears! Isn't that nice?"

"Now you listen to me—" Vimes began.

"No, you listen to *me*, Commander. Yes, I knew you'd come to Koom Valley, because the Summoning Dark would come here. It needed you to bring it. No, *listen* to me, because we don't have much time. The Summoning Dark symbol commands an entity as old as the universe. But it has no real body and very little physical strength; it can cover a million dimensions in the blink of an eye but could barely make it across a room. It works through living creatures, especially ones it finds . . . amenable. It found *you*, Commander, a cauldron of anger, and in small, subtle ways it saw that you got it to this place."

"I believe him, sir," said Angua quickly. "It was the one called up as a curse by one of the miners. Remember? The one who drew the sign in his own blood? On a locked door? And you—"

"There was a door that stung when I touched it, I remember . . ." said Vimes. "Are you telling me that *behind* that door he— oh, no . . ."

"He was already dead by then, sir, I'm positive about that," said Angua quickly. "We couldn't have saved him."

"Helmclever said—" Vimes began, and Bashfullsson must have seen the panic rising in his eyes, because he grabbed both his hands and spoke fast and urgently: "No! You didn't kill him! You didn't even touch him! You were afraid that if you did, I'd say you'd used force, remember?"

"He dropped dead! How much force is that?" Vimes shouted. His voice echoed, and heads turned all across the cavern. "There was the symbol, wasn't there?"

"It's true that the . . . creature tends to leave a, a signature on events, but you would have had to touch him! You did *not*! You did not raise a hand! I think you would have resisted even then! Resisted and won! Do you hear me? Calm down. Calm *down*. He died of fear and guilt. You must realize that."

"What reason did he have to feel guilty?"

"Every reason, for a dwarf. That mine bore down so heavily on him." The grag turned to Angua. "Sergeant, could you get the commander some water? It's as pure in these pools as anywhere in the world.

Well, it is if you pick one without a body floating in it."

"Y'know, you could have avoided that last sentence?" said Vimes. He sat down on a rock. He could feel himself shaking now.

"And then I got the damn thing here?" he managed.

"Yes, Commander. And it got you here, too, I suspect. Cheery says she saw you drop into churning water half a mile from where we are now. Even a champion swimmer wouldn't have survived that."

"I woke up on a beach—"

"It got you there. It swam your body for you."

"But I was all knocked about!"

"Oh, it wasn't your *friend*, Commander. It needed to get you here in one piece. It didn't have to be a good-looking piece. And then . . . you disappointed it, Commander. You disappointed it. Or, perhaps, impressed it. It's hard to tell. You wouldn't strike the helpless, you see. You resisted. I had the sergeant here bring you down because I was frightened that the struggle inside would rip your tendons from your bones."

"They were just frightened old men . . ."

"And so, it appears to have let you go," said the dwarf. "I wonder why? Historically, anyone subject to the Summoning Dark dies insane."

Vimes reached up and took a mug of water from Angua. It was teeth-aching cold and the best drink he'd ever tasted. And his mind worked fast, flying in emergency supplies of common sense, as human minds do, to construct a huge anchor in sanity and prove that what happened hadn't really happened and, if it had happened, hadn't happened much.

It was all mystic, that's what it was. Oh, it *might* all be true, but how could you ever tell? You had to stick to the things you can see. And you had to keep reminding yourself of that, too.

Yeah, that was it. What had really happened, eh? A few signs? Well, anything can look like you want it to, if you're worried and confused enough, yes? A sheep can look like a cow, right? Ha!

As for the rest, well, Bashfullsson seemed a decent lad, but you didn't have to buy into his worldview. Same with Mr. Shine. That sort of thing could spook you.

He'd been wound up about Young Sam, and when he'd seen those devil guards, *of course* he'd gone for them. He hadn't been getting much sleep lately. It seemed like every hour brought some new problem. The mind played funny tricks.

Surviving the underground river? Easy. He must have kept himself afloat. There were a lot of things the body would rather do than die.

There . . . some logical thought, and the mystic becomes . . . well, straightforward. You can stop feeling like some puppet and become a man with a purpose once again.

He put down the empty mug and stood up— purposefully.

"I'm going to see how my men are," he announced.

"I'll come with you," said Bashfullsson quickly.

"I think I need no assistance," lied Vimes, as coolly as he could.

"I'm sure *you* do not," said the dwarf. "But Captain Gud is a little nervous."

"He'll be a lot nervous if I don't like what I see," said Vimes.

"Yes. That's why I'm coming with you," said Bashfullsson.

Vimes set off across the cavern a little faster than he felt comfortable. The grag kept up by skipping at every other step.

"Don't think you know me, Mr. Bashfullsson," Vimes growled. "Don't think I took pity on those bastards. Don't think I was merciful. You just don't kill the helpless. You just don't."

"The dark guards seemed to have no trouble with the prospect," said Bashfullsson.

"*Exactly!*" said Vimes. "By the way, Mr. Bashfullsson, what kind of dwarf doesn't carry an axe?"

"Well, as a grag, my first resort, of course, is to my voice," said the grag. "The axe is nothing without the hand, and the hand is nothing without the mind. I've trained myself to *think* about axes."

"Sounds mystical to me," said Vimes.

"I suppose it would," said Bashfullsson. "Ah, here we are."

"Here" was the area that the newly arrived dwarfs had occupied. Very military, Vimes thought. A defensive square. You're not sure who your enemies are. And neither am I.

The nearest dwarf regarded him with that slightly defiant, slightly uneasy look he'd come to recognize. Captain Gud straightened up.

Vimes looked over the dwarf's shoulder, which was not hard to do. There were Nobby and Fred

Colon, and both of the trolls, and even Cheery, all sitting in a huddle.

"Are my men under arrest, Captain?" he said.

"My orders are to detain everyone found here," said the captain. Vimes admired the flatness of the response. It meant: I am not interested in a dialogue at this time.

"What is your authority here, Captain?" he said.

"My authority comes threefold: the Low King, mining law, and sixty armed dwarfs," said Gud.

Bugger, thought Vimes. I forgot about mining law. This is a problem. I think I need to delegate. A good commander learns to delegate. Therefore, I will delegate this problem to Captain Gud.

"That was a good answer, Captain," he said, "and I respect it." In one movement, he pushed past and headed for the watchmen. He stopped dead when he heard the sound of drawn metal behind him, raised his hands, and said: "Grag Bashfullsson, will you explain matters to the captain? I have stepped *into* his custody, not out of it. And this is not the time or place for rash action."

He walked on without waiting for a reply. Admittedly, banking on the fact that someone would get into trouble if they killed you would probably come under the heading of rash action, but he'd just have to live with that. Or, of course, not.

He hunkered down by Nobby and Colon.

"Sorry about this, Mister Vimes," said Fred. "We were waiting on the path with some horses and they just turned up. We showed 'em our badges, but they just did not want to know."

"Understood. And you, Cheery?"

"I thought it'd be best to stay together, sir," said Cheery earnestly.

"Right. And you, Detr—" Vimes looked down, and felt the bile rise. Brick and Detritus both had chains on their legs.

"You *let* them shackle you?" he said.

"Well, it seemed to be gettin' all poll-itical, Mister Vimes," said Detritus. "But say der word and me an' Brick can have 'em off, no trouble. Dey're only field chains. My granny could've bust out of 'em."

Vimes felt the anger rising, but put a lid on it. Right now, Detritus was being rather more sensible than his boss. "Don't do that, not until I say so," he said. "Where are the grags?"

"They're guarding them in another cave, sir," said Cheery. "And the miners. Sir, they said the Low King is on his way!"

"Good job it's a big cave, otherwise it'd be getting crowded," said Vimes. He walked back to the captain and bent down.

"You chained up my sergeant?" he said.

"He's a troll. This is Koom Valley," said the captain flatly.

"Except even *I* could bust out of chain that thin," said Vimes. He glanced up. Sally and Angua had regained their amour propre in their proper armor, and were watching Vimes carefully.

"Those two officers are a vampire and a werewolf," he said, still in the same level voice. "I know you know this, and you very wisely didn't try to lay a finger on them. And Bashfullsson's a grag. But you put my sergeant in weak chains that he could snap with a finger so you could kill him and say he was trying to escape. Don't even *think* about denying it. I know a dirty trick when I see one. Shall I tell you what I'm going to do? I'm going to give you a chance to show brotherly love and let the trolls out, right now. And the others. Otherwise, unless you kill me, I'll poison your future career to the very best of my ability. And you don't *dare* kill me."

The captain eyeballed him, but it was a game Vimes had mastered a long time ago. Then the dwarf's gaze fell on Vimes's arm, and he gave a groan and took a step back, raising his hand protectively.

"Yes! I'll do it! Yes!"

"See you do," said Vimes, taken aback. Then he, too, looked down at the inside of his wrist.

"*What the hell is this?*" he said, turning to Bash-fullsson.

"Ah, it left its mark on you, Commander," said the grag cheerfully. "An exit wound, perhaps?"

On the soft underskin of Vimes's wrist, the sign of the Summoning Dark blazed as a livid scar.

Vimes turned his arm this way and that.

"It was *real*?" he said.

"Yes. But it is gone, I'm sure. There is a difference in you."

Vimes rubbed the symbol. It didn't hurt; it was just raised, reddened skin.

"It's not going to come back, is it?" he said.

"I doubt it'll risk it, sir!" said Angua.

Vimes opened his mouth to ask her what she meant by that piece of sarcasm when yet more dwarfs trotted in to the cavern.

These were the tallest and broadest dwarfs he'd ever seen. Unlike most dwarfs, they wore simple mail shirts and carried one axe: one good, large, beautifully balanced axe. Other dwarfs bristled with up to a dozen weapons. These dwarfs bristled with one each, and they separated and spread out into the cavern with a purpose, covering lines of sight, guarding shadows, and, in the case of four of them, taking up station behind Detritus and Brick.

When they finally clattered to a halt, another group stepped out of the tunnel. Vimes recognized Rhys, Low King of the Dwarfs. He stopped, looked around, glanced briefly at Vimes, and summoned the captain to him.

"We have everything?"

"Sire?" said Gud nervously.

"You *know* what I mean, Captain!"

"Yes, but we found nothing on any of them, sire! We searched them, and we've gone over the floor three times!"

"Excuse me?" said Vimes.

"Commander Vimes!" said the king, turning and greeting Vimes like a long-lost son. "It is good to see you!"

"You've lost the bloody cube?" said Vimes. "After all this?"

"What cube would this be, Commander?" said the king. Vimes had to admire his acting ability, at least.

"The one you're looking for," he said. "The one dug up in my city. The one all this fuss is about. They wouldn't throw it away, because they're grags, right? You can't destroy words. It's the worst crime there is. They can't destroy it and they don't dare hide it. So they'd keep it with them."

The Low King looked at Captain Gud, who swallowed.

"It's not in this cave," he muttered.

"They wouldn't leave it anywhere else," said Vimes. "Not now! Someone might find it!"

The luckless captain turned to his king, seeking help there.

"There was panic everywhere when we arrived, sire!" he protested. "People running and screaming, fires everywhere! Complete chaos, sire! All we can be sure of is that no one got out! And we searched them all, sire. We searched them all!"

Vimes shut his eyes. Memories were fading fast as common sense walled up all those things that could not have happened, but he recalled the panicking grags, hunched over something. Had there been just a twinkle of blue and green specks?

Time for a long shot . . .

"Corporal Nobbs, come here!" he said. "Let him through, Captain. I insist!"

Gud didn't protest. His spirit was broken. A reluctant Nobby was produced.

"Yes, Mister Vimes?" he said.

"Corporal Nobbs, did you obtain that precious thing I asked you to acquire?" said Vimes.

"Er . . . what would that be, sir?" said Nobby. Vimes's heart leapt. Nobby's face was an open book, albeit the kind that got banned in some countries.

"Nobby, there are times when I'll put up with you mucking about. This isn't one of those," he said. "Did you find the thing *I asked you to look for*?"

Nobby looked into his eyes. "I . . . Oh? *Oh*. Oh, yes, sir," he said. "I . . . yes . . . we rushed in, you see,

you see, you see, and people were running everywhere and there was, like, smoke . . ." Nobby's face
glazed and his lips moved soundlessly in an agony of
creation, ". . . an', an' I was bravely fightin' when what
did I see but a sparkly thing rollin' and bein' kicked
about, an' I thought, I jus' *bet* that's the very same
sparkly thing Mister Vimes very specific'ly told me
to be lookin' out for . . . an' here it is, all safe . . ."

He pulled a small, glittering cube out of his pocket
and held it out.

Vimes was faster than the king. His hand shot
forward, closed over the cube, and was locked in a
fist in the skin of a second.

"Well done, Corporal Nobbs, for obeying my
orders so concisely," he said and stifled a grin at
Nobby's impeccably dreadful salute.

"I believe that is dwarf property, Commander
Vimes," said the king calmly.

Vimes opened his hand, palm up. The cube, only a
couple of inches across, gave off little blue and green
glints. The metal looked like bronze that had been
corroded by time into a beautiful pattern of greens,
blues, and browns. It was a jewel.

He's a king, thought Vimes. A king on a throne as
wobbly as a rocking horse. And he's not *nice*. It's not
a job where the nice last long. He even got a spy into
my Watch! I will not put my faith in kings. Right
now, who do I trust?

Me.

One thing I do know is that no damn demon got
inside my head, no matter what they say. I wouldn't
buy that even if they threw in a lifetime supply of cabbage! No one gets into my head but me! This damn

. . . burn is just a . . . coincidence. It doesn't mean anything! But you play the hand you're dealt . . .

"Take it," he said, opening his hand. On his wrist, the Summoning Dark glowed.

"I ask you to give it to me, Commander," said Rhys.

"*Take it*," Vimes repeated. And he thought: Let's see what *you* believe, shall we?

The king reached out, hesitated, and then slowly withdrew his hand.

"Or, perhaps," he said, as if the thought had just occurred to him, "it might be best to leave it in your celebrated custody, Commander Vimes."

"Yes. I want to hear what it has to say," said Vimes, closing his fist again. "I want to know what was too dangerous to know."

"Indeed, so do I," said the king of the dwarfs. "We will take it to a place that can—"

"Look around you, sire!" snapped Vimes. "Dwarfs and trolls died here! They weren't fighting, they were standing together! Look around you, the place looks like a godsdamn game board! Was this their testament? Then we listen to it here! In this place! At this time!"

"And supposing what it has to say is dreadful?" said the king.

"Then we listen!"

"I am the king, Vimes! You have no authority here! This is not your city! You stand here defying me with a handful of men and your wife and child not ten miles away—"

Rhys stopped, and the echoes bounced back from distant caves, tumbling over themselves and dying into a silence that rang like iron.

Out of the corner of his ear, Vimes heard Sally say: "Oops . . ."

Bashfullsson hurried forward and whispered something in the king's ear. The king's expression changed, as only a politician's face can, into careful amity.

I'm not going to do a thing, Vimes told himself. I'm just going to stand here.

"I do look forward to seeing Lady Sibyl again," said Rhys. "And your son, of course . . ."

"Good. They're staying in a house not ten miles away," said Vimes. "Sergeant Littlebottom?"

"Sir?" said Cheery.

"Please take Lance Constable von Humpeding with you and go down to the town, will you? Tell Lady Sibyl I'm fine," Vimes added, not taking his eyes off the king. "Off you go, right now."

As they hurried away, the king smiled, and looked around the cavern. Then he sighed.

"Well, I cannot afford a row with Ankh-Morpork, not at the moment. Very well, Commander. Do you know *how* to make it speak?"

"No. Don't you?" This is a game, right? Vimes thought. A king wouldn't take this kind of gobbyness from anyone, especially when you outnumber them ten to one. A row? You'd just have to say we got caught in a storm in Koom Valley, which is such a treacherous place, as everyone agrees. He will be greatly missed and we will certainly hand over his body if it ever turns up . . . But you're not going to try that, are you, because you need me. You know something about this cavern, yes? And whatever's going to happen, you want good ol' not-sharp-but-by-gods-he's-straight Sam Vimes to tell the world . . .

"No two cubes are alike," said Rhys. "It is usually a word, but sometimes a breath, a sound, a temperature, a point in the world, the smell of rain. Anything. I understand that there are many cubes that have never spoken."

"Really?" said Vimes. "But this thing damn well *gabbled*. And whoever sent it out of the valley *wanted* it to be heard, so I doubt it only starts talking when a virgin's tear falls on it on a warm Tuesday in February. And this one started chatting very smartly to a man who didn't know a word of Dwarfish, too."

"But the speaker would want dwarfs to hear it, surely!" the king protested.

"It's a two-thousand-year-old legend! Who knows who wanted what?" said Vimes. "What do *you* want?"

This was to Nobby, who had appeared beside him, looking with interest at the cube.

"How did tha— he get past my guards?" said the king.

"The Nobbs sidle," said Vimes, and, as a couple of embarrassed guards dropped heavy hands on Nobby's frail shoulders, he added: "No. Leave him. Come on, Nobby, *you* say something to make this thing start speaking."

"Er . . . 'say something or it'll be the worse for you'?" Nobby suggested.

"Not a bad try," Vimes conceded. "A hundred years ago, sire, I doubt if anyone in Ankh-Morpork knew many words of Dwarf or Troll. Perhaps the message was *intended* for humans? There must have been a settlement down on the plain, with all those birds and fish to eat."

"Perhaps some more human words, then, er, Nobby?" said the king.

"Okay. Open, speak, say something, talk, spill the beans, play—"

"No, no, Mister Vimes, he's doing it wrong!" Fred Colon shouted. "It was in the olden days, right? So it'd be old words, like . . . er . . . openeth!"

Vimes laughed as a thought struck. I wonder, he thought. It could be. This is not really about words, it's about sounds. Noises . . .

Bashfullsson was watching the attempt with a puzzled expression.

"What is the dwarf word for 'open,' Mr. Bashfullsson?" said Vimes.

"In the sense of 'open a book?' That would be *dhwe*, Commander."

"Hmm. That won't do. How about . . . 'say'?"

"Why, that would be *aargk*, or, in the preemptive form, *aork!*, Commander. You know, I don't think—"

"Excuse me!" said Vimes loudly. The babble of voices stopped. He moved the cube close to his mouth.

"Awk!" he said.

The blue and green lights ceased their sparkle and, instead, began to form across the metal a pattern of blue and green squares.

"I thought the artist knew no Dwarfish," said the king.

"He didn't, but he spoke fluent Chicken," said Vimes. "I'll explain later . . ."

"Captain, fetch the grags," the king snapped.

"The prisoners, too, even the trolls. *All* shall hear this!"

The metal seemed to be moving over Vimes's skin. Some of the green and blue squares rose slightly proud of the rest of the metal.

The box began to speak. There was a crackle that sounded like Dwarfish, although Vimes couldn't make out a single word. It was followed by a couple of loud knocking noises.

"Second Convocation Hubland Dwarfish," said Bashfullsson. "That would be right for the time. Whoever is speaking has just said: 'Art thys thyng workyng?'"

The voice spoke again. As the cracked, old syllables unrolled, Bashfullsson went on: "'The first thyng Tak did, he wroten hymself; the second thyng Tak did, he wroten the Laws; the thyrd thyng Tak did, he wroten the World; the fourth thyng Tak did, he wroten ay cave; the fyfth thyng Tak did, he wroten a geode, ay egge of stone; and in the gloamyn of the mouth of the cave, the geode hatched and the Brothers were born; the first Brother walked toward the light, and stood under the open sky—'"

"This is just the story of the Things Tak Wrote," Angua whispered to Vimes. Vimes shrugged, and watched as some of the bodyguards hustled the old grags in the circle, Ardent among them.

"It's not new or anything?" Vimes said, disappointed.

"Every dwarf knows it, sir."

"'—He was the first Dwarf,'" Bashfullsson translated. "'He found the Laws Tak had wrytten, and he was endarkened—'"

The crackling voice went on, and then Bash-fullsson, who had his eyes closed in concentration, opened them in shock. This time, he didn't bother with olde-world language.

". . . uh . . . 'Then Tak looked upon the stone and it was trying to come alive, and Tak smiled and wroten: "all thyngs strive,'" said the dwarf, raising his voice above the growing commotion around him. "'And for the service the stone had given, he fashioned it into the first Troll, and delighted in the life that came unbidden. These are the thyngs that Tak Wroten!'" He was shouting now, because of the noise level.

Vimes felt like an outsider. It seemed that everyone except him was arguing. Axes were being flourished.

"'I WHO SPEAK TO YOU NOW AM B'HRIAN BLOODAXE, BY RIGHT OF THE SCONE THE TRUE KING OF THE DWARFS!'" Bashfullsson screamed.

The cave went silent, except for the echoing scream returning from distant darkness.

"'We were washed into the caves by the flood. We sought one another, voices in the dark. We are dying. Our bodies are broken by the terrible water with teeth . . . of stone. We are too weak to climb. Water surrounds all. This testament we will entrust to young Stronginthearm, who is still nimble, in the hope that it will reach the daylight. For the story of this day must not be forgotten. This outcome was not meant! We came to sign a treaty! It was the secret, careful work of many years!'"

The box stopped speaking. But there were faint groans, and the rush of water somewhere.

"Sire, I demand that this should not be heard!"

shouted Ardent among the grags. "It is nothing but lies upon lies. There is no truth in it! What proof is there that this is the voice of Bloodaxe?"

Captain Gud is looking a bit uncertain, Vimes thought. The king's bodyguard? Well, they mostly looked like the stolid kind who stayed loyal and didn't pay much attention to politics. The miners? Angry and confused because the old grags are yelling. This is going to go bad really *fast*.

"City Watch, to me!" he shouted.

The background noises from the cube died, and another voice started to speak. Detritus looked up quickly.

"Dat's Old Troll!" he said.

Bashfullsson hesitated for a moment. "'. . . er . . . I am Diamond King of Trolls,'" he said, looking desperately at Vimes. "'Indeed, we came to make peace. But the mist came down upon us and when it rose, some trolls and dwarfs cried, "Ambush!" They fell to fighting and would not hear our commands. So troll fought troll, and dwarf fought dwarf, and fools made fools of all of us as we fought to stop a war, until the disgusted sky washed us away.

"'And yet we say this. Here, in this cave at the end of the world, peace is made between dwarf and troll, and we will march beyond the hand of Death together. For the enemy is not Troll, nor is it Dwarf, but it is the baleful, the malign, the cowardly, the vessels of hatred, those who do a bad thing and call it good. Those we fought today, but the willful fool is eternal and will say—'"

"This is just a trick!" Ardent shouted.

"'—say this is a trick,'" Bashfullsson continued,

" 'and so we implore: come to the caves under this valley, where you will find us sharing the peace that cannot be braken.' "

The rumbling voice from the box stopped speaking. There was, once again, a rustle of half-heard voices, and then silence.

The little squares moved about for a moment like a sliding puzzle, and the sound came back. Now what issued from it was shouts and screams, and the clash of steel . . .

Vimes was watching the king's face. Some of this you knew, right? Not all of it, but you didn't look surprised that it was Bloodaxe speaking. Rumors? Old stories? Something in the records? You'll never tell me.

"*Had'ra,*" said Bashfullsson, and the cube fell silent. "That means 'stop,' Mister Vimes," the grag added.

"And so we are under Koom Valley," sneered Ardent. "And what do we find?"

"We find you," said Bashfullsson. "We always find you."

"Dead trolls. Dead dwarfs. And nothing more than a voice," said Ardent. "Ankh-Morpork is here. They are devious. These words could have been spoken yesterday!"

The king was watching Ardent and Bashfullsson. So was every other dwarf. You don't have to stand and argue! Vimes wanted to shout. Just chain the bastards up and we can sort it out later!

But being a dwarf was all about words and laws . . .

"These are venerable grags," said Ardent, indicat-

ing the robed figures behind him. "They have stud-
ied the Histories! They have studied the Devices!
Thousands of years of knowledge stand before you.
And you? What do you know?"

"That you came to destroy the truth," said Bashfullsson. "You dared not trust it. A voice is just a
voice, but these bodies are proof. You came here to
destroy them."

Ardent snatched the axe from a miner and was
flourishing it before any of the bodyguards could
react. When realization caught up with them, there
was a massed move forward.

"No!" said Bashfullsson, holding up his hands.
"Sire, please! This is an argument between grags!"

"Why do you carry no axe?" Ardent snarled.

"I need no axe to be a dwarf," said Bashfullsson.
"Nor do I need to hate trolls. What kind of creature
defines itself by hatred?"

"You strike at the very root of us!" said Ardent.
"At the root!"

"Then strike back," said Bashfullsson, holding out
his empty hands. "And put your sword away, Commander Vimes," he added, without turning his head.
"This is dwarf business. Ardent? I'm still standing.
What do you believe in? *Ha'ak! Ga strak ja'ada!*"

Ardent jerked forward, axe raised. Bashfullsson
moved quickly, there was the thud of something
hitting flesh, and then a tableau as motionless as
the brooding figures around the cavern. There
was Ardent, axe raised overhead. There was Bashfullsson, down on one knee, with his head resting
almost companionably against the dwarf's chest and

the edge of one hand pressed hard against Ardent's throat.

Ardent's mouth opened, but all that came out was a croak and a trickle of blood.

He took a few steps back, and fell over backwards. The axe struck the white, wet, stony waterfall, and smashed through the drip of millennia. Time fell in shards around.

Bashfullsson rose, looking shocked and massaging his hand.

"It is like using an axe," he said, to no one in particular, "but without the axe . . ."

The uproar began again, but a dwarf, dripping with water, pushed through the mob.

"Sire, there's a band of trolls coming up the valley! They asked for you! They say they want to parley!"

Rhys stepped over the gurgling body of Ardent, looking intently at the hole in the waterfall of stone. Another piece fell down as he touched it.

"Is there something unusual about their leader?" he said in a preoccupied voice, still staring into the new darkness.

"Yes, sire! He's all . . . sparkly!"

"Ah. Good," said the king. "He has his parley. Bring him down here."

"Could that be a troll who knows some very powerful dwarfs?" said Vimes.

The Low King met his eyes for a moment. "Yes, I imagine it is," he said. Then he raised his voice. "Someone fetch me a torch! Commander Vimes, could you just . . . look at this, please?"

In the depths of the revealed cave, something shone.

On this day in 1802, the painter Methodia Rascal dropped the glittering thing in the deepest well he knew. No one would ever hear it down there. The Chicken chased him home.

It would be a lot simpler, Vimes thought, if this was a story. A sword is pulled out of a stone, or a magic ring is flung into the depths of the sea, and with general rejoicing, the world turns.

But this was real life. The world didn't turn, it just went into a spin. It was Koom Valley Day, and there wasn't a battle going on in Koom Valley. But what was going on here wasn't peace, either. What was going on . . . well, what was going on was *committees*. It was negotiation. Actually, as far as he could tell, it hadn't even got as far as negotiation yet.

It hadn't got past talks about meetings about delegations. On the other hand, no one had died, except maybe of boredom.

There was a lot of history to be unpicked, and, for those who weren't actually engaged in that delicate activity, there was Koom Valley to tame. Two cultural heroes were down there in the cavern, and all it needed was one good storm and a few misplaced blockages for a white flood laden with grinding boulders to wipe the whole place away. It hadn't happened yet, but sooner or later the dynamic geography would get around to it. Koom Valley couldn't be left to its own devices, not anymore.

Everywhere you looked, there were teams of trolls and dwarfs surveying, diverting, damming, and drilling. They'd been engaged in this for two days. It would take them forever, because every winter changed the game. Koom Valley was *forcing* cooperation on them. Damn Koom Valley . . .

Vimes thought that was a bit too pat, but nature can be like that. Sometimes you got sunsets so pink that they had no style at all.

One thing that had happened fast was the tunnel. Dwarfs had cut down quickly through the soft limestone. You could stroll down into the cavern now, although, in fact, you'd have to queue, because of the long line of trolls and dwarfs.

Those in the line going down eyed one another with uncertainty at best. Those in the line coming up sometimes looked angry, or were close to tears, or just walked along looking at the ground. Once they got past the exit, they tended to form into quiet groups.

Sam, with Young Sam in his arms, didn't have to queue. News had got around. He went straight in, past the trolls and dwarfs who were painstakingly reassembling the broken stalagmites (it was news to Vimes that you could do that, but apparently if you came back in five hundred years they'd be as good as new) and into what had come to be called the Kings' Cave.

And there they were. You couldn't argue with it. There was the dwarf king, slumped forward across the board, glazed by the eternal drip, his beard now rock and at one with the stone, but the diamond troll king had remained upright in death, his skin gone cloudy, and you could still see the game in front of him. It was his move; a healthy little stalactite hung from his outstretched hand.

They'd broken off small stalagmites to make the pieces, which time had now glued into immobility. The scratched lines on the stone were more or less invisible, but Thud players from both races had already pored over it and a sketch of the Dead Kings' Game had already appeared in the *Times*. The troll king was playing the dwarf side. Apparently, it could go either way.

People were saying that when this was all over, they'd seal the cave. Too many people in a living cave killed it in some way, the dwarfs said. And then the kings would be left in the dark to finish their game in, with luck, peace.

Water dripping on a stone, changing the shape of the world one drop at a time, washing away a valley . . .

Yes, well, Vimes had added to himself. But it'd never be that simple. And for every new generation, you'd have to open it again, so that people could see that it was true.

Today, though, it was open for Sam and Young Sam, who was wearing a fetching wooly hat with a bobble on it.

Brick and Sally were on duty, along with a couple of dwarfs and two more trolls, all watching the stream of visitors and one another. Vurms covered the ceiling. The game gleamed. What would Young Sam remember? Probably just the glitter. But it had to be done.

The players were genuine—on that, at least, both

sides agreed. The carvings on Diamond were accurate, the armor and jewelry on Bloodaxe were just as history recorded. Even the long loaf of dwarf bread that he carried into battle, and which could shatter a troll skull, was by his side. Dwarf scholars had, with delicacy and care and the blunting of fifteen saw blades, removed a tiny slice of it. Miraculously, it had turned out still to be as inedible now as the day it was baked.

A minute was about enough for this historic moment, Vimes decided. Young Sam was at the grabbing age, and he'd never hear the end of it if his son ate a historic monument.

"Can I have a word, Lance Constable?" he said to Sally as he turned to go. "The guard changes in a minute."

"Certainly, sir," said Sally. Vimes strolled off to a corner of the cavern and waited until Nobby and Fred Colon marched in at the head of the relief.

"Glad you joined, Lance Constable?" he said, as she hurried up.

"Very much, sir!"

"Good. Shall we go up to the daylight?"

She followed him up the slope and into the damp warmth of Koom Valley, where he sat down on a boulder. He looked at her while Young Sam played at his feet.

He said: "Is there anything you'd like to say to me, Lance Constable?"

"Should there be, sir?"

"I can't prove anything, of course," said Vimes. "But you are an agent of the Low King, aren't you? You've been spying on me?"

He waited while she considered her options. Swallows swooped overhead in squadrons.

"I, er, wouldn't put it quite like that, sir," she said eventually. "I was keeping an eye on Hamcrusher, and I'd heard about the mining, and then, when it all started to heat up—"

"—becoming a watchman seemed a good idea, right? Did the League know?"

"No! Look, sir, I wasn't spying on *you*—"

"You told him I was headed for Koom Valley. And the night we arrived, you went for a little fly-around. Just stretching your wings?"

"Look, this isn't my life!" said Sally. "I'd joined the new force in Bonk. We're trying to make a difference up there! I did want to come to Ankh-Morpork anyway, because, well, we all want to. To learn, you know? How you manage to do it? Everyone speaks highly of you! And then the Low King summoned me and I thought, where's the harm? Hamcrusher has caused trouble up there, too. Er . . . I never actually told you a lie, sir."

"Rhys already knew about the Secret, right?" said Vimes.

"No, sir, not as such. But I think he had some reason to suspect there was something down there."

"Then why didn't he just go and look?"

"Dwarfs digging around in Koom Valley? The trolls would, er, go postal, sir."

"But not if the dwarfs were merely investigating why a copper from Ankh-Morpork was chasing some fleeing criminals into the caves, right? Not if the copper was good ol' Sam Vimes, who, everyone knows, is as straight as an arrow even if he's not the sharpest knife in the drawer. You can't bribe Sam Vimes, but why bother when you can pull the wool over his eyes?"

"Look, sir, I know how you must feel, but . . . well, there's your litle boy there, playing in Koom Valley, with trolls and dwarfs all 'round, and they're not fighting. Right? I didn't lie, I just . . . liaised a little. Wasn't it worth it, sir? Hah, you really worried them when you went to the wizards! Shine hadn't left the city! Rhys had to fly him in by night! All they really did was follow your lead. The only person who fooled you was me, and it turns out I wasn't very good at it. They needed you, sir. Look around and say it wasn't worth it . . ."

A hundred yards away, a house-sized rock rumbled across the stone, pushed and steered by a dozen trolls, dropped into a sinkhole and blocked it like an egg in a cup. There was a cheer.

"Can I mention something else, sir?" said Sally. "I do *know* Angua is standing behind me."

"It's Sergeant Angua to you," said Angua, by her ear. "You didn't fool me, either. I told you we didn't like snitches in the Watch. But for what it's worth, sir, she smells like she's telling the truth."

"Do you still have a route to the Low King?" said Vimes.

"Yes, and I'm sure he'll—" Sally began quickly.

"These are my demands. The grags and what's left of their guards are coming back to Ankh-Morpork with me. That includes Ardent, though I'm told it'll be weeks before he can talk again. They're going before Vetinari. I've got promises to keep, and no one is going to stop me. It'll be tough to make any big charges stick, but I'm bloody well going to try. And since I'll bet my dinner that Vetinari is in on all this, I expect he'll pack 'em off back to Rhys in any case. I imagine *he's* got a cell that's deep enough for comfort. Understood?"

"Yes, sir. And the other demands?"

"The same as that one, repeated in a louder voice," said Vimes. "Understood?"

"Absolutely, sir. Then I'll resign, of course," said Sally.

Vimes's eyes narrowed. "You'll resign when I tell you to, Lance Constable! You took the King's Shilling, remember? And made an oath. Go and liaise!"

"You're going to keep her?" said Angua, watching the vampire disappear into the distance.

"You said yourself she's a good copper. We'll see. Oh, don't make that face, Sergeant. It's all the rage in politics these days, spying on your friends. That's what I'm told. Like she said: look around."

"This is a bit unlike you, sir," said Angua, giving him a look of concern.

"Yes, it is, isn't it?" said Vimes. "I had a nice sleep last night. It's a nice day. No one is actively trying to kill me, which is nice. Thank you, Sergeant. Have a nice evening."

Vimes carried Young Sam back in late-afternoon light. Just as well the girl *had* been working for Rhys. Things might have been a bit tricky otherwise. That was the plain fact of it. Keep her on? Maybe. She'd been very useful, even Angua admitted. Besides, he'd been practically forced to take on a spy, in times of more-or-less war! If he played that right, no one would *ever again* dictate to him who he took on in the Watch. Doreen Winkings could rattle her false canines as much as she liked!

Hmm . . . was this how Vetinari thought *all the time*?

He heard his name being called. A coach was coming across the rock, and Sybil was waving from the window. That was another step forward; even wagons could get up here now.

"You haven't forgotten the dinner tonight, have you?" she said, a hint of suspicion in her voice.

"No, dear." Vimes hadn't, but he'd hoped that it might evaporate if he didn't think about it. It was going to be Official, with both kings and lots of important lesser kings and clan leaders. And the Special Envoy from Ankh-Morpork, unfortunately. That would be Sam Vimes, scrubbed up.

At least there weren't going to be tights and plumes. Even Sybil hadn't been that farsighted. Regrettably, though, the town had a decent tailor who'd been very keen to use all that gold braid he'd bought by accident a couple of years ago.

"Willikins will have a bath run by the time we get back," said Sybil as the coach moved away.

"Yes, dear," said Vimes.

"Don't look so glum! You'll be upholding the honor of Ankh-Morpork, remember!"

"Really, dear? What shall I do with the other hand?" said Vimes, settling back into the seat.

"Oh, Sam! Tonight you'll walk with kings!"

I'd sooner be walking all by myself along Treacle Mine Road at three in the morning, Vimes thought. In the rain, with the gutters gushing. But it was a wife thing. She took such a . . . a *pride* in him. He could never work out why.

He looked down at his arm. He'd sorted *that* out, at least. Exit wound indeed! It was just the way the burning oil had splashed on his skin. It might look a *bit* like that damn symbol, enough to put the wind up the dwarfs, but no floaty eyeball was going to get past *him*. Common sense and facts, that's what worked!

After a while, it dawned on him that they weren't going into the town. They'd gone down almost as far as the lakes, but now they were heading back up on the cliff path. He could see the valley below them, opening out.

The kings were working their subjects hard, reasoning that tired warriors are less keen to fight. Teams swarmed over the rock like ants. Maybe there was a plan. There probably was. But the mountains would sneer at it every winter. You'd have to have squads here all the time, you'd need to scout the mountainsides to find and smash the big boulders before they caused trouble. Remember Koom Valley! Because, if you don't, your history is . . . history.

And maybe, behind the thunder and in the roar of the waters flowing underground, you'll hear the laughter of dead kings.

The coach came to a halt. Sybil opened the door.

"Get down, Sam Vimes," she said. "No arguing. It's time for your portrait."

"Out here? But it's—" Vimes began.

"Good afternoon, Commander," said Otto Chriek cheerfully, appearing at the doorway. "I haf set up a bench and zer light is just right for color!"

Vimes had to agree that it was. Thunder light made the mountains gleam like gold. In the middle distance, the Tears of the King fell in a line of glittering silver. Brightly colored birds skimmed through the air. And all the way up the valley there were rainbows.

Koom Valley, on Koom Valley Day. He'd had to be there.

"If her ladyship vill be seated viz zer little boy on her lap and you, Commander, standink with your hand on her shoulder . . . ?" He bustled around his big black iconograph.

"He's up here taking pictures for the *Times*," Sybil whispered. "And I thought, well, it's now or never. Portraiture must move on."

"How long is this going to take?" said Vimes.

"Oh, about a fraction of a second, Commander," said Otto.

Vimes brightened up. This was more like it.

Of course, it never is. But it was a warm afternoon, and Vimes still felt good. They sat and stared with those fixed grins people wear when they're wondering why a fraction of a second takes half an hour, while Otto tried to get the universe sorted out to his satisfaction.

"Havelock will be wondering how to reward you, you know," murmured Sybil as the vampire fussed around.

"He can go on wondering," said Vimes. "I've everything I want."

He smiled.

Click!

"Sixty new officers?" said Lord Vetinari.

"The price of peace, sir," said Captain Carrot earnestly. "I'm sure that Commander Vimes wouldn't settle for anything less. We are really stretched."

"Sixty men—and dwarfs and trolls, obviously—is more than a third of your current complement," said the Patrician, tapping his walking stick on the cobbles. "Peace comes with a rather large bill, Captain."

"And a few dividends, sir," Carrot said.

They looked up at the circle-and-bar symbol over the door of the mine, just above the yellow-and-black rope used by the Watch to warn off intruders.

"The mine falls to us by default?" said Vetinari.

"Apparently, sir. I believe the term is 'eminent domain.'"

"Ah, yes. That means 'theft by the government,'" said Vetinari.

"But the grags bought the freehold, sir. They're hardly going to contest it now."

"Quite. And the dwarfs really can make watertight tunnels?"

"Oh, yes. The trick is almost as old as mining. Would you care to step inside? I'm afraid the elevator is not working at the moment, though."

Lord Vetinari inspected the rails and the little carts the dwarfs had used to shift spoil. He felt the dry walls. He went back upstairs and frowned as a one-ton slab of iron came through the wall, whirled past his face, passed through the opposite wall, and buried itself in the street outside.

"And was that supposed to happen?" he said, brushing plaster dust off his robe.

An excited voice behind him shouted: "The torque! It's impossible! Amazing!"

A figure climbed through the wall, holding something in one hand. It rushed up to Captain Carrot, vibrating with excitement.

"It spins once every six point nine seconds, but the torque is immense! It broke the clamp! What powers it?"

"No one seems to know," said Carrot. "In Uberwald—"

"Excuse me, what is this about?" said Lord Vetinari, holding out a hand imperiously.

The man glanced at him and then turned to Carrot.

"Who's this?" he said.

"Lord Vetinari, *Ruler of the City*, may I present Mr. Pony of the Artificers' Guild?" said Carrot quickly. "Please let his lordship see the Axle, Mr. Pony."

"Thank you," said Vetinari. He took the thing, which looked like two cubes, each about six inches on a side, joined together on one face, like a pair of dice joined at the sixes. In relation to the other, one turned—very, very slowly.

"Oh," he said flatly. "A mechanism. How nice."

"Nice?" said Pony. "Don't you understand? It won't *stop* turning."

Carrot and Pony looked expectantly at the Patrician, who said: "And that's a *good* thing, is it?"

Carrot coughed. "Yes, sir. One of these drives one of the biggest mines in Uberwald. All the pumps, the fans that move the air, the trucks that haul the ore, the bellows for the forges, the elevators . . . everything. Just one of those. It's another type of Device, like the cubes. We don't know how they're made, they're very rare, but the other three I've heard of have not stopped working for hundreds of years. They don't use fuel, they don't *need* anything. They appear to be millions of years old. No one knows what made them. They just turn."

"How interesting," said Vetinari. "Hauling trucks? Underground, you say?"

"Oh, yes," said Carrot. "Even with miners in."

"I shall give this some thought," said Vetinari, avoiding Mr. Pony's outstretched hand. "And what could we make it do in this city?"

He and Carrot turned questioning faces to Mr. Pony, who shrugged and said: "Everything?"

Plink! went a drop of water onto the head of the very, very late King Bloodaxe.

"How long are we going to have to do this, Sarge?" said Nobby as they watched the line of visitors shuffle past the dead kings.

"Mister Vimes has sent for another squad from home," said Fred Colon, shifting from one foot to the other. It seemed quite warm when you first came into the cave, but after a while, the clamminess could get a man down. He reflected that Nobby wasn't affected by this, being blessed by Nature with natural clammy.

"It's starting to give me the creeps, Sarge," said Nobby, indicating the kings. "If that hand moves, I'm going to scream."

"Think of it as Being There, Nobby."

"I've always been *somewhere*, Sarge."

"Yeah, but when they comes to write the history books, they'll—" Fred Colon paused for thought. He had to admit, they probably wouldn't mention him and Nobby. "Well, your Tawneee will be proud of you, anyway."

"I think that's not to be, Sarge," said Nobby sadly. "She's a nice girl, but I think I'm goin' to have to let her down lightly."

"Surely not!"

"'Fraid so, Sarge. She cooked me dinner the other day. She tried to make distressed pudding like my ol' mum used to make."

Plink!

Fred Colon smiled all the way from his stomach. "Ah, yes. No one could distress a pudding like your ol' mum, Nobby."

"It was awful, Fred," said Nobby, hanging his head. "As for her slumpie, well, I do not wish to go there. She is not a girl who knows her way around a stove."

"She's more of a pole person, Nobby, that is true."

"Exactly. An' I thought, ol' Hammerhead, well, you might never be sure which way she was lookin,' but her buttered clams, well—" he sighed.

"There's a thought to keep a man warm on a cold night," Fred agreed.

"An,' y'know, these days, when she hits me with a wet fish, it doesn't sting like it used to," Nobby went on. "I think we are reaching an understanding."

Plink!

"She can crack a lobster with her fist," Colon observed. "That's a very portable talent."

"So I was thinking of speaking to Angua," said Nobby. "She might give me a few hints on how to let Tawneee down gently."

"That's a good idea, Nobby," said Fred. "No touchin,' sir, otherwise I shall have to cut yer fingers orf." This was said, in a friendly tone of voice, to a dwarf who had been reaching in awe toward the board.

"But we'll still be friends, of course," said Nobby as the dwarf backed away. "So long as I can get into the PussyCat Club for free, anyway, I'll always be there if she needs a helmet to cry on."

"That's very modern of you, Nobby," said Fred. He smiled in the gloom. Somehow, the world was back on course.

Plink!

Wandering through the world, the eternal troll . . .

Brick headed after Detritus, dragging his club.

Well, he wuz goin' up in der worl' an' no mistakin'! Dey said it hurt if you come off of der stuff, but Brick had always hurt, all his life, and right now it wasn't too bad at all. It wuz, like, *weird* der way he could fink to der end of a sentence now an' still remember der start of it. An' he wuz bein' given food, which he wuz gettin' to like once he stopped frowing it up. Sergeant Detritus, who knew everythin', had tole him if'n he stayed clean an' smartened up he could rise as high as lance constable one day, makin' heapo money.

He wuzn't too sure what had been happnin' to cause all dis. It looked like he wasn't in der city anymore, an' dere had been some fightin', and Sergeant Detritus had showed him dese kinda dead people and smacked him aroun' der head an' said "Remember!" an' he wuz doin' his best, but he'd been smacked aroun' der head a hole lot harder many, many times and dat one was *nuffin'*. But Sergeant Detritus said it wuz all about not hatin' dwarfs no more and dat was okay, cuz really Brick never had der energy to waste hatin'. What dey had been doin' down dat hole was makin' der worl' a betterer place, Sergeant Detritus said.

And it seemed to Brick, as he smelled the food, dat Sergeant Detritus had got dat one dead right.

Trolls and dwarfs had raised a huge roundhouse in Koom Valley, using giant boulders for the walls and half a fallen forest for the roof. A fire thirty yards long crackled inside. Ranged around it on long benches were the kings of more than a hundred dwarf mines, and the leaders of eighty troll clans, with their followers and servants and bodyguards. The noise was intense, the smoke was thick, the heat was a wall.

It had been a good day. Progress had been made. The guests were not mixing, that was true, but neither were they trying to kill one another. This was a promising development. The truce was holding.

At the high table, King Rhys leaned back in his

makeshift throne and said: "One does not make demands of kings. One makes requests, which are graciously granted. Does he not understand?"

"I don't think he gives a *tra'ka*, sir, if I may be coarse," said Grag Bashfullsson, who was standing respectfully beside him. "And the senior dwarfs in the city will be right behind him on this. It's not my place, sir, but I advise acquiescence."

"And that's all he wants? No gold, no silver, no concessions?"

"That's all *he* wants, sire. But I suspect you will be hearing from Lord Vetinari before long."

"Oh, you may be sure of that!" said the king. He sighed. "It's a new world, Grag, but some things don't change. Er . . . that . . . thing *has* left him, has it?"

"I believe so, sire."

"You are not certain?"

The grag smiled a faint, inward smile. "Let's just say that his reasonable request is best granted, shall we, sire?"

"Your point is taken, Grag. Thank you."

King Rhys turned in his seat, leaned across the two empty places, and said to the Diamond King: "Do you think something has happened to them? It's past six o'clock!"

Shine smiled, filling the hall with light. "I suspect they've been delayed by matters of great importance."

"More important than *this*?" said the dwarf king.

. . . and, because some things *are* important, the coach stood outside the magistrate's house, down in the town. The horses stamped impatiently. The coachman waited. Inside, Lady Sybil darned a sock, because some things are important, with a faint smile on her face.

And floating out of an open upstairs window was the voice of Sam Vimes:

> "It goes *HRUUUGH!* It is a *hippopotamus!*
> That is not my cow!"

Nevertheless, it was close enough for now.